OPERATION STEALTH SEED

OPERATION STEALTH SEED

GEORGE AMABILE

Doug Whiteway, Editor

Cover design by Doowah Design.
Photo of author by Annette Willborn.

This book was printed on Ancient Forest Friendly paper.
Printed and bound in Canada by Hignell Book Printing Inc.

We acknowledge the support of the Canada Council for the Arts and the Manitoba Arts Council for our publishing program.

Library and Archives Canada Cataloguing in Publication

Title: Operation stealth seed / George Amabile ; Doug Whiteway, editor.

Names: Amabile, George, 1936- author. | Whiteway, Doug, 1951- editor.

Identifiers: Canadiana (print) 20190177888 | Canadiana (ebook) 20190177896 | ISBN 9781773240558 (softcover) | ISBN 9781773240565 (HTML)

Classification: LCC PS8551.M32 O64 2019 | DDC C813/.54—dc23

Signature Editions
P.O. Box 206, RPO Corydon, Winnipeg, Manitoba, R3M 3S7
www.signature-editions.com

1

The Caribbean
September 2011

A hundred miles offshore, the U.S. cruiser *Corregidor* out of Pensacola rocked gently in a blaze of sun. Some sixty fathoms below the foam-flecked swells, Lieutenant-Commander Edward McLaren turned and cruised back along the drop-off shelf that was his point of reference. He bunched himself up and dove deeper. The battery-powered quartz headlamp opened a glowing cavern in which schools of brightly coloured fish hovered for a moment, then veered off into the shadows.

He was no longer aware of the wet suit, or the breathing apparatus. It felt as though he had been swimming in this miraculous world from the dawn of time. Then something stirred deep in his memory. A word surfaced. *Rapture.* Then another, and another: *The rapture of the deep.* He struggled to convince himself that this onset of euphoria was a danger point beyond which he could not allow himself to drift. Resentfully, he checked the dials on his wristband.

Three hundred and eighty-six feet, an hour and forty-two minutes. Working mechanically, driven by months of training and sheer will, he disengaged the mouthpiece, unzipped a shoulder pocket and brought the clear tube with its compartment of white powder up to his mouth. The plastic felt unpleasantly foreign, but he forced himself to bite hard, releasing a flood of fresh water and the bitter, slightly acidic taste of NS2-7.

It was an awkward manoeuvre, but they had not been able to make the complex chemical work in a simple pill, a liquid or an injection. It had to be catalyzed by water. It also had to be ingested immediately. After a few minutes, if it did not combine with elements in the blood, it would break down.

He forced the chewed tube from his lips and watched it unfold as it sank. Trash, he thought. Human litter. He replaced the mouthpiece, kicked and stroked briskly until he felt his head clear, then swam as hard as he could toward the surface, though all his training and previous experience told him how dangerous this was. He knew how it felt to have nitrogen gas bubbling up in your blood. That's why they called it "the bends." It doubled you over with excruciating pain and could put you down for good.

Now, as he rose through brighter and brighter light, he felt his muscles tighten involuntarily, as though expecting the worst. But it didn't happen. The damn stuff was working. With that little tube of water and magic dust, divers could operate all day at tremendous depths and come up fast in an emergency without risking serious injury. The military implications astounded him.

As he exploded into the bright afternoon, he gave a pumped fist salute to Admiral Hawley and Commander Tritt who stood at parade rest in their dress whites while the short, stocky Dr. Kee from Sarbitt Chemical leaned out over the rail in his black suit, running stubby fingers through his brush cut and grinning wildly.

The celebration didn't last. By the time he had gotten out of his gear and down to sick bay for testing, he'd begun to feel queasy and his pulse accelerated, skipping beats and scaring the hell out of everyone. Lying on the examination table, hooked up to a series of sophisticated machines, he felt anxious and irritable. His bones ached, the muscles in his legs and feet developed severe cramps, and he was so weak he couldn't lift himself to an upright position. Just before he passed out, he remembered being warned by the older men twelve years before: Never volunteer for a goddamn thing.

In the wardroom, Admiral Hawley took off his cap and placed it carefully on the teak table beside the tumbler of Scotch, which he had poured but had not drunk. The skin on his face was taut and shiny, with hairline wrinkles that deepened around the pale blue eyes when he frowned. His close-cropped hair was still thick, but had gone very grey. He looked up at Commander Tritt who stood with his broad hands folded on the back of a chair, then back at Dr. Yueng T. Kee. He was not a happy man.

"I thought you said you had it licked, Kee. What the hell went wrong?"

Kee shifted his thick body and stared back at Hawley for several seconds before answering.

"Let me remind you, Admiral, that McLaren came up from over 300 feet in thirty seconds with absolutely no free nitrogen in his bloodstream. I hope you understand what that means."

"Of course, I understand. But the man was sick as a dog, and he's lapsed into a coma. What the fuck was that and how soon can you fix it?"

"I can't tell until I see the test results, but it looks like NS2-7 has a whole spectrum of nasty side effects. Unfortunately, I'm not sure it *can* be fixed."

2

New York
April 2012

Dr. Yueng T. Kee sat in the comfortable leather chair in the sumptuously appointed office and realized that he was not at all comfortable. When Sarbitt Chemical was acquired by the agro-giant Lang & Baine, Kee was kept on as the CEO, but was required to report to one of the partners at L&B. Now, as he watched his new boss pore over the NS2-7 file, he tried to read his expression, but there was no way to tell whether his nitrogen suppressant for deep-sea divers would survive the afternoon. After a while, the man looked up and his voice was noncommittal.

"Tell me how this all got started, and where you are now."

"A lab tech, Abe Sinden, was examining samples from one of the L&B manure slurries you were using to develop your new fertilizer, Accel 3."

"Yes, we were monitoring the nitrate levels."

"Which had been getting higher and higher. That's why Sinden couldn't believe what he saw under his microscope. A bacterium no one had ever catalogued. It shouldn't have been there. No microbe could survive in such a lethal environment."

"But it had."

"Not only that, it was reproducing wildly. The severely hostile conditions had triggered a genetic adaptation, a polyvalent sequester which bonded with the whole range of nitrogen oxidation states and made them chemically inert."

"And it was your idea to see if this sequester could be used to suppress nitrogen in the blood of deep-sea divers and allow them to surface quickly without suffering the ravages of caisson disease?"

"Yes. I pitched the idea to the Department of Defense and they provided substantial backing."

"But the tests on Lieutenant-Commander McLaren show severe, allergenic, immune system reactions which you haven't been able to counteract."

Kee hesitated, tried to think of something he could say that would at least extend the conversation, but could think of nothing and just nodded, yes. Here it comes, he thought.

Eighteen months of work down the drain, along with the Defense Department contract. But the L&B exec went on to ask about an update Kee had added to the report.

"Tell me more about this reverse sequester." Although the man's tone remained neutral, his eyes showed intense interest as he listened to Kee explain:

"Not much to tell. As the original sequester succeeded in neutralizing nearly all the nitrogen in the slurry, the level got too low and the bacterium developed a molecule that would reactivate enough to build and maintain its colonies."

"You were able to produce large quantities of the original sequester, is that right?"

"Yes, as you know, L&B started using it to clear the slurries of high density nitrates, as required by law in some countries, and it cut nearly eighty per cent from your cleanup costs."

"We will, of course, continue to use significant quantities for that purpose, but can you produce the reverse sequester just as easily?"

"I can't think of any reason why not."

"Good. Very good. I want you to triple production of NS2-7 and put together the best team of transgenic engineers you can find."

3

Langley, Virginia
A year later

It took some time, but because of his contacts at the Department of Defense, Kee was able to arrange a meeting with Dr. Rydell, director of the African Desk at the CIA compound in Langley.

Kee introduced the L&B exec who began the conversation with a question for which he already had the answer.

"Is it true that your agency has an ongoing interest in President Kamoro Baku of Mawabi?"

Claude Rydell was tall and slender, with thinning sandy hair. He drew a pipe from the pocket of his tweed jacket and filled it with an exotic-smelling tobacco from a pouch but didn't light it.

"Is that why you've come, to enquire after a Third World head of state?"

It wasn't a response the L&B exec expected, but he managed to maintain the slight smile that was his trademark, a smile that said, with an air of casual superiority, "I know something about you that you don't know I know."

"Well, yes, but also to offer a proposal that might help jump-start your somewhat stalled career, Dr. Rydell."

It was true. Rydell had been passed over twice when he was next in line for the deputy director's job. Then he'd been moved laterally, to the African Desk, and had not moved since. He studied the man who sat across from him for several seconds before he answered, noted the Savile Row suit, the two-hundred-dollar haircut, and the eyes, alert, but unforthcoming and hard to read.

"Your information is correct. We are interested in President Baku."

"I've a fair idea why, but it would be helpful if you could elaborate."

"Certainly. First of all, we believe the elections in which he won a landslide victory were rigged in some way. His status as a democratically elected leader is therefore questionable.

"Lately, he has begun to show dictatorial tendencies. He has nationalized the banks and all public utilities, as well as the country's oil and gas producers. He continues to express sympathy and support for occupied Palestine, Hamas and Hezbollah. But our most urgent concern is Mawabi's production of yellowcake uranium. A sale to Iran could greatly accelerate their nuclear weapons program and would provide Baku with much needed capital for the broad range of entitlements which have tripled Mawabi's national debt."

"Thank you. I assume that you are considering a range of options that might neutralize this imminent threat to our national interest."

"Yes, but I'm afraid that information is classified, and your visitor's clearance doesn't reach that high."

"Understood. But what would you say if I told you our project for Mawabi could destabilize the regime by creating a national crisis? Baku and his corrupt cabinet would be held responsible. He would lose his populist support base and conditions would become strained enough to justify an immediate humanitarian intervention. Your man Loyuba, who is waiting in Chad, could easily be reinstalled to stabilize the country and support US interests there."

Rydell smiled. "I'd say you've been reading our mail, but I'd also have to remind you that your firm lost its bid to run the cash crop mandated by IMF and World Bank loans in Mawabi."

"The contract was awarded to Curtiss James of Great Britain, so I'm not sure what project you're referring to." The L&B exec slid the file folder he'd been holding across the desk. "The details are all here. If you like what you see, we can talk further."

"Very well. And how much will this little sideshow of yours cost American taxpayers?"

"Nothing. Not a red cent. All we ask is that our project be shielded from investigation and/or prosecution under whatever national security protocols apply."

Rydell raised an eyebrow. "I'm not authorized to make those kinds of guarantees, but I will discuss this with the deputy director and our associates over at the National Security Agency, Homeland Security and the Department of Defense. If we think your proposal can deliver the results you've described, I expect we can work something out."

In the limo on the way to the airport, Kee seemed lost in thought and a little confused. His boss picked it up right away. He laughed. "Okay, Kee. Spit it out. What's bugging you?"

Kee shook his head. "I can't even guess what that was all about."

"Ah, yes, well, it's about making the world a better place, and making a whole lot of cash for L&B at the same time. Let me draw you a picture, uh, no, a sketch, of what's going on in the world of bread and butter. There's a drought, Kee, a drought that's been getting more and more severe in most of the high-yield wheat-growing regions on the planet, Russia, Egypt, South America, China, our own great plains and central Canada, to name a few. And the commodity index price keeps rising. Mawabi is only a trial run. By this time next year, we'll have control of the world wheat market."

"Okay, but I don't see what that has to do with deposing Baku."

"Of course, you don't, and I'm not going to tell you. L&B doesn't discuss corporate strategy with its subsidiaries. We *decide* policy and you implement it."

4

They stared at the squat building that occupied half a block where Merritt crossed Light Street in the Bronx. It was after six and the neighbourhood of warehouses, shipping depots, scrap-metal auto-wreck yards and trucking dispatch terminals was deserted.

Detective Buzz Alteri was getting restless. "We sure about this, Nicola?"

His partner and team leader, Lieutenant Nick Cortese, nodded. "All the intel checked out and this is the Bravos' home base."

"Wish there was a way we could get in there, see what's going on."

"Maybe we can. That fire escape leads to the roof. If we take off one of those vent covers we can worm in through the air ducts."

He opened the Motorola HT1000 and briefed the rest of the team.

"Listen up, guys. Buzz and I are going in through the roof. I want you to cover all exits. When the Colombians leave, pick them up as soon as they hit the street. We'll have to keep radio silence and won't be able to give you a heads-up, so stay sharp."

The captain of the 49th Precinct, Liam "Wolf" Donovan, had his SWAT team on a roof across the street. Nick thought this was overkill. It was his case and he had set up the raid, but the 49th wasn't his precinct and the guy outranked him, so he'd let it go. Now, as he put in the call on his two-way, it worried him.

When Donovan answered, Cortese brought him up to speed. Then he added,

"So here's the deal, I need you to stand down, absolutely stand fucking down."

"I don't know if I can do that, Cort*eeze*. I got my orders, too, you know."

"Yeah, you can, and you will. It's my collar and it's my call, so just make sure everyone up there knows what's up and tell them to lock their weapons."

Cortese shut down the Motorola and nodded to Alteri. They crouched low, ran across the intersection and climbed up the fire escape to the roof. Buzz took out the Swiss Army knife he'd carried everywhere since high school and undid the four screws that held the air vent cover in place. Carefully, silently, he lifted off the cap and set it down on the tarred rooftop. Then he climbed up and slipped into the opening. Nick was right behind him.

After a few dozen yards, the light from the opened vent on the roof petered out and the duct ahead of them was dark. There was just room enough to crawl on all fours, but it was stifling, and coated with dust that rose in a fine cloud as they inched along, trying to breathe quietly, trying not to cough or sneeze. As they came to a place where one section was joined to another, the metal creaked and buckled and the seam opened. They stopped, kept very still.

Were they made? They listened intently, but there were no shouts, no indication that anyone had seen or heard the duct give way. Maybe no one was there and the whole operation was a false alarm. Maybe there had been a deal but the Bravos had been tipped and called it off. Then they heard voices, far off, but unmistakable. Nick felt an urge to move quickly but suppressed it. He brought up an image of the warehouse building plan he'd scanned to his iPhone and confirmed that the duct they were in branched off to the left and led to a grate in the office located at the top of a set of stairs. From there, they could observe what was going on without being seen.

After what seemed like a long stretch of squirming through blind twists and turns, the blackout began to dissipate up ahead, and as they approached the screened grating they could hear the voices more clearly. It sounded like a deal was going down, which meant they had to move, fast. But the grating was screwed in from the outside and if

Alteri kicked it in, their cover would be blown before they could make the arrest.

Nick nudged his partner from behind and his voice was a hoarse whisper. "Use the knife!" At first Buzz didn't understand. It was impossible to unscrew the grating frame from inside; then he realized he could cut the screen.

The grating was positioned above a desk and they were able to climb down quietly and set up on either side of the office door. Through the glass panel they had a good view of the warehouse floor. On one side of a long shipping table, two men in dark suits were closing silver attaché cases. On the other were four Bravos in leather jackets. One of them, who looked like the leader, was weighing plastic bags of cocaine on a balance scale and packing them back into a suitcase. When he was done, he nodded at the dark suits. They shook hands, then the Colombians turned and walked toward the front of the building. When they were gone, Nick and Alteri burst through the office door, guns and badges raised.

"NYPD! Keep your hands where we can see them!" They came down the stairs carefully, one step at a time, alert for any sign of resistance, but the Bravos had their hands in the air. They didn't look at all disturbed and it looked like the bust was going to go down without a hitch. That's when it happened.

A shot rang out outside the warehouse, then there were several answering rounds followed by burst of heavy gunfire.

When the Bravos heard the gunshots, they panicked. One of them yelled, "They're not cops!" and went for his weapon. Then everyone started shooting. Nick felt a bullet whizz by him and hit Buzz in the chest. He cringed from the impact, but the vest saved him and he returned fire, bringing down a Bravo who had started to crouch behind the table. The others turned and ran, firing as they did. Before they reached the stairs to the office, Nick winged one of them, then another, but one of their shots took Buzz in the neck and he went down. Nick shot the Bravo who was climbing the stairs and he fell across the railing, hit the floor and did not move. The other two were wounded, but kept firing, and Nick ran over to the table, upended it, and returned fire till his clip was empty. He reloaded and this time took careful aim at the two who had run behind a stack of wooden crates. He knew those boxes wouldn't stop a 9mm round and he shouted, "The building is surrounded, you can't get out. Throw out your weapons and advance with hands on your heads."

There was a long silence, then they started firing again. Nick shot one, then the other, in the head, through the flimsy slats of the crates. By this time Price, Mifflin and Malone had broken in through the three exits. Nick told them to check the four Bravos and ran back to where Alteri lay on the floor, his eyelids fluttering, his breath broken in quick gasps. Blood oozed then pulsed from his neck. He tried to speak, but his eyes rolled up and his head fell to the side. Nick made the officer-down call, then lifted his friend and cradled his upper body across his thighs.

It only took six minutes for the ambulance and the medical team to get there. Nick rode with Alteri, holding his hand in a tight grip, as if he could keep him from slipping away. When he regained consciousness, it looked like there was a good chance he'd make it. Nick talked to him, tried to keep him from passing out again.

"Hey Buzz, we can fix this, you hear? Hang in there, buddy. Stay with me."

"Nico, you there? Yeah, Nico's always there, Nico, Buzz and the Fifth Street Strikers...sure did strut around a lot back there in the day, snatching apples and pears from Librizzi's, kickin' ass and takin' names..." He coughed. Blood came up and trickled from the left side of his mouth. He was grinning, "We always got in shit, you an' me, all those years..."

At the hospital paramedics raced Alteri through Emergency Services to Intensive Care. A team of interns hovered around him, working with visible urgency, hooking up scanners, connecting an IV to his wrist, listening to his heart and lungs with stethoscopes while Nick stood outside with his face to the glass partition, frantic, helpless, dazed.

But there was something he desperately needed to do. He took out his iPhone and called Alteri's wife. Her phone rang and rang, but a message came on and told him she was unavailable. He felt a brief sense of relief, then guilt, then he was furious with himself, took a deep breath and auto-dialed Johnny Alteri, but before his partner's younger brother picked up, there was movement behind him and he turned just as Catherine came running full tilt into the corridor. When she saw him, she screamed, "*Nico, Nico,* is Buzz okay, is he…?" Before he could answer she had stumbled into him and he held her trembling body against his chest. Her whisper had the force of a shout, "Is he… dead? What did you do? How did this happen?"

Nick walked her over to a bench and they sat side by side. He told her about the cocaine bust, but she was distracted, confused, kept shaking her head, and he realized it would be a long time before he could explain it to her, or even to himself.

Then Catherine's eyes cleared and her face changed. "What the hell, Nico, why did you take him in there? What were you thinking?"

He was trying to frame an answer when a voice interrupted them.

"Lieutenant Cortese?"

Nick turned to face a stocky older woman dressed in operating room scrubs spotted with blood. She looked profoundly defeated, drained, and Nick hesitated for a long heartbeat before he answered. "Yes, I'm Cortese, how is he?"

She shook her head. "There was too much shock, too much blood loss. She paused. "And I hate how stupid it sounds to say I'm sorry."

As she walked away, looking like a soldier heading back to some unwinnable war, Catherine screamed, once, an uncontrollable shriek that felt like a knife in Nick's chest. She leapt up from the bench. "Damn you! He trusted you! You were his big brother, his hero! You had to protect him!" Her fists hammered against his arms, his face. Then she turned, closed into herself and wept until she was empty.

5

By the following morning, the shock had begun to wear off but the pain had only got worse. Nick sat at his desk, his head in his hands.

He'd spent most of the night with the Alteris. He and Buzz and Johnny had spent their entire childhood in and out of each other's houses. It was like having two brothers, two sets of parents. He couldn't bear the grief in their eyes. They were his family and he had betrayed them. Catherine was right. He should never have taken Buzz into that warehouse. He should never have let the SWAT team cover the bust.

These thoughts repeated themselves like sharp blows, for hours, but slowly, as he went over everything that had happened, other thoughts began to surface. Donovan knew that he and Buzz were inside. Some cowboy on the SWAT team had disobeyed a direct order to stand down and had fired on the Colombians before Nick's team could arrest them. He still felt a deep emptiness, still felt he could have acted differently, *should* have acted differently, but he began to feel anger too. He had to find out who fired that first shot. Whoever it was had to be stopped before he got other cops killed.

Instead of going through channels and filing a report, Nick drove up to the 49th Precinct.

He wanted to have a talk with Donovan first. He didn't know what he expected but when he entered the captain's office after having to wait for half an hour, Donovan ignored him, flipping through a manila folder, arranging stacks of paper on his desk, looking busy and annoyed.

Finally, he looked up.

"Oh, it's you. Whaddaya want, Cort*eeze*?"

Nick bristled. "I wanna talk to you about the stupid sonofabitch who got Alteri killed!"

Donovan looked away, smirking. "Well," he said, "that might just be the asshole who took him in there."

A slow rage began to build, but Nick took a deep breath and controlled it. "I called in the order to stand down and you agreed. I want the name of the shooter."

"Can't tell you that, but what I *can* tell you is that we were under orders to fire if the perps tried to leave the scene."

"I know the drill, Captain. A warning shot, then you get on the hooter, announce that you're the NYPD, they're under arrest and must surrender their weapons."

"Yeah, something like that. But they fired at us."

"Yeah, after you shot one of them, and never told them who the fuck you were. Of course, they fired at you."

Donovan's voice rose and he came halfway out of his chair. "They're scum! They would have shot anyway!" Then he settled down. "We didn't identify because our megaphone was out, batteries or some damn thing. We don't use it all that much."

"I want the name of your cowboy, Captain."

"No way. It was a good shoot. But, hey, you're free to file a report. I'll see that it gets in with the papers we send upstairs."

6

Three weeks later Nick sat at his desk, reading the letter that had just been delivered by courier from the mayor's office. The file Donovan sent to the commissioner's review committee and Internal Affairs included Cortese's report. Nick had described what happened inside the warehouse. Chaz Malone and Eddie Mifflin confirmed Cortese's order to stand down, and that it was ignored when the SWAT team fired on the Colombians without warning before Nick's team could arrest them.

That should have done it, but Donovan and his team constructed a very different series of events, which they swore to and signed under a notary's seal.

Donovan had been around for thirty years. He had friends and favours owed all over the department. His team outnumbered Cortese's three to one and he had added a paragraph suggesting that, given the close, long-standing relationship between Cortese and his partner, it was understandable how, in the throes of personal grief, the lieutenant could have misremembered or misinterpreted what he saw and heard at the warehouse, and how his team would feel they should back him up.

Apparently, the brass agreed, because the SWAT shooting had been judged an "appropriate application of deadly force, to prevent the escape of dangerous and high priority offenders."

Nick crumpled the letter, tossed it at the wastepaper basket and left the office. He walked three blocks to Rafter's, a watering hole frequented by precinct regulars while they unwound and tried to make the sometimes stormy transition back to civilian life. He sat at the far end of the bar, ordered a double martini and felt his frustration build as he thought about what to do next.

He hated to let the committee's decision stand, but he knew that an appeal would involve a long, uphill battle. He'd been through this before, had been bounced like a Ping-Pong ball from office to office and from one ranking officer of the U.S. Marine Corps to the next, was given so many "big picture" and "for the good of the Force" and "bad press helps the enemy" lectures, he finally agreed to back off.

His train of thought was interrupted when a group of suits from a neighbouring precinct came in and sat at the bar to his left. One of them was a captain Cortese had only met once or twice and had disagreed with about something he could no longer remember. They nodded curtly to each other and Nick had already turned back to his martini when the captain, Thomasson, started talking about what he called "that drug deal balls-up, up in the Bronx."

There was an unmistakable barb in Thomasson's voice and it was pretty clear where this was going. Normally, Nick would have dropped a bill on the bar and left, but something he didn't recognize as part of his everyday self kept him rooted.

Thomasson went on in a loud, harsh voice and this time the big Icelander looked straight at him. "Whoa," he laughed, "some fuckin' disaster. What the hell were you thinkin', Cort*eeze*?"

Nick stared back, felt his body tense all the way to his feet, but kept his mouth shut. Thomasson turned to the others, "Buncha bleedin'-heart pussy bullshit! I'da gone in there and lit up the lot o' them."

Maybe it was that phrase—"lit up"—which he'd heard for the first time in Iraq, but something seemed to take charge of Nick's brain. The punch began below Thomasson's waist and his fist turned viciously just before it caught the man between the jaw hinge and his left ear.

As the captain toppled from the stool and rolled into a heap, Cortese went into combat stance and waited for the bigger man to get back on his feet. But he didn't. Some of the men took hold of Cortese's arms while others helped Thomasson get up and steered him off toward the men's room.

When it became clear that Nick had calmed down, they released him. He looked confused, as though he couldn't quite relate to what had just happened. But it wasn't long before reality began to sink in. He had just decked a superior officer. Three tours with the Marines had taught him what that meant. He could forget about challenging the SWAT team ruling. He'd be lucky if he could stay out of jail.

7

Captain Jenette Hendricks was still puzzled by the report. She'd read through it several times and had spoken privately with some of those who were involved. It had been a difficult meeting that tested her administrative and diplomatic skills. She was a confident, reasonable, well-balanced person who had accomplished a good deal more than she could have imagined when, in spite of well-meaning warnings from parents and some of her friends, she had applied and been accepted as a cadet by the Police Academy. But the going had not been easy. Although she was respected for her exemplary record as a policewoman on patrol, where she had been wounded in a crack house raid, as she passed exams and was promoted ahead of her male peers, many of them began to resent being outdone and then commanded by a woman. The complaint in the report had been filed by one of Jenette's most outspoken critics, and to make matters worse, it was against a detective who had been one of her few supporters and who had become a good friend. She closed the folder and looked up.

"I don't get it, Nicola. This just isn't you. You're the cool one, remember? How did Hemingway put it, 'grace under pressure'? What the hell happened?"

Nick felt his whole body shrink and he wanted to get up and leave, but Hendricks was one of the few brass he knew well and admired. He shook his head. "Beats the hell outta me, Jen. I guess I just lost it."

He didn't know what else to say, so he stared out the window at clouds building and rolling in the autumn sky. The axe would fall and he'd have to accept it.

Hendricks glanced back at the report. Her face still had a puzzled expression, but she shook it off. Her voice took on an official timbre. "Looks like you dodged a bullet on this one, Lieutenant."

Cortese stared at Hendricks in disbelief.

"Thomasson didn't know how close you were to Alteri," Hendricks continued. "When I explained that you had grown up together and were more like brothers than partners, he withdrew the assault charge."

Cortese continued to stare. Hendricks grinned. "You caught a break, Nicola. Stop looking like a dope and get back to work."

On his way back from Hendricks's office, as he passed an open window, Cortese was nearly blinded by a flash of intense light and heard an immense explosion. He leaped to his right and ducked behind a desk, screaming, "Incoming! Incoming! RPG's! Get flat!"

Then rain hit the screen and he came out of it, looked around and got slowly to his feet. No one said a word.

He went down the hall, slipped into his office and closed the door.

There was a bottle of Glenfiddich in the desk and Nick took it out. He looked around for a cup but didn't see one so he twisted off the cork top and took a deep pull from the bottle. He sat down and stared, shook his head. What the hell was that, he wondered. He took another drink, put the cork back in the bottle and laid the bottle back in the drawer. Then the phone rang. And rang. Five times before he picked up.

"Detective Nicola Cortese, Homicide." His voice was hoarse.

"I know who it is, dummy."

He sighed. It was his ex. "Yeah, well, if I knew it was you I'd have hid in the closet."

"It's not a joke, Nicky. Where's that child support payment? You said you made the deposit but you didn't. I'm warning you, I'll talk to your boss. I'll have your salary garnished."

Her voice was like an insect in his ear. "I made the deposit, Ronnie."

"Yeah? Well, the money's not there."

"Don't have a nervous breakdown, okay? I'll check with the bank and get back to you."

"Well, you better. Your daughter needs braces and books and clothes for school. You have no idea what it costs to raise a..."

Before she got to the lecture on responsibility he hung up the phone.

The bank wasn't open yet, but someone would be there. He dialed the number, spoke with the assistant manager for a few minutes, then called Ronnie.

"I just talked to my bank. The money will be transferred within the hour."

"Well, for your sake, I hope so. What happened anyway? You overdrawed again?"

Nick counted to three. "They tried to make the transfer yesterday, but the computer at your bank went down before noon."

"They should have sent it earlier."

"Ronnie, they sent it. Your bank's computer was down."

"Well, that's your story. It just better be there when..."

"Goodbye, Ronnie."

8

Cosimo Chorniak got to the precinct early the next morning. He stood waiting in the hall by the open door of his office. He had his right hand on the knob and when Nick came in from the street he slammed the door, hard. The bang startled Cortese. He leaped over the booking desk's counter and pressed his back up against it. Chorniak's beer gut jiggled with hilarity and he yelled, "Gotcha!"

Cortese came out from behind the counter and walked calmly down the hall. As he passed Chorniak, he said, "Very funny, fat boy." It was like a slap in the face and Chorniak grumbled. "Some people don't know how to take a joke."

Later that day, Cortese was seated at one of the workstation computers. He had earphones on and was listening to a tape that had been transferred from a wiretap. Before anyone could stop him, Chorniak came up behind the lieutenant, blew into a paper bag he had saved from lunch, and popped it inches from Cortese's ear.

No one, least of all Chorniak, could have predicted what happened next.

Instead of diving for cover under a desk, Cortese came out of his chair turning sharply to his right, pulled Chorniak's arm into a hammer lock, but didn't stop there. He kept moving, spun and lifted the man's 286 pounds into a throw across his right hip and over his shoulder. Chorniak flew some eight or ten feet across the hall and broke through the upper panel of an office door. He hung there like a sack of corn, bleeding from a broken nose, unconscious, his left ear half severed, what was left of the plywood jutting into his gut. He was wedged so tight they had to cut the doorframe apart before the paramedics could wheel him out.

9

The room had become very quiet. Cortese hesitated before he spoke. He was trying hard to remember, but he looked confused, uncertain.

"After the gunshot, I just, I don't know…all those years of taekwon-do, then special forces training with the Marines, it just kicked in."

Internal Affairs Bureau chief Connolly shook his head. "There was no gunshot, Lieutenant."

"I know that *now*, but that's what I heard, and I reacted. It wasn't as though I had time to make a rational decision."

"It says here that Officer Chorniak had played a trick on you that morning and you took it badly."

"I didn't think it was funny, and I told him so, but that was it. I wasn't looking to get him back. I was working, at a computer, with earphones on."

"So you didn't know it was Officer Chorniak behind you?"

"All I remember is seeing some kind of uniform, the rest is a blur."

Connolly looked thoughtful. "When did you realize who it was?"

"I don't know. I guess it was just before he hit the door. I don't recall seeing his face until then."

Connolly looked around the room and asked, "Does anyone have any questions?"

No one did. He turned back to Cortese. "Do you have anything you'd like to add or correct?"

Nick shook his head.

"Okay. Captain Hendricks has provided us with a copy of your service record, your many commendations, and her personal evaluation of your abilities and achievements. It's very impressive. Also, you've never done anything like this before and there seems to have been no personal malice involved in the incident. So, it's the decision of this committee that you will not be suspended, but we don't believe you can continue to function effectively in your present position. You will be reclassified as detective second grade and transferred over to Operations. This is not a permanent move and will be revisited periodically. We suggest, no, we strongly urge that you see a department counsellor. We have good people specially trained to deal with things like this."

Connolly stood, reached over and shook Nick's hand. "Good luck, Detective." Then everyone filed out and left him sitting alone at the conference table.

Back at his office, Nick stood looking down at the cardboard box in which he had packed his personal belongings. There were surprisingly few—two coffee mugs, the bottle of Glenfiddich, a Waterman pen and pencil set, a file of departmental papers documenting his career in the force, and two framed photos. One of them was of Nick and his daughter, Terry. They were holding hands in the sun on the boardwalk at Asbury Park. She was six years old. Her hazel eyes and freckled face smiled brightly at the camera. She was a teenager now. Soon she'd be a young woman.

The last thing he put in the box was a photo of his parents. His mother wore a pink blouse and a rose-coloured skirt. His father was in uniform. He had served as a paratrooper in Vietnam. When he retired with the rank of major, they'd gone to live in Hawaii. Suddenly, Nick felt a tightness in his chest. It felt like he couldn't breathe. He staggered over to the window, pulled it up and leaned on the sill trying to get more air into his lungs. Spots danced before his eyes, but before he passed out, whatever it was eased and he stood up.

He felt shaken as he looked around the room he had worked from for half a dozen years. It was no longer his and he thought, *I should just pack that box in my trunk, drive off and never look back.* The idea was appealing and the weight he'd carried around for days began to lift, but he knew he couldn't do it. He'd stick it out. He'd get his old life back.

10

Operations was dismal and boring. Once every week, Nick sent a letter to IAB and copied Captain Hendricks. He wanted another hearing. He'd had no further episodes. He was ready to be sent back to his old job at the Sixth. And every week a notice came back that said *not yet* in department police-speak.

But the paperwork job left most of his evenings free, so he decided to do something he'd thought about but never had time for, and it brought a new person into his life, Dr. Claire Kim Tran. She had a passion for her subject and her lectures on criminal psychology were totally absorbing. More and more he found himself staying after class with questions she seemed happy to discuss. One evening, during the last week of the course, he bit the bullet and asked her out. He didn't think she'd accept, but she did, and he loved her suggestion about where to meet for lunch.

It had been a while since he'd ridden the subway. The crowds, the dirt, the screech of steel wheels on steel rails—they were all a bit overwhelming, but as he swayed with the press of bodies as the car careened around curves, he felt the life of the city in a way he never did inside a cruiser.

The train rocked and roared in the tunnels between stations and he watched the passengers—men in suits behind their newspapers, teens with their headphones and glazed eyes, women with shopping bags and toddlers in tow, oldsters locked in their private thoughts—all of them, like him, united briefly by a need to be elsewhere.

He came up into sunlight and a warm breeze, walked north to 79th then west across town through honking yellow cabs, exhaust fumes, the crush and rush of too many people trying to do too much in too little time, and into the green shade of Central Park.

She was waiting for him just inside the entrance, dressed in a blue track suit and still flushed after her run from Hamilton Heights where she had an office at City College of New York.

"Ah, there you are! Very punctual, Detective."

"One of my few virtues. But it's only because I hate to be kept waiting myself."

"Well, I hope you're not really starving, because I'd like to walk for a while and cool out before we eat."

"Lead on, Doctor."

She set a relaxed pace and he was content to watch her appreciative observation of everything around them. It was almost childlike, but keener, more focused.

As they passed Belvedere Lake, the Great Lawn and Belvedere Castle, she said, "Marvellous. It always makes me feel like I've travelled back to the twelfth century."

Her sense of wonder was contagious and he became vividly aware of the delicate shapes of leaves reflected in still water, the earth-scented air.

"Hard to believe this is actually New York," he said. "Except, of course, after dark."

"Yes. When I was in college, someone I knew was raped in the park. It was brutal. She never fully recovered. I think that's why I specialized in criminal psychology. I wanted to understand.... I don't know why it happened, the mental state that caused it, and how it could be fixed."

"Can it be fixed?"

She smiled. "You took the course and passed with flying colours. What do you think?"

"It should be possible..."

"But?"

"Maybe we're going about it the wrong way. Most violent perpetrators don't rehabilitate. They repeat their crimes, go back to prison, come out and do it again. It's as if they have a calling, a way of life, and won't give it up. Sometimes it bewilders me. If they worked that hard at a day job they'd probably end up rich."

She laughed. "Hard work is admirable?"

"Sure, but not when it's wasteful and destructive. We work hard at a lot of things we ought to avoid like the plague."

"Such as?"

"Oh, I don't know, war, politics, junk food."

"Speak of the devil, here we are!"

They stood in the small crowd at the Sabrett cart and waited their turn. Nick ordered a footlong with onions and mustard. Claire got a classic with sauerkraut. They took their dogs and two orange sodas over to a bench and sat in the shade. A light breeze stirred the leaves above them, sprinkling spangles of sunlight over their clothes.

Nick finished first and watched with admiration as Claire skillfully demolished her skinless frank with small white teeth. Then his cellphone warbled its corny tune. Not a good time, he thought. I should just let it ring.

Claire looked up, stopped eating and tilted her head.

"Police business?"

Reluctantly, Nick checked the number. He hadn't had a call from her since the last time they spent a weekend together, and that had been one tick short of disaster.

"No, it's my daughter, Terry."

Claire smiled. "Well, if she's your daughter, she probably hates to be kept waiting too. You'd better take it. Really. I don't mind."

Nick got up and walked off a way before he brought the phone to his ear. "Hi, sweetheart."

"Hi, Pops."

"I'm really glad you called."

"Yeah, thanks, but maybe you won't be when I tell you why."

"No worries, Terry. What is it?"

"It's Mom, and Willie."

"What about them, they having meltdowns or something?"

"You mean like you guys used to?" Terry laughed. "No, nothing like that, we're just having a disagreement."

She hesitated, and Nick waited while she decided what she should tell him. "They're going on a two-week getaway thing and they say I have to go with them."

"Sounds like fun, what's the problem?"

"Geez, Dad, don't you get it? They're boring. There'd be nothing to do, just lying around on a sun chair watching them guzzle those stupid drinks with umbrellas in them."

Nick heard voices in the background, then Terry said, "Mom wants to talk to you."

While he waited for his ex to come to the phone, he looked up and Claire caught his eye.

She pointed to her wristwatch and mouthed the words, "Gotta go!"

He watched her jog off till the path curved and she was out of sight. She had a light, graceful stride, and he was thinking how easy she was to be with when Ronnie's annoyed, put-upon voice yanked him back.

"That daughter of yours, she's really hard to handle these days."

"You sued for full custody, remember? Have you changed your mind?"

"Of course, I haven't, for chrissake. I just need a break now and then."

"Hire a babysitter."

"She *is* a babysitter. She's almost sixteen." This was going nowhere. Nick sighed. "You want me to take her for a while?"

"Would you? I'd really appreciate it."

"Let me think about it."

Silence.

"Are you still there?" he asked.

"Yeah. Well, the thing is, uh, we have these plane tickets all arranged."

"No shit. Where to?"

"Jamaica."

"Bad idea. It's real expensive, and they knife tourists after dark."

"Stop foolin', Nicky. We tried convincin' her but she's pigheaded like her father. She won't leave New York and we can't leave her in the house. She wants to stay with you."

Nick scratched his head and wondered, why me, Lord? But as he thought about it he realized he liked the idea. They had barely said boo to each other since her last visit, and she was growing up fast. It might just work. He had more time now and they could do things together.

"OK, I'll pick her up after school tomorrow."

"Thanks. I knew you'd come through for me."

"It's not for you, Ronnie. Not at all."

"Oh, well, you know what I mean."

After he rang off, Nick thought about Claire. Was something happening there? Would she ever go out with him again?

11

Nick pulled up to the wrought iron security gates and stopped. A guard in a green uniform with military braid on the shoulders came to the driver's window and asked to see some identification. Instead of showing his driver's licence, Nick flashed his detective's badge. The guard looked annoyed but waved him through.

He'd memorized the instructions he'd been given but the grounds were extensive—acres and acres of lawn under old shade trees behind an eight-foot fence, buildings with gothic arches done in New England granite, paths and picnic grounds, playing fields and an enormous duck pond.

Terry was sitting on the front steps of the St. Mary's School for Girls Library, her chin in her hands, her longish wavy chestnut hair lifting in the breeze from Long Island Sound. One knee poked through her ripped, stonewashed designer jeans and the oversized navy blue sweatshirt made her look like a waif.

She was not in a good mood and made no move to come to the car. Nick just watched her. Even though her expression was suspended halfway between a sulk and a pout, he could see that her face had begun to lengthen ever so slightly, giving her high cheekbones and blue-green eyes a hint of adult seriousness. She was going to be one hell of a woman, Nick thought, and felt a tug of pride. Finally, she got up and came to the car, carrying a ratty orange knapsack.

Nick leaned over and let her in. She threw her pack into the back seat, slammed the door and looked out the window.

"What's the matter, Terry?"

"Nothing."

"Right. So, is this your new personality, the tragically unhappy bitch princess?"

She turned quickly. Her eyes flared, then she suppressed a smile. "Yeah. I been workin' on it."

"I'm no expert, hon, but I'd say it's ready to take on the road."

Her smile opened. She almost laughed, really pleased now, but she didn't say anything else.

"How about some dinner?"

"You buyin'?"

"Of course, I'm buyin'. I'm your father."

"Good. Let's go to McDonald's."

Nick's face twisted up in a very good imitation of a man suffering from indigestion before he answered.

"Look, let's make it a festive occasion. I know this great Indonesian place..."

Terry did a good imitation of his imitation, even gave a little shudder of disgust. Then she said, "I want a big fat burger with fries."

Nick thought about that for a while. "Okay. But let's go someplace where we can get a *real* one."

She smirked, considered it for a while, then nodded.

Rorie's was a small restaurant on the ground floor of an older building. It was done in very dark wood, with heavy, scarred trestle tables along both walls, and four-by-ten rafters with imitation Tiffany lamps overhead. The specialty was a half-pound, very lean chuck steak burger on a freshly baked Kaiser roll.

They sat near the open door and enjoyed their food. Nick ordered a second draft Heineken while Terry finished her parfait.

"Your mother said it was your idea to stay with me while they're in Jamaica. Is that right?"

She shook her head, swallowed a mouthful of ice cream and hot fudge sauce. Nick waited for her to explain.

"It was Mom's idea for me to stay with you. I wanted to stay in the house on my own. I told them you could drop by now and then, to check up."

I don't blame you, Nick thought, picturing the large, six-bedroom clapboard Cape Cod with its wrap-around veranda, spacious lawn and octagonal gazebo. A two-week, nonstop party.

"Did you really want to take care of that monster house all by yourself?"

"No way. We pay people to do that."

"Too bad, then. Maybe next time."

"Doesn't have to be."

"Come again?"

"Doesn't have to be next time."

Nick still didn't get it, so she told him, lowering her voice and leaning across the table.

"I know where they hide the key. You could drop me off and, you know, check up now and then. They'd never know, and I'd be outta your hair."

He stared at his daughter. She was persistent all right, pigheaded as her father. "You're not *in* my hair, Terry, and I promise not to get in yours. Besides, I'm seeing someone and I won't be around that much."

He thought, there goes our chance of doing things together. And as for seeing someone, well, at this point it's just a wish and a prayer. It came as a mild shock that he had just lied to his daughter.

Her eyes lit up a little, considering the possibilities.

"In fact, I have to go back into town tonight, so you'll be on your own."

"Why do you have to go back to Manhattan?"

"To see some friends, guys I used to work with."

"Oh."

"Would you like to come?"

"And watch you guys get drunk? No way."

Nick smiled. There was something about his daughter's prickly manner, her forthrightness, that tickled him.

"Okay. So if you need anything, Mrs. Hennessey will take care of it."

"Who's Mrs. Hennessey?"

"My housekeeper."

"Does she live there?"

"No. I just asked her to work some extra hours till you get settled."

"Geez, Dad. I don't need a *baby*sitter."

"Housekeeper, hon. Besides, you'll like her. She's a no-bullshit person like yourself."

12

Corbie Price and Chaz Malone were sitting at a corner table in the newly remodelled Kettle of Fish when Nick arrived. Price, with his orange-paisley-bandana-wrapped head and gold earring looked like a Somali pirate, but he was probably the best street detective in the Borough. Chaz wore faded jeans and a white T-shirt with a pack of cigarettes rolled up in the left sleeve. He was blond, blue eyed and cut like a weight lifter. There was a tattoo of an anchor and the words Davey Jones on his shoulder.

Price looked up and grinned. "Well, lookit here, if it ain't that big old desk jockey yusta yank our chain when we wuz kickin' ass in the Sixth. Take a load off, Lieutenant."

Nick scowled. "It's 'detective' now, paper grade. And thanks, I will."

Malone asked, "So, whazzup, Doc?"

"Not a helluva lot, Chaz. How about you?"

"Just bustin' our butts as usual. You heard about Hendricks?"

"No, what about her?"

"Rumour is she's due to get kicked upstairs, to borough commander, or bureau chief. She's not lettin' on though, gets kinda cranky when you ask her about it."

"Yeah, that's Hendricks. Plays it close to the vest. Not a bad idea, the way shit flies around the department."

The waiter came by and Nick ordered a draft, but Malone said, "Why don't we just get a pitcher and save this guy some time."

"Hell, let's order two. You guys are way ahead in the cheer department. I'd like a chance to catch up."

Price held up his half-full glass in a toast. "Here's to the sportin' life, which ain't egzackly the life of sports, but close enough."

Malone started to speak, but stopped, wondering whether he should mention it, then he said, "Chorniak's back."

"Yeah? How's he doin'?"

"Okay, I guess, kind of subdued these days. Hasn't pulled one of his silly-ass pranks in a while, and they sewed his ear real good, it just sticks out a little bit more than the other one."

Price laughed. "Sheeit, he looks like a mutt with one ear flopped!"

"Well, I'm sorry to hear that. I never meant to disfigure the jerk."

Malone looked uncomfortable. "Everybody knows it wasn't personal, Nico." He paused, then added, "How you feelin' these days, anyway?"

"What do you mean? I'm feelin' fine 'cept for, you know, paper cuts and eye strain."

"Yeah, good, well, we were just wonderin'..." He hesitated and Price cut in, "Let's just lay it out, Chaz. Nico, it's boring as tapioca these days. The new lieu is a tight-ass number cruncher. We want you back bustin' our chops like the old days."

Nick was touched. "I'd like that too, Corbie, I surely would, but it's not up to me."

Malone said, "Well, actually, it kinda is, or, uh, you know, it might be?"

Price shook his head. "What monkey mouth is tryin' to say is that IAB would take another look pronto if you'd do a few rounds with a counsellor."

Nick felt himself getting hot, and his breathing quickened. He felt surrounded, smothered, trapped.

The beer came and he poured himself a glass, took a long drink before he answered.

"Yeah, well, I thought about it, but I don't see what good it will do."

"We ain't saying anything's broken, bro, it's just, you know, for the brass." Malone added, "They want to move you back, but they need some paper."

"Paper? Fuck, don't they have enough paper in the NYPD? The department's drowning in paper. Besides, I haven't had any, uh, incidents since I left the Sixth. I've been sending them letters telling them so every week. That should be good enough. I'm not gonna spill my guts to some office boy with a bullshit degree."

Malone looked disappointed. He opened both hands in a conciliatory gesture and shrugged. "Hey, Nico, I'm sorry I brought it up."

Nick chucked him on the arm. "I understand. And it means a lot that you guys want me back. I just don't see myself sittin' there like Tony Soprano mouthing off about anxiety attacks and stuffing myself with downers."

Price started laughing, and it went on, got deeper, like something had really tickled him. "Oh shit, I love it, Nico Soprano, Capo Sensitivo, it breaks me up."

Nick didn't know whether to be offended or take it as a compliment. All he said was, "Enough about shrinking heads. It's a big bad city, boys. What do you want to do next?"

13

The familiar signs were all there. Thick tongue, thick head, queasy stomach and a profound reluctance to move. As he lay gathering up the strength to launch his day, he heard voices: Mrs. Hennessey's strong, no-nonsense cadence and the more buoyant no-nonsense voice of his daughter. She sounded in a good mood.

On his way to the shower, he remembered leaving the Kettle of Fish and walking out into the New York city night, lots of people in the streets, almost a carnival feeling, lineups in front of rock clubs and jazz clubs and strip clubs, bouncers in tight T-shirts or sweats guarding the door, and the swarm of taxis, buses with hissing doors and the smell of exhaust fumes mixed with hamburger smoke and the steam from hot dog stands. They barhopped till after two. Price and Malone were ready for more, but Nick begged off.

As he towelled himself he caught whiffs of French roast, fried bacon, onions, toast and something he couldn't quite place. It lifted him out of his self-inflicted misery, and he felt almost alive again.

The kitchen was bright with morning sun. The table was set, and Mrs. Hennessey's sturdy, handsome face beamed at him. He gave Terry a hug and kissed her on the forehead. She steered him to a chair and sat him down. While he poured fresh coffee, she loaded his plate with fluffy eggs, thinly sliced potatoes fried with onions, breaded, lightly browned rounds of green tomato and a large tangle of crisp bacon. She fixed herself a plate, another for the housekeeper, brought over a stack of buttered toast, and they began to eat.

After the first mouthful, Nick looked up at Mrs. Hennessey and grinned.

"This is really spectacular. Exactly what I needed this morning."

Mrs. Hennessey laughed, her eyes twinkling and a tinge of colour flushing her ruddy complexion.

"It warn't none of my doin', Mr. Cortese."

Nick turned to his daughter, his mouth half open with surprise. "It's fabulous, hon. Just fabulous. Where did you learn to do potatoes like that?"

She poked him. Pretended to look hurt. "From you, you jerk. Remember? That summer we went up to Lake Parsippany?"

It all came rushing back, the little cabin, the tumbling brook, that remarkable eighty-year-old schoolteacher who ran the small resort, Mrs. Thurston, how bright she thought Terry was, the rabbit his nine-year-old daughter caught in a trap she had made herself out of old window screen...and the way he himself had learned, from his grandfather, how to slice the potatoes and onions paper thin, to fry them slowly till they were crisp and brown but soft inside, in the magical days of his own summer childhood.

Emotion swelled in him and he struggled to control it. I'm coming apart, he thought, I'm losing it. Then he thought, no, it's not that. I'm just grateful to be reminded that I didn't entirely miss her growing up. I was there. Not often, and not for very long, but it might be something to build on. He smiled at his daughter.

"Yeah. Thanks, I remember. I guess we had some good times after all."

"One or two, I guess." Terry gave him that half-hidden, half-amused smirk that was so much of what she had become these last few years, and he knew that she sensed what he'd been feeling.

As he was clearing the dishes, she looked up at him. "You got a minute?"

"Sure, hon. What is it?"

She glanced at Mrs. Hennessey, who read her perfectly and left the kitchen.

"We have to talk."

"Okay."

He sat back down at the speckled Formica table. She leaned toward him and her face became calm but at the same time animated with an urgency she kept out of her voice.

"There's an Islanders game on Friday night. I'd like to go."

"That's great. I'll pick you up after school, we can grab a bite and..."

She looked sad for a moment, sorry, and her voice was very adult, very tender, the voice of a woman tactfully refusing a date.

"Oh, thanks, that's really sweet, but, uh, a bunch of the kids are going and I wanted to go with them."

Nick tried, not very successfully, to hide his disappointment. The idea of taking Terry to the game had really appealed to him. After a short silence, he said, "Kids from the school?"

"Well, yeah, an' some of the guys from St. Peter's."

"Ah, I see. Boys."

"It's not like that. They're just friends," she said a little sharply, beginning to be annoyed at the direction the conversation was taking.

"Any parents or teachers?"

She looked almost shocked, almost insulted. "No, why?"

"Well, you know, to keep an eye on things. It can get pretty wild sometimes when the Islanders play Montreal."

"So what could happen? It's a public arena, cops are all over the place."

Nick's face darkened a little. Not the police, not patrolmen. Cops. That's how she and her friends saw the NYPD. He felt a flurry of conflicting emotions. Her interest in hockey was one of the things she had learned from him and one of the things they still shared. But she was in his care and he really had no idea where his responsibility lay, or how Ronnie would handle such a request. Was she into boys already, dates, drinking beer and going out afterward for pizza, wrestling with some horny jock in the back of a muscle car? As he looked at her serious face, he saw very clearly that she was no longer a child, that he would have to stop thinking of her that way. When he nodded, she jumped up and hugged him hard.

"Wait, wait, wait...there are some rules, hon."

"Sure, what?"

"No drinking, no speeding, and you've got to be home by eleven."

"Okay, that's fair. But with traffic and all, how about eleven-thirty?"

It was his turn to hug her, and another emotion, pride, rose from the cross-currents that had swirled through him over the last few minutes, pride, because he knew he could trust her to keep any promise she made. That was one thing that had not changed about his daughter. She could be stubborn and bratty and even manipulative, but she had always been an honest kid. Still, he knew how many things could go wrong, how many things could happen over which she had no control, and as soon as he thought this, he began to worry.

She felt his new tension, could see what he was thinking and she leaned back, put both hands on his shoulders.

"Nothing will happen, okay?"

She'd grown up a lot since her last visit. He wanted to tell her so, he wanted to tell her many things, but the time felt wrong and all he said was, "Okay."

14

They stood for a moment looking up at the sun disk and wings of the sky god carved in the Nubian sandstone above the gate before they walked through it into the Temple of Dendur.

Claire spoke first. "It's Egyptian, but the Romans built it, in 15 BC, I think. Seems like each time we meet we go back further in time."

Nick laughed. "Big jumps too, from the twelfth century to 15 BC. What's next? Cave man drawings, then dinosaurs, then the big bang?"

As soon as he said it, he nearly blushed with embarrassment at the unintended sexual innuendo, but Claire was amused.

"Might take a while to get that far. What say we have a snack first?"

They sat at a small table in the museum dining room, sipping black tea. While they waited for their food to arrive, they talked. Nick said, "I'm so glad you called. I didn't know if you'd want to see me again."

"Why wouldn't I?"

"That telephone interruption, family intrigue, ex-wife, grown daughter—not the most attractive first impression."

"Oh no. I felt badly abandoning you that way, you know, just running off, without even a sunset to run off into?"

The food arrived and they were quiet while they ate. She sensed a tension building in him and when they were done, she reached out, laid her long, slim fingers over his crossed hands.

"Is something wrong?"

"Oh no, no, nothing wrong. It's just that…well, I know I shouldn't say this, and I'll probably regret it, it's not the way things are supposed to go, but I really like being with you and I'd like to go on seeing you if you think…I mean, our lives are so different…"

"In some ways, yes, but I also think we're a lot the same."

He looked surprised. "How so?"

"For one thing, we're both on our own, and for another, we share a keen interest in crime. Also, we both seem married to our jobs with not too much going on in our lives."

"I didn't know..."

"Of course not, no way you could, but I'll bet there's a lot more about us that's not so different too. Sooner or later we're going to have to divulge our deep dark secrets, so why not get that done and see where it goes."

"Isn't that sort of talk supposed to happen, I don't know, later?"

She laughed. "Are we really that conventional?"

"I guess not. But I've never been comfortable talking about myself."

"Neither was I, till I spent two years in psychotherapy. But I soon realized that there is very little in most people's lives that is truly private. Most of our secrets are about things that involve other people. So no matter how uncomfortable some event in your life may be, someone already knows about it. Once I figured that out the rest came easy."

"I don't know, Claire. What you say makes sense, but it still feels awkward."

"No worries. Maybe some other time."

Nick shook his head. "No, I'm being silly. I do want to know you better, and it won't happen if I won't let you know me." He hesitated, frowned as though he were figuring something out, then he said, "Okay, so how do we do this, flip a coin to see who goes first?"

"Now, why didn't I think of that?"

"Seriously?"

"No. I'm the one who brought it up, so I'll start. My parents came here after the war. My father had worked with the Marines as a translator so there was no language barrier and he did well. I was born in New York, but I was raised in a traditional Vietnamese family. It was confusing, but I loved and respected my father, and when he chose the man he thought I should marry, I agreed. He was eight years older than I, but a good man, a warm person, educated, professional and kind. We were happy together for several years but when I won a post-grad scholarship and went on with my education, he was uncomfortable. A wife's duties were in the home and I was clearly headed elsewhere. I assured him I could do both, but of course I could not, or at least not up to the meticulous standards he expected. Then I became seriously ill. The infection spread and turned into pelvic inflammatory disease. When I recovered I was told the PID had left so much scar tissue I'd never be able to have children. The grief he felt over that was so deep I knew it was over between us. We talked about adoption, but he was not keen.

"Finally, we agreed that our lives had diverged in some irreversible way. It was a painful but not an unfriendly divorce. We are still close. He is married to a marvellous woman who is an excellent housekeeper, a charming hostess and the happy mother of three kids."

Nick was quiet for a moment, taking it in. He fidgeted in his chair, started to say something but stopped, thinking it over.

Claire said, "I know this isn't easy for you. Just begin anywhere. I'm not going to grade you for organization."

"Okay. I guess, like you, I always had great respect and admiration for my father. He served in the military, and I was raised to trust those in authority."

As he said those words, he felt a tightness in his chest, and saw brief flashes of the warehouse disaster and scenes from his tours with the Marines. He shut them down and continued, "I was an altar boy, joined the CYO, a sort of Boy Scouts of America for Catholics, and in high school I was good at sports, got elected to student council, had good grades. I did ROTC in college, then joined the marines."

He stopped again, shook his head. "That's not it. What I want to tell you about is my marriage. It was a disaster. Well, not at first.... We'd grown up together. Her father owned the saloon on the corner and she was the most beautiful girl on the block, had her own little retinue of retainers, like a little countess or something, and a long line of boyfriends knocking on the door. She was younger than me, nearly seven years. I never thought about her that much, till I got back from college. Then she sort of, I don't know, set her sights for me. She seemed to show up everywhere, gave subtle hints, called me up, ran into me at odd times, I don't know.... She was like a cat, not stalking exactly, but she was very determined. We started dating. I was flattered, our parents were pleased, the sex was fantastic, and Ronnie decided it was time, so we got hitched."

He paused.

Claire said, "Ronnie. It sounds like a boy's name."

"Yeah, that ain't the half of it. Her mother had her baptized Rosalinda. She wanted to name her after the actress Rosalind Russell but the grandparents and some of the in-laws objected that it wasn't Italian. Rosalinda's not Italian either. I think it's Spanish, means something like 'pretty rose'. Ronnie always hated it. She hated it even more when the kids started calling her Rosa and Rosina and Rosie. She thought Ronnie sounded very trendy, very *au courant*."

"It does. I like it. So tell me what happened to your storybook romance."

"It was okay for a while. But Ronnie is a very demanding person. She was used to people crowding around her day and night and here she was married to this hotshot who she saw for maybe an hour a day and two on Sundays. After 9/11, I was shipped out, first to Afghanistan, then to Iraq, so we were apart for several years. Ronnie didn't like it at all and when I got back, she said I was different, moody. I joined the NYPD and spent all my time on the job. Or I'd go off by myself for days, sometimes a whole week at a time. She started dropping hints. She told me it felt like she was a widow but without the advantages. When I asked what those might be, she said widows could sleep with anyone they felt like and even get married again. I laughed, but it was no joke. She got more unhappy, complained, had tantrums, and the more she got on my case, the less I wanted her company."

"And then she had an affair."

"Is it that obvious?"

"Well, it happens."

"Yeah, but I sure as hell didn't see it coming. We fought a lot. I promised to spend more time with her and our daughter. But I never did. When she told me she was going to work, I only half believed her, and when she got a job I figured it might not be a bad idea. We needed the money and she seemed happy. Too happy, I guess. Way too happy. Three months later she told me she was in love with her boss and that she was leaving.

"The divorce was not friendly. Lawyers piling up hours and billing every time they sneezed. In the end she got Terry, the house, the car. I got the TV, the VCR, eight cartons of books, some paintings Ronnie never liked, and a lot of space. Two years ago, she remarried."

"Her boss?"

"No, he dumped her after she became a free woman. She married some German dude named Willie, pulls in around eight hundred large, after taxes. I've never been able to understand what he does. Something financial. Anyway, Ronnie ended up with our daughter. But as soon as she had her she found it was too much work. I think she wanted custody...well, not to spite me exactly...but I guess it was part of our war and she wanted to win."

"What would you have done if you had won custody?"

"I've thought about that. I'd have had to hire someone, a housekeeper, and find a new line of work."

"Could you have done that?"

"I really don't know. Sometimes I think I ought to. But I also really want to get back on the street."

"I understand. Both of our jobs are demanding, difficult, frustrating. Sometimes I think I should pack it in too. Also, neither of us connected with anyone after our marriages failed, so you see, we do have a lot in common."

He nodded, smiled. "Okay, are we finished now?"

"I hope not."

"Sorry, what I meant to say was, now that we know each other so well, will you have dinner with me?"

Claire looked rueful. "I'm teaching tonight, and I always eat alone before a class. Sort of a get-ready-to-perform ritual. It works, and I'm still superstitious enough not to mess with whatever works."

15

When Claire called on Friday and invited him to supper at her place, he felt uncomfortable and almost told her he couldn't make it. Terry was going to the hockey game and he wanted to be there when she got back, or if she needed anything, or if she got into trouble. But that wasn't the only reason. Along with the excitement he felt about spending time with Claire, there was an undertow of uncertainty. His feelings for her had intensified so quickly it scared him. She totally delighted him. She was her own person in charge of her own space, and he loved her cheerful, radiant independence.

It had been a long time since he'd felt what he was feeling now. A very long time. Or maybe never. And that's what worried him. It felt like the real thing, but he was still upset by his own recent disruptions, the flashbacks, the panic attacks, the sudden, over-reactive combat responses, the bad dreams. And when he compared this to her clarity, her strong, confident, light-footed stride as she came around that screen of rhododendron leaves in Central Park, he felt woefully inadequate. The comfortable distance between teacher and student had dissolved into a deepening intimacy that could go anywhere, but where was it going, did it have any chance at all, and even if it did, was it fair?

She had no idea how confused he was. He was coming apart. How could he sustain a relationship when he could barely control his own thoughts, his own feelings, his own behaviour? And it might get worse, he might become dangerous, or incapable of doing what was left of his job; then where would they be? Did he expect her to support a mental invalid for the rest of her life? But all those questions receded as he thought about spending an evening with her and he said, "Sure, eight o'clock, I'll be there."

Terry had bought flowers on her way home from school and was arranging them in a glass vase when Nick got home from work. She looked up and grinned.

"Too much hang-tough and live-with-it décor around here, Pops. Thought I'd lighten it up a bit."

Nick took in the subtle array of colours and textures suffused with late afternoon sun and knew his daughter had trusted him with another small, but very private part of herself. He didn't know how he should respond, but before he could think, another part of him said, "They're beautiful Terry. Thanks."

He paused. He was still worried about not being there when she got back from the hockey game. He wanted to keep his time with Claire free for whatever might happen, but Terry might need him, so he said, "Look, I know you can take care of yourself. I taught you some kick moves myself; but I'm trying to be a father here, and I suck at it, so help me. Promise me one more time, you'll call if you get in trouble, or need anything, anything whatsoever?"

Terry turned away, walked over and sat down behind the coffee table on the ratty sofa. "We've already done this, Pops. What more do you want?"

"Nothing, really, I just want to give you an address where I'll be. Just in case."

Terry looked puzzled. "In case of *what*, for god's sake?"

"I don't know, hon. In case you can't use your phone. In case you need to get away fast in a cab..."

As soon as he said the words he felt like a cartoon. But Terry laughed.

"Okay, okay, I'm the daughter of a police lieutenant. I'm at risk of losing my access to the real world."

"You know, hon, I'm not really sure *what's* real these days, but please..."

"Shoot me the address, I'll..."

"No, not on your iPhone, let me write it down on a card from the Stone Age, so I can come galloping out of the past and rescue you with a club."

Terry gave her father a look that said, *You are really weird, but you're okay for a cop,* and read what he had written on the NYPD detective card he gave clients he hoped would call back.

She came to the door dressed in a yellow, knee-length jacket with three-quarter sleeves, a stand collar and splits from hem to waist at each side over a pair of matching silk pants. He caught the subtle fragrance of leather and violets and mimosa in her perfume and she nearly squealed with delight when he handed her the single yellow rose he had bought on impulse from a flower girl on the street.

"My favourite colour, how did you know?"

He stood there grinning foolishly, thinking how sometimes you're just in the zone and you don't know it.

"Come in, come in," she said, "supper's almost ready, you can open the wine."

He followed her into the kitchen where she clipped the flower and pinned it into her blue-black hair, which was tucked up in a mass of overlapping whorls.

All through dinner he watched her eyes, moving through subtle changes, like the light under swaying palms, and the tiny dimples that appeared and disappeared at the corners of her mouth as they talked. She was animated, buoyant, reached out and touched his hand sometimes to emphasize a point, and he felt the attraction build, slowly, effortlessly, until a shadow of self-doubt cut across it, and what he'd wanted, needed in his life for a long time became the same thing he was unsure of.

When they were through eating, he helped clear the dishes and stack them on the counter in the kitchen, but as he reached down to open the dishwasher she stopped him, took his hand and led him toward the bedroom. He didn't resist, but wondered how it would go, what he should do. Didn't she need to know about his problem before they found themselves naked in bed?

They stood very still, face to face, for a long moment before he leaned over and kissed her on the mouth, lightly at first, then with more pressure, moving his lips over hers, tracing their shapeliness, their firm swell and curve. He felt desire rise in him like a warm tide and his pulse, his breath, quickened. She parted her lips and moved her mouth over his, flicking his tongue with her tongue while she reached up and began to unbutton his shirt. When she was done, he pulled it loose from his belt while she slipped out of her jacket and dropped it to the floor. She was wearing a pale gold blouse which she pulled off over her head and he felt her body heat, caught a heady waft of her perfume, and an overwhelming flood of emotion poured through him, left him weak, really weak in the knees, and he froze, didn't know what to do next. Though he had been with many women before Claire, all his experience seemed to fall away, as though it belonged to a different person or a different life and was utterly useless to him here, with her, now.

She read his uncertainty immediately and her clear eyes told him she understood. She undid her bra, unbuckled his belt and stepped back. Slowly, they finished undressing, stood before each other as though before a mirror, drinking in the pleasure they saw each take in the other, and when they lay down together, they were both ready, open, totally present, and as he entered her she sighed and moved with him. They found each other's rhythm and rode it, higher and higher until it crowned and eased off. It felt like this had never happened before, and also like they had made love many times, in many places, intensely fresh and intensely familiar all at once, like coming home after a long time away.

They had both dozed off, lightly, without saying a word, and when they woke it was already dark. He didn't know what time it was and it caused him some concern. He wanted to be home for Terry. He tried to calculate how long they'd been asleep and how long it would take him to drive back to Queens, and whether he should leave pretty soon, or immediately. But leaving in a rush bothered him too. How rude would that be, to eat, go to bed and run? Claire was nestled against his shoulder. When he looked down he was surprised to see that she was smiling.

"You'll have to leave pretty soon if you want to be there when your daughter gets home. Call me tomorrow."

It was just after eleven when he got back to his apartment. He turned on the TV, couldn't concentrate, turned it off. He flipped through an issue of *U.S. News & World Report*, but it bored him. He kept checking the clock. At eleven-forty he began to worry, and by the time midnight inched by, he was frantic. He should never have let her go. What if she got in a car with some drunk preppie and is lying right now in a heap of twisted metal bleeding to death? Or getting gang raped in some soundproof basement?

He opened the bottle of Glenfiddich and poured himself a shot. He threw it back and was about to pour another when the buzzer rang and he let her in. While she was on the elevator he tried to calm himself. He wanted to tear a strip off her for being almost an hour late and putting him though the tortures of the damned, but when she came smiling in through the front door, he was so happy to see her safe, he just hugged her and asked, "How was it?"

"It was fantastic. Islanders won four to three."

He wanted to kiss her, but somehow it seemed inappropriate. "Sorry I missed that. Maybe some other time, eh?"

"Sure, yeah, that would be great."

"Okay, we'll do it before your mother gets back from Jamaica."

"I wish they were staying longer, I like it here."

"No worries, hon. You can visit any time you like and for as long as your mom will let you."

"I'll work on her about that. And Dad?"

"Hmm?"

"Thanks for trusting me."

16

Cortese lay in tangled sheets, soaked with sweat. The dream had surfaced again and woken him just after midnight. He didn't get back to sleep till well after four.

When the phone rang, he jerked up as if yanked by strings and stood before the bedside table, staring at the alarm clock till his eyes cleared and he picked up the receiver.

"Yeah, hello?"

"Good morning. Is this Detective Nicola Cortese?"

"Yes."

"This is Baxter Chase. Captain Hendricks has been promoted to borough commander for Manhattan South and I've taken over as her replacement."

Nick wondered what that had to do with him. "Uh…congratulations, I guess. Glad to hear about Hendricks, she deserves it."

"Thank you. I've petitioned to bring you back to the Sixth and with Hendricks's support IAB has agreed. I'm also promoting you to detective-investigator second class. It's not lieutenant, but the pay is better than what you get at Operations."

Nick was stunned. "I don't know what to say. Thank *you*, Captain."

"Don't thank me yet, Cortese. What you did to Chorniak and Captain Thomasson, along with all your other crap, is entirely unacceptable in a member of service. You're a loose cannon, totally out of control. Hendricks covered for you, and there's nothing I can do about that now, but I'm putting you back in the real world because I'm betting it won't be long before you freak out or pull some crazy shit. And when you do, I'll be there to make sure you get what *you* deserve."

Nicola felt like he'd been hit with a hammer.

"Of course, you can save yourself and the rest of us a whole lot of trouble. You can resign from the force. Tomorrow's your RDO, so you'll have all day to think about it. Think hard, Detective. And get your ass down here at eight sharp Tuesday morning."

Before Nick could think of something to say, Chase hung up.

Later that day Nick was still wrestling with a swarm of conflicting thoughts and emotions. He was very angry, but also worried that Chase might be right, he might not be able to control his responses, and worried too about how being back on the job might affect his relationship with Claire. He wanted to see her, to talk, but he knew he wasn't ready yet.

Her voice was bright and cheerful when she answered her cellphone.

"Nico! So glad you called. I've been thinking about you."

"I've been thinking about you too. All day. Are you free tomorrow? It's my regular day off…"

As though she had picked up on his urgency, her voice became more serious.

"Yes, I'm free, but it sounds important. If you want, I can meet you somewhere now."

"Well, yeah, it kind of is, but I need to finish up here and there are some things I have to do later on." It sounded lame so he added, "I've just been transferred back to my old precinct, so I'll be on the job again Tuesday morning."

"Good news? Or not?"

"Ah, Claire. You read me so well. I don't know. That's what I'd like to talk about. Can we go somewhere tomorrow, maybe take a drive in the country, have a picnic in a park or at one of those rest stops with green wood tables on the parkway?"

"Sounds lovely and it will be good to get out of the city for a while. I'll pack us a lunch."

17

Kenneth Lang watched with a scowl as the electronic security system rejected his ID for the third time. A pair of Sunday strollers stopped and stared. *Screw off*, he thought, *I own this building.* Finally, he gave up and pounded on the glass. A uniformed guard left his coffee and magazines and took his own sweet time crossing the marble floor. He pressed a button and spoke into the intercom, his voice broken by static.

"What are you doing?"

Lang waved the ID card. "I can't get this damn thing to work. Open up."

"Can't do that without authorization," the guard replied then added, "Sir."

He raised the stainless steel hatch about half an inch. "Slide your card through there. I'll check it out." Lang did as he was told.

The guard sauntered over to his desk, switched on the computer and punched some keys. Light from the screen flickered over his face. He frowned, chewed at his lip, then got up, came back and unlocked the door. As he handed back the card Lang snapped, "What's your name, fella?"

"Tomlinson, Jake Tomlinson." His voice had lost its confident briskness.

"All right, Tomlinson. You're a pain in the ass, but that's what I pay you for."

The worried look melted from the young man's face. He came to attention and looked straight ahead.

"Thank you. Sir!"

There was something unmistakably military in that, and Lang responded with a brief salute. It was automatic, the reflex of a former lieutenant-colonel.

He crossed the sunlit foyer with its trees and shrubs and stood before the brushed chrome doors of the elevator. After six-and-a-half years, he still felt a twinge of pride when he entered this building of white stone with windows like smoky X-ray prints that swept gracefully up and back from the street.

He got out on the thirty-seventh floor and let himself into a spacious, well-lit room he had furnished in flagrant violation of the building's austere decorum. The centrepiece was a large antique desk, flanked on one side by a flag from the Revolutionary War, and on the other with the Gadsden flag of 1775, yellow, with a coiled rattler and the words Don't Tread On Me in brown ink underneath it.

There were bookshelves stocked with first editions, a glass case of sports trophies, civic awards and war medals. Artifacts from Africa and the Third World were placed unobtrusively around the room. And there were photographs, including an eleven-by-fourteen colour shot of Lang with Bill Clinton, shaking hands.

He walked to the bar, leaned over its cowhide armrest, selected an old-fashioned glass from the shelf and poured two fingers of Jack Daniel's. He took it over to his desk, drank half an ounce and worked steadily for several hours.

At three-thirty he put in a call to Senator Alvin Tillis. When the senator finally came to the phone, Lang said, "Happy birthday, Al. How many years you got now anyway, old dawg?"

Tillis laughed. "Ken Lang, for god's sake, how the hell are ya?"

"Not too bad, though Baine keeps reminding me it's customary at my age to delegate the small stuff, accept a decreased workload, and think about, God save us, *retirement*."

"Out of the mouths of babes, eh? But I hear you're expanding, talking with DOD and Langley."

"Yeah, when we acquired Sarbitt Chemical, we took on some projects that involved federal agencies. Some of those contracts need to be renegotiated. Next time I get to DC we should spend an evening together."

"Excellent. Let me know when your plans firm up."

"Will do. In the meanwhile, have a great day, old friend."

"Thanks, Ken. Talk to you soon."

Lang finished the last of the sour mash, washed the glass at the bar sink and placed it back on the shelf. He glanced at his watch. He was in good time for the train back to Greenwich.

Halfway across the lobby, he stopped and turned to the security desk. "Tomlinson!"

The guard's head came up from his magazine, a puzzled look on his face. "Carry on, soldier."

Tomlinson threw him a quick salute and grinned as Lang left the building.

Out on the street, Lang scanned Fifth Avenue for a cab and noticed that the Lincoln Town Car parked at the curb was occupied and had its motor running. Two dark-skinned men in dark suits got out and approached him. He sensed danger in their body language. Then he saw that the driver was holding what looked like an assault rifle and felt a jolt of adrenalin. One of the suits tried to force his right arm behind his back, but Lang braced his fist against his hip and swung his elbow back into lean ribs. The man grunted and released his grip. Lang turned to his left and nailed the other man with a straight right that scattered a couple of teeth and sent him spinning. He felt something like a bee sting in his upper back as he swung his forearm into the bridge of the other man's nose. By this time the first attacker had recovered and was pulling him into the back seat of the Lincoln.

He watched through waves of nausea as Tomlinson ran from the building, unholstering his Smith & Wesson. But before he could get off a shot, the driver fired two short bursts through the open passenger window. Tomlinson hit the sidewalk and rolled into a heap, one leg bent under the other, his uniform stained with patches of red. The glass door behind him held a pattern of white, spider-web cracks before it collapsed. And that was the last thing Lang saw before the

Lincoln's acceleration pressed him back into plush upholstery that soaked up the last thought in his mind.

18

Malcom Duplessis adjusted the burgundy smoking jacket around his hefty frame. He walked over to the dimmer switch near the door and turned the lamplight down to a soft glow. Then he picked up the snifter of Otard XO and eased himself into the big leather chair. There was a fire in the hearth and the faint scent of roses lingered in the air. He warmed the snifter in the palm of his hand, swirled the cognac in slow circles and brought it up to his nose. The heady fumes filled him with satisfaction, but his enjoyment was bruised a little when Connie came out of the bedroom and staggered down the hallway, literally bouncing off walls and spilling her drink on the Persian rug.

She swayed to a stop and stood beside the armchair, pouting.

"I'm bored, Malcom. I want to go to the club."

"I detest the place, Consuela, you know that."

"Not you, *me, I* want to go."

"You can't go to a place like that on your own, and I won't take you."

"Don't have to. Get Victor. Puhleeeeze? He can bring me in the limo, pick me up later."

Duplessis thought about it. Victor was a chauffeur, but he was also a bodyguard. He'd keep her out of trouble if paid to wait.

"Okay, but he's not to leave you there, you hear? He'll stick around till you're ready to go."

She put her arms around his neck and kissed him.

"Thank you, daddums. I'll go change."

After she left, he poured himself a second cognac, put on some music and thought about his very young wife.

The first time he saw her, working a badly lit street in Soho, she took his breath away.

He had been with street girls before, but she was different, still fresh, unbroken by The Life. He came back night after night, then bought all her time for a considerable sum from that weasel Ricky Sanchez.

But he wanted more.

When he proposed, she giggled, did a little dance around the room and said, "Sure, Malcom, can I wear white?"

Of course, it meant nothing to her. When the money ran out, so would she.

The cellphone's warble interrupted his dismal reverie. He checked the caller ID and what he saw surprised him. It was a business number.

"Malcom Duplessis, how may I help you?"

"Glad I caught you, Malcom. We've got a job for you."

"What sort of a job?"

"Oh, the usual, but this is big. The client is willing to go as high as 600 large."

If that was the first offer, Duplessis knew he could get eight, or a mil. "That's an interesting fee, but I'll have to think it over."

"No problem. You've got thirty minutes. I'll call you back."

He was sorely tempted. His hands weren't as steady as they used to be. In a few years he wouldn't be able to work at all and he needed the money, now more than ever. But he had to be there when Consuela returned from the club or God knows what she'd get into. He felt his chest tighten. He had to decide and there wasn't much time. He hoisted himself from the chair and headed for the bathroom.

He badly needed a tranquilizer, but when he opened the medicine cabinet, they were nowhere to be seen. *Consuela. She's done it again, walked off with my pills.* But he remembered the last time this happened and hoped she'd squirrelled them away in the same place.

As he rooted around in the top drawer of her bedside chest, he noticed an opened envelope. It was vellum, with no stamp or address, but had *Consuela Ramirez* written on the front in purple ink. He knew he should leave it alone, but he couldn't. He drew the letter out and opened it. As he read, he felt an uncontrollable rage build in his blood.

19

On Monday morning, the phone rang before the sun came up. Nick was not happy to be roused in the dark on his day off. But he thought it might be important, so he picked up.

"Cortese here."

It was Baxter Chase.

"Change of plans. I've got a case for you."

"Wait a minute. You said I'd have a day to think about it."

"Well, your time ran out. You've got about sixty seconds, then shag your ass."

"Fuck you, Chase."

"Good, that's very good, Cortese. Keep that wop temper of yours stoked up and you'll be gone in no time. Or does that *fuck you* mean you quit?"

"I don't quit, Bassett."

"Baxter, it's Baxter Chase."

"That's what I said, Basket Case. What are you yammering about at six in the a.m. anyway? Somebody snatch some lingerie from a Macey's mannikin?"

"It's a homicide, Detective, in the Village, 32 Charles Street."

"Who caught it?"

"Uniforms from the Sixth."

"And you want me to handle it?"

"No, Cortese, I want you to screw it up."

Nick checked the clock. It was way too early to wake Claire and change their plans for the day. He'd do that later, and he could leave Terry a note, with money for a cab to school and Mrs. Hennessey's home number in case she needed anything, but she should be all right. She might even enjoy having the morning to herself.

He strapped on the shoulder holster with his Glock 20 10mm., slipped on a loose jacket and left the apartment.

The sky was overcast and by the time he got to Charles Street it had begun to drizzle. A TV truck was pulled up on the sidewalk and a crew of cameramen was swarming around, shooting. Three patrol cars blocked the street, two of their turret lights still twirling. The temporary headquarters van was parked in front of the apartment building and a squad of uniforms stood around, waiting for their assignments.

Nick parked in a loading zone, pulled the ID plate from the visor and tossed it onto the dash. He fished out his shield wallet and clipped it to a thong, which he looped around his neck.

As soon as he got out of the car, he was accosted by Alycia Huston from WKBL. She strode over and shoved a microphone in his face.

"Are you in charge here?"

"Not yet, Ma'am. I just arrived."

"Come on, we know there's been a homicide, we need some details."

"I don't have any details. Talk to me after I've done my job."

"And when will that be?"

"As soon as you get out of my way."

He brushed past her and headed for the temporary headquarters van.

As he climbed into the cramped, stifling space a middle-aged patrol sergeant with an ample gut and a large freckled face held out his hand.

"Dale Keagan. Good to see you're back on the job, Detective."

"Thanks, Dale. What notifications have you made?"

"We've called the borough, the chief of detectives, and the Major Case Squad. They told us to wait on you for further instructions."

"Good. I hate to make extra work for you guys, but those media vultures will be poaching the police band frequencies, so I want you to use landlines."

"No problem. Anything else?"

"The usual drill. Set up a detail roster and an assignment log. We'll also need the Crime Scene Unit and the medical examiner. See if you can get Kaprisky from Bellevue."

Keagan nodded. "Will do," and Cortese left the van.

He flashed his shield and ducked under the tape. At the entrance to the building, he checked in with Patrolman Onofreo who recorded his name, number and time of arrival in the crime scene log. Nick asked him for the steno pad and scanned it.

"Okay. I want a tight rein on all personnel. No one gets in who doesn't have an assignment. And if any of the brass show up, keep them here and send for me."

Onofreo grinned. "Tight as a tick's ass, Detective." He unhooked the rope that blocked the entrance and let Cortese through.

As he came into the lobby, he heard Corbie Price's high, musical laugh rise from the low-key buzz of male voices. When Price saw him, he came over and chucked him on the arm.

"Great to have you back on the street, Nico."

"It's good to *be* back, but what's up with this Chase guy?"

"Ah, he's an uptight, rulebook desk jockey, but he's all right."

"If you say so, Corbie, I'll hold my nose and try to believe it. What have we got here?"

"Call came in last night at 2:47. Neighbours heard screams, were unable to gain entrance and called 911. RMP's from the Sixth were on the scene at 3:08. Sergeant Keagan's squad had to force entry upstairs, in 14-B. They found a young woman, early twenties, DOA, looks like her neck was broken. Notifications were made to the chief of detectives and the borough commander. Chase called back and set up a special op code through the Major Case Squad. Said you were the whip."

"Okay, let's get this lobby cleared."

Price went over and talked to the half-dozen uniforms who were standing around smoking. They dropped their butts and ground them out on the marble floor, then filed out to begin canvassing the neighbourhood.

Two officers were talking to a thin, balding man in shirtsleeves who was nervously sucking on a Camel straight and shaking his head. Cortese introduced himself and they shook hands.

"Paul Hillerman. I manage the building." He lit another Camel from the butt and shook his head. "Nothing like this has ever happened here, Officer. How can I help?"

"A detective will take your statement shortly. For now, just try to relax, and stay out of the way as much as possible. You can also make sure that tenants who enter or leave are kept away from the roped-off areas."

Hillerman nodded enthusiastically, happy to finally have something to do.

As they rode up in the elevator, Cortese asked Price for his read.

"Hard to say. The doorman has the victim coming in around 2:00 a.m. Her husband's driver," Price checked his notes, "one Victor Luzov, dropped her off. She was high, but otherwise undamaged. He was on till 6:00 a.m. and didn't see anyone else enter or leave, but that part of the lobby between the entrance and the elevator isn't visible from his office."

The elevator whirred to a stop, the doors slid open and they stepped out into a hallway crowded with uniforms and tenants, all talking excitedly.

Cortese and Price pulled on surgical gloves, then flashed their shields to the patrolman who stood in front of the apartment door. It was splintered and hung from one hinge. Cortese checked the lock and didn't see any scratches or other signs that there was a forced entry before Keagan's foot broke it down. Inside, a few uniforms had gotten into the liquor cabinet and were drinking single malt Scotch from crystal glasses.

He felt his temperature rise, strode into the hallway and shouted, "Listen up, you whisky-sucking fuck-ups. I want you checked at the Temporary Headquarters van and out on the job in two minutes flat."

The hubbub dwindled to a tense silence as they knocked back the last of their drinks and filed out. When the scene was cleared, Cortese and Price did a walk-through. Nick talked and Corbie wrote in his notebook.

"Living room. Fingerprint detail. Snifter on side table."

They moved on. "Dining area, glass tabletop. Gold-plated single-edged razor blade, traces of white powder, probably cocaine."

In the kitchen, Cortese bent over with his hands behind his back and sniffed at an old-fashioned glass. He looked up at Price. "Vodka. Collect the dregs and have the glass dusted."

In the bathroom, the medicine cabinet held a collection of blue vials B Dilaudid (hydromorphone), Percocet and Halcion (triazolam). They were all prescribed by a doctor named Murray Gimmelman. Price copied the name into his notebook and bagged the drugs.

In the study they found a lease and a marriage licence. The apartment was paid for by a man named Malcom Duplessis who had been recently married to the victim, Consuela Ramirez, a woman less than half his age.

They crossed the narrow hallway and entered what looked like the dead woman's bedroom. The lamp on the bedside chest was still lit and the top drawer was halfway open. There was a blue vial of Valium on top of the chest and an empty envelope with *Consuela Ramirez* written on the front in purple ink. The letter, written with the same ink, was lying on the bed. Cortese picked it up and read it.

It won't be long now, Darling. Mo made copies of the keys. Here are the ones you gave me. Put them back as soon as you can. We'll have the passport and other ID tomorrow. Just think, with all that money the world will be ours, we can go anywhere we want. Stay with the plan, don't get too high, and think about how it will feel to be free. I love you. Rhea

He gave the letter and the envelope to Price. "These go into evidence and see if you can get one of the uniforms to use a public phone and put out an APB on Malcom Duplessis. I think we've got a person of interest here."

Nick moved out of the bedroom and into the hallway. A young patrolman stood before the body of a young woman who lay face down, partially covered by a man's overcoat. Cortese stood there shaking his head in disgust.

"Was the body found this way or did someone cover it?"

The young officer looked away and mumbled that he had taken the coat from a closet and draped it over the body. He was visibly upset. "I know it's not procedure, but my god, she was lying there all exposed. Should I remove it?"

"No, just leave it. What's your name, Patrolman?"

"Driscoe, sir."

"Okay, Driscoe, I do respect your commitment to the laws of decency. But in future, please remember your commitment to the rules of evidence. I don't think any harm's been done this time, but I've seen too many perps walk because of some officer's carelessness. You are relieved. Check out and report to the TH van. Then I need you to take down the licence plate numbers of all civilian vehicles in a five-block perimeter. Someone might have seen something."

Driscoe saluted smartly and left.

A uniformed officer came over and announced that the Crime Scene Unit and the ME had arrived. Price briefed the CSU from his notes, and the ME examined the body while Nick briefed the forensics team.

"I'll need a crime scene sketch with full triangulation. Detective Price has given you my instructions for fingerprints and evidence collection. I want the entire apartment stripped. Collect address books, wallets, letters, bank books, clothes, anything that might give us information about the victim and anyone else who might have been here in the last two weeks. Once you've got a line on next of kin, contact Benson at the Sixth."

Nick took the crime scene photographer, Scotty Mackenzie, aside and said, "Shoot the entire apartment. And I mean everything. Every wall. Every window. Every closet. I'll need the disk of jpegs on my desk in an hour. And Mac, use the Nikon."

Mac brightened. "You got it!" and started setting up the high voltage lights.

Nick walked back to where the victim lay on the oak floor. The lab techs had finished and had not replaced her bra or bikini panties. There was a thickening welt behind her right ear and a bruise on her temple. As he stood before the young woman's naked body, Nick was nearly overcome with grief and rage.

Even in death her face was extraordinarily beautiful, child-like, almost angelic in the soft light that filtered into the hallway. He felt a chill that began at the base of his spine and rushed up his back. There was a wave of nausea. His heart was racing, then he couldn't feel it any more, or his clenched teeth. It was as though he had left his body. The room went out of focus and was replaced by a field of diffuse light. There was the sound of water, moving fast, and another sound, like children crying, then gunshots and a woman running from a house. She was wearing a torn shirt and nothing else. She was bleeding profusely from the neck and her left arm hung uselessly as she ran. Before she reached him, she cried out and fell. He rushed to her side, knelt and felt for a pulse. She was unconscious and she wasn't breathing. He was shouting, *Medic! Get a medic over here!* He was giving her mouth-to-mouth, but it wasn't working. He became frantic, lifted her and began to run. Then everything floated away and he found himself standing in the rain, on a street in Greenwich Village, with a dead woman in his arms.

20

Nick was rattled, confused, and all the way back to the precinct, he kept trying to figure out what had just happened. He fully expected Chase to be waiting at the door with a suspension order, but he told himself, whatever, just suck it up, soldier. You've got a case to solve, so do what you need to as long as you can.

But Chase didn't meet him or call him in, so he took the CD with the Nikon jpegs to the mainframe and ran high-resolution prints, which he took back to his office. As he looked through them he began to get excited by what he saw. There were four prints of the hallway, shot from different angles, and one of them showed a thin line in the varnished wainscoting.

It was midday and the precinct was nearly empty. The only one still on duty eligible to go on patrol was Pratt Finch, an up-and-coming fast-track rookie with connections and a powerful "rabbi" in the department. He was smart, well groomed, well mannered and really good at sucking up without letting it show too much. Nick would have preferred to take Price or Malone, but there wasn't time, so he walked over to the neatest desk in the room and said, "Finch, I've got a job for you, come with me."

"Where to, Detective?"

"Back to the crime scene at Charles Street."

Finch frowned. "Excuse me for asking, sir, but what for? It's already been processed by CSU."

Nick laid the file folder he was carrying on Finch's desk and opened it.

"Look at this print and tell me what you see."

Finch studied it for a minute, then shook his head. "Nothing out of the ordinary, a hallway, with wood panelling all lit up with sun from a window."

"Good. Now look right here."

"Looks like, uh, a joint line, maybe a piece that was damaged and had to be cut out and replaced?"

"Yeah, or maybe it's some kind of hinged flap, a door with a spring lock. Some sort of hiding place. I want to check it out. And I don't want to be interrupted so I need you to keep an eye out while I'm inside."

"Will do, but don't we need a warrant?"

"Nah, it's a crime scene, remember?"

The door at 14-B had been replaced and there was a strip of yellow tape across it.

Cortese broke the seal and let himself in with the key he had gotten from the superintendent. Now that he was actually there, he began to understand what the joint line he'd seen in the print might be, and it wasn't good news. The wainscoting was crisscrossed by grooved bands about an inch wide and even if the joint was there, it might signify nothing more than the way the wainscoting was attached to the wall, in large squares fitted together so the seams were hidden in the grooved woodwork. But the square he'd been studying in the print showed a joint line running across the grooves more than halfway down, and it wasn't part of the design.

He looked at the print again and counted over to the square he wanted to examine. He pressed his cheek against the wood and sighted toward the source of the light. From that angle he could see that the line in the photo was real. He took out his pocket knife and tried to insert the smallest blade into the crack, but it wouldn't fit. He scanned the entire wall for any knobs, hooks, doorstops, anything that might act as a lever.

At the centre of each square, there was an ornamental rosette about two inches in diameter. He felt a spurt of excitement, but when he tried to move it up, down, left or right, nothing happened. He pushed it in, tried to pry it up. Still nothing. He tried rosettes in the surrounding squares. Above, below, to the left, to the right. Nothing. But when he pushed upward on the rosette two squares above the one where he'd seen the joint line, the whole piece clicked and slid forward revealing a drawer fifteen inches square and about eight inches deep.

There were only two items inside, a nine-by-twelve leather-bound album or scrapbook and a small heavy manila envelope. The envelope contained two keys. They looked like they belonged to a mailbox or strongbox or locker. They were almost certainly the keys mentioned in Rhea's letter. The album's vellum pages were about three quarters filled with signatures, like a guest book, or a collector's autograph book. Nick flipped through but did not recognize any of the names, and almost returned it to the drawer, but decided to keep it for future reference.

21

As Nick pushed open the front door to Colin Hewitt's locksmith shop, a bell jingled over his head and Colin looked up.

"Nico Cortese! How are you, dear boy? It's been a frightfully long time."

They shook hands and Colin asked, "What have you brought me this time?"

"Keys, what else? But I'm not sure what kind."

Colin shook the keys from the envelope and nodded.

"Safe deposit keys."

"Great. Can they be traced?"

"Depends where they're from. Let's see what I can find out. Will you wait or do you want to leave them?"

"I'll stick around and watch you work if you don't mind."

"Very well. It's not complicated, but it will take a while. Would you like something to drink—tea, sherry, a splash of that Glenfiddich you're so fond of?"

"Thanks, Colin, but I'm good, and very curious."

"Righto. If you have any questions, just speak up."

He took the keys over to a counter and photographed them using a digital camera with a high-powered close-up lens. He took out the memory stick and transferred the photos to his computer, then selected a program from the start menu and let it run. When the results flashed up on the screen, he shook his head. "Sorry, old boy, but only one of them caught a match. It's from the First National Bank at Chalmers and Broadway. The other's not from the State of New York and we haven't a national directory at this point in time."

"One for two, you're batting 500. Thanks, Colin."

"Baseball?"

"Right, and you just hit 100 points higher than Ty Cobb in his best season."

Nick felt a slight chill as he came through the glass door into the severely air-conditioned lobby of the bank at Chalmers and Broadway. He showed his ID to a teller and asked to see someone about getting into a safe deposit box.

"I don't think that will be possible without a warrant, Officer, but if you'll come with me, I'll introduce you to our manager who handles the safe deposit accounts."

Nick followed the trim, athletic figure of the teller across an open space and stood before a glass-walled office while she knocked, spoke with the manager, then introduced him as Mr. Omar Renfrew and left. Renfrew invited Nick in and closed the door.

"Ms. Hollister tells me you are requesting access to a safe deposit box."

He was a heavyset man with a thick neck, crinkly reddish hair and very short, nearly white eyelashes around his pale blue eyes.

"That's correct. It's come up in a homicide investigation and we believe it contains information that may be crucially probative."

"I understand. Please be seated while I confer with our legal department." Renfrew got out of his chair, excused himself and walked awkwardly around Cortese's chair. When he got to the door he said, "I won't be a minute. Can I have the girl bring you something?"

Nick declined and, while he waited, tried to calculate how much time he had before Captain Chase got the CSU Report and closed him down. End of the day at the outside and probably sooner.

He watched through the office's vertical yellow blinds as Renfrew talked with an older man in a dark suit. It didn't take very long and it did not look good. When he came back across the lobby Renfrew's pudgy, acne-scarred face had a look of resolute determination.

Nick stood as Renfrew came in and waited for what he knew was coming.

"Of course, we are always more than happy to cooperate with law enforcement, Detective Cortese, but I'm very sorry to tell you that we have very strict rules when it comes to safe deposit accounts. We can't allow anyone other than the client to open an SDB, even if they have a key and a very good reason. What you'll need in this case is a search warrant or court order."

He stood there, stolid and unmovable. It was clear there was no point trying to persuade him.

Nick sat in the car and cursed his impatience. He should have known the trip would end like that. He *did* know, but there wasn't time to do what he'd have to do now. He opened his cellphone and made a call to the Honourable Brian Cullen Williams.

"Judge Williams. How may I help you?"

"Good morning, Your Honour. Detective Nicola Cortese here, and I need a warrant."

"Hello, Nicola. Heard you were back on the street. What have you got?"

Nick gave Williams the relevant information and the judge said, "Understood. But I can only issue authorization for a limited search. You'll only be able to remove objects or documents that have direct evidentiary relevance to the homicide. Of course, that will be a judgment call and might be challenged when what you find appears in court."

Nick thanked him and drove back to the precinct.

Baxter Chase met him at the door. His face was red and he was shouting, "What the hell are you doing, Cortese? This is an open-and-shut case. Happens all the time. Husband finds out his wife is gonna clean him out and vamoose with her lover, so he loses it, offs her, and now he's in the wind. What I need you to do is stop violating crime scene seals and harassing bank managers. Get off your ass and track down Duplessis."

It made sense, but somehow Nick didn't believe it. Something was missing, and he only had a few hours to find out what.

22

Chaz Malone sat with his feet up on his desk and his hands behind his head. He looked like he might be daydreaming or taking a nap, but Nick knew that he was analyzing details, details, details, so he went over to talk to Price.

"I need you to pick up a warrant from Judge Williams at the courthouse, then go to the First National at Chalmers and Broadway. The manager's name is Renfrew. Show him the warrant and ask him to open the safe deposit box of Malcom Duplessis. Here's the key."

Price laughed. "Where the hell did you get this, Nico?"

"Shhh. Not a word. Baxter will fry your ass if he finds out."

"He'll find out soon enough, bro."

"True, but by then we'll know what the hell's in there."

After Price left, Nick pulled out the yellow pages and scanned the directory of physicians and surgeons till he came to Dr. Murray Gimmelman. He just wanted to ask about the Duplessis prescriptions and he was surprised to see that Gimmelman was listed as a plastic surgeon. He dialed the number and waited while it rang.

The receptionist's voice had a nasal twang and it sounded like she had a mouthful of bubblegum.

"I'm sorry, the doctor is in the Ba*hay*mas through the end of the month."

"This is Detective Nicola Cortese, NYPD. Can you give me his address or telephone number there?"

"I'm sorry, 'yum not authorized to release that inform*ay*shun."

Before he could muster his powers of persuasion, he was confronted with a dial tone.

"She hung up on me," he said, out loud, to the empty office. "Brilliant. You handled that like a pro."

That's when Captain Baxter Chase came in, waving the Crime Scene Unit report, and yelling, "You're a raving lunatic, Cortese! You completely contaminated that crime scene. I've been on the phone with IAB and they've agreed to suspend you pending a psychiatric evaluation. You've got five days and it's your responsibility to call the counsellor and set up an appointment. I'm ordering a drug test as well."

Nick expected the suspension, but the drug test was bizarre.

"What the hell do you need a drug test for?"

"It's right here in the report. You've been acting like you're seeing things. You know, hallucinating? Like you're high on some goddamn chemical."

23

The first thing he did after turning in his gun and shield was to call Claire. It rang three times, then her voicemail kicked in. Nick hesitated, wondering if he should leave a message. In the end, he hung up and dialed her office at CCNY.

"Dr. Tran, psychology."

He was relieved to hear her voice but wondered what she'd say when she heard his. "Hi, Claire, it's me. I'm so sorry…"

"Nico! Where are you? I waited till ten, then I thought I'd come in and get some work done."

As she spoke Nick tried to gauge her mood. She didn't sound pissed off exactly. Disappointed, he decided, and that might be worse. The goddamn job, he thought, it's all happening again. Now he would have to explain himself and hear how lame it sounded.

"I got called out on a homicide around five-thirty. I didn't want to wake you. Then I got to the scene and lost track of time. I'm really sorry."

Silence. He hurried to fill it. "Are you free for lunch?"

"I don't think so, no. I've gotten into something here that I really should finish. It will probably take all afternoon."

After a very pregnant pause she added, "But why don't you come by for a late supper, around eight."

"Super. I'll bring a bottle of Meursault."

"Nico?"

"Yes?"

"Are you all right? You sound sort of…I don't know, distant, distracted."

"I'm fine, really. It's just been a helluva day. I feel wrung out."

"Okay. After dinner I'll give you a Thai massage and tuck you into bed."

When he got home, he was too exhausted to think, much less to decide what he should do next. He took a shower, drank a can of apple juice and set the alarm to go off in two hours. But just as he lay down, the telephone rang. It was Corbie Price.

"Nick, glad I caught you. What the hell, bro? Back in the shithouse, eh?"

"Looks that way, but I don't buy Baxter's theory of this case and I'm not letting go."

"Do what you gotta do, but you're gonna need help on the inside."

"Thanks, Corbie, but I can't let you do that."

"Why the hell not?"

"You know why not, it could get your ass fired."

"Well, it's my ass, and there's no way I'm gonna let you have all the fun. Far as I'm concerned, you're still the whip on this one. And I'll talk to Malone. He loves this cowboy shit."

Nick sighed. "Okay, but watch your back. Chase knew I'd been at the crime scene again and I sure as hell didn't tell him. It was Finch. I took the little creep with me 'cause there was no one else in the house."

"No surprise there. What else?"

"Did you get Renfrew to open the box?"

"Yeah, but all I found was a diamond tie pin, a gold watch on a chain, a locket with a picture of someone who looks like she might be Duplessis's mother and some old letters."

"Fuck a duck, I thought for sure there'd be something we could use. We got anything on the dead girl?"

"They ran a check and came up with two priors for prostitution. Bail was paid by one Ricky Sanchez."

"I know that scuzz. He runs a section of the stroll over in Soho."

"Want me to sweat 'im, see what he knows?"

"No, but see what you can find out about this Rhea person."

"Already got a line. Malone talked to a hooker he did some favours for over on West Broadway. The chick's name is Carson, Rhea Carson, another one of Ricky's girls, older though, and off the street for a while now. We'll run the name through R&I and get back to you."

Nick felt a jolt of adrenalin. He still had a team and a case to solve, in spite of Baxter Chase. He turned off the alarm and turned on the TV.

There was a breaking news story on CNN.

"Early this morning, the mutilated body of Kenneth Lang, senior partner of the agro-multinational Lang & Baine, was found in an abandoned tenement. Lynn Sawchuck has the story."

The image on the screen cut to a young woman with short blonde hair in a dark suit buttoned up to the neck.

"Thank you, Anderson. Police responded to an anonymous call and found Lang strapped to a chair and shot in the head, execution style. There were unmistakable signs that he had been tortured. An extremist wing of an African nationalist organization in Mawabi claimed responsibility for the crime."

"Do we know anything about why they did this?"

"Yes. Apparently, Lang had sold a new, classified chemical weapon to Chad, Mawabi's hostile neighbour and historical enemy. The terrorists intended the assassination as a warning."

"Thank you, Lynn. We go now to an interview taped earlier today with L&B's junior partner, Jeremy Baine, and Kenneth Lang's wife, Vanessa."

"Our sincere condolences to both of you. I'd like to begin with you, Jeremy. What can you tell us about the alleged sale of a chemical weapon?"

"I am deeply saddened to report that, unfortunately, the sale did take place. Apparently, Kenneth thought it would help deter Mawabi's jihadist president, Kamoro Baku, from selling yellowcake uranium to Iran. Ken's intentions were unimpeachable and I'd bet the farm on that. All he wanted was to protect this country any way he could."

"Can you give us more information about the weapon?"

"Well, it was developed by our subsidiary, Sarbitt Chemical, for the Department of Defense, and it's classified, so I can't divulge its technical name or composition, but I can tell you how it is delivered and what it does. It's versatile, can be administered as a spray, a gas, or a direct injection. Its immediate effect is to disorient and immobilize the target. But the secondary effect, which kicks in almost immediately, is to make him or her completely obedient to and compliant with commands delivered by someone in authority. It was designed to save lives by removing the will to fight and was seen as an effective way to control rioters or disarm enemy combatants, and to do so without collateral damage."

"Is the induced condition reversible, and are there side effects?"

"It does wear off after a day or two. The immediate side effects include dizziness, moderate headaches and nausea, but it's new and we have no long-term data."

"Thank you, Jeremy. Mrs. Lang, you've heard what Mr. Baine has told us, would you like to respond?"

"I most certainly would." Her voice was shaky at first and sounded as though she had been crying. But it got stronger as she spoke. "First of all, Baku is not a jihadist and has never offered to sell uranium to Iran or anyone else. Secondly, Kenneth would never sell weapons to a foreign power. If the sale was made, it was done without his knowledge or consent. Chad is harbouring the former Mawabian dictator, Pierre Loyuba, and has refused to extradite him for trial on charges of genocide and crimes against humanity. Kenneth would never support a man like that."

Baine broke in before he was asked a question. "I was shocked too, Vanessa, I didn't want to believe it, but we have his signature on the invoice and the bill of lading."

"I don't care what you've got. It could never happen. There's something going on here, and I won't stop till I find out what it is."

24

The current was cold and strong. He was fighting it, pushing hard toward the deeper channel at the centre of the stream. And there was something else in the river. He could feel it beneath him, churning. Bubbles rushed up around him. He felt it climb up his legs and he went under. He thrashed and swerved but couldn't shake it. The water got muddier the deeper they went until he couldn't see more than a few inches in front of him. He couldn't hold his breath much longer, and just before he took in water, he managed to twist and kick out with all his strength, lunging toward the faint light he could still see some twenty feet above his head. After what seemed like an eternity, he broke back into the air with a gasp.

It was dark. At first, he didn't know where he was. Then he heard a voice, very loud, but not far away, "Nico! You're dreaming, wake up!" and he realized that he was in Claire's bed and she was not.

"Claire, are you all right? I'm so sorry, I don't know what happened."

"I'm fine, except for the damage to my self-esteem. I've never been kicked out of bed before."

He was so relieved by her wry remark, he couldn't think of anything to say.

All through dinner he had evaded her questions and struggled with himself. He wanted to confide in her. He knew it was wrong to keep her in the dark about the suspension and the conditions that were responsible for it. If he couldn't share these things, the relationship would never last. Still, he couldn't bring himself to talk about that part of his life, huge as it was, because it would almost certainly change the way she thought of him and change it permanently for the worse. She wasn't the kind of woman who would stay with a man who couldn't keep a job or control his own mind. But now there was no way to hide the fact of his nightmare, and the next thing she said forced him to make a decision.

"It's happened before, hasn't it?"

"Yes."

"The same dream?"

He was surprised and annoyed by her professional manner. Was she psychoanalyzing him? It hardly mattered. And having gone this far there was no point dodging what had to be said.

"With minor variations, yes."

"How often, Nico? And is it always so strong?"

"Two or three times a month, and it seems to be getting more intense."

"Can you describe it to me?"

Nick wrestled with that for a full minute, then he shook his head.

"I really can't. It bothers me too much and I don't know why."

"Maybe that's something you need to find out. Have there been any other disturbances?"

It was the question he dreaded. He got out of bed and walked over to stand by the open window. Breathing the cool night air, he felt something release itself inside him. He closed his eyes for a minute before he went back and sat on the edge of the bed.

He told her about the warehouse, the death of his partner and childhood friend, the episodes with Thomasson and Chorniak, and finally, the bizarre behavior that had got him suspended that morning. When he was done she looked deeply concerned.

"I have to ask you this, Nico. Please think hard before you answer."

He nodded. "Okay, shoot."

"Can you see a connection between the dreams, the incidents you described, and your experiences in Afghanistan and Iraq?"

He took his time, trying to remember. He had to be absolutely honest, and he sensed that Claire would know if he was not.

"I didn't think so, but now I can see, I don't know, traces, flashes of quick pictures, smells, sounds, like a fractured movie, and everything's bigger and faster and scarier than it should be."

"How many days would you say you were in the field?"

"I don't know. Because of the stop-loss policy, I did three tours, and we didn't get much R&R. That's a lot of days, I guess."

Claire was silent and it looked like she was trying to decide where to take the conversation, or perhaps how far.

"What I'm going to say is not a diagnosis, or anything like that, Nico, but from what you've told me, my guess is that you're suffering from PTSD."

The acronym struck him like a slap in the face. He shook it off.

"No way. Combat doesn't do that. It just triggers things in those who had mental problems before they joined up, and I never did. Some of the guys, well, maybe more than some, faked it to get out of patrol duty, and that's why there's so much talk about it and all those big numbers. But I never met anyone who actually had it."

Claire nodded. She seemed unwilling to press the issue much further, but what she said next was something he'd never heard before.

"Since PTSD was first included in the *Diagnostic and Statistical Manual of Mental Disorders* in 1980, psychiatrists have arrived at a consensus. It's not unanimous, but most believe that the threshold is between 280 and 300 days of combat. Beyond that almost everyone has symptoms, and with as much combat as you've had, the onset of full spectrum PTSD is nearly universal. It doesn't mean there's something wrong with your mind, it's a normal reaction to severely abnormal conditions."

When Nick didn't respond, Claire went on to make a suggestion.

"I know someone who can help. He's a retired Marine, two tours in Vietnam. He's worked with veterans who served in Iraq and Afghanistan. He's been having spectacular success with a new technique. It doesn't require a lot of disclosure, so it's minimally invasive. You don't have to commit, Nico. Just go talk to him, see how it feels. He won't try to sell you and I can brief him so you won't have to start from scratch."

Nick looked away, withdrawing into an angry determination to deal with his problems himself. But he couldn't leave it there. Claire was only trying to help and she deserved better.

"Okay, I'll think about it, but the department has ordered an evaluation from one of their counsellors. I'm supposed to talk with her in a few days."

Claire nodded. "That's good. She'll be familiar with your working conditions."

Nick just sat there, feeling deflated and spent. Claire smiled, came over and put an arm around his shoulder.

"You're exhausted, Nico. Let me give you that Thai massage I promised and see if you can get some sleep."

It was tempting, but it was too risky. He might have another nightmare. He stood up, leaned over and kissed her. It was a tender but regretful kiss.

"I'm afraid I might hurt you, Claire. I've got to go."

25

They were waiting for him when he got back to his apartment after dropping Terry off at school, two blue suits with red ties. One of them was a blunt-looking, thick-necked heavy who said nothing but stared with unblinking hostility while the other one introduced himself as agent Robert O'Hare from Homeland Security. He was slight, light haired and pink skinned, an unlikely looking Fed, but he seemed very sure of himself.

"Now, Mr. Cortese, we know that you broke the police seal on an active crime scene, opened a secret compartment in the wainscoting and removed evidence which you did not log in to the evidence room. We also know that part of that evidence was a safe deposit key to a box at a branch of the First National Bank for which you conned Judge Williams into signing a search warrant. That warrant was served by Detective Price. Whatever he, or you, or anyone else found in that box is now the exclusive property and under the exclusive jurisdiction of the federal agency that has taken over the case as a matter of national security. We are investigating possible terrorist activity that may involve one Malcom Duplessis. You are required to surrender those materials."

"I'd like to see your credentials, Mr. O'Hare."

O'Hare's lips tightened into a white line and he stared at Nick as though he'd been personally insulted.

"Your superior officer, Captain Chase, has already seen my credentials."

"This may come as something of a shock to you, Bob, but I am not Captain Chase."

"You're not much of anything, Cortese. You've got no badge, no gun, no credibility and I'm told you are mentally unstable."

"That may be, but so far all I see is a skinny little pop tart in a bad suit. I need to know who the fuck you are."

O'Hare turned very red, but fished out his ID, flashed it and returned it to his pocket.

"Thank you, Agent O'Hare. Now I need to see some proof that you have jurisdiction. Do you have a court order? A memo from the Justice Department? A federal warrant? What?"

O'Hare smiled a nasty little smile.

"I don't need any of that. I have the power to arrest you and hold you without charge, without reading you your rights, without letting you see a lawyer, or anyone else, and not for twenty-four or seventy-two hours, but for the rest of your miserable life if I so choose. And if Homeland Security can persuade the President to designate you a threat to the Republic we can execute you anywhere anytime."

Nick didn't believe it. *Could this be true?* He knew there had been some changes after 9/11, but this was ridiculous.

"What happened to habeas corpus, innocent until proven guilty, the Bill of fucking Rights?"

"Gone, Mr. Cortese, all gone, along with most of the Constitution. It's a new world out there, and your country needs your cooperation. Don't you realize we're at war?"

Nick thought, *don't talk to me about war, you hairless pussy*. What he said was, "Well, if the law doesn't matter anymore, I should just hit you so hard you'd puke and shit your pants before I hit you again and broke your neck. Then I could toss your body guard through that window."

"Oh, but the law does matter, Mr. Cortese, and it still applies, to *you*, not to us."

"What applies to you, Bob, are the laws of physics, a fist crushing your sternum."

O'Hare went red again, then white.

Nick shrugged, "But why would I? Detective Price didn't take anything from that safe deposit box because there was nothing there worth taking."

"Do you have a list of the contents?"

"No, but you don't need it, just haul your red-white-and-blue Gestapo ass over to the First National and take a look yourself."

O'Hare thought about that for a minute, then he nodded.

"All right, Mr. Cortese, but if we discover that you have lied to us, we'll be back, and I warn you, that will be very unpleasant."

Robert O'Hare stared down at the open safe deposit box and shook his head. He took out his cellphone and made a call. When Rydell picked up O'Hare said only three words: "It's not here."

He turned to Omar Renfew.

"Who was the last person to access this box?"

"That would be Detective Price."

O'Hare gave a grimace of annoyance. "Yes, of course, but before that?"

"Malcom Duplessis's wife, Consuela Ramirez Duplessis."

O'Hare remembered the letter. Finch had made a copy for him. It mentioned fake ID.

"And when was that?"

"Monday morning, sir."

O'Hare perked up. Consuela Duplessis was dead by then.

"Can you describe this Mrs. Duplessis?"

"Well, she was blonde, in her late thirties, I'd say, blue eyes, with a longish, boyish face, and she was tall, around five ten or eleven."

26

The clamshell grab dredger clawed the seabed, raking up bay mud and loading it onto a barge. It had been working through the night to clear a shipping channel east of Staten Island. The operator cursed as he heard the bucket clank and strain the cable as it came slowly up. What the hell's it picked up this time, he wondered.

As it came out of the water he saw that it was a boat anchor, good sized, gunmetal grey, with a chain that trailed off into the chop. The bucket rose higher and swung on its crane toward the barge. That's when he saw that there was something attached to the other end of the chain. It didn't come out of the water and he couldn't make out what it was, but he stopped the cranking winch and started up the motor. He drove the boat to Midland Beach and used a grappling hook to drag the chain out of the water. That's when he called 911.

Two radio motor patrols twirled their lights out on the sand and several uniforms stood around the body of a man dressed in a blue blazer, grey pants and a white shirt. He looked middle aged, or older, with grey at the edges of his dark hair. He was hefty, and about five ten, but he was lying on his stomach and his features were partly buried in the sand.

When the Crime Scene Unit and the medical examiner arrived, they turned him over and were shocked to see that most of his face was gone. At first they assumed that it had been picked apart by crabs, but on closer inspection, the ME discovered shotgun pellets embedded in his sinuses and forehead. There was nothing in any of his pockets, no money, no credit cards, no ID. They took his fingerprints before they zipped him into a body bag and sent him to the Bellevue Morgue.

Nick was on his computer scanning the National Defense Authorization Act for information about Homeland Security and its extraordinary powers when the phone rang. It was Price.

He was excited as he told Nick about Duplessis.

"He didn't have no concrete slippers, but it sure looked like a mob hit till they ran his prints. Turns out he did some work for the CIA, freelance, had a high security clearance. Of course, the files are classified so there's no details, but it looks like it ain't your everyday family affair."

"Guess who I got a visit from this morning?"

"Your closest friend and president of the Nico fan club, Baxter Be Good?"

"Wrong. He sent me a thug and a baby rabbit from Homeland Security."

"No shit?"

"I shit you not, bro."

Price whistled, "This is getting way deep, *compadre*."

"You got that right. What did R&I throw up on Carson?"

"Couple of busts, prostitution and a pot possession. But we got her address, a cold-water fourth-floor walk-up on uh…" he paused, "Renwick Street on the Lower West Side, near the Holland Tunnel."

"Escape route to New Jersey."

"If this is anything like it's beginning to look, she better get further than that."

"Look, Corbie, can you sit on a plant, and if she shows, pick her up?"

"Sure, boss. You want her booked?"

"No, let's keep this off the computer."

27

Cortese and Lazlo Kaprisky sat in the tiny office at Bellevue Morgue, drinking black coffee. The assistant medical examiner was describing the results of an autopsy he had conducted on the corpse of Malcom Duplessis.

"This is going to sound rather bizarre, but I'm sure the perp used a shotgun because he wanted to destroy the victim's face. He was only partly successful. There was enough left to show that Duplessis had reconstructive surgery and a hair transplant that would have made significant changes in his appearance. Tissue was relieved from the back of the ears to flatten them against his head. His earlobes were also shortened. Unfortunately the nose was blown off, but the bridge just under the eyes is still intact and it shows that the cartilage has been resectioned."

Nick sat up in his chair.

"Can you tell how recently this was done?"

"From the condition of the scar tissue and the new hair follicles, four to six months."

Nick looked thoughtful for a moment.

"It's beginning to come together. The initial canvass produced witnesses who described him in wildly different ways, but they present two distinct pictures. For some reason we're not aware of yet, he went through a lot of pain and expense to change the way he looked. Of course, he'd just married a much younger woman, but I'm betting there's another reason, one that also accounts for his death."

Kaprisky nodded. "There's more. His left eye socket was three quarters intact and I found tiny fragments of green plastic lodged in the outer edge. At first, I thought it was from a shotgun shell with a special load, something like the Teflon in a Glasser safety slug, so I ran some tests. What I found was completely different. The plastic fragments were the remains of tinted contact lenses, the kind that are worn to change the colour of a person's eyes."

"Is there any way you can reconstruct his face?"

Kaprisky looked doubtful. He took a long sip from his coffee and thought for a while. "It's a long shot, Nick. The real problem is that we're not working from the original skull.

"We have to reconstruct a face from a face that has already been reconstructed. There are very few people who do this kind of thing well. There's Mikhail Gerasimov who worked out of the Laboratory for Plastic Reconstruction at the Russian Academy of Sciences in Moscow. There's Dr. Richard Neave at the University of Manchester's Department of Anatomy who had such spectacular success with the Karen Price case in 1990, and here in the USA there's the Clyde Snow–Betty Gatliff team in Oklahoma.

"For our purposes though, the most promising possibility would be the laser and computer techniques developed by Dr. Robin Richards at the Department of Medical Physics at University College Hospital, London. It's painstaking, time consuming and hideously expensive. From what you've told me so far, I'm not sure NYPD would foot the bill."

"Lazlo, I need this. I'm convinced that Duplessis is part of a deeply covert operation with explosive international implications."

"Well, I have to admit that I've been dabbling in this sort of thing myself, though I'm no expert. I have a good friend, a forensic anthropologist who's had some impressive results using the same laser and computer techniques that were developed in England. If we can have an Identikit team assigned to work with us we might get somewhere. I'll give him a call. He loves a mystery as much as you do, Nicola."

After he left Bellevue, Nick called Price again.

"I hate to do this to you, Corbie, but I need to see the evidence that was collected from 32 Charles Street. Can you get me in, or take a look yourself and give me an inventory with digital pics if possible?"

"There's no way I can sneak you past the evidence officer, but I'll see what I can find and call you back."

Ten minutes later Nick's cell warbled.

"I don't fuckin' believe it. Everything's been moved and sealed. It's now under federal jurisdiction and they say it's all classified. Even Chase can't touch it. Hell, the chief can't touch it. NYPD is locked out, top to bottom. Looks like it's gonna disappear into some black box in a storeroom buried under some intelligence complex in Virginia."

"I can't let that happen, Corbie."

"I hear ya. Whatever I can do, bro, just holler."

"Well, right now I need to get back on the force. Chase has given up on the case and he won't back anything I do while I'm suspended. I'll call you if I need your help. And Corbie?"

"Yeah?"

"Thanks."

Nick drove home but he didn't go to his apartment. There was a neighbourhood bar a block away and that's where he sat, nursing a Red Cap ale for half an hour trying to decide on his next move. He was scheduled to take a drug test and undergo a psychological evaluation by a department shrink. It made him anxious. He knew the drug test would come up negative. He hadn't smoked dope or sniffed cocaine since he got back from Iraq but he no longer trusted Chase and his buddies. They were too hooked up to department politics and it looked like the NYPD wanted this one to go away. After struggling with himself through another Red Cap he got on his cell and called Claire.

"Nico! I'm so glad you called. I've been trying to reach you. Are you all right?"

"Not really. No. And I've been thinking about what you said. Can you give me the number of that Marine psychiatrist, what was his name, Sanderson?"

"I can do better than that, I'll fill him in and set up an appointment for you."

"Great. Thanks. But I hope you can do it quick. Things are moving fast and I've got to get back on the force, like, yesterday."

"I'll tell him, but he's really busy, Nico, and I don't know how soon he can see you."

"Okay, as long as he knows it's urgent, that's the best you can do, and thanks. You were wonderful the other night. I can't believe how you took it all in stride and how helpful you were. I felt supported and cared for without being pushed or managed. Hope you know how much that means."

"Glad to help, Nico. I'll call you when I've got a date and time."

There was nothing more he could do, and Nick felt restless. He sat in the booth and stared. He tore strips off the Red Cap label. Then he paid up and left.

When he got to his car he knew what he needed to do to clear his head. He'd take a drive in the country, park somewhere in Connecticut, go for a long walk in the woods.

28

She was wearing a Trekker backpack and carrying a sizeable duffle bag, looking a bit the worse for wear as she got out of the taxi and made her way down the block toward 36 Renwick.

Price got out of the unmarked Chevrolet Cavalier and met her just before she reached the front door.

"Excuse me, Miss, but you're Rhea Carson, right?"

"Oh shit. Who wants to know?"

He flashed his badge. "Corbie Price, NYPD."

"What the hell do you want?"

"We'd like you to come with us."

"Us? Who the fuck is us?"

"Well, me, and my partner, that scruffy-looking dude in the Cavalier."

"Am I under arrest?"

Corbie shook his head. "No, nothing like that, Rhea. It's…I'm really sorry, I guess you haven't heard."

"About what? The Mayan-fucking-apocalypse?"

He looked away, then back at the drawn, tired face, like the face of so many women he'd seen on these streets for so many years.

"No, it's about your friend, Consuela Duplessis."

Rhea tensed, her whole body set to defend, to deny. But when Price told her, she stood for a moment like a frozen sculpture, went white, then curved into herself, and cried out. She sobbed, her legs folded and she curled up on the sidewalk, keening with an anguished sound that came from deep inside her.

Price waited till she was totally still before he spoke.

"Duplessis knew about your scam, he found your letter, but he didn't kill Consuela. We don't know who did, but we think you can help us. Will you talk with the only man I know who can find out what the hell happened?"

She looked up, her face streaked with tears, her lips twitching with the effort to control her pain, and she shook her head, hard, whipping her long blonde hair around her face.

"I can't deal with this. Leave me alone!"

Price went back to the Cavalier and leaned in the open window. He talked with Malone for several minutes and came back to stand a few feet from where Rhea was slowly coming out of her clenched anguish, getting back on her feet. As she stood before him again he could see that something fierce had come into her face.

"You say this guy knows who killed my baby?"

Her voice broke on that last word, and Price waited a beat before he answered.

"No, but he's the only guy I know who has a snowball's chance in hell of finding out. So let's go talk to him."

"And what about me? Am I a suspect? Are you fuckers going to put me down for this because you found that letter I wrote to Consuela?"

"All we've got on you is conspiracy to commit fraud, but it's pretty thin. We don't want you, Rhea. We want the people behind this."

"Behind what?"

"They just found Malcom Duplessis dead at the end of an anchor chain off Staten Island."

29

Rhea sat in the back seat with her eyes closed as they drove south on Pennsylvania Avenue, turned left on Flatlands and south again on Remsen. When they came to Seaview they parked. Cortese was waiting for them. He came over to the Cavalier, opened the back door and told Rhea Carson who he was. She just sat there, a look of utter hopelessness on her face. Then her jaw tightened and she climbed out of the car, clutching the backpack and khaki duffle bag as though they were the only things she had left in the world.

As Price and Malone pulled away, Nick took Rhea's elbow, a light grip, a courtesy. They walked till they came to a bench but they didn't sit down. It was getting on toward mid-afternoon and the light was already deepening in the piled clouds over Jamaica Bay. The air in Canarsie Beach Park was rich with sea scents and the voices of children. It was all too beautiful. He wished he were somewhere else.

Rhea lit up a Virginia Slim, let the smoke drift from her narrow nostrils into the breeze.

Her voice was husky and barely under control. "What do you want with me?"

"Nothing, Rhea. I just need some answers. What can you tell me about Duplessis?"

"Not much, just what I got from Consuela. He worked for the Feds on some sort of secret operation. Personally, I think it's bullshit."

"Maybe not. That's what we're trying to find out. What about the keys?"

"What keys?"

"Rhea, we read your letter, remember?"

"Okay, okay. Safe deposit boxes. One in Shreveport, the other here in New York."

"Is that where you were, in Shreveport?"

"Yes."

"Looks like you spent some time on the Gulf. You've got a tan."

"A few days. I wasn't due back till...they returned from the Bahamas."

"You're using Consuela's ID: passport, credit cards, driver's licence, marriage certificate. Her name is signed with your handwriting. How did you do it?"

"It was quite simple, really. Once she and Duplessis were married, she applied for credit cards. I had no idea what this guy was worth but the cards were gold and platinum. When he was out, I just came over and signed her name on the back. The driver's licence, passport and marriage certificate were a different ball of wax. We needed help with those."

Nick said, "Mo Zimmerman."

"How the hell...?"

"Your letter mentioned Mo. We had him in our files. But no big deal. I'm not going to arrest Mo Zimmerman." Nick paused for a moment. "Why you and not her? I mean, why didn't she just empty the safe deposit boxes herself?"

"It wasn't that simple. Duplessis wouldn't let her out of his sight. When we realized how suspicious he was, we worked out a plan. Consuela had talked him into going to the Bahamas. They were supposed to leave on Monday. While they were away, I would empty the bank accounts and the safe deposit boxes. Mo drafted a letter giving Consuela access to the accounts and forged Malcom's signature."

"So what did you find down in Shreveport?"

"Mostly cash, a lot of it, probably his life savings."

Rhea gave him the duffle bag. He opened it, scanned the contents. There were nineteen bound sheaves of thousand-dollar bills. He nodded, then handed it back.

At first, she didn't understand what he was doing. She frowned, tilted her head. Then her mouth fell open and her eyes got wide as it dawned on her that he was giving it to her.

She took the duffle bag and started to zip it up, but hesitated, debating with herself. Then she handed Nick one of the bundles.

"I know I shouldn't push my luck, but could you give this to Mo Zimmerman?"

Nick surprised himself when he said, "Why not?"

They looked at each other without speaking. She sat very still, but waves of emotion played softly across her face. In her whole damn life she'd never been given a break by a man. Not even her father. Not even her ex-husband, the tattooed sailor. She wanted to tell this cop that he was a good person, that she would never forget his kindness, that she...but it all seemed pointless now. It was Nick who finally broke the silence.

"We know the other key is for the First National at Chalmers and Broadway. But there's nothing worth taking there and you don't have much time. The people who killed Duplessis are after something and they think you have it."

She went pale. "Maybe I do have it. I emptied the box at First National before I left for Shreveport."

Nick felt a jolt of excitement.

"What did you take and where is it?"

Rhea opened her backpack and took out a leather portfolio. It contained $645,000 in bearer bonds. There was also a small manila envelope.

"What's this?"

"I'm not sure."

Nick opened the envelope and immediately recognized it as the kind of audio tape brought in by undercover detectives who'd been wearing a wire. He was excited, but he'd deal with that later. His first concern right then was Rhea Carson.

"We've got to move. I'll walk you to the taxi stand. Take a cab to some other city. Maybe Wilmington or Baltimore. Then get the hell out of the country as fast as you can. You should have enough money to start a new life."

She leaned over and gave him a kiss on the cheek. It was an impulsive, childlike gesture and it surprised him. He could feel the warmth rise under his collar. He thought, *I don't fucking believe this, I'm blushing*. As they started to walk he said, "I like your perfume."

30

Dr. Drew Sanderson had an office on the Upper West Side, a restored brownstone with original steps and balustrade and double oak doors. Nick pressed the brass intercom button and a deep, relaxed voice answered, "Come right up, Detective, I've been expecting you."

Sanderson was standing at the top of the stairs. He was nothing like the psychiatrist Nick had envisioned. A big man, heavy in the arms and shoulders, his rust-coloured hair and beard streaked with grey. Instead of a suit or a white coat, he wore jeans and a checked shirt. He looked like a lumberjack or a ranch hand, but Nick could sense intelligent eyes reading him, carefully, thoroughly, without judgment and with considerable human warmth.

They shook hands firmly, then Sanderson stepped aside and ushered Nick into his office.

It was spacious, with birds'-eye maple flooring and a high ceiling framed by crown moulding. There were prints on the walls, which Nick recognized from his university course on modern art—Kandinsky, de Kooning, Rauschenberg, Calder, two leather chairs and a sofa arranged on a large oriental rug. There was also a desk near the window that looked out onto the street, but Sanderson didn't go there. Instead, he made a gesture with his arm that indicated the entire room. "Wherever you feel most comfortable. Walk around, get used to the place. I need a short trip to the head."

When he got back, Nick had taken one of the chairs closest to the corner and away from the windows. Sanderson sat on the sofa, across from him, well outside Nick's personal space, but not so far they had to raise their voices.

"Claire brought me up to speed on your symptoms, and because this new technique is not psychodynamic or cognitive, you won't have to give me your life story. There are very few things I need to know before we can begin."

"I have some questions first."

Sanderson nodded. "Ask away."

"How long is this going to take? I need a psychiatric evaluation by the end of the week."

"Not likely. Can you get an extension?"

"Normally, yes, but the precinct captain wants me out."

"I see. Can you appeal to a higher level in the chain of command?"

Nick laughed. "By the time the paperwork got to the right desk upstairs, I'd be gone. But, look, why don't you just sign an evaluation form, keep the axe from falling while we work on whatever needs work."

Sanderson smiled. "I can't do that. It would falsify the whole process. What I *can* do is clear some time outside my normal office hours."

Nick looked as though he was going to argue but stopped himself.

Sanderson continued. "Before we start, you need to understand that you are not crazy, you're just having a normal reaction to an extremely abnormal experience."

That's what Claire had said. Nick felt a wave of relief and promised himself he'd see this through, no matter what.

"What do I have to do?"

"The hardest part will be going back there, over and over, until it gets reprocessed and resolved. Traumatic events are not processed like other experience. Part of the brain's limbic system, the hippocampus, which fixes the event within the timeline of your personal history, is suppressed. Without it, the trauma floats free. It can be reactivated spontaneously, and inappropriately, in response to cues or triggers that remind us of the event."

Nick nodded, drinking it in.

"But why now, after four years?"

"I'd say you managed to cope with the memories by suppressing them, with drink, with work, and by not talking about them with anyone, even your family or other vets. Then they got shaken loose by what happened at the warehouse. What you have to do now is re-experience the traumatic events until they are processed, resolved and placed in the past, in the war zone, not on the streets of New York."

Sanderson paused, waited. When Nick didn't respond, he went on:

"We'll start by deciding which traumatic events need processing. We'll pick one and you'll describe it. After the first run-through, I'll ask you to go back to the part that has caused the most distress. As you re-experience it, I'll pass two fingers back and forth diagonally in front of your eyes. This is called a set, and it will last for up to two minutes before we stop and talk. We'll keep doing sets until the stress level comes down."

"Seems too good to be true, too easy, like waving a magic wand. Is there more?"

"Yes, two things. First, in order to keep control you need to establish a safe place, a harbour, so to speak, where you can go in your mind if the memory gets too strong and you feel yourself flashing back. It can be an activity that is pleasant and soothing, a person you trust, or a place about which you have positive feelings."

Nick became quiet and Sanderson let him search his memories for several minutes without interruption.

Asbury Park, on the Jersey shore. He's walking in the sun with his daughter, Terry. She's eating saltwater taffy and chatting happily about her dog, her friends, her dancing lessons, her busy life in grade six. There's a fresh breeze from the Atlantic. He can hear the distant rush of waves mixed with scraps of music from a carousel. The air is laced with traces of barbecue, sea scents and cotton candy. They're just walking, holding hands.

When Nick spoke again, his voice was softer, further away, and his face was relaxed. "I've got it. Now what?"

"We'll use a scale from one to ten to measure your stress levels. We call these SUDs or Subjective Units of Distress. We'll keep doing sets until that number comes down. Tell me about your flashbacks."

"Really freaky. I know I'm here, but all my senses, instincts, are operating there, in the war zone." Nick paused, letting a memory organize itself into words before he went on. "Sometimes, when I need a break from work, I'll take a drive in the country. I was up in Connecticut and I wanted to walk a bit, so I pulled over and parked on the shoulder. There was a trail which looked kind of...peaceful, so I followed it into the woods. After a mile or so, it rose up over a knoll. Below me, I could see a river and a bridge. That's when it happened. Shell bursts, adrenalin rush, and I'm running through the trees, diving for cover. On my way back to New York, every time I crossed a bridge, I felt this surge of...combat alert, as if I could be blown away any second. I was coming up on the Queensboro. I could see it in the distance, arching over the river. A flash of sun from the water split me in two. I could still see the bridge, but it looked like there was a dirty window in front of it. The rest of me saw another bridge, another river, and my pulse went crazy even before I heard the explosions. They came closer and closer till one of them blinded me and I panicked, almost ran up over the sidewalk into a restaurant."

"Was this a flashback to a particular event?"

"I think so, but I can only remember bits and pieces."

"What was your stress level during the flashback?"

Nick took a moment then he said, "Eight and a half."

"Let's start with that. Just tell me what happened. If you feel like you're losing awareness of where you are or if you feel too much stress, you can stop."

Nick's eyes glazed over and he seemed to sink deeper into himself.

"It starts out in the dark. We're on recon. We had intel about a large force of Ba'ath Party loyalists and Al-Qaeda jihadists. They've set up a command post–training camp on Lake Tharthar between Ramadi and Tikrit. Our job is to see how much information we can gather about them. Helo insert is rejected because it might alert them and create a hot landing zone, so they bring us in by boat in a high wind at 0500 hours. We disembark on a rocky spit that curves out into the water. From there we hunker down and duckwalk north. I'm on point. As I come up over a dune, I surprise a young man who seems to be just standing there."

Nick's voice cracked and he struggled to control it. When he continued, his breathing was shallow and his eyes were tightly closed.

"I don't know what to do. I yell at him, *sallama*, surrender! He turns and I see he's carrying an AK-47. I drop and roll over on my back, firing as I fall. The burst from my M-16 catches him full in the chest as he's raising his arms. He hits the ground and lies curled up on his stomach. I know he's dead, but I turn him over with my foot to be sure." Nick paused, his face pale with horror. "He can't be more than twelve years old."

Slumped down, his shoulders hunched, arms loose between his knees, Nick looked exhausted. Sanderson sat still for a moment, assessing Nick's stress level, then said, "I know how hard this is. Would you like to stop?"

Nick shuddered awake. His eyes were clear, but he was still tense, straining. "No," he said. "Let's do it."

"Okay. Try to rate your stress level."

"Nine and a half."

"Good. Now choose a statement that expresses your self-belief about the event."

"I really screwed up."

"How do you feel about that?"

"Terrible."

"Can you be more specific?"

"I feel guilty, responsible, really sorry, sad."

"Where in your body do you feel it?"

"In my throat, my chest, my gut. My whole body feels heavy."

"Okay, focus on that. Now tell me what you'd rather believe?"

"That I did the right thing."

"How true do the words 'I did the right thing' feel to you on a scale from one to seven?"

"Maybe a one, just barely."

"I want you to think about the boy you shot and, without moving your head, let your eyes track my fingers."

Sanderson started moving his hand in quick, short diagonals about a foot in front of Nick's face. After a minute or so, he asked, "What do you get now?"

"About the same...no, wait, as the boy turned he was raising the AK and it was aimed at my chest."

"Good, let's do another set." This time Sanderson slowed the hand movements and kept the set going for almost two minutes. Nick's face changed, as though something had occurred to him.

"I thought he was going to shoot. I expected him to drop his weapon and raise his hands but he didn't."

After the next set, Nick said, "I gave him a chance to surrender. I didn't ambush him or shoot him in the back. I just reacted."

Two more sets and he nodded. "I didn't know he was a child, I shot at a trained combatant."

"Good, think of that. What's your SUD level?"

"It's down, maybe a two or three."

"What would get it down to zero?"

"I don't know. A child was killed. That won't go away."

Sanderson nodded. For a moment he looked like he was remembering his own wars. "Fair enough. Now think about the words, 'I did the right thing' and give me a Validity of Cognition rating from one to seven."

"I feel okay about what I did now. I'd say a six or six and a half."

Sanderson smiled. "Looks like eye movement desensitization and reprocessing is the right way to go. We've still got lots to do, Lieutenant, but you've made a great start."

"I really do feel better. It's like, I don't know, some kind of spell that changes reality."

"I'd say it's seeing reality more clearly. If you feel up to it, I'd like you to tell me about the recurring nightmare."

"Okay. The light is very dim though it's not night. There's this fog or mist. I can smell raw earth, machine oil, cordite. There's a roar...fire rushing out in a stream and bursting, flaring again, crackling in a dense cloud. Then it changes. Water. A river that looks shallow and quick, but when I start to cross, the bottom drops away and something wraps itself around my legs, dragging me down till I can't breathe and I wake up."

"Do you know what that's about?"

"No, I don't. Do we have to go into that now?"

"No, we've done enough for one day. But I'd like you to try something. It's called *in vivo* exposure. It means exposing yourself to real-life situations that are flashback triggers. In this case, one of those bridges over the East River. Don't drive over it, just park somewhere, approach on foot and see what happens. If you find yourself losing control, focus on your breathing. Slow, long inhale, hold, long exhale that totally empties the lungs, hold, then inhale again. Increase the hold time with each new breath."

Nick brightened. "Of course, *Dan Jun*. It's something I used to do for taekwondo."

"Yes, exactly. It should keep you connected to the here and now. Do you think you're ready to try this before our next session?"

Nick was silent for a half a minute before he answered.

"I really don't know. I just hope I don't have to call you from Bellevue."

31

The yellow cab looked entirely out of place, raising a trail of dust on a dirt road in rural Georgia. It slowed as it came into town, made several turns and stopped before a small house that might once have been white, but was now the colour of weathered wood.

Rhea Carson got out, reached into the pocket of her jacket and took out a single bill. When she handed it to the cabbie, he looked at her in disbelief. "You gotta be kiddin'."

"I don't have anything smaller, sorry."

He turned the bill over, snapped it a couple of times, held it up to the light. "I saw a bank back there. If this ain't real, I'll be back. With the cops."

He opened his wallet and counted out her change. She gave him all the smaller bills as a tip. As he drove off she turned and pushed through the leaning wooden gate with missing slats and marched up the weedy, cracked sidewalk. The grass in the yard was sparse and brown and strewn with discarded tires, a smashed TV set, a small refrigerator without a door, a broken chair and a rusty bicycle with one flat tire.

Rhea climbed up onto the tilted porch, set down the duffle bag, slipped off her backpack and rapped twice on the aluminum screen door. It banged loosely against the frame. When no one came, she knocked again, harder this time, and longer. Nothing. She pounded the door and shouted, "Danni, goddammit, I know you're in there, open the door!"

The blind in the window on the other side of the porch moved. One of the slats lifted, then quickly dropped back. After a few seconds, it happened again. Then Rhea heard slippered feet shuffle across linoleum. The door opened a crack. A pair of bloodshot, pale blue eyes stared up at her.

"Rhea? What the fuck? I thought you were dead."

"I will be if you don't let me in out of this fucking heat."

Danni laughed, a squeaky giggle. "Shit, it's hotter inside this dump than it is out there."

Rhea came into the small, stifling room and looked around for a place to sit. She dumped the duffle bag and backpack on the Formica table and slumped into the chintz-covered seat of a tube chair. It creaked under her weight.

Danni looked at Rhea like she was some sort of apparition. She shook her head, accepting the most unexpected turn her day could take.

"You wanna drink?"

"Of course."

Danni sloughed over to the refrigerator and came back with a half-gallon of cheap Tokay. She opened it and set it on the table, went back to get an unwashed glass from the pile of dishes in the sink. Rhea held the glass up to the dim light bulb in the kitchen ceiling and made a face.

She put the glass on the table and took a long drink straight from the bottle.

Danni kept standing, as though she were waiting for Rhea to leave.

"Soooo, whaddya want, Rhea?"

"I don't want anything. I'm here to save your sorry ass."

Danni laughed, a burst of incredulous mirth. "You, save me? That's a good one."

"Well, it's true. I'm going to make sure you've got a steady income."

"How the fuck ya gonna do that?"

"I hit it big this time."

"Big? What's big?"

"Big enough. And this is what's gonna happen. You're gonna come with me to the nearest bank and I'm gonna set up a trust fund. You'll have enough for daily expenses and rent in a better neighbourhood. And if you go back to school, like you been pipin' about for the last ten years, I'll pay tuition, books, everything. But you gotta go into detox and rehab and you gotta show receipts for all your purchases to the trustee."

"Yeah, and who's that, you?"

"I'd like it to be, but that's not gonna happen."

Danni frowned. "You in some kinda trouble, are ya?"

"You might say that, but I'm cool. I'm leavin' the country for a while."

"Cops?"

"Worse, but hey, you up for this or what?"

"I dunno if I believe you, but even if I did, I'd have to ask, what's in it for you?"

"If it works, I get my little sister back."

32

Nick had a second session scheduled with Sanderson, and as he drove toward Manhattan he thought he'd try taking Brooklyn Bridge instead of the Midtown Tunnel, but he remembered what Sanderson had said about driving, so when he got to Brooklyn Heights he pulled over and parked about six blocks from the river.

It was a beautiful morning, but he grew increasingly nervous as he approached the bridge. Just as the water came into view, a cloud covered the sun and the day went dark. In that moment, his heartbeat accelerated, his breathing grew shallow and rapid, his hands felt cold and his mouth dry. His whole body tensed and he looked up into a jagged, wind-swept mountain range, waiting for the first shell to explode. With an immense effort, he completely emptied his lungs, took a slow, deep breath, counted to four and exhaled slowly. He could feel the cold numbing his face, he could smell the lichen-spattered boulders, but he could also see the bridge and the water, as though through a scrim of thin cloth. It felt as though his mind had split and he was inhabiting two worlds at once, with New York vague as a faded dream and the Hindu Kush range closing all around him.

He wanted to run, to find shelter, but he forced himself to hold his ground and breathe, breathe. He tried to focus on the bridge through the wall of stone that rose from the Pech River valley. The first shell burst overhead and he winced, ducked away, but came up again, stood still and waited. Slowly, very slowly, he was able to steady his gaze on the first massive tower of the bridge. The two Gothic arches filled with nothing but sky looked something like a cathedral. Slowly, but clearly, he began to remember things he had read. Once those towers were the tallest structures in the city. As he followed the huge cables that swept up, across the pylons, then down again on the other side of the East River, a scrap of poetry surfaced from that English class in his life before the war. *O harp and altar…How could mere toil align thy choiring strings!* then he noticed the seagulls, easy as snowflakes on the soft air…*wings…Shedding white rings of tumult.* It all still seemed unreal, and he could feel the sweat crawl down his neck as another shell burst overhead, but it was quieter, further away. Then the day brightened as the cloud passed and the sun seemed to burn off the chill and his pulse grew steadier, still high, but a bit slower every time he exhaled. After a few minutes, though he still felt tense, the panic was gone and he knew where he was.

On his way back to the car, he noticed things he hadn't seen before. A hopscotch template drawn in chalk on the sidewalk; two scrawny kids pitching nickels against a brick wall; a girl in frayed cut-offs with raven hair carving her initials in the asphalt; steam rising out of the steel grid of a manhole cover. Everything seemed brightly etched in his mind's eye. He wasn't *in the zone,* and his pulse and breathing seemed normal, yet he felt charged with attention and seemed to glide over the grass-tufted cracks, the tiny splinters of glass that flashed from the sidewalk. He could smell the river and the dry odour of old paint from the peeling storefronts.

When he reached his car he hesitated. He wanted to go ahead and drive over the bridge, but he knew he'd had enough for one day. As he made his way through the heavy morning traffic, he did something he hadn't done for months. He turned on the radio and listened to FM jazz all the way downtown.

33

Standing in line to buy a ticket to Belize at the Atlanta airport, Rhea noticed that one of the passengers was being asked to produce his passport. A light bulb went off and she realized that her own passport, along with the one that identified her as Consuela Ramirez, had almost certainly been red flagged by now.

She left the line and walked over to the traveller's information booth. "Is there service to the main bus terminal downtown?"

"Yes, but you just missed it and there won't be another for an hour and a half."

She thanked the woman and walked aimlessly for a while, trying to formulate some kind of plan. That detective, Nick, was very clear. She was in danger. She had to keep a low profile and get out of the country, at least until whatever it was blew over. But how in the hell could she do that with a fake passport the authorities knew about. They also knew who she was, and probably had her picture too.

There was an airport restaurant up ahead. She went in and stood at the bar. It still surprised her that she could afford anything she chose from that wall full of expensive bottles. She ordered the house Chardonnay and when it arrived she sipped it, slowly, and considered her options. She couldn't fly anywhere, and there was no legal way she could cross the border into Mexico. She could go back to New York and Mo could make her a new set of IDs with a new name, but that would take time, and it was risky too. If Cortese knew about Mo, so did whoever killed Duplessis. She could go somewhere like Idaho or Nebraska, and lie low for a year or two, but she was really frightened by what Cortese had told her. She believed whoever they were had the power to find her wherever she went as long as she stayed in the U.S. She could only think of one other thing to try, and if that didn't work she was finished.

When the Greyhound arrived in El Paso, Rhea picked up her luggage and hailed a cab.

"Where to, Ma'am? Can I suggest a hotel?"

"Not just yet. Where's the stroll in this berg?"

The cabbie came to attention, smiled. "You buyin' or sellin'?"

"I'm looking for someone."

He nodded. "Friend of yours?"

"I sure hope so."

It didn't take long to find a street that looked all too familiar. Three working girls were displaying their wares in tight skirts and shorts. Rhea paid the driver, lit a cigarette and checked them out. One was a runaway, not more than sixteen, scared and defiant. The second was a two- or three-year veteran trying to look bored, wearing a red mini-skirt and net stockings. At the seniority spot, on the corner where the traffic was four-way, a thirty-year-old redhead in a light blue jumpsuit leaned against a store window. She was tall and thin. Too thin, almost emaciated.

As Rhea approached she could see that the redhead looked tense, drained, tired, as though she were coming down from a high, probably crack cocaine, or meth, and was beginning to get that edgy, desperate look around the eyes. She stood in front of her and without saying anything, offered her a Virginia Slim. The woman took it and as she lit up, Rhea asked, "How many more tricks do you need to get straight?"

"Who wants to know?"

"I'm not a cop."

"You lookin' for a date?"

"I need some info. I'll get you fixed and buy you the best dinner in town if you help me out."

The woman looked wary, but shrugged, "Okay, what's the deal?"

Rhea hesitated, not sure how much to reveal, then she said,

"My passport's fucked and I have to get into Mexico, like yesterday."

The redhead laughed. "That's a new twist. Lotsa people tryna get out, but I never heard of illegals tryna get *in*."

"You got something for me?"

"I know some people. But it'll cost ya. Three hundred, and you can skip the dinner."

Rhea counted out six fifties and the redhead opened her cellphone.

She sat in a booth at the back of the Silver Saddle bar and nursed a Jim Beam. She was ready to order another when a young Hispanic in a black cowboy hat, jeans and tan boots pushed open the saloon-style double door and looked around. He eased into the room and an older man with a crew cut and sunglasses followed him. When they spotted her they sauntered over and slipped into the bench seat across from her. The older one waved off the waitress, looked Rhea over and shook his head.

"No way we can run you south, *chica*, but there may be a better way."

"Whatever works, *hombre*."

"Well, see, there's this border guard we work with sometimes. He's been known to look the other way for a price."

"What kind of price?"

They looked at each other, then at Rhea.

"Of course, it's not just him. There's a few other palms that's gotta get greased, and we need to make a little something too, you know, like a finder's fee."

The cowboy hat smiled, and nodded, as though he liked the idea of a finder's fee.

Rhea made a face. She didn't like these two. She almost got up and left, but where would she go? And corrupt officials in Mexico were normal as chicken tamales.

"Let's cut the shit. How much?"

"It'll only cost ya five large, in small bills. Twenties will do. And oh, yeah, we'll need a copy of your passport."

Rhea frowned. He explained.

"Ya know, so he'll reckonize ya and let ya thru the gate."

Rhea was standing in line at the pedestrian crossing into Ciudad Juarez. She was getting really nervous. She had no idea what the bought guard looked like, and if this guy was not him, she'd be cooked. She could still go back, try to disappear somewhere, and ride it out, but as the line got shorter she could see the guard's name plate. It said Dario Gutierez. She felt the tension leave her body and she smiled when she handed him her passport. He smiled back, opened it and laid it flat on his scanner. After a few seconds, a message she couldn't see came up on the computer screen. He picked up his phone and dialed, waited, said something in Spanish, then looked at her and smiled again.

"It's nothing, Señorita." His voice was calm, reassuring. "Just take a seat while we verify your ID. A few minutes, no more."

Rhea walked over toward the waiting area where she started to sit on a bench, then bolted toward the exit. Before she reached the door two brown uniforms caught up with her. They knocked her down, growled something in Spanish, twisted her arms behind her and cuffed her wrists. When she fought back, they punched her in the face and dragged her, struggling and screaming, across the station to an interrogation room.

After what seemed like hours a man in a blue suit and a woman with dyed blonde hair and zircon ear studs came in and sat across from her at the table where Rhea rested her elbows and held her head in her hands. The woman carried a file folder, which she opened and read from.

"On Monday last, you fraudulently presented yourself as one Consuela Ramirez Duplessis and using a counterfeit passport removed certain contents from a safe deposit box."

She looked up. Rhea said nothing, did nothing. The woman continued speaking in a clipped, indifferent voice.

"You need to surrender them, immediately."

Rhea sat up. Her eyes were streaked and her face drawn. But she was not ready to play ball with these people who had not even identified themselves or called her by name.

"Who the hell are you, Immigration? What?"

"We represent Homeland Security and this is a federal matter."

"I want a lawyer."

The man in the blue suit laughed, a harsh, condescending snort.

"Don't be ridiculous. This isn't some cop show on TV. This is a national security threat and you have no rights at all. Just give us what you took from the bank."

"There wasn't anything worth taking, some jewellery and old letters."

The blue suit deferred to the woman. She crossed her hands and when she spoke she sounded like a flight attendant reeling off a memorized script.

"This is how it is. You need to tell us what you know, right now. If you don't, we can hold for you as long as we want, without charge, without a lawyer, in solitary, in a very ugly jail. We can pressure you in all sorts of ways that are no longer considered torture, but believe me, they'll have you screaming bloody murder. We can also classify you as an enemy combatant and execute you without ever going to court."

"I took the bearer bonds."

"What else?"

"Nothing else. I swear."

The blue suit laughed again, shook his head.

"One more chance. We know there was something else in that safe deposit box. Now hand it over."

"I don't have it."

"What did you do with it."

"I never took anything but the bonds."

"We know about your co-conspirator."

"What are you talking about?"

"Those thousand-dollar bills you took from Shreveport were paid to Malcom Duplessis by the Defense Intelligence Agency. Their serial numbers are on file. You used some of them to set up an account for your partner in a terrorist plot that has already resulted in the assassination of a prominent corporate executive. If you do not give us what we want, Danni will be in that jail cell right beside you, and on the waterboard, and before a firing squad if it comes to that. So I'll ask you again, what did you take from the First National Bank at Chalmers and Broadway, and where is it now?"

Rhea held out for several minutes more before she broke down and told them.

34

It was hot in the room and Clay Noireau had just loosened his tie when the phone rang. The voice on the other end was his hush-hush employer, recommended and sanctioned by the CIA, DIA, NSA, DOD and DHS. Noireau sounded pleased with himself as he reported that Homeland Security had gotten the necessary information from Rhea Carson and had her in custody. The voice on the phone did not seem impressed.

"So we know who has the wire tape. But it's not us, is it?"

Noireau was six-five, with fierce amber eyes and a scar that ran from his left cheekbone back to his ear. He was heavily muscled and trained to kill. He looked down at the receiver and thought, if this mouthy creep were in the room, I'd snap his neck. But he wasn't in the room and Noireau calmed himself.

"Your guys never bothered to frisk Duplessis for a wire. You let him record you while you were offering him the job. And you know what, asshole, he would have given it to you if you'd paid him what you promised. But you tried to screw him and now a cop has your balls in a vice."

As he was saying this, Noireau had a thought. Whatever this pompous fuck is into, it's going to mean big bucks. Nothing wrong with a little retirement insurance. He reached down and hit the record button on his answering machine.

There was hard breathing from the phone and the words that came after it sounded like they were being pressed through tight lips.

"I paid him a cool mil up front, in bearer bonds. He wanted the rest in cash. I didn't have it."

Noireau snorted. "That's bullshit. You weaseled him."

"You think I give a shit what you think? Just get the tape."

"We'll get it, soon enough."

"You're sure of that, are you? Let's review your brilliant performance up till now. Your quiet abduction of Kenneth Lang turned into a gunfight that left a dead guard on Fifth Avenue. Your B&E expert did not find the keys he knew were somewhere in the Duplessis apartment, but he did manage to leave another corpse, which drew the boys in blue like flies."

"Fuck you. I told you that couldn't be helped. She wasn't supposed to be there. We knew from the phone tap that she was at the club and we got Duplessis out of the apartment for one last job, but the stupid bitch came back and was sitting there in her underwear, snorting coke when our man showed up. She freaked and he had to shut her up. Then there was no time to do anything else, so he blew. And we did get rid of Duplessis, as planned."

"Did you? You were supposed to dis-a-fucking-pear the guy, not dump him in the Bay."

"We dumped him ten miles out, the tide brought him back."

"That it did. And where are we now with this detective? Why haven't you picked him up and squeezed him till he squeaks?"

"Wouldn't do any good. He's a Marine, Special Forces. He'd probably croak before he told us more than his name, which we already know. Maybe we should just take him out."

"Kill a cop? Another corpse on the street? Then what? NYPD is not in love with him, but he's still one of theirs. It'd be like stirring up a hornet's nest. Stupid move, Noireau. Stop trying to think and just do what you're told. There are many ways to squeeze a U.S. Marine."

35

As he climbed the oak banister stairs, Nick could feel Sanderson reading his body language. The big former Marine looked pleased.

This time Nick sat on the sofa and the therapist settled in behind his desk near the window.

"Have you had any flashbacks or other symptoms?"

He told Sanderson about his experience in the shadow of the Brooklyn Bridge.

"I almost lost it, but the breathing thing you suggested, the one I recognized as *Dan Jun*? It helped keep part of me in the present, in New York, and I got through it."

"At our first session you told me you weren't able to recall the events that triggered those flashbacks in Connecticut and at the Queensboro Bridge. Let's go back to that and see how it goes."

Nick nodded, and reached back into his mind to retrieve the memory. His face twisted into a grimace of pain as he tried to hold back the flood of emotion that threatened to overwhelm him.

Very quietly, Sanderson said, "Okay. This time, don't describe it. Just see how much you can remember and when you've got a fix on that bridge, let me know and we'll begin the eye movements."

Nick's whole body tensed as he tried to force his mind back, but after a short time he shook his head. "Can't find it. All I'm getting is flashes."

"Let's brake for a minute or two. Go to your harbour."

Nick let himself relax into the memory of his walk with Terry in the summer sun and it steadied him.

"Better. Can we start again?"

"Yes, but this time I'd like you to begin by remembering the other men on your team. Just let them come easily into your mind if you can."

"There are six of us. Joey Solera, the one we call Scout, a New Yorker, small, wiry, able to crawl easily into tight dark places. He carries a chrome-plated ice pick, amuses himself by nailing spiders and centipedes from ten yards away. Pudge Bayliss is my radio man, short, chubby, but quick, and quiet as a cat on patrol. Kenny Sawchuck is the outrider, unpredictable, but no one's better in emergencies. Big Mo, short for Motown, because he's always singing those rhythm and blues tunes from the fifties, and big because he's about six-five and two-sixty.

"And Russell. Sergeant Russell Haynes. My second in command. Tall, thin, never says much, but when he does, with that slow, Oklahoma drawl, it's worth hearing. He thinks the war is wrong, but never bitches about it, never bitches at all. And we're close, went through basic together. I trust him completely. On most patrols, we leapfrog point, and he's better at it than I am, calmer, with better eyes."

"Great. Now see if you can find your way to the bridge."

"We're doing recon out of Camp Blessing in the Pech River Valley. It's up in the Hindu Kush range near Pakistan. We have intel about foreign fighters setting up a command post there, transporting troops and ordnance across the border. It's afternoon, but the wind is already steel cold and cuts like a knife.

"We've just come up over a ridge and Russell, our point man, raises one fist. We freeze. We can hear voices and motors, but far off, and below us. When Haynes motions me forward, and the valley comes into view, I see a river with a bridge, and halfway across it a halted convoy of trucks, mortars, personnel carriers and troops on foot. They're smoking cigarettes and joking."

When Nick paused, Sanderson waited. He realized that Nick was describing the event as though it were happening in present time.

After closing his eyes to focus, Nick went on.

"I pull out our maps, locate the coordinates of the bridge and signal for the team to withdraw into cover on the other side of the ridge we've just climbed. I tell Bayliss to radio artillery on the PRC-77 and request a strike from their .155 Howitzers. We hunker down and wait. And wait. Then the first shell explodes. Close. Too close. They're falling on top of us. We scatter and hit the ground. I can't believe what's happening. When the shelling stops I crawl over to...him...Russell, he's...on his back. His...face...it's...not there.... I turn away, then I see it, hair, the whole scalp, and his forehead too, and some of his nose and eyes...I'm frozen, can't breathe, can't move, but I'm squad leader and I have to. I crawl further into the hard rock shadows and find Big Mo, then Bayliss and Scout. They're out. Sawchuck is a dozen yards further on, curled up against a tree trunk."

Nick shook his head. Tears filled his eyes. His voice was choked, horrified.

"It's my fault. I gave Bayliss the coordinates. I got them wrong, horribly, fatally wrong."

Sanderson only said two words. "*Dan Jun.*"

Nick took a few minutes to get his breathing under control. When Sanderson asked if he was able to go on, Nick nodded and braced himself.

"This is going to be really hard, but you have to remember it again while your eyes follow my fingers."

As Sanderson's hand waved back and forth, the scene unfolded again. About halfway through the set, Nick looked as though he'd thought of something he hadn't remembered before. Sanderson asked him what he'd just seen.

"There was cloud cover, a storm was building and there was static on the PRC-77. Maybe the information got garbled..."

"Good, let's do it again."

This time Nick remembered something else. The artillery team was supposed to fire an illumination round to check the target location before they sent in live shells. But they never did. That's one of the things that shocked him, the first shell exploding on the ground a few feet away instead of in the air as a warning.

Another set. No change. Then another and Nick looked like he'd caught something else.

"It's a bit later, after we got back to Camp Blessing. The artillery radioman told me he wrote down the coordinates I sent and checked them on the map before he gave them to the gunners. They were correct."

After two more sets, Nick looked like he had just discovered something else. "I talked with the gunnery sergeant. He told me they had been firing those 155s at other targets and the guns were still hot when our call came in. They have a ten- or twelve-mile range and our target was right at the edge of that limit. It didn't surprise him that the first barrage went off target. He apologized about the illumination round. They had run out but the call was urgent and they didn't want to wait for replacements to be brought from the armory."

One more set.

"Anything new?"

"Yeah, one thing. After we got hit, I had Bayliss call artillery again. They made an adjustment, hit the bridge and knocked out a good chunk of the convoy."

"Good. When you talk about Pech River and the bridge now, you talk about it in the past tense, back there in the war where it belongs. How's your Subjective Unit of Distress reading?"

"It's down, maybe a three. But it still sucks. The violence, the waste of such a remarkable life. I'm sad about it, and angry, but it's different, the feeling I mean, I don't still think it was my fault."

Sanderson nodded. "Really good. This is maybe the hardest thing for those of us who lead. We bond with our men, we promise ourselves we won't let anything happen to them, but you know, we don't have that power. No one does. War destroys, and it doesn't just kill the bad guys. When it kills those we care about, it tears a piece out of us. We feel rage, and a lot of guilt because we survived and those we were responsible for did not. We think those feelings are right because we feel them so strongly, but they're not and they do a lot of damage, to ourselves, sure, but also to those we go on living with."

"The strange thing is, I didn't even know what I was feeling. I mean, I knew it didn't feel good, but I just tried to get on with it, like it was normal."

"And it wasn't, will never be. You've walked another long mile today, Lieutenant, but I don't think we're out of the woods."

"Okay, what should we do next?"

Sanderson thought for a moment before he answered. "Why don't you decide?"

"Okay. Did Claire tell you about the flashback at the crime scene?"

"Yes, you carried the young woman's body out to the street before you came out of it."

"I was completely disoriented, didn't know where I was or what I was doing. I'd like to clear that up."

"Those memories seem deeply buried. I expect they're so painful they can only manifest themselves in REM sleep. Can you recall anything, anything at all, about where the flashback took you?"

"I remember calling for a medic, so it must have been in a combat zone, and the woman in the flashback was alive."

"Do you remember what you were feeling?"

"Very chaotic—grief, rage, helplessness."

"Good. Try to get back those feelings and anything at all from the place you flashed back to."

Nick sat back and began to concentrate. He tossed from side to side as if trying to free himself from something that had taken hold of him. Sanderson told him to go to his harbour but Nick didn't hear him. His face, his whole body, convulsed. He cried out and leaped to his feet knocking the chair over behind him. He opened his eyes but didn't recognize his surroundings. He looked around frantically and when his eyes found the door he bolted and fled from the room.

By the time he got back to his apartment he had calmed himself down. He knew he should go back, keep working, force himself to remember what had shaken him so deeply, but he could not. He wasn't ready. He might never be, but he was ashamed of the way he'd left Sanderson's office. The man had made time for him, he deserved better. With a deep sense of regret, he picked up the phone. Sanderson's voice was warm, with no trace of recrimination.

"Hello, Nicola. I'm glad you called."

"I just wanted to apologize. I shouldn't have run like that."

"No problem. We tried to go too deep too fast. But there's still work to be done. Can you come by this evening around seven-thirty?"

There was a long pause while Nick thought about it. He could say he had other commitments, but that wasn't true.

"I'd like to, I want to, but I'm just not ready. I'm not backing out, I just need time…"

There was another long pause then Sanderson said, "Okay, let it settle for a while. You have my card. Call me, at any of those numbers, any time, day or night. And I do mean day or night, understood?"

"Understood. And thanks, I will."

After he hung up he tried to put the whole thing out of his mind. He had gotten this far on his own. He'd just have to suck it up and keep moving. When he got enough evidence to close the case there'd be time enough to do the procedure and get reinstated. For now, he needed to get back to work. He called Price and asked him to come over, then he found the tape Rhea Carson had given him and slipped it into his machine.

36

Terry was sitting on the library steps when a Chevy Cavalier pulled up and stopped. The uniformed policewoman who got out was blonde, in her early thirties, very trim, and she was smiling when she came around the front of the vehicle.

"You must be Terry, there's a definite family resemblance. I'm Officer Mulholland, Denise."

She held out her hand. Terry reached over and shook it, lightly, but did not get up. She looked worried.

"What's up? Is my dad okay?"

"Oh yeah, he's fine."

"So what are you doing here?"

"Mrs. Hennessey got delayed, phoned your dad to say she couldn't pick you up and your dad called me."

"You a friend of his?"

"More like a, you know, co-worker."

"Funny, he never mentioned you."

"Well, we weren't partnered or anything. We were on the same shift before he was transferred to Operations."

Reluctantly, Terry got to her feet and walked across the sidewalk. When Mulholland opened the back door of the unmarked cruiser, Terry stopped.

"Uh, I want to ride in the front."

Mulholland frowned politely. "Sorry, no can do. Regulations." Then she smiled again. "But, hey, let's just pretend this is a taxi."

As they drove back toward the city, Terry began to feel uncomfortable. She wasn't sure, but it didn't seem like they were going in the right direction.

"Where are you taking me anyway?"

Mulholland had to think for a second and the hesitation raised Terry's pulse a notch. "We're not going to Astoria, Nick's going to meet us in the Bronx. He'll drive you home."

Terry tensed but told herself to stay cool. "What the hell is he doing in the Bronx? He doesn't know anyone up there."

Mulholland shrugged. "Business, I guess. Police business. You can ask him yourself when I drop you off."

37

Corbie Price sat at the kitchen table while Nick listened to the wire tape one more time. He'd been running it all afternoon. The identity of the man who hired Duplessis hovered just at the edge of Nick's aural memory. He had heard that voice before but couldn't place it. He was sure it was no one he knew, even casually. More like a public voice, a TV personality, or a politician. It was a very smooth, very guarded voice, the voice of a man used to giving orders, and confident to the point of arrogance.

Duplessis: *"Your offer is alarmingly generous. What's the catch?"*

Unidentified Voice: *"Very astute, Malcom, there is a catch. In addition to your usual skill set, we'll be asking you to impersonate someone for an hour or two."*

"I don't see how I can do that, I'm no actor."

"You won't have to be. In fact, you won't have to say a single word. But it will be necessary to make some changes in your appearance."

"Dye my hair, lose ten pounds, what?"

"I'm afraid it will be a bit more substantial than that. We've engaged one of the best plastic surgeons in the country. The reconstruction will be painless and will only take a couple of weeks to heal."

There was a long silence. Then Duplessis said, *"Will the changes be reversible?"*

"Not entirely, no, but I'll bet the farm you'll be very pleased with your new face, once you get used to it."

"What if I want my old face back?"

"That won't be possible, but you can have a second round of procedures that will bring you closer to the old look than the new one."

"This all sounds very high risk. What does it involve, and who am I supposed to impersonate? What happens when he finds out?"

"I can't tell you that, but I can tell you that there's no risk to you, none at all. We're covered by the CIA, Homeland Security and the Department of Defense, so don't sweat it."

Duplessis whistled. *"I don't know, my gut is telling me to get the hell out, right now!"*

"Okay, see how your gut reacts to this. You've been involved in a number of criminal enterprises over the past eleven years, and we have enough evidence to send you to a very unpleasant institution for maybe the rest of your life. On the other hand, if you accept this assignment, we'll double your fee, one million up front and one point six when the job is done."

"That's a very tempting offer, but I'll have to think about it. I don't believe you can send me to jail, so your big stick's just a toothpick. But the money would be enough to retire on, so I'll consider it and get back to you, though I should probably just tell you to fuck off and die."

"Think fast, Malcom. We're on a tight schedule here. You've got twelve minutes. After that you'll be apprehended by DHS and you'll disappear."

Another long silence, then Duplessis answered, his voice very quiet, almost a whisper. *"Before I decide I need to see your money."*

"No problem. We brought an attaché case with the first installment. There's also a ticket to Washington where you'll meet the man with the knife. We'll see you again in two weeks with further instructions…"

Nick played it again, and it almost triggered something he'd heard somewhere in the news, or on a police bandwidth. He took off the earphones and laid them on his desk.

"Who does that guy sound like?"

"Dunno, but he ain't no shitkicker."

"Right. Got that Master of the Universe thing about him, don't he?"

"Yeah, but I bet he'd piss himself if he knew he was singin' to the cops."

Nick shook his head. "Not much of a song, really. The first part of the tape is corrupted and this little tête-à-tête goes to fraud, at the most, and some intra-corporate power game at the least. Not too damaging. Of course, whoever the guy is, he doesn't know the tape has been damaged. He thinks it could fry his ass and he wants it. That gives us an edge. But who the hell is it? I know I've heard that voice before."

"Don't sweat it, boss. You heard the dude's voice before, you'll remember it."

"Thanks, bro, I hope you're right."

He rewound the tape and they listened to it one more time.

When the phone rang, he checked the caller ID before he picked up and was surprised to see that it was Mrs. Hennessey.

"Nora, what's wrong, have you picked up Terry?"

"I'm so sorry, Mr. Cortese, but I couldn't get off to the school."

"Why not, why didn't you call sooner?"

"Well, I'll not be making much sense of it, but there's someone here who's wanting to speak with you."

Another voice came on the line. Nick recognized it immediately.

"Detective Cortese?"

"Well, who the hell do you think it is? You called me."

"This is Agent Robert O'Hare of Homeland Security."

Nick became cautious and furious at the same time. He'd checked out the new laws and knew that O'Hare's description of his extra-legal prerogatives had not been entirely off the wall.

"Good afternoon, Agent O'Hare, may I ask why you have detained my housekeeper?"

"There seem to be certain, uh, irregularities, and we have become curious about your recent meeting with a person of interest. Mrs. Hennessey has been most cooperative but seems to have no knowledge we can use."

"What do you want?"

"Want? We don't want, Mr. Cortese, we just take what we need to protect the interests of the United States."

"It's *Detective* Cortese, and I'd like to know what you think you need?"

"I believe you know very well. We'll be in touch with instructions shortly. In the meantime, I can assure you that we have no further interest in Mrs. Hennessey. We will release her, but only with the understanding that you will tell her nothing whatsoever about these proceedings."

"Proceedings? What proceedings? What are you talking about?"

"Have a nice day, Detective."

Price was looking at him, waiting for an explanation, but Nick knew he couldn't say a word about what had just transpired.

"Something's come up. I've got some calls to make. Go on back to the shop and I'll call you later."

"You sure, boss? You look a bit rattled. Anything I can do?"

"No, no. Just a misunderstanding. I'll talk to you later."

As soon as Price left, Nick called St. Mary's School for Girls.

"Hello, this is Detective Nicola Cortese. Do you know if my daughter, Terry, is still there? The woman who was supposed to pick her up was detained and I'd really appreciate it if you could tell her that I'll be there as soon as I can. She's probably sitting on the steps of the library waiting for her ride."

"Glad to, but I'll have to put you on hold while I see what I can find out."

"Yes, I'll hold, but hurry, please!"

Nick waited and waited, drumming his fingers, feeling his pulse rise and his mouth grow dry. Three minutes later the receptionist came back on the phone.

"I'm sorry, Detective. She's not waiting at the library, and I didn't see her anywhere in the vicinity. She probably got tired of waiting and took a bus?"

"Okay, thanks. She's probably on her way home."

Nick took a long breath, then let it out slowly. He told himself she was all right, but he didn't believe it.

38

Price sat in the Cavalier and called Malone.

"Chaz, I've just been with Nick. He got a phone call and it really rattled him. He wouldn't tell me what's going on and I'm kinda worried. Maybe he's having one of those episodes, or maybe he's in some deep shit, I don't know."

"Sounds serious, what should we do?"

"I think we ought to check it out."

"You mean tail him? He's the boss."

"So what? He might need our help. We'll just keep an eye on him, a long leash, okay?"

"Hell, if you want to do it right and he's in trouble, let's run a double, I'll take the radio and we'll leapfrog him."

"Okay. I'm set up outside his place now. Get here as soon as you can."

The silence in the apartment got heavier and heavier till it felt like a hand closing around Nick's throat. He didn't know what he should do. Maybe she did take the bus, or several buses, and it would take hours for her to get home. Or maybe she went to a friend's house, got into something and forgot to phone her father. But he couldn't follow that lead—he had no idea who her friends were, where they lived or how they could be contacted. All he could do was wait.

Outside, across the street from Nick's apartment building, Malone sat in a Ford Crown Victoria talking on the radio phone to Price.

"Looks like he's not in a hurry. Maybe it's cool."

"I dunno, Chaz. I gotta feelin something's goin' down. Let's hang in for a while."

"Ten four. I'll wait on your signal."

Nick went into his bedroom, dialed the combination lock on the safe and took out one of the unregistered weapons he kept for emergencies. He strapped on the ankle holster and secured the Heckler & Koch 9mm. M13. It was a compact semi-automatic that held thirteen rounds in the clip and one in the chamber. He took off his jacket and shirt, removed the Kevlar vest from its hanger, shrugged it on and adjusted it. He got back into his clothes, checked his watch, and sat down to wait a little longer.

Then the phone rang. His first thought was, *it's Terry*! and he felt a great wave of relief, but when he picked up, his worst fears were confirmed.

"We have something that belongs to you, Cortese." The voice was cold and smug.

Nick shouted back. "Where is she, you piece of shit?"

"...and you have something that belongs to us."

"I need to know she's all right."

"She's fine. And will remain so as long as you cooperate. Right now, she's eating a Whopper with fries."

"Let me talk to her."

Nick could hear footsteps moving away from the phone. A door opened and a few seconds later he heard two sets of footsteps coming back. When Terry came on the phone, he almost broke, overwhelmed by a mixture of anguish, guilt that he hadn't seen this coming and relief that she was okay.

"Dad! What's going on? Who are these guys?"

She sounded nervous, but not yet really scared. He struggled with how much he should tell her. But before he could decide she said, "This woman cop picked me up and brought me to this creepy place up in the Bronx. Come and get me, I'm on..."

There was the sickening sound of a slap, then a sharp cry and shoes scuffing over linoleum, a door slamming, silence.

Nick's voice was razor-edged and quiet. "If anything happens to her you're all dead. I'll find you, you twisted fuckers, and I'll burn you alive."

A different voice answered. It was cool, measured.

"No need for threats. This is a simple business proposition, a *quid pro quo*. You know how it goes. Bring the item. Don't talk to anyone. We'll give you instructions on how to proceed. You will follow them to the letter. You will be watched at all points, so don't improvise. If you comply, your daughter will be returned to you safely."

"All right. But I have some conditions of my own. We make an even trade, out in the open. If I don't see my daughter alive and healthy, you don't get your fucking item."

"Fair enough. Leave the apartment within three minutes and drive east. We'll provide further directions on your cellphone."

Nick's Sebring came out of the parking garage and Price watched it turn left. He waited till there was another car behind it then he started the Cavalier and eased out into the street. He followed at a distance of five car lengths and after a mile or so got on the radio phone to Malone.

"He's on the move. Doesn't seem to be in a hurry, but he keeps changing direction, like he can't decide where he's going. I'm gonna drop back. Pick him up at the next intersection."

The cellphone warbled again and Nick put it on speaker. Though the voice was not loud, it seemed to fill the enclosed space like a sinister spirit.

"At the next intersection, turn left, then take the next right. In the middle of the block there's an alley. Pull into it and stop."

He did as he was told.

"Malone to Price, over."

"Gotcha, Chaz. What's up?"

"Looks like he's just parked, waiting for instructions, I guess. He's in an alley halfway down the street. Can you come around and cover where it comes out in the next block?"

"Right. I'll take him from there."

Five minutes later, the cellphone rang and the voice gave Nick a new set of directions.

He was to drive north across the Robert F. Kennedy Bridge to Randall's Island Park, take the Bruckner Expressway east, then south to Ferry Point Park and across the Whitestone Bridge, continue south on Interstate 678 to the Belt Parkway, and over the Verrazzano-Narrows Bridge to a weedy, empty lot on Father Capodano Avenue at South Beach on Staten Island.

When the Sebring nosed out of the alley and turned left, Price hunkered down and counted to ten, then he straightened up and reached for the key in the ignition but didn't turn it. He watched Nick cross the intersection and waited for him to get another half block lead before he started the Cavalier. But a red Nissan 300Z pulled out in front of him. Price let it get twenty feet away, then started his car and followed.

Two blocks later, when Nick turned right, the Nissan did too and Price turned after the Nissan. Two more turns and Price got on the radio phone.

"Malone?"

"Yeah."

"Look's like he's picked up a tail. They're heading for the expressway. If they get on it, let's see if one of us can get close enough to see what they're up to."

As he approached the bridge, Nick had a moment of near panic as he felt the onset of a flashback that could drag him almost entirely back to the war-torn combat zones of Iraq and Afghanistan, but he forced himself to think about Terry, recalled the memory he had used as a safe harbour during his sessions with Sanderson, and managed to stay focused on the bridge, drive across, follow the signs and get to the entrance ramp for the Bruckner.

Traffic was building on the expressway but Malone pulled out and eased past the red Nissan. Without turning his head or staring, he could see that there were two men in the front. The driver was a short, slight, fair-skinned man with very blond, almost white hair. The passenger was taller, heavyset, with a thick neck and doughy jowls. He was talking into a cellphone and smiling. It was not a pleasant smile.

Malone dropped back, called Price and told him what he'd seen.

"Looks to me like the Nissan's giving instructions and Nick's going wherever they tell him to. That's why his movements haven't made much sense."

Price came back with a question. "What's your read?"

"I'd say they're tryna make sure no one's following him."

Price laughed. "Well, they fucked that one up."

"Sure did. They have no idea we're on them. It's got to be some kind of meet, unofficial, so they can make their pitch where no one's likely to see them."

"Either that or it's a set-up. Suppose they've sucked him in, you know, got him to go somewhere with no backup, then wham!"

Malone's face went grim. "We got that covered too, *compadre*."

It was getting dark. Nick sat in the Sebring in the empty lot for twenty minutes before the voice came back with new instructions. He was to cross the Bayonne Bridge into Jersey, then take the Holland Tunnel back to Manhattan.

It made no sense, but that was the point. As he continually did what he was told, like a robot, he would be forced to confront and accept his absolute helplessness. And it was working. Driving through neighbourhoods that millions called home, he was intensely aware of his isolation, the danger he faced, and the threat to Terry. All those people went on with their lives, coming home from work or school, cooking and sitting down to supper, talking about their day, getting up and watching TV. None of them knew what he faced, and none of them could help him.

39

He parked the Sebring in front of a shabby apartment among the factories, warehouses and industrial properties on Hudson Street and waited. Nearly five minutes later the cellphone voice that had become a live-in ghost, haunting him wherever he went, came on and gave him final instructions.

He turned off the headlights and got out of the car. The bulb in the street lamp had been shattered and he found himself in a sinister world populated by looming shapes and stretches of impenetrable darkness.

As the voice had promised, the entrance to the apartment building was unlocked. When he pulled it toward him it lurched and sagged on its hinges, scraping the sidewalk. He closed it behind him and walked through the dim hallway to the back door. It opened onto an unlighted alley. He stepped out onto a gritty spritz of pulverized glass on cracked concrete.

Across the way, barely visible, there was a warehouse, and, directly in front of him, a parking lot or loading zone. Suddenly he *felt,* he *knew,* someone was there. The skin tingled at the back of his neck and his body came awake, shrugging off fatigue like a lead coat.

He knelt, pretending to retie his shoe, and slipped the H&K M-13 from his ankle holster into his jacket pocket. He stood up and scanned the darkness, trying to make sense of the jumbled, nearly invisible forms that lurked there. Slowly, as his eyes adjusted, a sports car seemed to materialize, though only as a silhouette, at the far end of the lot.

He felt the adrenalin hypersensitivity, the brittle, almost crystalline quality of sight and sound he had experienced in Iraq and Afghanistan. Everything was magnified and his reflexes felt like coiled springs.

When the headlights came on they blinded him, and he leapt to the cover of a dumpster he didn't know he knew was there.

He heard a car door open. The man who got out was just a dark shape behind the glare of the high beams but he looked familiar. When he spoke Nick knew who it was.

"You follow directions very well, Mr. Cortese."

"Where is she, O'Hare?"

"She's, uh, resting. Wasn't quite up to the trip."

"You promised an even trade. You said you'd bring her."

O'Hare laughed. "I lied. But I hope you didn't. Where's the tape?"

"Somewhere close by."

"Now, now, Nicola, don't be coy. Time to show your wares."

"Not until I see my daughter."

O'Hare made a gesture with his right hand and the other man hoisted himself out of the Nissan and lumbered over to stand next to him.

"This is one of our associates, Mr. Clemson. He's a specialist. And a very persuasive one. Show us the tape and we'll take you to your daughter."

And then you'll kill us both, Nick thought. His mind was racing. If he gave them the tape, he'd have nothing left to trade for Terry. If he didn't, they'd probably shoot him and find it eventually. And they'd kill Terry anyway, to cover their tracks or just for spite. He had to stall till he could figure out how to turn it around, disarm them, force them to tell him where they were keeping her. But before he could tell them they'd never find the tape without his help, Clemson drew an ivory-handled, long-barrel .357 magnum from the holster under his meaty left arm. He pointed it at Nick's crotch.

"You got ten seconds to tell and show, otherwise it's bang bang and no more bang for Cortese."

"I lie, too, Clemson, just like your boss. Do you think I'd bring it? It's where you'll never find it in a—"

A voice came out of the darkness behind the Nissan.

"NYPD! Freeze! Drop your weapon!"

Clemson turned and fired. Price shot him through the head and he was dead before he hit the ground. O'Hare ran back to the Nissan, but Malone cut him off. When he saw O'Hare reach inside his jacket, Malone hit him, hard, with an elbow chop to the neck. He heard something crack and O'Hare went down. O'Hare lay in the glass-peppered dirt of the empty lot, on his side, barely breathing. His eyes rolled up into his head and he was gone.

Nick rushed over and knelt beside O'Hare's motionless form. He lifted him by the shoulders and shook him.

"Wake up, you fucking weasel!" His voice broke. "Where is my daughter?"

He looked up at Price and Malone. They were standing with their heads bowed.

Nick screamed at them. "What the fuck have you done? Do you even *know* what you've done?"

Malone opened his mouth but didn't say anything. Nick stood up and said, very quietly, "Look at me." Then he shouted, "Look at me!"

They both looked up, then looked away.

"Didn't you hear what we were talking about? How could you be so thick? They have my daughter. Now one of them is dead and the other one will probably never wake up. How the fuck am I going to find her?"

40

It was stuffy in the small kitchen and there was the musty odour of mildew and rotted wood. Clay Noireau hauled his six-foot-five frame up from the table, walked over to the window and yanked it up. But there wasn't even the hint of a breeze. The safe house was in a part of the Bronx that looked like a bombed-out city. There were no streetlights and no one lived in the tenements that had been ransacked and wrecked. He cursed under his breath, went into the living room where he stood for several minutes, staring out into the deserted street before he came back and sat down again.

Jocko Birdick ran a hand through his thinning hair and poured himself another Baileys. After he knocked it back, he gave a short, dismissive grunt. "Relax, Clay. You'll blow a gasket."

Noireau growled, "I don't like it. They should have called in by now and Clemson's not answering his cell."

"Ah, he's probably just doin' what he gets paid for."

Noireau ignored him, opened his cell, found the number and punched the call button. He held it to his ear, listened while he drummed his fingers on the table then slammed it shut.

"Something's wrong. I'm gonna go downtown and check it out."

Jake shrugged, took a slug from the bottle. "Do what ya gotta do."

Noireau gave Birdick a long, hard stare. "Make sure you look in on the little bitch every ten minutes. If she gets loose, it will be your ass."

Jake made a clumsy salute. "Whatever you say, Mastah Noireau, suh!"

"What I say is keep your slimy hands off the merchandise, Birdick. And lay off that Irish pussy booze you been suckin' up since you got here."

While Price called in the shooting, Nick went through O'Hare's jacket and pants, but all he came up with were the keys to the Nissan. Malone stood by, watching, looking like he'd rather be stretched out on a bed of nails.

"They won't hurt her, Nick, not while you've still got what they want. They'll be in touch."

It made sense, but waiting was the one thing Nick could not do. He looked at the key fob he was holding, thought for a bit, then opened the door and got behind the wheel. He turned on the ignition and scanned the dashboard as it lit up. Over on the right-hand side of the instrument panel, there was what looked like a computer screen. He pushed one of the buttons below it and the screen came on.

It was a Garmin GPS Navigator. Nick brought up the menu, activated the recent trips tab and found the long list of twists and turns the Nissan had made as it followed him all around New York. It was something he could use, but it would take hours to retrace every single one of the directions he had followed and by then, they'd know something had gone wrong and they'd move her. Or worse, they'd send him messages, like her ear or one of her fingers. The thought terrified him. He studied the image, played with the controls and realized he could follow the route back to its point of origin right there on the screen. It was an address in the Bronx and he remembered Terry telling him they'd taken her to that part of town. He set it as his new destination and the computer started a new blue line. Without alerting Price or Malone, he started the motor and took off in a spray of glass chips and dirt and smoke from his squealing wheels.

He drove north on Hudson, then left on Houston and right onto West Street. He turned north again, with the Hudson River to his left, Eleventh Avenue, Twelfth, the Lincoln Highway, Joe DiMaggio Highway, and the Henry Hudson Parkway. At 151st Street, Route 9A veered west again toward the river and a strong breeze came up.

He felt a burst of adrenalin and the hyper-arousal that signalled the onset of a flashback.

This time it wasn't a bridge but the sound and the smell of water that brought it on. Suddenly the air grew murky. He couldn't see more than a few inches in front of him. He couldn't breathe, he was drowning. Something was tangled in his fingers, dragging him deeper. His legs were like lead and his feet felt as though they had grown roots. He couldn't kick free, couldn't swim, and just before he blacked out there was an enormous thud as though he'd been hit by something in the water. It shocked him and he came awake. He'd jumped the curb and jammed the Nissan's right fender into the railing of the entrance ramp to Interstate 95 East. He braked to a stop on the walkway in a screech of scraped metal and the motor stalled. He took long, deep breaths and when he was centred again he checked the GPS. The screen was locked and when he tried to get it working again, it just went black.

He remembered the address he was trying to reach, but he hadn't spent much time in the Bronx since his first few months on the force, and though the street sounded familiar, he had no idea where it was or if he could find it without the Garmin.

41

Jocko Birdick drained the last dribble from the fifth of Baileys and tossed the bottle at the sink but missed. It bounced on the counter, fell to the floor and rolled back under the table.

He cursed, got to his feet and stumbled over to the ancient refrigerator. There was another bottle stashed in the produce tray.

When he'd gotten the top off and had another drink, he felt better. He took it with him into the bedroom. She was there all right, no worries, her wrists handcuffed behind her back, her left ankle handcuffed to a front leg of the bed. After she almost gave Cortese the address, Noireau had stuffed a handkerchief into her mouth and tied a rag around it.

She just sat there looking at Jocko. The little slut had guts, he'd give her that. And she was a looker, too. He wondered how old she was, wondered how she would look without her clothes. Did she have hair on her thing?

Noireau said to keep hands off, but he didn't say anything about a peek. He walked over to the bed and she got up, started to run but the cuff stopped her. He pulled her back, pressed her down into the mattress with his knee. He reached behind her head and untied the rag, took the gag out. He still had the Baileys in his left hand. He held it out. "How's about a little drink, sweetums."

She shook her head, hard.

He laughed. "Oh, she's a toughie. Well, if you won't have a drink with old Jocko, we'll have to find some other way to entertain ourselves."

"Get the fuck off me!"

Jocko laughed again, leaned down and licked her ear. She screamed and turned her face away. He shook his head. "Go ahead, bitch. Make all the noise you want. Ain't nobody in this building. Hell, ain't nobody in the whole damn block 'cept you and me and some rats."

He put the bottle down on the floor and stood studying her. He couldn't get her clothes all the way off without getting rid of the cuffs, but that was too risky. He'd have to make the best of a bad situation.

"Let's unwrap this tasty little package, see what we got here."

He pushed her back again and reached down to undo the top button of her jeans. She didn't scream, she just brought her right knee up into his testicles. He stepped back, couldn't believe the shock of it, and the pain that made him weak. She kicked him again, this time with her foot and he nearly passed out. In his haste to get beyond the range of her kicks, he stumbled, tripped over the Baileys and curled up on the floor till the pain passed.

When he got back to his feet, his face was contorted with rage and humiliation.

"All I wanted was a little friendly drink, and a peek, that's all, just a peek."

He reached behind him and brought out a 9mm semi-automatic, cranked a round into the chamber and pointed it at Terry.

"You're a nasty piece of work, you know that? So this is what's gonna happen. You're gonna lie real still. And the price just went way up. You want to stay alive, bitch, you don't say a fucking word. Your pants are gonna come down, and your panties. Then I'm gonna turn you over and do you, alive or dead, it don't matter to me."

Jocko approached the bed like a boxer, with his left foot forward and his torso turned away from Terry's feet. He shifted the Glock to his right hand and reached for her jeans, but she writhed and kicked and he hit her across the face with the gun barrel. She fell back and when he raised the gun to hit her again a shot rang out.

The front of his head blew off and he fell to the floor.

Nick climbed in from the fire escape and ran to his daughter. She was unconscious but breathing normally and except for the laceration on her cheek, she seemed unharmed. He undid the handcuffs and her eyelids fluttered. As she regained consciousness, she kicked out.

"It's okay, hon, it's me. You're safe now."

She looked up and her eyes changed. "Dad! Thank God it's you." She closed her eyes and held onto him. He lifted her from the bed and began to carry her, but she struggled and shook her head.

"No, I'm fine, I can walk."

They moved quickly to the kitchen window, but before they could climb out onto the fire escape, a silver-grey Lincoln Town Car drove into the alley and parked beside the Nissan. They stepped back into the room before being seen and Terry followed her dad as he ran to the front door.

Nick felt a stab of panic and took a deep breath. Think, he told himself. Whoever it was in the Lincoln would be relieved to see the Nissan and would assume Clemson and O'Hare were back with the wire tape. He would not be expecting any trouble. Before he discovered the truth Nick would have a free shot and he would not miss. But suppose there were two of them, or three. He couldn't afford a firefight, not with Terry in the room.

He moved out into the hallway and looked around. At the far end there was a narrow flight of stairs leading up into absolute darkness. They ran to it and climbed up to a narrow door he hoped would lead to the roof. He turned the knob and pushed, but it was stuck. He could hear footsteps on the stairs three floors below. If he kicked the door open they would hear it and there would be gunfire. He turned and braced his back against the door. He used all his strength, pushing up with his legs and shoulders. The door creaked but held. He relaxed, took a deep breath and heaved again. This time it moved but did not open. The footsteps grew louder; one floor away now as he made a last effort, pushed through and fell out onto the roof. He got back on his feet, helped Terry climb out, then closed the door and bunted it shut with his shoulder.

The tenements were built wall to wall and he could see that the way was clear to the last building on the block. Moving quickly, they climbed over the low walls that separated one rooftop from the next until they came to the end. Nick tried the door that led down from the roof but it was locked and he couldn't budge it. He took his daughter by the shoulders and his voice was intense.

"Listen, I have to leave you for a few minutes. I'm going to climb down the fire escape and get in on a lower floor. Then I'll come back up and open this door from the inside so we can get out of here."

She nodded to let him know she understood, then hugged him hard and stepped back.

He went to the edge and began to climb over but pulled back when he saw lights at the other end of the alley. They were high headlights, like those on a half-ton truck, and up where the roof of the cab would be there was a powerful spotlight that swept left and right as the vehicle advanced. He ducked low and ran to the front of the building. When he peered over the edge he saw an empty street and breathed a sigh of relief until the silver-grey Lincoln nosed slowly around the corner. He wondered how many more of them were out there, scanning the neighbourhood. And how long it would be before they started searching the tenements, one room at a time, from the basement up to the roof.

42

Nick opened his cellphone. But who could he call? It would take too long for help to arrive from the Sixth. Besides, he was suspended and had just shot a man through the head, without identifying himself and without a warning.

He pulled up the list of NYPD precincts and punched in the number for the Detective Squad at the Forty-second. When the duty officer answered, Nick said, "This is Detective Nicola Cortese, from the Sixth."

He gave them his badge number, told them there had been an assault, that the perp was still at large and the victim needed medical assistance. It only took them three and a half minutes to get there. They never checked to see if his badge was valid.

At the hospital Nick showed his ID, explained how Terry got hurt and made an unusual request. "I'd be grateful if she could be registered as a Jane Doe. And you can skip the insurance paperwork, I'll pay cash for her care."

"I don't think we can do that, Detective."

"Is Doctor Neville Chambers on call tonight?"

"I'll check."

The receptionist pulled up a screen on her computer and nodded. "Yes, he is. Shall I page him?"

"Please, and is there someone I can speak to about keeping my daughter's identity anonymous? I hope you understand that her life is in danger, and though I respect your security arrangements, I'd rather be safe than sorry."

"Well, if Dr. Chambers agrees, I see no problem."

Nick thanked her again and went back to sit next to Terry while they waited for the doctor. She was subdued but seemed calm and he hoped that her injury was as superficial as it looked. His one concern, besides the laceration and the trauma of being attacked, was a possible concussion from the blow with the gun barrel. He'd mention that to Chambers as soon as he arrived.

Half an hour later, Terry was still being attended to by her physician and Nick was frantic to see her, but he knew he had to wait until she'd been thoroughly examined and X-rayed. He opened his cell and put in a call to Corbie Price, then he paced up and down the corridor for what seemed like an eternity before Dr. Chambers came through the glass door and shook his hand.

They sat in the waiting area and Chambers brought Nick up to date.

"First of all, the good news. There was no concussion from the blow and the laceration is deep, but clean. It will heal and I don't think there will even be a slight scar. But she has been terrorized. Apparently, her assailant repeatedly attempted to strip her, and when she fought back, he promised to rape her then hit her with a pistol and knocked her out. She is exhausted, disoriented and in a state of mild shock. She's been sedated and needs to rest. We'd like to keep her overnight for observation."

Nick felt like he'd been kicked in the stomach. Dr. Chambers rested his right hand on Nick's shoulder and spoke quietly. "She's a very brave girl, Nick. She'll be all right."

"I want to see her."

"Of course. I'll take you to her."

When he came into the softly lit room, Terry smiled weakly and held out her arms. He sat on the bed and held her for a long time. He had explained the little that was explicable on the way to the hospital. Now there was nothing to say. After a while, she asked, "Are *you* all right?"

Nick smiled. "I'm fine."

The sedative was beginning to kick in and she gave a big yawn. She lay back on the pillow and looked like a five-year-old. It wrung his heart. But before she drifted off, her eyes grew bright and her face looked anguished.

"What is it, babe?"

"I'm ashamed to tell you."

He stroked her hair, looked at her very seriously. "There's nothing you can't tell me, Terry."

"I wanted to kill him, Dad. I'm glad he's dead."

"Nothing wrong with that, hon. You had good reason, and so did I. He won't abuse anyone else, ever."

He waited till she drifted off to sleep, then left the room quietly and took the elevator down to the lobby. Price and Malone were standing next to the coffee machine, talking in subdued voices. When they saw him they came over and shook hands.

"Is she okay, Nicky?"

"Yeah, Corbie. She's asleep. The doctor says recovery will take a couple of weeks, and there will probably be nightmares for a while after that, but she'll be all right."

Malone smiled. "Really glad to hear that, Nick. We're both so sorry. We didn't hear what those guys were saying to you. All we saw was that big dude waving his cannon..."

"I know. I should have told you what was doing down. But the truth is, if I had, and you stayed out of it, they probably would've killed me, and Terry as well, so thanks for being there. As it turned out, you saved us both."

They both looked like a great weight had been lifted from their shoulders. Price filled Nick in on what happened after he had roared off in the Nissan.

"When backup arrived, they treated it like a normal crime scene, called in the CSU, ME, and the medical team. They impounded your car, too, but it wasn't involved in the shooting so they released it."

"Where is it now?"

"It's parked outside."

"How the hell did you get it here? I've still got the key."

Malone looked sheepish. "I, uh, hotwired it. Hope you don't mind."

"Why should I mind? You think I like flagging taxis? Thanks, Chaz. Really."

"No problem. But you know there's going to be an investigation. We both gave formal statements and we'll have to file a report."

"How much do they know?"

"We told them the guy I shot and that skinny pink dude Malone clobbered had kidnapped your daughter. But they didn't believe us. Turns out one of them was some sort of pro, a former Blackwater contractor working as a floater, and the other was Homeland Security."

"I'll file a report corroborating your statements. What do you think will come down?"

"Well, knowing Chase, it will be by the book. But the shoot was to protect the life of a police officer who was being directly threatened by an armed assailant. We identified as NYPD and shot in self-defence."

"Sounds pretty straight. What about the Homeland Security agent?"

Malone answered, "He ain't dead, but I guess I broke his neck. Hasn't woke up yet. Might be an assault charge, but he resisted arrest and was attempting to flee, so we'll see what happens. I'm not really worried. They were kidnappers, for Chrissake."

"Yeah, but they were *official* kidnappers, connected high on the totem pole, and guarding our national security, so they're probably covered. Or maybe DHS will just cut him loose as a rogue. What about that address up in the Bronx?"

"Looks like a cleaner got there first. Probably CIA. It was completely stripped. Not even a rat turd anywhere."

43

Noireau was beginning to hate the voice on the phone. His well-connected, deep-pocketed but anonymous employer sounded like he was about to go viral.

"I thought Blackwater, Xe or whatever the fuck you call yourselves, was supposed to be top of the line. Rydell said I could depend on you, but you're a pack of incompetent morons."

Noireau walked over to the window and looked out at the lights of New York. He wondered how long it would take to find the prick and teach him some manners. When he spoke again his voice was filled with contempt.

"Getting a little agitated, are we?"

"You bet your black ass I'm agitated. Your entire operation has been a disaster. I want that fucking tape, right now."

"Think you could have done better, do you?"

"A Girl Scout could have done better, you stupid gorilla. Do you still have that Carson whore?"

"No. I told you, she's in custody at DHS."

There was a long silence. When the voice came on again it was back in control.

"Okay, what's done is done. Here's what I want you to do next. And your performance had better improve, expo-fucking-nentially, or your fee's gonna get so small it won't buy you a barbecued chicken."

44

After Price and Malone left, Nick sat in the coffee shop and thought about his next move.

If he turned the wire in to the evidence room, Chase would agree to let the Defense Intelligence Agency or Department of Homeland Security or some other Feds claim it and whoever was incriminated on it would walk. It was well hidden, but he'd have to make a copy and make sure it got into the hands of someone he could trust. And that was the least of his problems. What worried him most was the safety of those he loved. He should never have let Terry stay with him after he got transferred back to the Sixth. He should have seen that she might be in danger. He wouldn't make the same mistake with Claire.

It was after eleven by the time Nick got to her apartment but the lights were still on, so he pressed the intercom and waited.

"Yes, who is it?" She sounded guarded, apprehensive.

"It's me, Claire, did I wake you?"

"Nick! What a nice surprise."

She buzzed him in and he took the elevator up to the seventh floor. As soon as she opened the door and saw him, her face became serious.

"What is it, what's wrong?"

"Terry's been kidnapped."

"Oh my god. When?"

"No, it's okay, we, I, got her back. Sorry if I sound confused. I have so much to tell you and I wish that none of it were true."

"Come and sit. Let me get you a drink. Scotch all right?"

"Yes, thanks."

He sat, tried to find the right words, but by the time she brought the Glenfiddich, he knew that the words didn't matter.

"Okay. The people who kidnapped Terry wanted to exchange her for a piece of crucial evidence. I still have it and they still want it. I didn't call before I came because I was afraid your phone might be tapped. Not likely, but if they know about Terry and have already used her to get to me, they might do the same with you."

"I'm in danger?"

"I'm not sure, but I think you might be, if not now, soon."

"Goddammit, Nick, what am I supposed to do with that?"

"That's what I want to ask you. Can you leave New York for a few days?"

"And go where?"

"I don't know, somewhere that's not obvious, not your parents or a close friend."

"And what about my job, my classes, my work?"

"I know. It's an invasion. From the beginning I was worried about how the job might derail our relationship, and it looks like I was right. I don't know what to say. If you stay here I'm not sure I can protect you."

She walked away, stood near the window thinking, then she came back and sat down. She reached out and took his hands in hers, gripped them hard.

"I know someone who can help. I haven't seen her for several years, but we were close in school and she's not someone my friends or colleagues here would know about."

"Is this going to get you fired?"

"Fired? No, not fired, but it might shoot down my merit pay."

"I'll make it up to you."

"Out of your vast financial resources?"

"I will, I promise. What about your classes?"

"I'm not teaching tomorrow and I can call in a few favours, have someone cover till the end of the week."

"Thank you, you're being very understanding. This can't be easy for you."

"It's not. I know it's not your fault, but it angers me. And even more so because the only option I'm left with is to run. I don't even know who I'm running from, or why."

"There's still a lot I don't know, but I'll tell you what I can if it will help, even a little."

"Hold that thought. I'm going to phone my friend. It's an hour earlier there and she's a night person so I'm sure she's still awake."

"Claire?"

"What?"

"Just one more thing. You've got to take Terry with you."

Claire looked stunned. Opened her mouth to speak, closed it again. When she finally answered, her voice was careful but uncertain.

"I don't know, Nick. I've never even met her. Can't you find someone else who knows her better?"

"Probably, but it would be someone they'd know about. I'm betting they don't know about you yet. If they did they'd have made a move by now."

"You said my phone was tapped."

"I thought it might be. But now that you mention it, maybe you should use your cell or an outside line when you call your friend."

"Nick, if my phone is tapped, they know who I am, and where I am and they'll soon know where I'm going. They're probably watching us even as we speak."

As she talked Nick could see that she was becoming more and more agitated. He held up a hand. "Right. You're right. I should have done this as soon as I came in. I'm sorry. It's been a very bad day."

He got up from the table, walked over and picked up the phone. He unscrewed the mouthpiece, and soon had all its innards open on the table. There was nothing there. While he was putting it back together, Claire relaxed enough to give him a smile.

"Where did you learn to do that, police academy?"

"No, my aunt was a telephone company supervisor, taught me all sorts of tricks."

"Good for her. And you're right about Terry. She'd be safer with me if no one knows who I am."

"Oh, god, thanks, Claire. Thank you."

She was silent for a long minute, then she said, "If you can get her released, I think she should stay here tonight. We can leave before the city wakes up. I'll give you a number where we can be reached. Call me when this third-rate cop show is over and I can get back to my nice, boring routine. But, Nico, this is the last time I'll let your job interfere with my life."

45

Terry was not happy to be roused out of her sedative-induced sleep. She kept diving back under the pillow. But when Nick told her he had signed her out, she perked up a little, got dressed and followed him out to the car.

They drove for about ten minutes through the night city with Terry leaning back in her seat and looking drowsily out of the window. Suddenly she straightened up, frowned and turned to her father.

"You missed the turnoff. Where are we going?"

"You're still in danger. I'm taking you to a friend's apartment. You'll be going with her on a trip out of the city."

"I don't want to go out of the city, I want to go home."

"I know, I know, but home is exactly where they'll be looking for you."

"You're a cop, right? Can't the police protect me?"

"Maybe, but it's risky. And you'd have to stay locked down in the apartment."

"I couldn't go to school, to the mall, anywhere?"

"No, you'd be, uh, totally grounded."

She looked like she was going to cry. "How long?"

"I don't know, Terry. Until whoever they are can't hurt you."

She stiffened, tightened her jaw, stared out the window. "I should never have agreed to stay with you. It's screwed up my whole life."

When they got to Claire's apartment and Nick introduced them, Terry shook hands but did not make eye contact and did not speak. Claire had made up her study as a guest room. She explained where the bathroom was, and that she had laid out towels, soap, a fresh toothbrush and a clean nightshirt. Still, Terry said nothing. She looked around like she was checking for an emergency exit, then went into the study, closed the door and locked it.

Claire shook her head. "This is not going to work, Nico."

"It's got to, I don't know what else to do."

"I understand. But if she decides to just walk out of here..."

"She's tired. She'll come around."

"What if she doesn't? I can't handcuff her to the bedpost."

Nick sighed. "Can't you, you know, use your powers of persuasion, I mean, you are a psychologist."

"I already told you. I don't get on well with teenage girls."

46

On the drive back to Astoria Nick could not shake the disturbing thought that he was responsible for damaging the lives of the two people he loved most in the world. But there was no way out of it, and only one way back. He had to finish what he had started and stop these people so he could get his life on track again and make it right with Claire and Terry.

The first step was to make copies of that tape and make sure they were secured in several places. Then he'd have to get some help identifying the voice of the man who hired Duplessis. But it wouldn't be the NYPD because Chase would confiscate the tape, hand it over to DIA or DHS and the whole case would disappear.

He parked in the underground garage, popped the hood and opened the lid of the windshield-washer fluid tank. It was still there, wrapped in plastic and looking none the worse for its immersion. He unwrapped it to make sure none of the fluid had gotten through. It was hard to tell in the dim light, but it looked okay. He tucked it back into the white plastic opening, locked up the Sebring and started walking toward the elevator. Something made him stop. A movement off to the side, between a Toyota and a Dodge truck. He felt that sudden adrenalin rush he'd felt in combat, and lately when there was a loud noise or some other trigger. He took a deep breath and waited, easing back behind a concrete pillar. But it was only an elderly neighbour coming home late. She nodded as she passed and Nick nodded back.

He wondered if he'd ever be able to get beyond this…thing that was happening to him, uncontrollably and without warning. He told himself to just relax, he was home now, he'd feel much better after a good night's rest.

But as soon as he stepped into his apartment he knew something was wrong. There was a faint scent he didn't recognize in the air, vaguely medicinal. Before he could switch on the light to investigate, strong arms grabbed him from behind. He snapped his head back and could feel the cartilage in his assailant's nose give way. The arms around his chest loosened and Nick slipped down out of their grasp, turned and drove the heel of his right hand into the diaphragm just under the heart. As the man staggered backward and fell, Nick felt a pin prick in his shoulder. He spun around into a stocky blonde woman in a white uniform. She had hard grey eyes and a grim mouth. He shoved her away and his momentum sent him stumbling forward. When he regained his balance he was facing a tall, muscled black man who held his hands in a karate stance and smiled. Nick started a body kick but before it landed he was hit on the side of the head with what felt like a military baton and there was another pinprick in his right thigh. He fell to the carpet, tried to get back to his feet but only made it to his hands and knees. A savage kick to the ribs turned him over on his side. As he lay there, the drugs he'd been injected with began to take effect and he felt paralyzed. A foot turned him over on his back. A voice said, "Do your thing, Helga" and the woman in white loomed above him. "It's *Dr. Schraeder*, asshole," she snarled. "Get out of my way." Before he passed out, Nick felt a sharp pain in the area behind his scrotum.

47

He was rising through layers of darkness. As he became conscious and tried to move, his body felt like it was cast in concrete. *Fuck, I'm paralyzed!* The thought triggered a wave of panic so intense it snapped him into a sitting position. He still had his eyes closed. It took every ounce of will to force them open.

The room was still dark, but there were streaks of light overhead. Fascinated, almost hypnotized, he watched them fan out across the ceiling and cascade down the walls. It spooked him and he dove toward the shadows to his left, away from their movement. As he lay there panting wildly, memory clips like dim fragments of a macabre dream flashed and disappeared. *A chill invaded his lower body…he was lying on his back, unable to move and there was a woman in white…a grim face…*

He felt an excruciating pain, as though someone had driven a nail up into his prostate. It brought him almost fully awake. He began to recognize details. He was still in his living room. But it was beginning to melt at the edges and he felt deeply, wildly afraid before he remembered *Dan Jun* and got control of his breathing. In his heightened state, his mind flitted from image to image, thought to thought, and he was aware of a fragrance that seemed like a hallucination it was so strong. A name came with it. *Poison.* How did he know that, where had he learned it? Then the word seemed to magnify itself into a chain of echoes…

The hallucination passed but the fragrance remained. It was like a magnet that drew every cell of his body toward the guest bedroom, though every cell in his body was filled with dread. It was Terry's room. His daughter. His baby. He blacked out briefly and when he came to he was standing in the open doorway.

On the bed, in the dim light that filtered through from the alley, like an image developing in a bath of photo chemicals, the body of a woman took shape. She was lying face down, her hair spread like a gleaming fan across her back. He took a step toward the bed and tripped over something that was lying inside the room. He fell to his knees. He felt suddenly cold and a shiver passed through him.

He curled up in a ball and closed his eyes, struggling to control the fear that felt like it would shake him apart. When the seizure passed he lay breathing quick, shallow breaths until he was steady enough to open his eyes. When he saw what had tripped him it triggered memories he barely recognized as his own and he nearly passed out again. But it wasn't a body bag, it was a Trekker backpack. Slowly, wearily, his body heavier than he could believe, he got to his feet.

He knew he had to act, turn on the bedside lamp, face everything that was there to face.

He reached out blindly and fumbled for the switch. The light nearly blinded him before it dimmed to a soft glow. The woman was naked and lightly tanned, except for a triangular pattern of pale skin where she'd worn a bikini. She was beautiful, but her back was puckered with stab wounds that had swollen till they looked like wet mouths. She was wearing silver bracelets and anklets that shone softly then hardened into handcuffs that tethered her to the four posts of the bed. Finally, he let himself see, in her back, between her beautifully rounded shoulders, the Victorinox chef's knife from the boxed set in his kitchen, its satin steel reflecting her clean, bright hair.

Suddenly he was filled with a thirst so strong it was like a dry heat in his flesh. And he heard a faint, distant wail, like the keening of a wounded animal. As it came closer he recognized the siren of a radio motor patrol, and he lapsed again into unconsciousness.

48

He felt his body grow lighter as though he were shedding strata of geological time. He became aware of something that looked like a blurred moon over his head. He let himself drift until the furry disk became a fluorescent light and he could hear voices. When he tried to sit up he found that he was strapped to a bed in what looked like a hospital room. There were bars on the windows and the light that filtered in was dull grey. A clock with a white face and black hands on the opposite wall read 8:27. He struggled ineffectively and lay back.

A few moments later, he heard someone say, "The perp is coming around."

Nick recognized the voice and as his vision cleared, he watched Captain Baxter Chase turn to a heavyset, scowling patrolman and bark, "Okay, Armagh, read him his rights."

Thomas Armagh came forward, droned the Miranda warning and stepped back, his eyes glaring with self-righteous anger under bushy eyebrows. Chase tilted his head and gave Nick a look of practised, professional concern.

"Is there anything you want to tell us?"

Nick took his time, trying to read Chase's face before he answered. He did not like what he saw there.

"I think I was drugged. When I woke up I found Rhea Carson's body."

Armagh growled, "Drugged my ass, you raped her, you murdering fuck!"

Chase held up his hand and Armagh backed off.

"Do you understand that you are charged with the rape and murder of Rhea Carson?"

"I'm not the one you should be talking to. I didn't do it."

"Give it up, Nick. We know everything."

"You don't know shit."

"Oh, but we do. You made a deal with Rhea Carson to split the money she stole from the safe deposit boxes of Malcom Duplessis. She tried to short you and you got a little excited. You handcuffed her face down on the bed, sodomized her, then tenderized her back with a chef's knife from your kitchen. Your fingerprints are all over it. Or maybe you tenderized her first then fucked her corpse. I should never have let you back on the force."

"That's a bedtime story, Chase, a fairy tale."

"I'm afraid not, Nick. We found semen in Ms. Carson's rectum. Genetic fingerprinting matched the DNA with samples of your blood. So stop the crap, okay? Talk to me. It might help you bargain a plea. You've got a lot going for you, three combat tours with the Marines, your medals, your NYPD commendations, the attack on your daughter and your PTSD. Frankly, though, I'd rather see you fry."

"There's no death penalty in the state of New York, Baxter, so can the melodrama. Clear the room and I'll talk to you off the record."

When Chase had convinced Armagh and the others to leave, he came back and sat beside the bed.

"We're alone, Nick. You want to tell me what happened?"

"When's the arraignment?"

"Day after tomorrow. But you haven't answered my question."

"Don't pull my dick, Baxter. We both know I'm being set up."

"I don't know anything of the kind. And why would you be?"

"For the same reason my daughter was kidnapped by a Blackwater contractor and an agent from Homeland Security. Don't you get it? Why do you think the Feds are so interested in a random, B&E homicide?"

"They won't say and I don't ask. And we have no idea who kidnapped your daughter. Besides, the whole thing is out of my hands. What you ought to be thinking about is saving your ass. You are in very deep shit, Nicky, and the only way out may be an insanity plea. The sooner you cooperate the easier it will be, for you, and for the NYPD."

Nick looked at Baxter Chase without blinking and let the silence stretch out. He considered telling him about the wire he'd gotten from Rhea Carson, but he was sure it wouldn't make any difference. Though it might identify the perp behind all the mayhem, it wasn't enough to convict him. He'd have to bide his time, and he'd have to get the hell out of wherever he was.

"Baxter, all I can tell you is that I was drugged and set up. But I can see you're not gonna buy it so we're through here."

Chase looked honestly perplexed.

"I can't believe you're being so pigheaded. If you won't confess and make a deal now, the gloves come off and you do down. You won't last a week in the joint. Ex-cops never do."

He left the room and came back with Armagh and the two uniforms.

Nick looked at Armagh and said very quietly, "Don't blow this on a technicality, Tommy. I've got a phone call coming. I want my goddamn phone call right this minute. And I want to see a lawyer."

Armagh smiled a mean little smile.

"Can't do it, Nick. You're still drugged up, you're not *cumpass mendes*. And tomorrow, when the case goes to Homeland Security and you're declared an enemy combatant, you got no rights at all."

49

The nurse held out a small paper cup in which there were two blue pills. She had a glass of water in her other hand.

"I've brought your medication, Mr. Cortese."

"What is it?"

She looked annoyed at the question. "It's just something to help you to sleep."

"I don't want to sleep."

She smiled. "You seem agitated. The pills will calm you and help you relax."

"That's not what I need right now. I need to think. Leave them, I'll take them later."

"I'm sorry, I can't do that. If you prefer, I can call an orderly to hold you while I administer the sedative with a hypodermic."

"What I'd *prefer* is two fingers of Glenfiddich."

"Entirely inappropriate, now take the pills."

Nick stared back at her until she blinked then sighed wearily and shook his head. He accepted the paper cup, tossed the pills into his mouth and slipped them under his tongue.

She handed him the water. He drank it and as he returned the glass she said, "Very good, now open up and say aaahh."

She took a long look inside his mouth, then nodded and left the room. As soon as she was gone, Nick coughed the pills into his hand. He looked for a place to dispose of them, but decided they might be discovered when the wastebasket was emptied so he hid them under his pillow.

This ritual was repeated every three hours. At noon and five p.m. she handed him two more pills. Each time Nick took them, hid them and pretended to sleep while he tried, frantically, to figure a way out. Now it was already dark outside as he opened his eyes.

McCloskey, one of the uniformed officers they'd left to guard him, sat in a chair next to the bed, drinking vendor machine coffee and reading a magazine. He looked really bored until he looked up and realized that Nick was awake.

"Welcome back to the land of the almost living, Detective. Have a good nap?"

"Never slept. Just closed my eyes and pretended to be somewhere else. How about you, all caught up on celebrity gossip, are ya?"

"News mostly. The war on this and the war on that. But they don't tell the half of it. I heard Baxter say you did three tours with the Marines. Were you in Afghanistan?"

"Yeah. Did some recce in the Pech River Valley near the Paki border."

"Uh huh. I was with an SF A-team on Task Force Hammer."

"Operation Anaconda?"

"You heard of it?"

"Heard it was pretty rocky."

"Confusion city. Central Command tried to run things from Tampa. Made a lot of stupid moves. Too many chiefs, too many tribes, and the big plan didn't fit the facts on the ground."

"How the hell did that happen?"

"The intel they started with said there were a couple of hundred Al-Qaeda in the Shahikot, in the villages on the valley floor. But there were over 1,000 of the fuckers, and they were dug in up on the high ridges. We sent troops into hot landing zones. They got shot up, or pinned down, and when one of the grunts fell out of a helicopter, the rescue team took heavy casualties."

"Was that you, on TF Hammer?"

"No, but we had our own problems. Special Forces trained and organized about 400 of Zia Lodin's Afghan fighters. They were supposed to be the main force. They'd enter the valley around the southern end of a humpbacked mountain we called the Whale and clear the villages. I was with Harriman's A-team. We were leading a small group of Afghans whose mission was to set up a blocking force in a narrow pass between the northern end of the Whale and a ridgeline called Gawyani Ghar. The idea was that the AQ's would surrender *en masse*, or try to run, and if they ran, we would cut them off. But shit happens, and, like Clausewitz said, as soon as the battle starts the plan goes out the window."

"He got that right."

"Sure did. We left the Gardez safe house just after midnight, driving without lights on the Zermat road, which wasn't really a road at all, but a muddy track, completely washed out in places where there were wadis up to fifteen feet deep. Several of the Afghan jinga trucks tipped over causing broken bones, a punctured lung and other injuries. The convoy stopped to reload the militiamen into spare trucks and evacuate the wounded."

McCloskey stopped to take a sip of cold coffee. Nick said, "After a scene like that, most of the Afghanis I knew would go back to their homes or their farms."

"Morale was way down, but these guys were keeners. Lodin was an inspired leader and his men would follow him anywhere, so no one quit, but they were not happy campers. The convoy started up again and the group I was with split off and headed east toward the pass. We didn't know it, but things were going to get a lot worse."

"Heavy machine guns and mortar fire from the high ridge, I'd guess."

"No, not till a lot later, but what we ran into was a nightmare. One of the main force leaders, Andy Thomas, got worried about coming into the valley through a narrow gap we called the Fishhook. It was a perfect place for an ambush. So he radioed Grim 31, the AC-130 Spectre gunship that was responsible for air support, and asked it to check out the area with its infrared and night vision scanners. Problem was, Grim's computerized navigation system was giving incorrect readings. They thought they were over the Finger, a ridge just south east of the Whale, but they were eight kilometres north of there. They scanned terrain that looked like the Fishhook and picked up a small truck convoy moving west. When Harriman heard the description the AC-130 sent to Thomas, he thought it sounded a lot like his mini-convoy, so he radioed his grid position, three times, and received confirmation that the enemy contingent the Spectre had scanned was six kilometres to the southeast of him. Harriman was still doubtful, but the Grim 31gunship crew was always cautious about identifying enemy targets. All U.S. and Afghan vehicles were marked with strips of glint tape, and when the Spectre "glinted" their target there was no flash from the trucks and no one on the ground reported having been glinted. So, Harriman radioed Grim 31 that it was cleared hot on those vehicles they'd scanned."

"And that was you?"

"And that was us. The AC-130 blew us to pieces. Harriman was killed with a racquetball-sized piece of shrapnel and three others were wounded. But we still had no idea what was happening. We thought we were taking incoming mortars. The only thing that saved some of us was that dawn came up and the Spectre had to head for home."

Nick could feel the onset of a flashback. He breathed deep but couldn't entirely stop it, and he could hear the shells bursting as he told McCloskey about his friendly fire experience in the Hindu Kush range above the Pech River Valley. When he was done, McCloskey looked thoughtful, but before he could say anything Nick asked, "Think you could get me one of those coffees?"

McCloskey smiled, "Sure thing, Lieutenant."

After he left, Nick took the blue pills from under his pillow, crushed them on the bedside table with a water glass and swept the powder into McCloskey's paper cup. He swirled it around for almost a minute before he set it back down. He wondered how long the sedative would take to work. Then he wondered if that many pills might be lethal. He was still struggling with that when the officer returned and handed him his coffee.

Nick took a sip and looked at McCloskey through the steam. McCloskey looked back.

"I've got to ask you this, Cortese, but you don't have to answer."

Nick nodded. "Go ahead."

"Did you rape and kill that woman?"

"No way, soldier."

"I didn't think so."

Nick took a deep breath, sighed. "But I just loaded your coffee with a dozen of those little blue pills I've been stashing under my pillow. It was the only way I could think of to blow this joint. My bad. They could have done you in."

McCloskey looked angry, then he thought about it for a while and nodded as though he'd made a decision.

"A mouthful won't hurt, and it will cover my ass when they come to spell me and find you're in the wind."

Out on the street in the dark, Nick was nearly overcome by the realization that he'd made a serious mistake. As long as he was in custody he was relatively safe. Even though DHS had the authority to execute enemy combatants, they'd never off him in a hospital bed. It would be too messy. They'd want to disappear his ass, and that would have to wait till after the arraignment, in spite of what Armagh said. But now he was an enemy combatant *and* an escaped felon. He'd taken McCloskey's badge and gun so he was also armed and dangerous.

The order would be to "apprehend with all necessary force," which was cop code for "shoot to kill."

And it wasn't just the NYPD. He'd be hunted by the FBI as well, and all sixteen intelligence agencies, wherever he went. But where would he go? In a couple of hours, after the new guard came on duty, they'd swarm all over the city. They'd set plants on his apartment, on Price and Malone, on Claire's place too, and even on his parents' condo in Oahu. He had to get to his apartment fast, pick up the car and drive out of town before they closed the net. Then he'd have to find a place where he could hole up while he figured out his next move, if he still had any moves left.

50

There was a Sebring on the second level of the parking garage under Nick's apartment building. It was a newer model than his and it wasn't a convertible, but if he exchanged the licence plates it might slow them down a little. With luck, the owner wouldn't be using his vehicle until morning, and that might give him enough time to get somewhere halfway safe and come up with a plan.

He found some tools in the trunk and had just gotten his back plate off when he was nearly blinded by a set of high-beam lights. He knelt there, frozen like a deer in the glare, with the plate in his hand and his pulse revved into overdrive when the silver Lincoln Town Car slowed and stopped.

As the passenger window came down, he scanned the row of parked cars for an escape route, but there was nowhere he could get to fast enough to elude the Lincoln. He reached for the 9mm Glock he'd taken from McCloskey and had it halfway out of his belt when a voice from the open window stopped him.

"Need any help with that?"

He slid the Glock back into his belt and took a deep breath.

"No, I'm good. Just putting on my new plates."

"Kinda late, ain't it?"

"Yeah, well, I kept forgetting about it and I just got pulled over. Gave me a warning and I figured I ought to change 'em before it slipped my mind again and I got a ticket. Anyway, thanks for asking."

"No problem. Have a good one."

Nick watched the Lincoln drive off and turn left toward the exit. He finished switching the plates, got behind the wheel and started the motor. He sat there for several minutes, then turned it off. He had no idea where he should go. It was pointless to wander aimlessly around the countryside till they tracked him down. He had to do better than that. He sat there racking his brain for several minutes. Then he remembered. He still had the numbers Sanderson gave him on his cellphone. Maybe the ex-Marine would be willing to help.

He dialed Sanderson's home phone and waited. When the voice mail message came on, he rang off and dialed the cell. Sanderson picked up on the second ring.

"Hello, Nicola, I'm glad you called."

"It's not what you think. I'm in a load of trouble and I need your help."

"Okay. I'm with a client, but we'll be through shortly. Meet me back at my office in an hour." And he hung up before Nick could explain.

It was nearly midnight by the time Nick got to the brownstone. But he had only been sitting on the front steps for a few minutes when he heard the roar of a cycle and Sanderson came up the street on a Suzuki Hayabusa.

"I've got to put this beast to bed. Why don't you go on up to the office. I'll be back in five."

He tossed Nick a set of keys and rode off down the block.

Nick had left the office lights off and when Sanderson came in he didn't turn them on.

They sat in the darkened room, lit only by what came in from the street, and Nick explained how he'd been drugged and framed, how he'd talked with McCloskey and gotten away, and the danger he was in as a result.

"What I need right now is a place to chill and think about what to do next."

"I'd say what you ought to do next is finish the therapy. Another hour, maybe two."

"I'm not ready for that. I've got to deal with this case first and they've got me boxed in."

"You've got yourself boxed in too. I don't see how you'll be able to think straight or operate at full capacity with a major unresolved trauma stuck in your nervous system. We need to clear it so you can proceed without that encumbrance. We already know what works for you. Just give it one more shot."

Nick was almost convinced, but as he felt his mind move back toward the war, he flinched and shuddered. He shook his head.

"Sorry, Doc. I know you're probably right, and I trust you completely, but I'm just not up to it."

Sanderson nodded. "Okay. There's a small guest room in my apartment, just down the hall. You're welcome to it. Get some sleep, but I have one condition."

"And that is?"

"We talk about this again before you leave."

Nick nodded and followed Sanderson to his apartment. After he got a tour of the kitchen, the bathroom and his quarters for the night, he hesitated.

"I think I'm going to need some help getting to sleep."

Sanderson grinned. "Don't have any warm milk, but there's a little blue pill that works almost as well. It's called Zopiclone and it's not addictive."

An hour later Sanderson was finishing up some paperwork when he heard Nick cry out in his sleep. It was a deep, strangled shout, filled with anguish, terror and revulsion. By the time he got to the guest room and opened the door, Nick was awake and sitting up in bed. He looked confused, as if he didn't know where he was. When he saw Sanderson, his eyes cleared.

"What time is it?"

"Just after two. Do you know where you are?"

Nick nodded, "Yes."

"I'm here because you cried out in your sleep. It sounded severe. Can you remember what happened?"

"It was a dream, a bad one."

"Not surprising. You've been under a lot of stress. Was it the same one we talked about before?"

"Yes. I was in the river, something was pulling me down."

"Okay, I don't mean to harass you, Nicola, but we've got to work through this. I wouldn't feel right letting you go without at least one more try."

Nick could feel his pulse accelerate and his chest grow tight. He had a strong sense of urgency, a need to move, to run, but he knew it wouldn't help and he took a deep breath, slumped back against the headrest.

"I know you're right, Sanderson, but I can't promise I won't freak out and split like I did the last time."

"The only promise I need is that you'll give it a go. If you can't hack it now, I promise to hold off till you believe you can."

"Okay, just give me a few minutes to get dressed and brush my teeth."

Sanderson looked thoughtful.

"I'd like you to get a good night's rest first. Another Zopiclone won't hurt if you need it, and I've got clients all day tomorrow, so you'll have some time to prep yourself before we start. Feel free to stay here, or to go where you want, but be back by eight tomorrow night and we'll get this done."

51

Nick woke feeling exhausted and apprehensive. He was still nauseous from the drugs they'd injected into his system during the attack at his apartment and he couldn't keep any food down. All day he subsisted on chicken broth and black coffee while he read the articles on eye movement desensitization and reprocessing by Dr. Shapiro and thought about the dream, trying to connect it to the flashback he'd had at the Charles Street apartment. What could have driven him to pick up a woman's corpse and carry it out of a crime scene into the rain?

Now, as he sat across from Sanderson with night coming on, memory traces began to surface and he felt a stab of panic. Sanderson saw it.

"Looks like you've got something."

"Yes, I'm starting to remember things, like you said, bits and pieces. It's not much and I can't be sure, but I think I know where whatever it was might have happened."

"That's good. See if you can go back to that place and that time."

"It was Iraq, southeast of Baghdad but not as far as Basra." Nick stopped and let the scene open slowly. "We were out on patrol when we heard gunfire and saw black smoke rising from a village off to our right. I left my crew on the road and went to investigate.

"As I come into the central square I see two soldiers standing outside the door of a hut. They're joking, smoking cigarettes. They look like they're on guard, but they're also waiting, I don't know for what. There's a lot of noise, screams, exploding grenades, popcorn rifle fire, flames crackling from some of the thatched roofs. A soldier comes out of the hut, buttoning his pants and grinning. The two who'd been waiting their turn start to enter but a young woman, her clothes ripped nearly off, runs past them, her eyes wild. When she sees me she changes direction, screaming, *Help me! Help me! No Al-Qaeda, No terrorist!*"

Nick hesitated, letting the details fill themselves in. He became more agitated as he remembered what happened next.

"Before I can answer, one of the soldiers shoots and her right hand disintegrates in a burst of blood, then her elbow twists and a red patch stains the front of her shirt. She falls and lies there, barely breathing. One of the men who had shot her comes forward and aims his rifle at her. I yell at him, 'Cease fire! Goddammit, stand down!' He looks up, sees that I'm not one of them and shakes his head. 'She was trying to escape.' Then he pulls the trigger and blows out the back of her head. Her eyes are still open, and she's so beautiful…I want to kill him. I don't know what stopped me. I wish I had. But, of course, it's too late. I should have done something when they first raised their weapons."

Nick paused and Sanderson decided it was a good time to take some readings. "Can you give me an SUD?"

"Very high, nine and a half or ten."

"Okay, do a body check."

"I feel…jumpy, restless, charged, hard to breathe, pulse erratic. I just want to run, fast, and as far as I can, away from this."

"Let's break for a minute. See if you can get in touch with your harbour."

It took a while, but Nick managed to find the image of his daughter and hold it until he felt calmer and his breathing slowed, but as soon as Sanderson indicated he could continue, he tensed up again and nearly choked on his words.

"I went looking for the officer in charge. It was like an insane carnival of extermination, carnage everywhere, machine gunfire; an elderly Imam, on his knees, explaining in good English that there were no insurgents in the area…he's executed in mid-sentence; a shot water buffalo that wouldn't fall is attacked by two grunts with bayonets; other animals explode when they stray into the compound, chickens, ducks, pigs, dogs, it's unbelievable. Someone throws an old woman down a well and shoots her. Iraqis coming out of their huts with their hands up are dropped in their tracks. On the other side of the village there's a low, swampy area. The reed houses are ablaze and most of the inhabitants have been herded down to the riverbank. Women with young children are separated from the main group. The others, old and young, male and female, are being pushed with M-16s, jabbed with fixed bayonets, kicked, or clubbed with rifle butts to move them down into the swale. They're crying, screaming, or trying to convince the soldiers that they are not the enemy. Then someone gives an order and they're all scythed down like a stand of wheat with machine gunfire. A toddler crawls away from the writhing bodies and the soldier who had given the order to shoot leans over, picks him up by one leg, throws him back into the pile and shoots him."

Nick stopped for a second, his eyes glazed and wet and far away. He shook his head and looked down at the floor as though he were looking into a bottomless pit. "Some of the men went into the swale and started cutting off scalps, ears, noses, tongues. And they slit the throats of anyone they found alive. I fired my M-16 into the air, grabbed the squad leader by the throat and pushed him against a tree trunk. I screamed at him, 'Are you out of your fucking mind? Where's your OC?'

"He stared at me like I was from some other planet. He tried to salute me and he sort of squeaked, 'That'd be Captain Wentworth. He's up on the ridge.' He turned and looked up to indicate a low hill a few hundred yards to the west. When I got there the captain was standing with his arms crossed surveying the carnage and it stunned me to realize that he looked pleased. I don't remember what I said, something about the men being out of control and you've got to order them to stand down, right now, but he just lit a cigarette and took his time answering.

"'First of all, you have no authority here, Lieutenant. I'm an army captain and you're just one of those recce night crawlers. This area is a free fire zone. A convoy was hit with IEDs, RPGs and mortar fire last night. Six of my company were killed, three others badly shot up.

These people are insurgents, son, and supporters of Al-Qaeda. We're just doin' what needs to be done. Now you better get back to your boys before I have ya arrested for interfering with a Central Command Operation'.

"I asked him if he'd ever read the rules of engagement and he said, 'yeah, long time ago, when I was an asshole like you'. That's when I hit him, hard, probably broke his jaw, and he was out like a light before he hit the ground. Then I got the hell out of there."

Nick stopped talking and sat hunched over and very still. His eyes had that thousand-yard stare Sanderson had seen so many times, in his office, and on the battlefield. He waited until Nick's awareness of where he was returned to him, then he asked, "What are you feeling?"

Nick looked away. "I feel like a bag of shit."

"You're angry."

"Yes."

"Down on yourself."

"Yeah, disgusted."

"Because?"

Nick stood up suddenly and shouted, his voice torn with rage and grief. "Because I should have done something and I didn't do a fucking thing but run."

Once again, Sanderson waited without speaking while Nick sat back down on the sofa and brought his breathing under control. This was even more difficult than he expected it to be and he decided to do something he almost never did. It might blur the clear line between professional and personal contact, but he felt in this case it was worth the risk.

"The dogs of war are truly savage beasts. We train our soldiers to think of the enemy as a lower life form, then we're surprised when they treat them like vermin. But massacres and atrocities are a lot more common than we care to admit. I've seen my share and I understand your belief that you should have done something. I also understand why it haunts you."

He paused. Nick looked interested, less closed on his own pain.

"But there *is* something you can do, right now."

Nick looked confused. "What can I do about it now? They're all dead."

"True, but you've come to a place where you can stop running."

Nick nodded. "I guess I have."

"Good. Let's begin with what you'd rather believe."

"That's easy. I'd like to feel that I did all I could to stop it."

"Let's do some sets. I'd like you to target the image of the young woman who was raped and shot. It seems connected to your whiteout at the crime scene. Just let your eyes follow my hand and see what comes up."

After the third set, Sanderson asked what Nick was getting.

"About the same. And the stress level is very high."

"Okay. This time try to think about what else you could have done."

Another set. Another. Nick shook his head. "They had M-60 machine guns, shotguns, mortars, M-79 grenade launchers and two flame-throwers. There was a gun-ship in the air and they had snipers along the defence perimeter. There were five of us against two companies with tactical support and they had the high ground. Maybe we could have killed the captain and a few squad leaders, but we would have been wiped out in minutes."

"And…?"

"It wouldn't have stopped the slaughter."

"And…?"

"Our deaths would be presented as evidence of significant enemy fire, which would validate the mission, case closed."

"Distress level?"

Nick sounded surprised. "It's down some, maybe an eight."

"Let's go on. What happened after you hit the captain?"

"I'm not sure."

"Just focus on that image and let your mind go."

Another set and Nick sat up, his body alert but relaxed as the images unfolded.

"I'm remembering something, but the geography is confused. I leave the village, running, but I get turned around and end up at the river instead of the road. I hear gunfire, laughter, the terrified voices of children. Half a dozen soldiers are separating a group of women from their offspring. They throw the kids into the water and hold them down with their boots. Some of the stronger ones manage to squirm loose. They're carried away by the current and the soldiers use them for target practice.

"I set my M-16 on semi-automatic and fire half a clip at their feet. They look around, then scatter and take cover in a stand of date palms. One of the older boys leaps into the stream and strikes out for the far shore, but the current is too strong and he goes under, comes up, cries out, goes down again.

"I sling the rifle across my back and run down to the small beach. I wade in. The river bed slopes down steeply and I'm up to my armpits before it levels out. I duck under but can't see him. When I come up for air, something grabs my legs and I stumble, go down, choking. Below me, I can see his body through clouds of silt. I lift and carry him, swimming on my back to the far shore. He's unconscious. I can't find a pulse and he doesn't seem to be breathing, but I administer CPR for several minutes until he comes to.

"When he recognizes my uniform, he's terrified. Then he sees that I'm dripping wet and he smiles. I pull him to his feet, tell him *adheb besr'eh*, go quickly, and he sprints into the underbrush."

Sanderson asked, "How do you feel now about the statement, 'I did all I could to stop it'?"

"I think it's true. Seven."

"Good. Validity of cognition is right where it should be. How about your distress level?"

"Better, but it's still a six or a five and half."

They did several more sets and Nick began to remember what happened after he got back to Baghdad. "I went to see my Marine CO, Major Bob Stanton, and explained what I had seen. He was very upset. He told me to write it up and he'd pass it on to Central

Command. A few days later I met with an army colonel named Jackson Lowe.

"He had my report on his desk and he looked as though he found it hard to believe. The first thing he asked me was if the other members of my team had seen what I saw. I told him no, I had ordered them to stay on the road and had rejoined them later. They witnessed the gunship strafing and heard ground fire, grenades, mortars, but had not seen anyone killed.

"He nodded. Said that presented a problem. This was a serious allegation and it might not even get to a court martial without corroborating testimony. He was sympathetic, said he admired my moral clarity, understood that what had happened was a war crime, an atrocity, but that we had to think carefully about how to proceed. He took a deep breath, sighed, stared out the window at the rain.

"'This is a crazy, brutal war, Lieutenant. We probably shouldn't even be here, but here we are, and most of the people we came to help hate us. We've got less and less support at home and the Iraqi army is useless, or worse. Now I'm inclined to believe you saw what you say you saw, not just because of your exemplary record, but because there are things in the official version that don't quite jibe. The number of enemy killed is very high compared to only three weapons recovered, and none, not a single one, of our men was hit. I find this disturbing.

"'Needless to say, what happened is inexcusable. It violates our rules of engagement, the Geneva Conventions and every known set of moral values humans attempt to live by, even on the battlefield.'

"He paused for a minute. Looked away. 'But there's another war. In the press, on the ten o'clock news. And on every radio or TV station in the Middle East. If we go public with this, what do you think Al-Qaeda, or the Taliban, will do with it? It's the propaganda equivalent of a nuclear blast. It could recruit thousands upon thousands of new fighters and destroy what little trust or credibility we have left. It would also completely dishonour the good name of all those decent men and women who have bravely fought and died because their country asked them to. And in the end, we'd never get a conviction anyway.

"'Now I can't, and I won't, ask you to scrap this report. All I ask is that we consider our options before we proceed. We can't help those who are already dead, but we can, and will, do everything we can for the survivors. And we can make sure that none of those who were involved will be allowed to do this again.'

"When I asked him how that could be accomplished he said they'd all be removed from combat status and given desk jobs or mustered out. I thought they should have to pay for what they'd done and told him so. He answered that they'd pay all right, because they'd be haunted by it for the rest if their lives.

"I spent the next week struggling with what he'd said and, in the end, I caved in. He congratulated me on making a mature and rational decision, but a few weeks later, one of the squad leaders who'd participated in the slaughter lost it, killed a command post CO and three of his clerks. A few months before the massacre he had opened fire on a crowd of Iraqis who were picnicking in a park. They ran to their cars and tried to get away but he kept firing. When he was ordered to cease and desist, he just yelled 'Negative, Negative!'

"At the court martial he was given extra guard duty for disobeying an order. But now that he'd killed a U.S. Army colonel, they arrested him and tried him back in the States. The thing is, if I hadn't given in to authority, one of the army's best officers and his staff would still be alive.

"It made me sick. I felt like I'd sold out any sense of honour I had left. I couldn't shake that feeling, so I buried it. Until now. And it's still there, strong as ever. I'm a moral coward. I betrayed my knowledge of right and wrong. I should have gone forward with the report, gone to the newspapers, written to my congressional reps and senators, done everything I could to see that those who did this terrible thing were brought to justice. But I let a superior officer talk me down."

"What are you feeling right now?"

"Angry, disillusioned, compromised. And I feel stupid too, gullible."

"Suppose you did what you think you should have done. What might have happened?"

"I don't know. I never thought it all the way through."

"Okay, let's do some sets and I'd like you to try and imagine the possible outcomes if you had acted differently."

Nick tried several times but couldn't seem to satisfy himself that he'd seen it clearly.

Before they tried again Sanderson initiated what he called a cognitive interweave.

"What was the official version of the massacre?"

"It was reported as a battle with a battalion of Al-Qaeda and foreign fighters from Iran."

"Was there anyone in the two companies under Captain Wentworth who came forward to challenge that story?"

"No."

"Did you talk with anyone who admitted what they did and agreed to testify about it?"

"No. I never got that far."

"Speculate."

Nick was quiet for a long time before he answered. "I don't think anyone would have said a damn thing."

"And...?"

"And without corroboration, no one would have been charged, much less brought before a court martial."

"And...?"

"The media would have run with it, but it would probably have been dropped quickly when they found that there was no real case, no hard evidence, no chance of convictions."

"What about the way the story would have been used by the terrorists?"

Nick sighed, shook his head. "I guess Lowe was right about that. It would have been hugely effective for enlisting recruits. More men, and women, and children, who would kill and be killed. But what I did was still wrong. Our soldiers committed horrible crimes and were never punished."

"Do you remember what happened after My Lai?"

"No, I was just a kid when that happened."

"Well, the Peers Inquiry recommended charges against twenty-eight officers and two NCOs for their attempt to cover up the massacre. Army lawyers only charged fourteen, including two generals and three colonels. Only one was eventually tried and he was acquitted.

"Of the forty-five men and a handful of officers involved in the actual killing, more than thirty were charged, but only one was ever convicted. Lieutenant William Calley. Do you know what happened to him?"

"No, but I bet you're going to tell me."

"He was sentenced to life imprisonment at hard labour for twenty-two counts of premeditated murder. But that sentence was later reduced, first to twenty years, then to ten. After three days in the stockade at Fort Benning, Nixon intervened and he was moved to house arrest. He was released on bail eighteen months later. Four months after that, he was rearrested and sent to do hard labour as a clerk typist at the detention barracks at Fort Leavenworth where he remained for four-and-a-half months before he was finally let out on parole."

Nick could barely believe what he'd just heard. "So no matter what I did, none of those murdering swine would have ended up in jail for life, or in a noose, or before a firing squad where they belong."

"Right. Most atrocities get papered over, at least by the side that commits them. If you lose a war, there will be tribunals. But if you win, or even if you just withdraw as we did in Korea and Vietnam, they tend to get remembered, if at all, merely as evidence of superior fire power."

"Hamburg, Dresden, Hiroshima, Nagasaki..."

"Exactly, and lots more, like No Gun Ri in Korea, or Son Thang-4 in Vietnam, nearly two years after My Lai."

"Never heard of them."

"Exactly. And after this you probably never will. But where does that leave us? What are you feeling now?"

"I'm still tense, unsettled."

"What's your stress level?"

"Four."

"What would it take to make it go away?"

"I don't know."

"Think about that and watch my fingers."

This time, Sanderson moved his hand in a slow, weaving diagonal pattern and Nick drew back into himself. After several sets he began to speak in what seemed to be an effortless but nearly hypnotic rhythm.

"I see it now. What triggered my flashbacks. At the warehouse, my best friend and partner was killed because I had caved in to authority once again." His face held a mixture of amazement and understanding. He nodded. "Because it was the same failure, to stand up, to insist on what I thought was right, all those things I never dealt with in Afghanistan and Iraq came rushing out."

Sanderson nodded. "Yes. That was the trigger, and it was another trauma you'll have to deal with before this is over."

"I know. I started to but I got sidetracked. This case..." He stopped and thought for a moment, then something seemed to become clear to him. "It's another example of corrupt authority, abusing power, using government agencies to further some private agenda. It's either big money or a power grab, I'm sure of it. So I've got to follow through on that as well. Maybe, if I can bring those high-ranking, privileged thugs down, those Subjective Units of Distress might come down with them."

"I think that's more than a maybe."

"I hope you're right, but whatever happens, this time I won't let go."

There was a short silence after which Sanderson asked, "So, have you drawn up a battle plan, Lieutenant?"

Nick's brief moment of clarity and exhilaration evaporated as he realized what was waiting for him out in the dark. Almost a full day had gone by since they'd relieved McCloskey and discovered his escape. They'd have surveillance up by now. The entire city, hell, the entire country and half the planet would be blanketed with photos and alerts and orders to apprehend with extreme prejudice. He shook his head.

"Haven't a clue."

"Might be a good idea to start with the bad guy. Do you know who he is?"

"No, I don't, not yet, but I've listened to him on a tape he didn't know was being recorded and I know I've heard that voice before."

As he explained about the Duplessis wire, something clicked into place. It jolted him and he stood up.

"Thanks, Doc. It just came to me. I know what I have to do next."

52

Traffic was light on the Merritt Parkway and Nick was still twenty miles from his exit when he picked up a tail. A Toyota Tundra came up quickly and pulled in behind him. Its high beams and a spotlight from the roof of the cab flicked on, flooding his rear-view mirrors and nearly blinding him. Before his eyes adjusted to the glare, he lost sight of the roadbed and swerved onto the shoulder. The truck accelerated and crashed into him from behind. There was a shriek of tires as the back end skidded and he almost lost control. He hit the brakes and steered into the skid until the front end came around, but the truck was still accelerating, trying to pin down the rear bumper and explode his tires.

A thought flashed through his mind so rapidly it was almost a reflex. He'd watched scenes like this a hundred times on TV. They had always puzzled him. Why would a driver in such a situation hit the brakes? A sports vehicle like the Sebring had a lower centre of gravity and could hold the road far better than a truck. His foot left the brake and hit the accelerator. The Sebring went into passing gear and pulled away but the Toyota sped up too and he realized that on a straight highway, he'd have a hard time out-manoeuvring the truck. As he approached the next exit, he braked, downshifted and turned sharply. His squealing tires nearly lost their grip on the ramp but they held and he could hear the truck screech to a stop after it missed the turn. It was already backing up as Nick drove through a flashing red traffic light and skidded onto a country road.

There was a long flat stretch ahead and the high beams were coming up fast behind him. He pushed the Sebring into the nineties and kept his distance until he saw a road sign indicating sharp curves ahead, then he slowed as he entered but accelerated quickly through the first turn. The truck had to slow down more than the Sebring and Nick pulled further ahead.

The road was a high-crowned, meandering two-laner and Nick drove the Sebring hard, holding his lead on the straight stretches and gaining on the curves. But as the road opened into a long uphill climb, the Toyota screamed to full throttle and started to close the gap. At the top of the hill, another sign showed a tight double curve with a safe speed of forty miles per hour. Nick slowed to fifty then sped up and came out of the second curve at sixty-seven. There was a light skid, but the tires held and as he pulled away he heard the Toyota screeching and skidding behind him. It came into view with smoking tires and tipped, riding on two wheels for several seconds before it went over, rolled and disappeared into the drainage ditch.

There was no explosion, but it was doubtful that the Tundra would be able to continue the chase. At the next intersection, Nick turned right onto a gravel road. He kept making turns, right then left then left again until he passed a sign that said Audubon Preserve. He pulled off into what looked like a hiking or cross-country ski trail and drove on until he was deep into unbroken woods, then he turned into the underbrush beneath a canopy of interlaced branches and stopped.

He'd outrun the truck, but he was sure they'd broadcast the switched licence plate number and all the agencies, including the state police and the various helicopter squads, would be gunning for him. He had no idea how far he was from his destination, but he'd have to ditch the car and make it the rest of the way on foot. He fired up the GPS and spent ten minutes memorizing the terrain between his present position and his destination. He had a good sense of direction and thought it would be safer to use the Audubon trails instead of the paved road and the highway.

Before he started out, he gathered fallen branches, twigs and leaves, which he spread over the cloth top, hood and trunk of the Sebring. It would make the car much less visible, especially at night.

He still had a dozen miles to go and he set off at a brisk trot. The trail was clear and he made good time, but after several miles, it branched, then branched again. He puzzled over which fork to take and chose the one to his left. He continued to run until the trail narrowed down, became a footpath and went downhill into a low-lying marsh. He remembered this from the GPS. It wasn't very deep and if he kept going he would be out of it in a mile or so. But it slowed him down. He wasn't dressed for slogging and every step made a squelching sound as the soft bottom sucked at his shoes and filled them with mud.

By the time he got to the other side and climbed up to solid ground again, he was breathing hard and his leg muscles burned with the effort. He stopped and looked around him. The trail had disappeared. He was in thick woods. It was very dark, with no moon or stars overhead, and as he stood there trying to see a way through the trees, it began to rain.

53

It was raining harder now and there was a stiff wind. Though Nick could only see a few feet in front of him, the trees seemed older, taller, with more space between them, and he kept moving. If his sense of direction hadn't failed him, he was headed toward a paved road that would lead him around a low rise to the other side of Greenwich. From there it was only another mile or two.

Lightning flashed and a second later there was a deep roll of thunder. As it faded he heard the faint *whap whap* of rotor blades and what looked like another slow sheet of lightning, but he quickly realized it was a searchlight. He watched it move off to the left until it was out of sight, then it returned and swept the area until it disappeared again to his right, but a bit closer.

He kept moving from tree to tree, but he hadn't eaten for thirty hours, was still working off the drugs, and felt fatigue lapsing into exhaustion. He was drenched to the skin and had begun to shiver. He didn't know how much longer he could continue without finding a place where he could rest, shield himself from the helicopter and build up some body heat to stave off hypothermia.

He began to feel dizzy, disoriented. He stopped and got control of his breathing before he went on, but after half a dozen steps he stumbled and went down. He rolled over, picked himself up and pushed ahead. Branches scraped his face and his feet dragged. A cobweb broke across his forehead. He reached up to brush it away and kept moving but the ground seemed to drop away and he lurched into a gully. As he came up the other side a fallen tree loomed in front of him. He started to go around it when he realized its top was tangled in the lower branches of other trees and it was suspended a few feet above the forest floor. He got to his knees and crawled under it.

The rain stopped pelting him and the ground felt dry. He sat with his thighs tight to his chest and his legs under him. The searchlight swept left, then right, closer and closer, till it seemed to ignite the fallen leaves all around him, then it was behind him, and further away with each pass. When he could no longer hear the whirr of the rotor, he set his internal clock for twenty minutes and eased into a light doze. He was still aware of the wind, the rain, the scent of pines and the earthy smell of rotted wood, and he did not dream.

When he woke it had stopped raining and a three-quarter moon had risen. It was bright enough to cast shadows and it wasn't long before he found another trail. He was still wet, and shivering, but no longer dizzy and as he came into a clearing he saw a small building off to the right.

There were two entrances, and both had lights burning above them. They were washrooms. He could hardly believe his luck, but when he tried the door of the men's, it was locked.

There was a glass transom above the door that looked like it would be easy enough to break, but he'd have to find a way to climb up there. A quick scan revealed that the door opened in and that it did not have a dead bolt. Nick took a plastic card from his wallet, bent it around the casing and forced it between the faceplate and the door jamb, releasing the latch.

It was warmer inside and the first thing he did was jam toilet tissue into the drain of the washbasin and fill it with hot water. He took off his shirt and undershirt and draped them over the hand blow-dryer. It came on automatically and he let it run. Then he went back to the sink, crossed his arms and immersed them up to his armpits, warming his blood and raising his core body temperature till the shivering stopped. He let the water out of the bowl and raked wet fingers through his hair.

When he finished drying his hands, arms and shirts at the blow-dryer, he dressed and stood before the mirror. What he saw wasn't going to make a persuasive first impression, but he felt much better and time was short. He gave his hair another quick finger comb and that's when he heard the latch turn and saw the door begin to open.

54

In two quick strides he was across the room with his back against the partition that stood between the entrance and the urinals. He could no longer see the door from there and he waited until two hands gripping a 9mm pistol edged cautiously into his field of vision. He held his breath.

Another step. One more. Then he chopped down with his left hand, dislodging the weapon, pulled the man toward him and hit him between the eyes with his forehead. There was the crunch of cartilage, a grunt of surprise, and as his assailant fell forward, Nick hit him behind the head with the blade of his right hand, separating the third and fourth cervical vertebrae. The man's paralyzed body crumpled and lay on the tile floor in a heap.

Nick went over and locked the washroom door, then searched the pockets of the blue suit and found an ID card that identified the man as a private security contractor. He worked for a company based in Virginia called Academi, formerly registered as Blackwater and Xe. He'd met some of them in Iraq and Afghanistan. Hired thugs. Well trained and very expensive. He wondered how many more there were on the grounds and as he did he heard the doorknob turn.

It turned again and when whoever it was realized the door was locked he hammered on it a few times and yelled, "Dennis, you fuck, are you in there? Dennis!" Then he mumbled something else and his footsteps crunched on the gravel as he moved off.

Nick waited for nearly twenty minutes before he opened the door, ran through the surrounding trees and found the hiking path a few hundred yards from the washrooms.

It took almost an hour to reach the paved road. He jogged along its moon-shadowed side close to the trees and came to a high field-stone wall, which he followed around to a double-winged, wrought iron gate that had the initials KL engraved on a bronze plaque. To the right, embedded in the stone, was what looked like a bell or buzzer button above an intercom.

Nick pressed it, but nothing happened so he pressed it again.

A light came on inside the compound and an elderly man in a guard uniform came out of a small fieldstone building to the right. He was wearing a weapon on his hip and did not look very welcoming. As he came toward the gate, Nick fished out the badge he'd taken from McCloskey and held it up. He spoke first.

"Sorry to disturb you, but I'm a police officer and I need to speak with your employer."

The guard looked him over carefully, noting the absence of a patrol car, the wet pants and muddy shoes. "You're not in uniform. Do you know what time it is?"

Nick didn't, but he ignored the question.

"I'm a detective, not a patrolman, and I know it's late, but it's absolutely crucial that I speak with your boss."

The guard did not look convinced.

"Not a good idea. Go home. Get cleaned up. Come back tomorrow."

This wasn't going anywhere and Nick decided to exaggerate.

"Tomorrow will be too late. Her life is in danger and it's imperative that we talk." The guard looked straight into his eyes for a moment, judged that his urgency was authentic, even if he didn't entirely buy the details, and he nodded okay before he returned to the guardhouse. A few minutes later he came back.

"She's agreed to talk with you, but I won't let you in. You can pick up the intercom and I'll monitor the conversation from inside."

Her voice was as he remembered it from the TV interview, throaty and firm.

"Who are you?"

Nick realized that an honest answer might end the interview, but if he tried to pose as McCloskey, and was found out, he'd blow any chance he might have of getting her help.

"I'm Nicola Cortese, NYPD."

There was a long silence. Then she said, "Apparently you missed the ten o'clock news or you wouldn't be here. You're famous, Mr. Cortese, a public enemy, much sought after by authorities everywhere."

It was exactly what he had feared, but her ironic tone was encouraging. Whatever she'd seen on TV, his presence didn't entirely terrify her.

"None of that is true, I was set up."

"And why would anyone want to set you up? Did you annoy them, use their toothbrush, sleep with their wife? I'm sorry, but if I let you in it would be aiding and abetting. I could be prosecuted as an accessory."

What she said was true, but when she hung up he felt a rush of anger, frustration, disappointment, anxiety. He wanted to smash the handset against the stone wall, but stopped, took a deep breath, held it, exhaled slowly and replaced the phone carefully on its cradle.

He could hardly blame her. Or the guard either. But what did that leave him? Where else could he go? He paced back and forth in front of the iron gate, racking his brain for something he could still do, something he hadn't thought of yet, some way to break out of the cul-de-sac he was trapped in.

A thought came to him. If he could contact Jen Hendricks, the borough commander might be high enough in the chain of command to fend off the Feds. For a moment it seemed possible, then he realized that they would have her covered too, her phone would be tapped, there'd be a plant on her house.

As he stood there thinking, Nick realized he was out in the open, under a streetlight, and he had a sudden sense of intense danger. He felt the trigger pull of a flashback, but it never came. He moved quickly, back into the shadows of trees, and kept going, though he had no idea what he should do next.

55

He kept close to the wall and followed it deeper and deeper into the forest. It angled off to the right where the underbrush grew thicker and his path was blocked by a heavy vine that snaked up into a tree, crossed the intervening space and clung to the fieldstone.

It was like an invitation, and without even thinking he reached up and pulled himself hand over hand until he came to the point where the vine gripped the stones. He jackknifed with all his strength and managed to get one leg over the vine. From there he could see that there were shards of broken bottle glass embedded in concrete, glittering like knives in the moonlight along the top of the wall.

Carefully, very carefully, he got his hands on the edge of the wall and pushed up into a handstand then lifted one arm to the other side, eased his legs back down and rested both knees on the inner ledge. He gripped the vine and slid his feet down till he was hanging full length for a moment before he let go. He landed in the soft earth of a flower bed, reds and yellows bleached almost grey in the moonlight, and as he turned the grounds of the estate spread out before him.

Directly ahead was a wide, rolling lawn. A road came up from the gate and curved into a circular drive in front of a colonial two-storey house with whitewashed stone walls and blue shuttered windows. To the left a stand of maples bordered a flagstone patio furnished with white wicker chairs and a glass-topped table. Behind the patio Nick caught a glimpse of tennis courts and a swimming pool. The drive led around to a five-car garage done in the same materials as the house but with a steeply peaked roof in which there were five dormers.

Nick walked out across acres of lawn toward a large and very old copper beech that spread its tall canopy between the garage and the right side of the house. The moon was so bright it cast his shadow in a black silhouette that skimmed the grass and shattered when he came in under the tree. He sat with his back to the trunk. He had a good view of the door and the patio from there. All he could do now was wait, and hope that she would talk with him before she called 911.

He dozed and woke, dozed and woke till the moon went out of the bright sky and a thin ridge of cloud over the horizon grew to a grey streak in the dawn.

When lights came on in the house he came fully awake. He sat very still. If someone from inside glanced that way and was able to pick him out in the shadows, the first he'd know of it would be the sound of tires braking to a stop on the gravel of the circular drive, or the wail of a siren, though that seemed unlikely under the circumstances.

There was nothing he could do. He watched. And he waited.

The sky grew lighter overhead, a pale, gradually deepening blue. Then the door opened and she came out.

At first, she didn't notice him sitting there under the copper beech. She was carrying an iPhone and it claimed most of her attention. But halfway to the patio she hesitated. It was just a split-second hitch in her stride, as though she sensed something unfamiliar at the edge of her vision. It didn't stop her though, and when she got to the patio she pulled out one of the wicker chairs and sat at the glass-topped table. She continued to work on her phone.

Nick decided it was time to move. He stood and walked out from under the tree, slowly enough so it wouldn't seem like an attack, but not so slow that it would look like he was being stealthy or was ready to run. He raised both hands, palms out, in a gesture of surrender.

She looked up and her face was calm. She did not seem surprised to see him. He decided to speak before she did.

"I came over the wall, and since you didn't invite me to, you can't be charged with aiding and abetting."

She smiled. Her voice was a rich contralto still husky with sleep. "Correct, but only if I turn you over to the authorities immediately."

"Please, just hear what I have to say before you call the police."

"You told my...doorman that my life was in danger. What was that all about?"

Nick hesitated for a second before he answered. "Uh, I guess I was exaggerating, a bit.... Well, maybe a lot, but I need your help and I had to get your attention."

"But why in God's name did you think I would help? I don't even know you and I have no idea what's behind all this. What I do know is that you're a fugitive, armed and dangerous."

"I can explain all that, but I've been investigating a series of homicides and I've come across information I think will be of vital interest to you."

"And what might that be?"

"It has to do with the death of your husband."

Vanessa Lang took her time considering this then, she stood up. She was tall, nearly six feet, raw-boned and vigorous, with short, reddish-brown hair, bright blue eyes and freckles under tanned skin that had spent countless hours on horseback in the West Texas sun. She took a step toward him and held out her hand.

"Welcome to Riverbend, Mr. Cortese. Won't you join me for coffee while we talk?" She picked up her phone and hit the speed dial button. "Good morning, Santos. It seems we have a visitor. Please bring two cups."

They sat in the maple shade and were served by an elderly but very fit gentleman Nick assumed was Santos. He poured coffee into tall ivory mugs and steam rose lazily in the cool morning air. When he was done he left the silver carafe on the table, gave a slight bow and walked back to the house. Vanessa watched him go and her smile was filled with gratitude and affection.

"My maître d'hôtel, sommelier, butler, chauffeur, landscape architect, head of security and manager of the estate. Wonderful man. Don't know what I'd do without him."

She turned and looked at her guest. Her eyes were clear, receptive, and her face was calm, but showed a trace of apprehension. She sipped black coffee while Nick told her about Malcom Duplessis and the wire Rhea Carson had taken from his safe deposit box.

"Duplessis recorded it secretly while he was being hired to impersonate someone and to perform another service that was never spelled out on the tape. He underwent extensive reconstructive surgery to alter his appearance, which suggests that the impersonation was more than a brief stand-in and had to hold up under close, maybe prolonged scrutiny."

Vanessa frowned and her jaw tightened as though she sensed where this might be going.

"Do you know who he was paid to impersonate and who hired him?" she asked.

"The other voice on the tape sounded vaguely familiar, a public voice like someone I might have heard on radio or TV, but I couldn't place it. Then something he said clicked with something I'd heard before, *You can bet the farm on that.* I remembered a similar phrase from the news interview he did with you on CNN."

Vanessa's eyes flared. "Jeremy!"

"Yes, Jeremy Baine."

"And he hired this man to impersonate Kenneth?"

"I can't prove that yet, but I believe so, yes. Whoever killed Duplessis destroyed his face with a shotgun, but our ME, Lazlo Kaprisky, and a colleague of his, are working with a new digital technology that may be able to provide a reasonable picture of what he looked like before he was shot. And we can subpoena his medical records from the surgeon who did the reconstruction."

"What else do you have?"

"Not much, but I don't think your husband was killed by terrorists from Mawabi."

"I've never believed that either. It doesn't make sense."

"You said as much on CNN. It was a long shot, but that's why I came."

"Well, I meant it. What do you need?"

"I need to know what other service Duplessis was hired to perform. We managed to find out that he worked for the CIA but that information is classified and they wouldn't release any details."

She nodded. "I know someone who can help, Senator Alvin Tillis. He's an old friend of Kenneth's and chairman of the intelligence oversight committee. But what about you, Nicola?"

"My daughter was kidnapped. They said they would exchange her for the tape, but after I got her back they drugged me and set me up. You saw the results on the news last night."

She looked thoughtful. "Tell me what happened and what you've been charged with. Don't leave anything out."

Nick described the attack at his apartment, his arrest and his escape from the hospital in minute detail. When he was done she considered his story for a moment before she spoke.

"I'm going to call a friend, Jason Endicott. He's one of the best defence lawyers in the country and he owes me several favours."

Nick shook his head. "I can't let you do that."

"Why the hell not?"

"I can't afford to hire someone like that and I won't accept charity."

Vanessa sighed. "Very high-minded, Nicola, but tell me, are you an active member of the NYPD?"

"You know I'm not."

"Then you're currently unemployed."

"Yes, very."

"Well then, I'm hiring you as a private investigator to look into my husband's death and to clear his name. You will not be paid a salary or a fee. Instead, you will receive legal representation by Jason Endicott."

Nick thought about that. He looked conflicted and didn't say anything, but after a long pause he gave a slight nod. She made the call and spoke to her friend for twenty minutes.

When she was done, she turned to Nick with a bright smile.

"He's on board and pretty optimistic, but he says you'll have to turn yourself in."

Nick knew he'd have to agree, but it worried him. What if Armagh was right? Under the National Defense Authorization Act, the president had extraordinary powers as commander-in-chief. If Homeland Security or the CIA could convince him and his counterterrorism advisers to add Nick's name to the enemy combatant kill or capture list they drew up once a week in the Oval Office, he could be arrested without being charged, confined in solitary indefinitely, assassinated on the spot, or whisked away to some secret detention centre in Saudi Arabia or Qatar and never be heard from again.

56

The ragged drone of the Cessna broke, sputtered and caught again as it banked right and crossed the river into Mawabi. Sean Doherty looked up from the folder he'd been studying since they took off from Lagos. He was stunned. Nothing in all that paper had prepared him for what he saw below.

On the Niger side, there were tilled fields and rolling pastureland, richly green after a month of seasonal rain. But in Mawabi, all the way to the horizon, the cash crop demanded by the World Bank as a condition of its loan was turning brown. It looked like he only had a few days, maybe a week, to figure out what had gone wrong and how to fix it. *And if it couldn't be fixed?* Before he could consider the disastrous consequences, the pilot turned and shouted above the din of the twin engines.

"We very far off course, Mistah Shahn. De compass stuck again."

"Can you tell how far, Aswari?"

"Sixty, seventy miles."

Doherty looked out through the scratched Plexiglas window. They were approaching an immense reservoir, named Lake Imibhotu after a guerilla leader killed during the revolution. It gleamed like a giant mirror among miles of dunes and the rubble of abandoned villages.

"How long till we get to Jankassa?"

"One hour, maybe somewhat further."

Doherty cursed under his breath. Every second counted and he wanted to take a strip off the pilot's hide, but it wasn't his fault. He let out a sigh and sat back in his seat.

As they flew low over the eastern edge of the lake, the battered Cessna banked left.

Before it had levelled out again, Doherty let out a cry of astonishment.

A few miles north of the lake there were hundreds of hectares of green wheat bending under the afternoon breeze beside a freshly paved road. He tapped the pilot on the shoulder, pointed down and yelled, "Can you land on that road?"

"Oh no suh, de road too thin, and also not in the flight plan."

Doherty pulled a fifty-pound note out of his wallet and the pilot nodded, then banked north again and began his descent.

They landed smoothly and even before they rolled to a stop on the gravel shoulder, Doherty opened his door and landed running. He knelt at the edge of the field and inspected the crop. It was wheat all right, and it looked as though it had been planted at the same time or just after the browned-out fields to the south and west. He took out a pocket knife, dug deeply around several clustered stalks, reached in with his fingers and lifted them out by the roots.

As he did so, he heard a popping sound. When he looked up he saw a small convoy of jeeps and personnel carriers coming over a rise about three miles to the east. Puffs of dust rose from the side of the road and he realized he was being fired upon.

Keeping as low as he could, he ran back and clambered aboard the Cessna. The plane turned and picked up speed as both motors went to full throttle. It got airborne just as the soldiers came within range and the frantic pilot banked sharply away from the convoy.

Doherty was still breathing heavily when the plane reached cruising altitude and levelled out. He leaned over and shouted in the pilot's ear.

"You know who those troops belong to?"

The pilot shook his head. He looked scared, and Doherty could sense that it wasn't just another bit of stagecraft. He handed the man a hundred-pound note.

"You did a good job back there, Aswari. Just get us back to Jankassa. And don't mention this to anyone."

The pilot's face relaxed.

"I b'lieve dat bunch work for Jonas Tumulu."

Doherty gave a low whistle. Tumulu was the minister of agriculture and mines.

57

As soon as they landed, Doherty ran across the tarmac, through the small booking office and out onto the dusty gravel road that led into town. It was hot, and the samples he'd dug up were already wilting in the fierce African sun. If he didn't get them to the Curtiss-James compound soon, they'd be worthless.

He looked around for a taxi, but there were none in sight. The first vehicle that came into view was a rusted flatbed truck. It rattled over the washboard roadbed and he flagged it down.

The driver didn't seem to be in any hurry to get where he was going and Doherty was encouraged by what he saw in the man's face—curiosity and a willingness to bargain.

"Thanks for stopping. I need you to drive me somewhere, you got time?"

"I got some time, but where you want to go, mistah?"

"There's a big industrial park on the other side of Jankassa. You know it?"

"No, but you tell me and I get you there. You payin'?"

They agreed on a price and Doherty climbed aboard, cradling the plants in his lap. The driver looked them over and shook his head. But he didn't comment or ask any questions. He just started to whistle a song as he drove.

It took them the better part of an hour to navigate through the streets of Jankassa, surrounded by bleats and brays, donkey carts and stalled traffic. Goats, oxen, asses and camels milled around the main square, jostling each other, or crouched in the thin shade of date palms, complaining. Street vendors hawked their wares, adding their voices to the clamorous uproar, which seemed to bother no one. Most of the faces they passed wore smiles.

Doherty was beginning to feel tense about the plants and he breathed a sigh of relief when they got out of town and swung onto a newly paved road. As they picked up speed over smooth macadam, he settled back against the ripped cloth seat and wondered what secrets the green wheat might contain and if they'd help reverse the mysterious brown-out.

The driver pulled up in front of a long, low building with the C-J logo etched into the floor-to-ceiling window glass. The compound had been constructed as soon as Curtiss-James got the contract to oversee the World Bank wheat crop, and everything looked spanking new.

Doherty stepped through the hissing, automatic door into chilled air that cooled the sweat on his face and under his shirt as he walked to the desk. The receptionist was a tall, thin Mawabian dressed in a brown suit and a tea-coloured, button-down shirt with no tie. His accent was British with African undertones.

"Good ahftahnoon, suh. How may I help you?"

"I need to see a lab tech, right away."

"And you are?"

"Sean Doherty. I'm here to investigate the brown-out."

"Please take a seat, Mr. Doherty. I'll phone the laboratories and have someone come over."

"Thanks, but it would be quicker if you could give me directions and call ahead to let them know I'm coming."

"You're right, probably it would be quicker, but I'm sorry to say regulations won't allow it. Please take a seat. I'll tell them it's urgent."

Doherty started counting to ten but only got to eight. He held up the plant samples, dribbling dirt on the polished mahogany counter top.

"What do you think this is?"

The receptionist looked momentarily apprehensive, as though he might be in physical danger. Then he shrugged and said, "Some sort of grass?"

Doherty told him what it was and where he'd gotten it. He added, "And if it dies before they can study it, we might never be able to save that crop. Curtiss James will go into receivership and what do you think will happen to your cushy job, suh?"

Now the receptionist looked scared in another way, and sincerely concerned for the fortunes of plant life in Mawabi. He glanced sympathetically at the wilted wheat, reached under the counter for a map and drew a twisting line in red ink.

58

After dropping off the plant samples Doherty had the receptionist call him a cab, which dropped him in front of the ten-foot, wrought iron gates of the presidential palace.

He showed his passport and diplomatic visa to the guard who wore a tall red hat, a red tunic, black pantaloons and boots. He held a Second World War .30-caliber M-1 carbine across his chest, did not take either document and did not move a muscle or change his facial expression. After several minutes, he turned abruptly and opened the gate.

Doherty walked up the curving, rose-coloured asphalt drive to the white, colonial building with Greek columns and three stories of red-curtained windows. At the entrance he showed his credentials to a second guard dressed in what looked like a blue policeman's uniform with gold trim. He was waved in and found his way to the general office. There was a large, pleasant-looking woman at the counter who smiled and asked whom he wanted to see.

"President Baku. My name is Sean Doherty and I work for Curtiss James. I have information about the crop failure and it's absolutely vital that I speak to him without delay."

The smile left her face and her voice became grave.

"Oh, yes, Mr. Doherty, you are expected. But the president is in conference. He is trying to prepare Mawabi for the terrible times we are about to experience, now that our wheat is dying. He has delegated all decisions about the crop to the minister of agriculture and mines. I'll call General Tumulu and make an appointment. I'm sure he will see you within the hour."

This was not what Doherty wanted, but there wasn't much he could do. He watched helplessly as the woman picked up the phone, removed a large, gold ring from her ear and made the call.

The ministry was housed in another white colonial building. It was set back from the road in a stand of trees. Inside, it looked as though it had been recently restored with rich wood, glass chandeliers, murals and an old world elegance it was difficult not to admire.

The clerk at the desk wore a military uniform. He was very polite, but Doherty had to wait for more than two hours before he was ushered into the office of Jonas Tumulu.

The general was seated at a large teak table on a raised platform. He did not rise when Doherty entered the room and did not invite his guest to be seated. He just stared with an entirely neutral expression, waiting for the visitor to begin.

Doherty decided on a direct approach. He told Tumulu what he had seen early that afternoon and explained that those few hundred hectares of healthy wheat might hold the key to preventing a widespread famine. Tumulu remained still, but could not entirely mask his alarm and discomfort. When Doherty asked for free access to the site for himself and plant biologists from Curtiss James, Tumulu shook his head.

"Those experimental fields are not as healthy as you might suppose, Mr. Doherty. They were sown with a slightly different strain of wheat, but they were planted later than the general crop. Unfortunately, they have already begun to die."

"Did Curtiss James oversee the experimental planting?"

"No. We did that on our own, but, alas," he spread out the fingers of both hands which he held before him in a gesture of defeat, "it has proven worthless."

"What did you hope to learn by planting it?"

"We thought it might do even better than the larger crop, might be even more suited to our particular environment. If so, we'd use it for future plantings, but now we know it was equally inferior."

"It's absolutely imperative that we be allowed access to that experimental planting. Even though it is failing, it might tell us something that could help reverse the brown-out."

Doherty's voice had become insistent and Tumulu went on the attack. He stood and glared down from behind the huge desk.

"That is pointless, Mr. Doherty, a waste of time. And there isn't much time, as you know very well. Ten days, no more, and the failure will be irreversible. I suggest you spend that time finding out what your company did to cause such a devastation."

The interview was at an end and Doherty knew it. But he thought he'd try one more question.

"May I ask the name of the person or persons who oversaw the experimental planting?"

Tumulu smiled. He was in control again and he resumed his seat behind the table. "Of course, you may *ask*, Mr. Doherty, but I am not at liberty to answer."

On his way back to the Hotel du Sahel, Doherty sat in the back of the cab and thought about his options. He had to find a way around Tumulu's roadblock. He leaned forward and gave the driver a new set of directions.

They drove west until Jankassa's paved streets gave way to the dirt lanes of the capital's shanty town, a sprawling collection of flimsy shelters thrown together from old crates, rusted metal, cardboard, scrap lumber and stained plastic.

The cab stopped before a shack with no door and a corrugated tin roof. There was soft light inside, a flickering, shadowy light that looked like it was thrown by candles. Doherty asked the driver to wait, walked over and knocked on the plywood wall. A tall male silhouette appeared at the open doorway. He had a child holding on to each leg, looking up with wide eyes and astonished faces, as though they'd never seen such a thing as a Doherty or even a taxi cab before. A young woman came into view behind him. She was laughing as she took the two little girls by the hand and led them back into the house.

Aswari Usama stepped out into the night air. He did not look happy. Doherty spoke first.

"Sorry to bother you at home, Aswari, but it really is urgent."

"No worries, Mistah Shahn. You want come in?"

"Thanks, but I think it would be better if we talk out here."

"Okay. What is this for, then?"

"I need you to fly me back to that patch of wheat near Lake Imibhotu."

Aswari shook his head vigorously. "No. I can't. No. Never go there again. Tumulu bad. Very bad man."

"We can pay you a good price, more than you could make in a month."

"Money no good. I go to jail, I be shot, who take care of the family?"

"I understand, but listen, Aswari, we have to go. If we don't, there will be famine, riots, police, Tumulu will take over the country and Loyuba will come back with an army from Chad. If I can get some photos of that wheat, Baku will listen to me and we can stop this madness."

"Loyuba comes back to Mawabi?"

"Yes, and it will be like it was before the revolution, before Baku."

"Them very bad times, Mista Shahn. Many people shot, chopped with machetes. Very bad time. You think we stop this?"

"Yes. I'm sure Baku will help if I show him the photos. And we don't have to land the plane at all, just fly over, take some shots and fly back."

Aswari was silent for a long time, remembering how Pierre Loyuba had sent death squads into the countryside, how thousands were executed without arrest or trial, how wages dropped to a dollar a day while corrupt politicians and their corporate backers built lavish palaces and stashed fortunes in foreign banks. Baku had changed all that and Aswari believed he would not let it happen again.

"We go, Mista Shahn. Tomorrow. You come in the taxi and we go."

59

Doherty slept for nearly ten hours and when he woke his legs were wrapped in a damp tangle of sheets. He pushed himself off the bed, scrubbed sleep-matted hair with his fingertips and stumbled into the bathroom. When he turned on the shower, the clang and clatter of pipes produced a short spurt that quickly slowed to a trickle. Cursing, he came back, dripping, into the bedroom and called the desk. Within a few minutes lukewarm water burst from the rusty nozzle and he was washing away a day and a half of grime and sweat.

He dried himself quickly, pulled on creased cotton trousers and a rumpled shirt. He needed to call the Curtiss James compound before he flew north with Usama and there was no phone in the room so he headed for the elevator. On his way down to the lobby, he went over what he knew, and didn't know, about the crop failure.

There was nothing wrong with the seeds. They had germinated and sprouted right on schedule and the first shoots were healthy. There was nothing wrong with the water supply either. Both his analytical ability and his intuition told him the problem must lie with the fertilizer, but those who tested it assured him it was state of the art, developed by Lang & Baine Enterprises. It contained a patented accelerator that enhanced the absorption of nutrients and was used for every agricultural project funded by the World Bank.

As far as he knew, that stretch of healthy wheat north of the reservoir was the only green patch in the country. He hoped the roots and soil he'd brought back might hold some clue that would solve the mystery.

He used the phone at the front desk to call the Curtiss-James compound. It took a while but he was finally able to talk with Maurice Currie, their head plant biologist.

"Have you learned anything from those specimens of healthy wheat?"

"Not yet, but I've sent half of the samples to our laboratory in Lagos. The facilities are much better there. In the meantime, we've replanted what we kept and it's doing well. I'll run some further tests and we'll know more this afternoon. I'll bring the report to your hotel and we can talk about how to proceed."

"Good. But I need to leave for a spell, and I won't get back till after lunch."

"No problem. I'll come by around three-thirty. I'll call before I leave the compound."

It had been forty-five minutes since they'd risen above the cloud cover and lost sight of the ground, but Aswari's normally cheerful face was still tense. He was not accustomed to instrument flying and he kept checking the compass against his flight charts every few minutes. Without the familiar landmarks of a countryside he knew as well as his own backyard, he had lost his confidence. The very real danger involved in flying over a restricted area bothered him too. He usually did his best to avoid trouble, but now he was flying right into it.

He checked his instruments and his maps one more time, then motioned to Doherty who was leaning forward in the navigator's seat. It was time to go back below the overcast to see if his calculations were correct.

He eased the Cessna into a slow descent and they came out of the clouds into drizzling rain. He had gone off course, as expected, but not by much. Lake Imibhotu was about a mile and a half to the west. He banked sharply and headed for it. Doherty snapped open the camera case, and removed his Nikon D5100 DSLR.

They were halfway across the large lake when they saw the smoke—tall, dark plumes rising into the overcast—and as they came closer they saw soldiers moving through the fields with flame-throwers. The entire crop was being scorched to the ground.

Doherty cursed and brought the camera up. He focused and shot, focused and shot.

But they would have to get closer. He turned to Usama and motioned for him to go down. The pilot looked frightened, hesitated, then nodded and took a steep run at the burning fields.

As Doherty zoomed in with the Nikon, he realized the soldiers were wearing different uniforms than the ones he had seen before. Beyond the flaming fields there were military vehicles, jeeps and armoured personnel carriers that bore insignia he didn't recognize, and there, standing by one of the jeeps, was the tall, thickly decorated figure of Jonas Tumulu.

Doherty caught everything on film, but when the forces on the ground became aware of the plane they raised their rifles and Usama pulled sharply up and to the right. A few moments later they were deep in grey mist.

60

Doherty sat at a table in the corner where sunlight ricocheted into the lounge from the small, stagnant swimming pool. It was comfortably cool in the high-ceilinged room with its teak arches and gold drapes. Behind him there was a bar and a streaked window that looked out onto the not very lush courtyard whose dusty fountain hadn't worked in years.

He ordered a Henninger Export. The waiter brought it quickly and left. As he sipped his drink and waited for Currie, he wondered if the photos he'd just taken would do any good. They'd prove Tumulu was up to something, and Baku would probably agree to look into it, but the experimental wheat was burned off and there might not be enough left in the ground to provide answers to questions that became more urgent with every hour that passed.

As soon as Currie entered the lounge, it was clear the news was not good. He looked tired, distracted, bemused, as though he'd exhausted every line of inquiry he could think of and run every test he knew how to run. He shook hands, then ordered Scotch, neat, and slumped into a chair.

Doherty was disappointed but sympathetic.

"Looks like you've hit a dead end." He said it quietly, without much intonation, and without judgment.

Currie shook his head. "For the time being, yes. We tested the soil from the wheat you brought back and what we found was hard to believe, so we tested it again. The results were the same as the ones we got when we did soil tests from the general planting. But they shouldn't be. In soil like that, the new wheat should be dying too, but it's extraordinarily robust. I don't know what else to tell you."

Doherty nodded. He described what he had just seen and photographed on the northern plateau.

"I don't think what we're dealing with is a natural disaster. The troops who were torching the healthy wheat wore uniforms the pilot recognized as Loyuba's presidential guard, and the armoured personnel carriers were stencilled with military insignia from Chad."

Currie's drink arrived. He sipped it and frowned.

"Well, that does explain what happened when we tried to get some of the seeds that were used for that northern planting. At first, the people we spoke to were very polite. They promised to help, but time went by and they never called back, so we called again and were shunted from one bureaucratic official to another until we spoke to someone in the ministry of agriculture and mines."

Doherty leaned forward.

"What happened then?"

"Not much. The man we spoke to, some deputy minister, I guess, said the seeds were unavailable at this time."

"What the hell does that mean?"

Currie shrugged, sipped some more of his Scotch.

"Beats me. We tried again and this time we talked with Tumulu. He was not helpful."

"I've got to show these photos to Baku, but I'm not sure I'll be able to get through to him. When you were trying to get those seeds, did you learn anything that might help me arrange a meeting with Baku?"

Currie finished his drink and thought about that for a while. He shook his head. "Nope. We never got anywhere near Baku. The presidential palace was off limits from the very beginning. I guess Tumulu has managed to effectively neutralize Baku's authority."

"What does that tell you, if anything?"

"Sounds to me like a coup is brewing. If the crop fails, it will initiate a total disaster."

"Famine, riots and enough instability to justify Loyuba's return with an army from Chad."

"My god, Sean, are you sure about this?"

"No, but I don't know what else to think, given what we know now."

"Okay. I'd better get back to the lab, see if we can speed things up somehow. If you think of anything we can do to help you see Baku, give a shout."

"Will do, and thanks. You and your team have worked hard on this. I'm glad to see you haven't given up."

Currie grinned as he rose from the table. "No way. We'll keep plugging till they kick us out."

After Currie left, Doherty sipped his beer, which had gone flat, and thought about the Chadian forces he'd photographed earlier that day. What kind of connection could exist between Tumulu and Mawabi's very unfriendly neighbour? He lit a Gauloise, blew out the harsh blue smoke and remembered something he had read in the massive files Curtiss-James had given him when they hired him on. Tumulu was a Serikole. So was Pierre Loyuba. But Baku belonged to the Puel tribe, the Serikole's ancient enemies, and tribal loyalties ran deep.

A scuffle of footsteps from the lobby interrupted his thoughts. As he stood to investigate, he was surrounded by half a dozen soldiers with angry faces and assault rifles at the ready.

Before he could move, or even think, they pulled the camera from around his neck and marched him across the room. A highly decorated officer barked orders in guttural Mawabian and the soldiers tied Doherty's hands behind his back. They started to drag him toward the exit, but he wrestled free and turned to face the officer.

"I was invited to Mawabi by President Baku. I demand to see him, immediately."

The officer sneered, "You are a foreign spy. I could have you shot." He made a dismissive gesture and the soldiers hustled Doherty out of the building. He wondered what would be done with him, but before he could ask, he found himself in the back seat of a personnel carrier between a grim-looking corporal and the officer whose chest was cluttered with silver, brass and gold dangling from rainbow ribbons. Though Doherty was infuriated by the man's arrogance, he tried to keep his voice off-hand and his face relaxed.

"Where are you taking me?"

"To a small airport on the other side of Tessili Tessoum. From there you will be flown back to Lagos."

Trying to get some authority into his voice Doherty tried again.

"Call Curtiss James. They will verify that I am here to help save the wheat crop. I'm a guest of your president. You don't have the authority to remove me."

The officer smiled and removed a 9mm semi-automatic from its holster. He pressed the barrel against Doherty's head and snarled, "I have all the authority I need." Then he leaned close and his voice seethed with anger. "You will not speak another word."

61

Rain lashed against the windshield as the rusted Checker cab bounced along a dirt track that looked like a string of tiny lakes. Out over the fields and trees, blurred sheets of it swayed and billowed in the wind under a thick grey sky. In the back seat, Doherty wondered if the Central African laboratories of Curtiss-James had made any headway with the samples they'd been sent from Jankassa. The compound was massive, but unpaved, a maze of tire tracks and pools that bounced in a white frenzy under the strafing rain.

He paid the driver and made a dash for the main building, stumbling and splashing through red-brown mud, his jacket pulled inside out over his head. By the time he got inside, it felt like he'd run through a waterfall, but the young African receptionist did not seem surprised to see a visitor dripping a trail of sludge and breathing hard as he approached the desk.

"Sean Doherty. I've got an appointment with Dr. Gregor Mandell."

"Ah yes, he's expecting you in greenhouse number seven."

Doherty headed back out into the storm. This time he just let it blow over him. Water pelted his face and ran in rivulets down his neck and arms. His shoes squelched loudly with every step and when he opened the greenhouse door, the wind almost ripped it out of his hands and he struggled to close it behind him.

Mandell was working at a long table covered with wooden flats. They were filled with soil samples and some of them were dotted with newly sprouted seeds. He'd been working for nearly three days with little sleep and when he looked up he seemed close to exhaustion.

Doherty introduced himself and they shook hands.

"When Currie called and explained how you got these samples, we found it hard to believe. If Tumulu had turned the brown-out around or managed a successful planting with a different strain of wheat, I was sure we'd know about it."

"That's what I thought, but there were soldiers guarding the area and they took shots at us. I went back to take some pictures of the crop, but a squad of what looked like soldiers from Chad and Loyuba's old presidential guard were torching it with flame-throwers. I need to know everything you can tell me about the wheat crop and those samples I collected near Lake Imibhotu."

Mandell nodded. "Okay, but I should start at the beginning. When we tested the soil samples from the failing crop, we used reagents. We wanted to see how much free nitrogen, potassium and phosphorus the soil contained. Because of the high-grade fertilizer, the levels should have been high. We were stunned by the results. Available nitrogen levels were even lower than those in the soil we collected from unfertilized areas. It made no sense, but at least we understood why the crop browned out. It had been starved to death."

Doherty felt a wave of fatigue and lit up a cigarette. Mandell waved away the smoke and continued.

"With the new soil samples from Jankassa, I ran the same tests and got the same results, but the plant specimens that were growing in what had tested as depleted soil were the healthiest I've ever seen. That was patently impossible, so I tested the soil again, this time using spectroscopic analysis. The results were mind-boggling. The spectroscope showed rich levels of nitrogen, but when we did the reactive test again, it didn't interact with our reagents. For some reason I have not been able to discover, the high level of nitrogen in the planted areas is not chemically active. It's there, but the wheat can't use it. Except for those few hundred hectares north of Lake Imibhotu. Those plants are able to reactivate the inert nitrogen. Not only that, they seem able to metabolize it at an accelerated pace that speeds up their growth rate and will shorten their maturation time by about two weeks."

Doherty was awake now. He'd begun pacing back and forth in the narrow space between the work tables. He stopped and looked at Mandell.

"Did you retest the fertilizer?"

"Yes, we did. And it tested out fine. Nitrogen is there in the advertised quantities and it reacted freely with the test chemicals. There is one strange thing though."

"What's that?"

"Well, we did a full spectroscopic analysis of the fertilizer, too, and it showed that almost three percent of the test sample had a chemical composition one would never expect to find in a fertilizer. Most of the lab techs think it's L&B's patented accelerator, but I'm not convinced. I haven't isolated or identified it yet, but I'm working on it and we should have a better idea some time next week."

"But won't that be too late? How long before the crop will be too far gone to save?"

"I'm not sure, but if the stems begin to die, we're probably past the point of no return."

"What's your best guess?"

"Anywhere from two or three days to a week. Of course, if we could find out who did that northern planting and get them to tell us all they know about it..."

"Not much chance of that. Tumulu has isolated Baku and disinformed the country's media." Doherty broke off, took a deep drag on his Gauloise, dropped it and ground it out under his shoe. Mandell didn't even wince.

"My sources tell me that Tumulu has managed to discredit both Curtiss-James and Baku's cabinet with the board of the World Bank," Doherty continued. "Apparently, he's shown them documents that prove malfeasance, corruption, kickbacks and the use of an inferior fertilizer which they say caused the brown-out." He paused, looked away. "I'm convinced that it was Tumulu who sabotaged the crop, probably with support from U.S. Intelligence. I assume that without this crop, the situation in Mawabi will deteriorate rapidly. I see famine, riots, disease, gangs of marauders roaming the countryside, a society coming apart at the seams. Do you think famine is inevitable if the crop fails?"

"I believe so, yes. Traditionally, the northern and eastern provinces supported small farms that produced locally grown food that the population at large could afford. But now, because the World Bank insisted on a cash crop in areas where ground nuts and millet were formerly grown, Mawabi has no indigenous food supply, and because of the crop failure, no cash with which to buy it from other countries, so there would be severe shortages and the inevitable epidemics that erupt among a malnourished people."

Doherty nodded. "Once that happens, Loyuba and his army will return from Chad. Mawabi will regress from a democracy to a brutal dictatorship in no time at all."

"Not a pretty picture. But how does that planting of healthy wheat fit in?"

"I'm not sure, but whoever planted it might be planning to use it later, much later I'd guess, to raise a new cash crop, repay the loan from the World Bank and justify Loyuba's *coup d'état*."

"We've got to find out how that healthy wheat was grown. Isn't there anything you can do?"

"I thought I might be able to get the UN or the World Court to intervene, but without hard evidence of sabotage there's not much they can do."

"What about the media?" Mandell asked. "If you can raise enough of a scuffle it might pressure Tumulu to come clean about the healthy wheat."

"That's a good idea, and I'll stay with it, but I haven't had much luck so far. I thought torching a healthy wheat crop in the company of foreign troops while the country faced starvation would be just the kind of international scandal CNN would jump on, but without those pictures, they declined."

"How about the newspapers?"

"I talked to Higgins at the London *Times*, Schwab in New York, and some of my contacts at the wire services. None of them will touch it. Even *The Guardian* won't touch it."

Mandell nodded, looked drawn and exhausted. He slumped back against the table. "What will you do now?"

"I'll book the next flight to New York."

"What's in New York?"

"There was a story in *The Times* recently, about the CEO of Lang & Baine. Apparently, he was assassinated by an extremist group of Mawabi nationals because he'd sold nerve gas to Chad. We're using L&B's fertilizer, so I'm going to check it out. There might be some connection to Loyuba."

62

As the squad car approached the three limestone arches of the Kings County Criminal Court building, Nick, sitting between two patrolmen in the back seat, felt a shiver of apprehension. It wasn't the sense of imminent danger that signalled the onset of a flashback, but it was close. In spite of Jason Endicott's reassurances, he'd half expected the Feds to appear and take him God knows where when he turned himself in. That hadn't happened, but it still worried him. He wondered if he shouldn't have just kept running. Or if he still could. Once he was on his own again, he might be able to get a confession out of Jeremy Baine, though he didn't know the man and he might just end up having to shoot him instead. But it would be dicey. There would only be a window of several seconds between the time the car stopped and the two hefty officers muscled him inside.

A call came in on the radio phone. It was filled with static, but Nick could tell it was asking for confirmation of the car's arrival at 120 Schermerhorn with the defendant. The driver gave a ten-four and got out. He came around to the curbside and opened the back door. The policeman on Nick's right climbed onto the sidewalk. His left wrist was handcuffed to Nick's right, and he gave it a tug.

"Here we go, buster. Your day in court. Let's move it."

Nick slid over, reached with his right foot and as he stood up he felt his left wrist drag the right wrist of the other officer. They were both big men and they were on combat alert. By the time all three were out of the squad car, he knew his chances for escape had dwindled to zero.

He let them move him along through the central arch, hoping the preliminary hearing wouldn't be short-circuited by DHS or the CIA, and that Jason's investigative team had come up with enough to get the case dismissed, but they hadn't had much time, and it didn't look good.

They unshackled him at the courtroom door and escorted him up the aisle to a table where Endicott stood at ease with his aide, a short, slender man in his mid-thirties whose blond hair and glasses made him look like a smart high school senior who excelled at math and table tennis. Endicott himself was fit, and tall, in a grey suit and vest. He wore a striped tie and white shirt under a well-trimmed beard. His full head of salt-and-pepper hair was carefully cut and his eyes were intent but showed no sign of tension. As Nick walked up and stood beside him, he could feel the man's confidence. He looked as though he had been in this situation so many times it was as comfortable as an evening at home in his living room or a stroll in the park.

Judge Giulio Carano was announced, took his seat and called the court to order. Jason spoke for his client and informed the bench that their intention was to plead not guilty should the case be bound over for trial. Everyone sat down and Truman Harris, the prosecutor, called his first witness.

"Please state your name and rank."

"Thomas Arthur Armagh, sergeant, NYPD."

"Now, Sergeant, were you first on the scene and the arresting officer in this case?"

Armagh cast a glance of angry disgust at Nick before he nodded. "That's right. The call came in at 5:36 am. My partner stayed in the squad car and I entered the building, then went up to Apartment 3-E. The door was unlocked and I entered the premises."

"Just for the record, who is the legal resident of that apartment?"

Armagh sneered and pointed. "Him, that scumbag, Nick Cortese."

"Thank you. Now tell the court what you saw upon entering the crime scene."

Jason objected that it had not yet been established that the place in question was, in fact, a crime scene. It was a trivial objection, but the judge smiled and sustained it. The prosecutor shook his head and gave a small sigh of exasperation.

"What did you discover after you entered the residence of Nicola Cortese?"

"A woman with long blonde hair was lying face down on the bed, naked. Her wrists and ankles were handcuffed to the bedposts and there were seven gaping wounds in her back. She did not move and when I felt her pulse there was none. I concluded that she was dead."

"Were you able to ascertain what caused the wounds that resulted in her death?"

"Yes. The murder weapon was a Victorinox Forschner twelve-inch chef's knife."

"Were you able to identify the owner?"

"Yes. The knife was part of a set we found in Cortese's kitchen."

"Thank you, Lieutenant." Harris turned to Endicott with a satisfied smirk. "Your witness, counsellor."

Jason conferred briefly with his aide. They whispered intently for half a minute, but so quietly that Nick couldn't hear what they were saying. Then Jason stood and took his time walking up to the witness box. He did not smile, nor did he greet the witness or make any statement to him by way of introduction. He just started asking questions.

"Where did you find the knife?"

Armagh scowled. "It was still stuck in the victim."

"Where, exactly?"

"In her back."

"What part of her back?"

"On the left side, near her shoulder."

"Try to remember the scene exactly and tell the court if the knife was standing straight up, or if it was slanted away from the vertical."

Harris rose to his feet.

"Objection, Your Honour, the question is irrelevant and immaterial."

Jason responded. "We will establish relevance, Your Honour, and we will show that this information is both probative and exculpatory."

The judge overruled the objection and Jason continued. "Was the knife straight or slanted?"

"It was slanted back toward the head of the bed."

"And when the call came in, what information did the caller give to the police?"

"He said he had heard screams and it sounded like a crime was being committed."

"Did he witness the crime?"

"No."

"Did he identify himself?"

"No, he did not."

"Did you ask or ascertain where he was calling from?"

"Yes, I asked but he refused to reveal his location."

"Were you later able to identify the phone number from which the call was made?"

"No. All we know now is that it was made from a disposable cell-phone. The owner could not be determined."

Jason nodded at Armagh, then turned to the judge. "I'm through with this witness, Your Honour." He returned to his seat and sat down. He smiled and gave a slight nod of gratitude to his aide.

The prosecutor called his next witness, a forensics expert from the Crime Scene Unit.

After the man was sworn in and had identified himself, he testified that they had been able to establish that the knife was, indeed, the murder weapon.

"The blade matched the wounds exactly and the blood on the knife was identified as the victim's."

"Did you test the knife for fingerprints?"

"Yes, we did."

"And what did you find?"

"We took two sets of prints from the handle."

"Whose were they?"

"They belong to the defendant, Nicola Cortese, and to Mrs. Nora Hennessey, his housekeeper."

"Thank you. Now, did you also use a rape kit on the victim?"

"Yes, and the swabs of her rectal area produced traces of semen."

"Did you run tests on the semen?"

"We did. DNA analysis proved that it belongs to the defendant, Nicola Cortese."

"Nothing further, Your Honour."

Jason began questioning the witness even before he left his chair. His faint West Texas drawl made it seem like he was initiating a casual conversation.

"Tell us, Dr. Chavez, was there any bruising, chafing, or other signs of sexual assault?"

"No sir, we found nothing like that on the victim."

"And did your rape kit produce any trace evidence such as pubic hair or epithelial skin cells?"

"No, there was no such trace evidence."

"Is it possible to violently sodomize someone and not leave that kind of evidence?"

"No. Even consensual sex leaves epithelials and genital hair. If it's rough sex, there would almost certainly be bruising or chafing as well."

"Now let's return to the murder weapon. Was there any other trace evidence on the knife?"

"Yes, there were traces of silicon powder, a lubricant found on surgical gloves, and molecules of a latex polymer used in their composition."

"So would it be fair to say that the perpetrator wore surgical gloves while stabbing the victim?"

Harris leaped to his feet and objected that the question called for a conclusion on the part of the witness. Jason explained that this was an expert witness who had been called for the express purpose of drawing conclusions. The objection was overruled.

"Yes, it is clear that the hand that held the handle of the murder weapon wore a surgical glove."

"And would it have been possible to leave fingerprints on the handle of the murder weapon while wearing surgical gloves?"

Dr. Chavez smiled. "I don't see how."

"Did you also collect evidence from the defendant's person?"

"We did. We swabbed his hands and sent the results to trace for analysis."

"Did that analysis show any signs that he had recently worn surgical gloves?"

"No, it did not."

"Let's turn to the victim's wounds. Did your examination provide any evidence about the person who inflicted them?"

"It did. Because of the position of the victim and the angle at which the blade entered the flesh, we concluded that the attacker was left-handed and no more than sixty-eight inches in height."

"Are you absolutely sure? Could he or she have been taller, if, say, his or her arms were much longer than the norm?"

"No. We factored that in to our calculations along with other variables and sixty-eight is the absolute maximum height possible in this scenario. Sixty-six or -seven would be more likely."

"Thank you, Dr. Chavez. Your testimony has been most enlightening." Jason turned to the judge.

"Let the record show that the defendant is right-handed and seventy-five inches in height. We would also like to enter a medical report that was the result of a thorough examination of the defendant when he was admitted to hospital. It states that he was unconscious for several hours after admission. This was caused by several toxic substances that were found when his blood was tested. He was under the influence of an animal tranquilizer, a hallucinogen, and an opiate. The report also describes sites of penetration by a hypodermic needle, two in his upper back, which could not have been self-inflicted, and one in the perineum. We offer this in support of our contention that he was drugged and unconscious when his semen was extracted and introduced into the victim."

The judge nodded and accepted the document Jason handed up to the bench.

"Is the examining physician available to testify at trial?"

"He is, Your Honour."

"Very well. Does the prosecution have any further evidence to present?"

Harris looked pale and uncertain as he rose to his feet.

"We do not, Your Honour. The prosecution rests."

Judge Carano turned to Jason and asked, "Does the defence rest as well?"

"Yes, and we respectfully ask that the case be dismissed on the grounds that the prosecution has failed to show probable cause."

"Thank you, Mr. Endicott, I will take your motion under advisement. Several documents presented by both parties require further study and consideration. I'm therefore calling a brief recess. We will reconvene in thirty minutes."

63

Vanessa Lang sat on the west deck, in the waning afternoon sun, sipping iced tea and thinking about Kenneth and the nerve gas shipment to Chad. He would never have approved, much less initiated, such a sale. In fact, Kenneth had confessed he was becoming more and more troubled by the chemical weapons research that Sarbitt was doing for the Pentagon. As she began to see a connection between Kenneth's death and his almost certain opposition to the nerve gas contract, she felt suddenly chilled by the implications.

Government officials from...what was it? The Defense Intelligence Agency? had assured her that Kenneth had been assassinated by a group of extreme Mawabian nationalists because he had sold the gas to their very aggressive enemies. She had been shown a handwritten note that said, "Death to the neo-colonial invaders." She knew what neo-colonialism was, had read Kwame Nkrumah's book, and had a good enough sense of history to understand the depth, the intensity, of Third World feeling against it. But the note made no sense. Kenneth had always been friendly and accommodating to emerging nations. It wasn't unusual to see him spending weeks and sometimes months teaching his Third World clients everything he knew about L&B products. He had sold them large orders on spec and had often worked in the fields alongside them until they felt comfortable with the new technology.

When she learned about the nerve gas contract she had been shocked and horrified by how neatly it explained Kenneth's death, and though she was convinced that they had killed the wrong man, she had accepted it as a grievous mistake. Now something else began to surface, and it made her blood run cold. What if Kenneth had been killed *because* he found out about the sale and had opposed it?

She refilled her glass and was still wrestling with this insight when the phone on the cedar table blinked and warbled.

It was Santos, her—as she liked to call him—chief of domestic operations. He had just spoken with his cousin at the gate. There was a gentleman who wanted to speak with her. He did not have an appointment, was not on the list of people who had regular access, but seemed straightforward if somewhat agitated. She wanted to scream, *not now!* but when Santos told her what the man wanted, she decided to see him.

A few minutes later, Vanessa received her guest in the sunken living room. Sean Doherty accepted her offer of a drink, and, looking a bit the worse for wear, seemed both impressed and slightly discomfited by the sheer good taste of his surroundings.

He stood before the bar, waiting, as she poured him a GlenDronach twelve-year-old. He carried his drink to the sofa where he remained standing while Vanessa took a seat and settled back to hear what he had to say.

"I'm sorry to invade your home, Mrs. Lang, but I was at the end of my rope. I've been trying to contact L&B Enterprises all day without success."

"Well, I'm not L&B, but you said you wanted to talk about my husband, so please do."

Doherty sighed and said, "This is going to be difficult. May I sit?"

She nodded and he eased his tired body into a leather chair across from the sofa.

"It seems that your husband met his unfortunate demise because he had sold Complianex-3, a nerve gas developed by Sarbitt Chemical, to Chad. I came to New York because I believe he may have been involved in a plot to destroy the cash crop required as a condition of the World Bank's loan to Mawabi, and to use the resulting crisis to pave the way for a *coup d'état* against the recently elected president, Kamoro Baku."

Doherty filled her in about the crop failure, the patch of healthy wheat that had been destroyed, his expulsion from the country, the curious test results, the accusations made by Minister Tumulu against Curtiss-James and President Baku, and his strong suspicion that the CIA had launched a scheme that would reinstate Pierre Loyuba.

Vanessa sat for a moment in stunned silence. As she gradually absorbed this information, she began to see how the sale of nerve gas fit into the larger picture. It angered and depressed her. But before she could tell Doherty about her own suspicions, he was talking again with an intensity that surprised her.

"We don't have hard evidence yet, Mrs. Lang, but I'm convinced that L&B Enterprises purposely sabotaged the wheat crop in Mawabi. I asked myself why, and except for the usual worship of profits, I couldn't think of an answer until I remembered that large uranium deposits were recently discovered in the north. Now, the U.S. has always been uncomfortable with socialist regimes, especially if they're democratically elected. The uranium raised their discomfort to serious alarm and they decided they had no choice but to reinstall a ruthless, but accommodating, dictator. Like most of the others the U.S. has supported over the years, from Papa Doc to Pinochet, Marcos and Mobutu, Loyuba is an iron fist, a murderer of his own people, but very friendly to Western interests. His brutal methods would stifle all signs of anti-American politics as long as they gave him money and arms."

Doherty paused for a moment while he drank the rest of the GlenDronach. He set the glass down on the coffee table and looked up. His face had become a grey mask.

"I have only one question for you, Mrs. Lang. How much will you personally profit by setting a struggling people up for famine, riots, disease and a civil war?"

No one had ever talked to Vanessa Lang that way, and she did not like it. She rose to her full height and seemed to lean out over Doherty as though she were going to fall on him like a tower of wrath.

"How dare you accuse me of things like that, you scruffy, mealy-mouthed little shit-for-brains?" The sheer volume of her husky voice surprised her and she settled back into her shoes. "Now you just sit in that chair with your mouth shut while I straighten you out about who's who and what's what at L&B."

Vanessa paced back and forth as she explained her own painful and very recent discoveries about her husband's death and her suspicions with regard to L&B's current CEO, Jeremy Baine. She also promised to do all she could to help rescue Curtiss-James and avert disaster in Mawabi.

"I apologize. I'm really sorry. I had no idea. I'm very relieved to hear this. Can you get into the L&B computer?"

"Yes. I managed to get the codes from a friend on the board, but I've been searching the files and there's nothing about Mawabi except for the failed bid they made for the cash crop contract and the subsequent sale of fertilizer to Curtiss-James. I don't see how they can help you."

Doherty hesitated, searching for a tactful reply.

"I'm sure you're very competent, Mrs. Lang, but in my line of work I've learned that different people see different things. Two heads are about five times more likely to find an answer than one."

Vanessa smiled, appreciating his polite way of telling her that he was a professional investigator and she was not.

"I'd be happy to open the files for you, Mr. Doherty. But perhaps you'd like another drink first. I'd suggest the Balvenie this time. It's very smooth."

They worked steadily and managed to find their way through L&B to the mainframe at Sarbitt Chemical. Every few minutes, Doherty stopped to scratch a note in his journal. Deep in the system there was a subdirectory, the Triticum Project. It meant nothing to Vanessa, but Doherty became excited. He reminded her that *triticum* was the Latin word for wheat. He clicked on the file menu and when a dialogue box opened asking him for a password, he re-entered the Sarbitt access code Vanessa had written out for him.

The circuits whirred furiously for about five seconds, then the whole system shut right down. A message came on the screen. SECURED SUBDIRECTORY. ACCESS DENIED.

64

Jeremy Baine nocked an Easton full metal jacket field point into his new Hoyt Spyder Turbo hunting bow, clipped the release onto the string's D-loop and pulled back to full draw. He held his hand tight to the anchor point at the corner of his mouth while he aligned the string sight with the top pin in the front sight window and the target 100 yards away. He was on the outdoor range of the Pinewood Archery Club but there was no wind to factor in to the shot, so he tripped the release trigger and the arrow flew, almost silently, and landed about six inches left at eight o'clock. He adjusted the fall-away arrow rest but before he could nock and draw for his second shot, he was interrupted by the musical clamour of a smartphone. He cursed, laid down the bow, fished the thing from his jacket and barked into it.

"I told you, no calls! I'm not available until tomorrow morning."

"I'm sorry, Mr. Baine, but this is a code red. Shall I put you through?"

He grumbled something unintelligible and Clay Noireau came on the line. His report was brief and to the point. Baine could hardly believe his ears.

"What? You can't be serious. I don't believe this. Is this what I pay taxes for, a police force that lets rapist murderers escape, and a court that releases them after they turn themselves in? It's a fucking joke!"

"No joke. He's out." Noireau was enjoying his boss's loss of composure.

"You've got to do something, Noireau. Right now."

"Okay. And what does our enlightened, infallible leader suggest?"

"Suggest? I'm *ordering* you to light a match under Homeland Security. Tell them to pick him up and sock him away in solitary for the rest of his miserable life. He's a threat to the national interest and he has to be stopped."

"Yeah, well, if he were just an ordinary asshole on the street, or if he'd been criticizing U.S. foreign policy in public or on the web, we could have him declared a terrorist supporter or an enemy combatant, but he's a New York cop and he ain't said shit about politics or the Middle East, so it's dicey. They haven't been able to get him on the president's kill or capture list. His name's been put forward, but it may take a while to convince the advisers to confirm it."

"We don't have a while. If he gets to the press or a TV reporter with that tape, the whole plan could go south. And there's another problem. That bitch Vanessa Lang has been snooping around in computer files that don't concern her. She could be as much of a threat as Cortese."

"You come up with a master plan, have you?"

"Yeah, I have. Screw DHS and the other Feds. Just grab her and that shithead detective. Take them somewhere they won't be found and waste them."

65

When Nick entered the Sixth Precinct squad room, all movement came to a halt, and conversations dwindled until there was dead silence. He saw confusion and uncertainty on the faces that turned to look at him. Time seemed to have suddenly stopped. Then someone clapped, once, twice, and others picked it up until the air was filled with applause.

Price and Malone were smiling as they got up from their chairs. There was a scattering of cheers as Nick walked over toward his desk.

But before anyone could shake his hand or slap him on the back, Baxter Chase came out of his office and shouted, "Cortese! My office! Now!"

The celebration died more quickly than it had begun and everyone got back to work.

Chase held his door open, then closed it when they were both inside. He nodded at the chair that stood in front of his desk.

"Sit."

Nick just stood where he was, leaned back against the wall and waited.

Chase looked at him. "You are one perverse sonofabitch, Cortese." He paused, then added, "Okay, so we were wrong. And, uh, we received the psychiatric report from Dr...." He looked down at the open file folder. "Sanderson. He gives you a clean bill of health. I just hope to God he's right, but I guess we'll find out soon enough. For now, you are reinstated without prejudice. But the two homicides you were working on are now permanently in federal jurisdiction and all materials, documents, evidence and information pertaining to them have been classified top secret. That means hands off. There is no case. It's over."

"They agree, then, that the homicides are related, that they belong to the same case?"

Chase looked disgusted. "Read my lips. There is no case. And that's from the chief of police and the mayor and the fucking governor. We're out of the loop. You screw with this, and you'll be compromising national security."

Nick nodded. But he wasn't agreeing, he was just nodding to himself because Chase had confirmed what he'd believed for some time now. Something big was being covered up, something that involved Jeremy Baine and some high-level agency people in Washington. It was heavy shit all right, and it was dangerous, as a lot of people had already discovered, but whatever the risk, he wasn't about to let them walk.

Chase grunted, closed the folder and put it aside.

"Right. So, I'm reassigning you. I'll have the details on your desk in the morning. Take the rest of the day off and get your head straight."

Nick went out into the squad room and it struck him that the mood had changed. He was one of them again and they just accepted his presence as a worker bee and let him do whatever it was he was doing. He walked over and sat down in the client chair next to Price's desk. Corbie read his face immediately and didn't look surprised when Nick said, very quietly, "I need you to do something for me. It's not on the case board and it might get Baxter's tits in a twist, so just say no if it's not something you'd do in my place."

Corbie frowned, thought, shook his head.

"Can't think of a thing I'd say no to, boss, if it's you who's askin'."

"Get the old narco squad together. I think we need to have another look at the warehouse where Buzz got shot. Talk to them one at a time, so it looks casual, like you're just bullshitting. Chase ordered me to take the afternoon off so I'm going back to my apartment. Meet me there in a couple of hours but don't all leave at once."

Corbie brightened, grinned. "Absolutely. I was wondering when we was gonna straighten that shit out."

"Don't know if we can, bro, but we got to try."

Not all the worker bees were absorbed in their own tasks and Nick's conversation with Price wasn't as private as he thought. After he left the building, Pratt Finch left too. He walked two-and-a-half blocks and made a call from the landline on the corner near the subway entrance.

A red telephone rang on a side table next to a leather sofa in an apartment on the Upper West Side. A woman with short blonde hair who looked like a track star answered. She wore a black body suit and a nickel-plated Heckler & Koch P7M13 in a shoulder holster under her right arm. Her voice was confident, cool, professional.

"DHS domestic surveillance, who's calling, please?"

Finch gave her his code name and she smiled. "Go ahead, Janus."

"Well, I was instructed to keep an eye on Detective Cortese and report if he did anything, uh, unofficial?"

"That's correct."

"Okay then. He's meeting with his old narco team later this afternoon and they're going back to the warehouse where his partner got shot in a friendly fire incident."

"Do you have an address for us?"

"Yeah, it's in the Bronx, corner of Merritt and Light."

"Good work, Janus. Your country thanks you."

When she told Noireau he looked uncertain about what to do. The big boss had ordered him to waste Cortese and Vanessa Lang. But he was still pissed about Ramirez and Tomlinson, and he wanted it done quietly. The problem was, it would take time to set it up so it wouldn't make a splash on the ten o'clock news, and time was running out. Noireau might have to act now, quiet or not. He needed more information.

"Do you know what happened at the warehouse?" he asked.

"Yeah, it was a drug bust. It went bad and a cop got offed, Cortese's partner."

"Who were the dealers?"

"Some Colombians and the Bravos."

Noireau came to full attention. "The Gun Hill Bravos?"

"I guess so, why?"

"Were any of them hurt?"

"Yes, there was a firefight, some of the Bravos were killed."

Noireau grinned. "That's great, Angela. This is how we'll set it up. Cortese and his boys just bought themselves a one-way ticket to gangland."

66

They parked the unmarked van on Kingsbridge Road and walked around to the other side of the warehouse. Nick didn't know what they were looking for, but seeing that squat, ugly building again triggered excruciating memories of Buzz Alteri's death and he felt the onset of a flashback. He took a slow deep breath, held it, exhaled slowly, totally emptied his lungs, counted to four and inhaled again.

When he had his feelings under control, he spoke to the others.

"I don't know what I expected to find up here, guys, but there's got to be something. I'd like you to spread out and see if there's anything that might help us get the review committee to reverse their decision. Who's got the camera?"

Malone held up the Pentax K-5 SLR.

"Okay, see if you can get up where the SWAT team shot from. Take half a dozen photos of the warehouse roof from that angle. I'm sure they had a clear view of me and Buzz going in through the vent."

Malone walked off toward south Third Avenue and the others began a detailed sweep of the area around the warehouse.

Across the street, there was a trucking company with a large parking lot and loading zone. The building was a converted factory five storeys high that was used now as a storage space for cartage transfers. Nothing unusual caught Nick's attention and he continued walking.

He turned the corner and looked up toward the roof from which Donovan's SWAT team had opened fire. It was two storeys higher than the warehouse. If Malone could get some good photos from that vantage point, they could challenge Donovan's version of the shooting.

As he stared up at the roof something occurred to him. It was a long shot, but he turned back the way he had come and broke into a run. When he came around the corner he slowed and scanned the loading zone, the parking lot, and the five storeys of Tri-State Transfer and Cartage. High in one corner he saw it, a small, black security camera that scanned the lot and the loading area. It was high enough to have an unobstructed view of the warehouse roof.

He knew that most of those cameras stored the recorded images for sixty to ninety days before they were erased. But the building was dingy with soot. Some of the windows were cracked or broken and several of their protective grills had come loose and were hanging at odd angles. With so much neglect and disrepair, what were the odds that the camera actually worked?

When the team collected again in front of the warehouse, Nick debriefed them.

"Tri-State Transfer and Cartage has a security camera that should include the warehouse roof in its regular scans. They're closed for the day but I'll get back up here first thing in the a.m. tomorrow."

They all high-fived, then piled into the van and drove east on Dock Street. At Edison they started to turn left and head up to Pelham Parkway, but the road was closed and a detour sign directed them south on Edison. After half a block the pavement came to an end and curved left into a dirt track that took them into what looked like a construction supply yard. Eddie Mifflin yelled, "It's a set-up!" Malone yelled, "Fuck!" as he screeched to a stop. There were dump trucks, half tons, front loaders and a few cars parked haphazardly around feed bins filled with sand and gravel. The way forward was blocked by a stockpile of concrete pads stacked on top of each other. He banged the wheel with the heel of his hand and started to back up but a semi-trailer pulled across the dirt track where it entered the yard behind him. Malone shifted gears, pulled forward and swerved right around a large pile of broken rock, but the lot came to an end at a concrete platform that dropped off into a spur of the Hutchinson River that ran down to Eastchester Bay.

Almost at once they took fire from a stand of trees along the narrow beach on the other side of the water. A short burst, then another ripped into the hood, the windshield and the instrument panel. They stared at the wreckage. Nick shouted from the back seat.

"The radio's fucked and I can't get a signal on my cell. We can't hunker down and wait for backup, guys, we've got to get out of the van and find some cover, now!"

Nick rolled out of the passenger door and ran toward a parked half-ton, keeping low and trying to fix in his mind the positions of the shooters. Corbie Price came out of the sliding door behind him, returned fire and tumbled in behind a blue dumpster. Malone opened the driver's door and a short burst from an assault rifle blew out the window, spraying him with glass and cutting a deep gash behind his right ear. He dropped to the ground and lay there, dazed, unable to move.

Hector was still in the van. Nick got his attention and signalled toward the east side of the lot. The back door slid open. Trojas dove to the ground, rolled and came up running a zigzag pattern toward a small storage shed. Gunfire erupted from the semi that was parked behind it and to the left. He felt something hit his left leg, stumbled, but made it to the shed and flattened himself against the wall. It felt like he'd been hit with a baseball bat. He looked down and realized that he'd taken a round in the hip. Miraculously, it had missed the bone, but the pain, which felt like a magnified bee sting, had already begun to intensify. He realized that he needed to keep going, to his right, to get around and behind the semi, but wondered how long he'd still be able to walk, much less run.

Eddy saw Hector get hit and hesitated. He fired at the semi, shattering the windshield and the left headlight before he leapt from the van and sprinted toward one of the feed bins that held several tons of sand and would provide good cover, but he only made it halfway before he was cut down. He lay still for a moment, then began to crawl forward and was hit again. This time all tension left his body and he lost consciousness.

Nick cursed, felt his pulse accelerate as he became hyperalert, and it was like he'd been beamed back to Iraq or Afghanistan, but this was the Bronx. Same difference, he told himself. Combat is combat, and he was in that zone where every sense, every nerve, was vibrating, his mind was racing but also rock still.

Three of his men were down, or wounded, and the whole team was pinned in defensive positions. Whoever set up the ambush knew what they were doing. They had triangulated firing lines that crisscrossed the kill zone. Nick knew that if they were going to get out of this alive, he'd have to outflank the shooters in the trees and take them down before his team could respond to the attack from the semi.

He scanned the area, looking for anything he might use for shelter. He fired three quick rounds and kept low as he ran from his position behind the half-ton. A small red dot followed him and rifle fire kicked up spurts of dirt that tattooed past him as he deked and fell in beside Price. Another volley strafed and whined off the edge of the dumpster. He returned fire and shouted across to Price, "What's your ammo like?"

"I've got seven in the cylinder and two reloads."

"Good. That should be enough. I'm gonna try to get across to the left of those trees across the river. If you can keep them occupied, I might make it, but be careful, they've got laser scopes—don't expose even a little finger."

Price nodded, reached around the edge of the dumpster and fired his Smith & Wesson .41 Magnum toward the trees. Immediately, half a dozen shots dinged into the heavy metal of the dumpster as Nick dove and skidded on his back behind a pallet stacked with cinder blocks.

When Price fired again, Malone, who had recovered and crawled under the van, saw what was happening and got off three quick rounds.

Nick used his knees and elbows to scrabble across the concrete pad to the edge of the lot. He took deep, quick breaths, hyperventilating for thirty seconds before he slipped into the slow, murky green current. He treaded water while he charted a course, then he ducked under and pushed off.

It was cold, and dark. On the third stroke he felt something tug at his thigh, and there was a sudden spurt of panic as the nightmare began to invade his consciousness. He shook himself awake and kicked forward. He couldn't use the *Dan Jun* breathing technique to steady himself while he was underwater and he felt an overwhelming urge to drive up to the surface, but he fought it, fought down the flashback, fought down the fear, but held on tight to a sense of danger. That was real, and he had to be fully alert when he came out of the river.

He had set out to swim on a diagonal across the intersection of the main channel and the backwater spur to the narrow beach just left of the trees, but he had no idea where he was by the time he felt the bottom beneath his feet. He fell forward and, dripping with stagnant water and strands of seaweed, crawled up the slope across slippery stones till a three-foot concrete wall stopped his progress.

He took a deep breath and felt the dizziness of oxygen deprivation clear. Slowly, he raised his head above the wall and his field of vision took in a paved lot. He pulled back and waited. When he was sure he hadn't been seen, he waited a bit more, till Price, then Malone, fired several rounds and he broke into a low run, across the lot and out onto a level stretch of grass. He followed a footpath down to the right beside a fieldstone fence that ran along the back of a small park dense with trees.

As he came up behind the thick trunk of a maple, he saw one of the shooters. He was in uniform complete with a MICH combat helmet and was holding an M-16 assault rifle with a laser scope. But he wasn't U.S. Army. There was a patch on his arm, a white bear's paw on black surrounded by a red oval. Nick recognized the logo from his tour in Iraq. Blackwater, then Xe, now Academi, a private security contractor hired by the Department of Defense. What the hell were they doing operating in the United States? And who were they working for? It was almost certainly Jeremy Baine. Whatever he was up to, it must be big. These guys were expensive.

Nick unholstered his Beretta M9 and hoped to God it would still work after his dunk in the river. He lined up his shot, just under the helmet, and fired. Even before the man fell Nick started running along the wall toward the other side of the park. As he ran he caught glimpses of the two other shooters who had turned around and were firing at the tree he had just shot from.

One of them was on the ground in a prone position, and the other was halfway up an oak tree, on the first, heavy branch.

Quickly, he analyzed the set-up and visualized a plan of attack. His Beretta had a double-action trigger and could fire two shots in less than half a second, but the targets were twenty yards apart and there was a sixty-degree difference in elevation. He'd have to sweep the barrel quickly from one to the other and that would make an accurate second shot difficult. The one on the ground would have the hardest time turning and aiming so Nick lined up the man in the tree first. He aimed for the heart, but then realized if the man was in full battle gear he probably had a Kevlar vest under his fatigues. A leg shot would put him down, but not out, and the head shot was obscured by a tree limb.

Nick repositioned himself, took a step to the left and went down on one knee. From there, he had a three-quarter view of the man's head and shoulders. Nick knew he had to be careful. If he wasn't completely focused there would be a tendency to pull the shot around toward the second target before the Beretta had fully recoiled and returned to its initial position. If he did that he'd miss and lose his advantage because they'd know where he was.

He raised the pistol with both hands and lined up the sights. He took a long, deep breath, held it, then completely emptied his lungs before he squeezed off the shot. The man's helmet flew off and his head flopped sideways. As Nick swept the barrel down and left, the other shooter had already started turning and his M-16 exploded, on full automatic, raking the grass and dirt with rounds that stitched up to the tree where Nick was kneeling. He caught one in the shoulder before he shot the man twice in the face.

He looked down. He was bleeding. It flowed steadily from the hole in his jacket. He moved his arm around and it felt like the bullet had gone straight through. There wasn't much pain yet but he knew the muscles would tighten up and get pretty sore as soon as the shock wore off. His team was on the other side of the river and he could hear gunfire from the construction yard where they were pinned down by shooters in the semi. He had to get back there, fast.

He got to his feet and ran to the contractor he'd just shot, checked his neck for a pulse and confirmed that the man was dead. He holstered his Beretta and picked up the M-16. The magazine was almost empty so he reached down and unclipped two full ones from the contractor's tactical duty belt and slipped them into his pocket.

As he came out of the trees he could see that the spur of the river he had crossed was very short and came to an end in a grey beach that sloped down from what looked like another open workspace for an asphalt paving company and a cement factory. There were feed bins of gravel and stone dust, piles of quarried granite and three storage tanks of liquid asphalt cement. There was lots of cover. If he moved to his left, around a fleet of cement mixer trucks parked against the wall of a squat brick building, and crossed the entire workspace, he should be able to set up somewhere behind and to the left of the semi without being seen. With the assault rifle, he wouldn't have to get real close.

Hector braced his back against the wall of the storage shed. His leg was seizing up and he knew he was no longer able to do more than hop and hobble, so he'd have to stay put. He tensed as he heard what sounded like heavy boots pounding the dirt. They were coming toward the shed from the left. As they came close, he moved the .38 police special to his other hand, stepped around the shed and fired three times at a shooter dressed in combat fatigues whose arms were extended in front of him with both hands around a Ruger Auto with a red-dot scope. The man yelled, spun and went down. A barrage erupted from the semi. As Hector pulled back behind the shed, its corner shattered in a burst of splinters. He went to his knees and curled up against the wall. What the hell kind of cannons were those guys using, anyway? And why was the U.S. Army trying to kill him?

He remained still and listened. There were two more gunshots across the river in the trees, then it was quiet. He hoped to hell Nick had been able to take them out, but the odds were not good—three against one, M-16s with laser scopes against a single Beretta. He looked for some way to get out of the yard without being ripped up, but it was no good. He was pinned, he could barely walk, and there were only three rounds left in the Colt's cylinder.

Nick sprinted across the cement factory lot toward the place where Edison Street had run into a dirt track and curved into the construction yard. The semi was still there, parked across the track, and there were shooters firing from behind the cab, from the back of the trailer and from its roof. Nick stationed himself behind the bucket of a front loader and scanned the semi with the scope off the M-16 he'd taken from one of the men he'd killed. The shooters were well positioned. All he could see that was anything like a target was the knee of a shooter in combat fatigues who was crouched down and spraying short bursts from the back of the trailer. Nick zeroed in, squeezed off a round, saw it rip into cloth and bone. There was a shout as the man grabbed his leg and fell back out of sight.

Nick ducked down and waited. The men in the semi returned fire but they didn't know where he was and they missed by a mile. A few seconds later, they resumed their assault on the van, the shed and the dumpster. Trojas, Price and Malone fired back, but they were low on ammo and their shots were sporadic. Outmanoeuvred and without tactical support, Nick knew the team couldn't hold out much longer. Sooner or later Blackwater would spread out and get behind them. They had to be stopped, but Nick didn't have a shot from where he was.

On the other side of the lot there was an asphalt processing complex, three rock crushers, conveyor ladders and belts, loading chutes and maintenance walkways, all steel and painted light blue, the colour of his jacket. If he could get to it across thirty yards of open ground, he could climb up onto a loading chute and pick off the shooters who were firing from the semi.

He waited until there was another exchange of fire between his guys and the semi, then he took off from the front loader and sprinted toward the asphalt plant. He only got a few feet out before the dirt flew up in front of him. He dove to his left, rolled and lay on his stomach behind a pile of quarried rock. There was no way he was going to make it all the way to the conveyor ladder or the blue girders he'd have to climb to get to the shooting position he envisioned behind one of the loading chutes.

Price saw Nick make his move and nearly get dropped. Bad luck. Now it was his turn.

He needed to move from where he was, to the right, and forward till he could come up behind the semi. There was a cement mixer parked in front of a feed bin about twenty yards out. It was risky, but he had to chance it. He motioned to Malone who was still under the van, making a pistol with the thumb and forefinger of his left hand, and when Chaz squeezed off a shot, Price took off. Just before he fell in behind the cement truck, he felt a blow to his chest. He was still wearing the Kevlar vest he'd put on that morning before the raid on a chop shop. It had kept the round from killing him, but it felt like he had at least one cracked rib and the pain was tightening the entire left side of his torso. He lay in the dirt while another barrage skittered and spit up dirt all around him. He was shielded now, but as he backed up against the cement truck's rear wheel, he knew there was no way he'd be able to outflank the semi.

Nick saw Price get hit and sprayed the semi with the M-16 till its magazine was empty. He shucked it, pulled a full one from his pocket and reloaded. There was something different about the new clip, but it seemed unimportant until he fired again. What came out of the assault rifle's muzzle startled him—a string of red smoke that trailed the bullet all the way to impact.

Tracer rounds. It was like having a new weapon, and almost immediately he saw how he could use it. He turned the selector switch to short burst and aimed the dot from the scope directly below the passenger door of the semi's tractor truck. Three red lines of burning smoke streaked across the lot and the diesel fuel tank on the Freightliner FL80 exploded. It lifted the tractor four feet into the air and threw the trailer back to the left. Its front wall was blown off and one of the shooters tumbled out. He was clothed in flame. He was screaming, running blindly with his arms up in front of his face. A shot from Malone's Glock took part of his head off. He fell in the dirt and lay there flickering like a spent flare.

Between the separated parts of the tractor-trailer, Nick could see one of the other shooters. He was in pieces, with his left arm and shoulder blown off and his right leg twisted at a hideous angle up near his chest under his left arm. But the shooter who had been up on the roof of the trailer was still alive. He had been thrown into the air, flipped a somersault and landed behind the semi in a feed bin of sand. The bin walls were like a fort and Nick didn't have a shot from where he was. He needed to get higher, but there was still too much open space between the rock pile and the conveyor ladder that angled up into steel grid-work and the loading chutes. He'd be cut down for sure before he got halfway there.

Malone had seen Price get hit and go down. But that was before the explosion. The way should be clear now for him to move up on the right. He crawled on knees and elbows, dripping blood from the cuts on his head, and made it to the edge of the yard where it stopped at the Hutchinson River. From there, he kept low and could run along the water without being seen. He was able to set up just beyond where the remains of the semi were flickering and giving off an intense stench of diesel fuel, scorched metal and burnt flesh.

Nick was still hunched behind the load of quarry stone. He wondered if any other Blackwater shooters had been deployed before the explosion. And if so, where were they now? There was no way he could find out if he stayed where he was, and he'd never make it to the conveyor ladder, so the load of granite was his only chance of getting to higher ground. He slung the M-16 over his shoulder and began to climb. The stone was broken in loose, uneven pieces and he clawed his way up, slipping and sliding as they rolled back under his feet.

He was breathing hard when he got to the top, but he had a much better view of the terrain. As he scanned the surrounding area, he became aware of a car turning right and cruising down Edison. It looked like a Ford Crown Vic and it was travelling fast. At first, he thought it might be an unmarked NYPD vehicle, but there was only one person inside and he waved at it to get back, but it kept going, passed the turn off into the supply lot and screeched to a stop. The driver's door opened and a tall, slender figure got out. It was a woman—athletic, late thirties, short blonde hair—and she was wearing a red beret and a red polyester jacket. Nick recognized the logo, an eye in a triangle inside a badge with wings—the Guardian Angels, a volunteer organization of unarmed crime patrollers. Usually they drove around in pairs, but she'd probably heard the explosion and rushed over to investigate on her own.

Understandable. But dangerous. And as he had that thought, the Blackwater contractor came around the wall of the feed bin and grabbed her before Nick could get off a shot. He was big, six-five or -six, and heavily muscled, a black man with amber eyes and a scar that ran from his left cheekbone down to his ear. He got his left arm around her chest, lifted her off the ground and pressed the muzzle of what looked like an FNP-45 Tactical against her head. He looked over at the rock pile and yelled,

"Cortese! I know you're there. Throw out your weapons and get your ass out here, hands high, or I'm gonna waste this collateral cunt!"

Nick shouted back, "Go ahead. I'm sure your employer will love it, lead story on the ten o'clock news, Volunteer Crime Fighter Murdered by Blackwater Thug. But you won't have to deal with that because, after you shoot her, I'll put a tracer through your right eye and out the back of your head. You won't feel a thing. You'll be dead before you fall down."

Nick was bluffing about the pinpoint accuracy of his marksmanship. True, he'd won the Marine sniper competition twice with record scores, but his left shoulder was swollen now, and he could hardly lift his arm. He'd have to rest the rifle on a rock to aim, and he'd have to shoot it with one hand. Not much chance of keeping the recoil from throwing the shot off centre. He hoped he wouldn't have to try it.

Nick waited while the Blackwater commander thought over his options. He looked frustrated, like he really wanted to shoot her. He started to say something, then changed his mind. He dragged her over to the car, opened the door, bent and moved the seat all the way back, then got in, holding her firmly in front of him. She tried to wrestle free. He hit her on the side of the head with the pistol and shouted right in her ear.

"Stop shakin' your ass. You move again and I'll shoot your cunt, your voice box, your knees, elbows, tits. You'll be a living *phee-nom,* if you don't bleed out."

Immediately, she stopped and sat very still.

"That's a good little pussy. Now reach over and close the fucking door."

She did that. He laid the FNP-45 on the passenger seat and smiled up toward Nick's rock pile before he started the car. He backed up Edison to where he could turn around, picked up speed and blasted through the Road Closed sign on his way to Pelham Parkway and the New York throughway system.

Nick scrambled backward down the slope of broken stone, landed on his feet and slung the M-16 across his right shoulder, but before he could turn and run across to the others, a voice stopped him. It was loud, husky, but also musical, a strong contralto, a woman's voice.

"Hold it right there! Take the rifle from your shoulder and toss it away. Then get rid of the Beretta and whatever you've got in that ankle holster. As an agent for Homeland Security I'm taking you into custody, unlimited and irreversible, without charge and without the right of appeal. I need you to command your associates to disarm and show themselves. You've been designated as an enemy combatant and if you don't comply with my instructions immediately, I have the authority to terminate with extreme prejudice."

Nick felt a slow rage begin to build inside his chest, but he held it in check and tossed his weapons away, one by one. She was behind him but he didn't know how far and his mind raced, trying to picture exactly where her voice was coming from. Maybe his only chance was to duck and dive to his left toward the rock pile. Before he could decide, a shot rang out, very close. He flinched, but felt nothing, could hardly believe she had missed, then he heard a body fall to the ground behind him and Malone came around the wall of the feed bin where the Blackwater contractor had landed when he fell from the roof of the semi.

They walked together to where the woman lay on her side, her helmet half off, her blonde hair tinged pink with the late sun, and her blue eyes staring. Malone looked down at the dead contractor and shook his head.

"I didn't want to kill her, but it was her or you, Nicola. I don't think I could have talked her down from where I was. If I'd been behind her..."

Nick put his hand on Malone's shoulder.

"You did what you had to do, Chaz. It was a righteous shoot."

Malone seemed like he was a still a bit dazed. "Hope you're right, but what the hell do we do now?"

"We've got three men down, we've got to get help."

"Sure, but the radio's out and we can't get a signal on our cells."

"I'll try mine again, but we're probably gonna have to take them to a hospital. Get the first aid kit from the van while I check to see how badly they're hurt."

Mifflin was out in the open, stretched out with one hand tucked under his chest and the other crooked beside his head. As Nick approached, images flashed through his mind. Eddy was the cutup on the team, unpredictable, a kidder, but he'd always had good instincts and was rock steady under fire. It was hard to see him like this, face down in the dirt and barely breathing. A memory surfaced from the war, Kenny Sawchuck curled up against a tree. It almost triggered a flashback, but Nick held on through an intense matrix of emotions that dissolved back into the present moment. *Sanderson's magic wand was working.* Nick felt a sense of gratitude and relief, but it was disrupted by apprehension about the men on his team. He examined Eddy more closely. It looked like he'd taken three rounds, one in the thigh, another in the back that may have punctured a lung, and a crease across the side of his skull, which probably made him lose consciousness.

When Malone came back with the first aid kit, they sterilized and bandaged Mifflin's head wound, put a compress on his thigh, but couldn't do much about the other wound. They agreed that it wasn't a good idea to turn him over or lift him and carry him to the van. One of them would have to take Price and Trojas to emergency, if they were up to it, and send back an ambulance. The other could stay with Mifflin so he wouldn't feel abandoned if he woke up.

As they walked over to check on Trojas and Price, they heard sirens and looked up. A cloud of dust rose along the dirt track all the way from where it left Edison Street. Two RMPs swerved into the yard and skidded to a stop, their dome lights twirling uselessly in the sun.

The driver of the first vehicle got out and stood behind it. He had a semi-automatic 9mm pistol aimed across the roof of the car. He shouted at them. "Down on the ground, on your knees, hands in the air!"

They did as they were told, but Nick managed to get out his police ID without getting shot and held it up.

"Lieutenant-Commander Nicola Cortese, Sixth Precinct."

"Don't move, don't fucking move a muscle." Then he shouted down into the car at his partner. "Go check him out, O'Meara."

The passenger door opened and a bulky, middle-aged officer ambled over to where Nick and Chaz Malone were kneeling. Nick handed him the ID. He examined it, handed it back.

"Sorry about that, Lieutenant, my partner's a little edgy these days. You can get up now."

Malone grinned. "I'm stayin' right where I am till you call off your doggie."

O'Meara called back over his shoulder, "They're okay, Collins, you can stand down."

Both doors of the other vehicle opened and all three officers came across to join O'Meara, who seemed to be the senior member of the group. They stood behind him, hands on their weapons while he asked, "What the hell happened here?"

"We ran into an ambush. Had one hell of a firefight. Three of my team are down and one of them's in serious condition."

O'Meara turned to Collins. "Radio for a rescue team and an ambulance."

Price and Trojas, who had watched the proceedings, got to their feet and limped over to where Nick was talking with O'Meara.

"There are three stiffs in the trees on the other side of that spur from the river. You're gonna need some body bags and a whole lot of paper on this one."

"Who are these guys anyway, they look...official."

"They're private security contractors. Blackwater, or Xe as they called themselves after their horrific behaviour in Iraq and Afghanistan caused such an uproar they had to change their name."

"So, they're at war with the NYPD?"

Nick grinned. "Looks that way, don't it. But no, they're freelancing. And they've got heavy backup. CIA, DIA, DHS, you name it."

O'Meara whistled. "I see what you mean about the paper."

"Wish you'd got here a lot sooner. We sure could have used the help. How did you find us, anyway?"

"That was Valorie, Valorie Wright. She's a Guardian Angel. Heard an explosion. Said she was going to investigate and would let us know what she found. She never called in. We wouldn't have thought much about it, but we got a 911 from a woman who was out walking her dog. She heard these unusual sounds, like moans, and thrashing. When we got there, we found Valorie, cuffed and gagged, inside a dumpster. We came as soon as she told us where to go."

At the Sound Shore Medical Center, Nick had his shoulder flushed, packed, wrapped and his arm put in a sling. He waited with Malone while the doctors worked on Eddy, Corbie and Hector. Chaz was leafing through old magazines and fingering the bandage that patched the lacerations behind his right ear. He didn't seem in the mood for conversation, and it was only then that Nick remembered to check his cellphone for messages.

There was a call from his daughter, Terry. All she said was, "Wow, Pops, Claire is a keeper. We're having a blast here in Whatever, Pennsylvania. Hope you're okay. Call us."

Then there was the usual telemarketing bullshit, and Vanessa Lang's husky contralto. She sounded really excited. "If you're free tonight, meet me at The Cherokee, 517 East 77th. Look for Tamas Berenyi, that's B-e-r-e-n-y-i, on the mailbox and try to get there around eight. Doherty found a locked file on the Lang & Baine main frame and I'm sure Tamas can hack into it."

Who the hell is Doherty, Nick wondered, and what's in that file?

67

The Cherokee was a century-old, six-storey walk-up. Sponsored by Mrs. William K. Vanderbilt and designed by Dr. Henry Atterbury Smith, it was built as low-cost housing for recovering tuberculosis patients and their families in 1911. On July 9, 1985, the New York City Landmark Preservation Commission designated it as an official landmark and in 1986 it was renamed the Cherokee Apartments and converted to a cooperative.

There were four buildings, each with its own central courtyard, open-air spiral stairs with double green handrails and wire glass louvres over the opening at each level to keep out rain and snow. Other distinctive features were cast-iron balconies supported by curved brackets and a green tile roof. There were no lobbies or front doors. Instead, the entries were Piranesi-like barrel-vaulted arcades with intricately patterned Guastavino terracotta tiles that ran from the courtyards to the street. Their large, squared openings were framed by heavy foliate mouldings divided into small sections and finished in a pineapple motif. Flanking each entranceway were large bronze lamps shaped to resemble torches and topped by a white globe. Every apartment had nine-foot, floor-to-ceiling, triple-sash windows that opened out onto the balcony and maple hardwood floors.

Nick scanned the rank of polished brass mailboxes till he found Berenyi. The studio was on the sixth floor, and by the time he reached it, he understood why there was an iron railing with a seat formed in it at the outside edge of each landing. Without them, tubercular patients who had difficulty breathing would never be able to make the climb. He was breathing hard himself when Vanessa greeted him at the door.

"Nicola! Glad you could make it. My god, what happened to your arm?"

Nick smiled. "That's a long story, I'll tell you later."

"Okay, well, I guess you're all right. Let me introduce you. This is Sean Doherty. He's investigating the massive crop failure in Mawabi, and that's Tamas Berenyi at the computer."

Tamas raised a hand from the keyboard but did not get up or turn around. He was stocky, looked to be five-foot-eleven or so, in his mid-fifties, with curly grey hair and a full, well-trimmed beard. Vanessa had told Nick he'd emigrated from Hungary as a young man, worked his way to the West Coast and through several degrees in computer science at the University of California.

He'd been a promising analyst and designer at Microsoft, IBM, Apple and Cray, but quickly found the corporate ladder too slow and too stifling. For a while he ran his own company but disbanded it and went freelance when it became clear that he'd rather manage microchips than people. He was one of the few techs in the country who could build a supercomputer like the Cray X1E from the ground up and develop software programs for an impressive range of applications.

He sat at the desk, chain-smoking Sobranie Black Russians and tossing the butts into a large ashtray stand, filling the room with layers of blue haze. He'd only been at the laptop for twenty minutes, and he'd already hacked through to a Sarbitt encrypted folder with the intriguing label Operation Stealth Seed. He skimmed briefly through its contents, then stood and offered the chair to Doherty.

"I think, what you told me? This is it. If you need something, I'm over there."

Doherty sat down and began reading, a look of utter astonishment on his face. When he'd scanned the entire folder, he began to tell the others what he'd learned.

"It started with a contamination test Sarbitt ran on Lang & Baine's manure slurries. The sample revealed a strain of bacteria no one had ever seen before. It shouldn't have been able to survive such a high concentration of nitrates, but the hostile environment had triggered a genetic adaptation, a positively charged molecule that could bond with a whole range of nitrates. This prevented the nitrates from reacting chemically and neutralized their lethal effect. Because the discovery was made in the Sarbitt lab complex near Johannesburg, the new strain was dubbed *Acidophilus africanus*."

Doherty paused and waited for questions, but there were only intent looks and thoughtful frowns. He continued, "When CEO Dr. Yueng T. Kee saw the report, he realized that the new bacterial strain could be grown in vast quantities, and its genetic adaptation, called a sequester, could be used to meet even the most stringent cleanup requirements by neutralizing high density nitrates, and this would cut costs dramatically.

"But Kee had another idea that excited the Pentagon and the Department of Defense. He thought the sequester, NS2-7, could be modified and adapted to inhibit the release of nitrogen gas in the blood of deep-sea divers. If Kee were successful, Navy Seals could stay down for hours and rise quickly without suffering the symptoms of caisson disease. The Feds put up a lot of soft money and signed a contract with Sarbitt."

Nick looked puzzled. "This may sound stupid, but I don't see how this is relevant. What has it got to do with destroying a wheat crop in Africa?"

Doherty looked up from the screen, his face bathed in its eerie light. "Not stupid at all, but it's a long and tangled tale. I'll try to be as brief as possible but I'll tell you right now, it's bloody diabolical, ingenious, incredible."

Nick nodded, "You seem to have the gist of it already. Please go on."

"Okay. It was a promising idea, but there were problems. The chemical had to be catalyzed by water, and it had to be used quickly or it would deteriorate. It took a while but Kee developed a product he thought would work and when they tested it in the Gulf of Mexico, the diver came up from over 300 feet in less than a minute without any ill effects. Until they got him to sick bay for tests. Then he developed life-threatening symptoms, and remained in a light coma for hours.

They revived him before he went into cardiac arrhythmia, but the NS2-7 Kee had adapted caused severe, allergenic, immune system reactions and was unusable on humans. Kee went back to the drawing board and that's where the Stealth Seed Agenda was born."

Vanessa had a question. "Was this before Lang & Baine acquired Sarbitt?"

"Yes."

"And after the merger, was my husband involved in the project?"

Doherty scrolled forward, opened another subfolder, scanned it and looked up. "He was able to renegotiate the Pentagon and Department of Defense contracts for NS2-7, then turned it over to Jeremy Baine."

"But Baine took the project in a whole new direction."

"Yes. Detective Cortese is right. The original NS2-7 deep-sea project didn't lead anywhere on its own, much less to Mawabi and wheat. But the research team at Sarbitt continued to test the slurries and they found that when all available nitrates had been neutralized, their unavailability threatened the survival of the bacterium, so *Acidophilus africanus* developed a reverse sequester that freed enough nitrates to build and maintain its colonies. When Kee told Baine about this new discovery, he organized a team of transgenic engineers who isolated the gene that produced the reverse sequester, RNS2-7. They spliced it into the DNA chains of a hard, red wheat L&B had developed by selective breeding from Canadian Triticale. They called the new strain Proto-Triticum, and because it was genetically enhanced, they were able to patent it."

Vanessa asked, "I'm not sure I see how this could destroy a crop, but the original sequester could."

"Exactly. By adding the sequester NS2-7 to the Accel 3 fertilizer they supplied to Curtiss James, they neutralized nitrogen in the soil and starved Mawabi's wheat crop to death. We tested the fertilizer, but it tested out fine because, as a dry compound, NS2-7 is entirely inert. It was produced by *Acidophilus africanus* to operate in a slurry, a very wet environment, and needs to be catalyzed by water, so it never neutralized the nitrogen in the soil until it was irrigated or rained on. After that, the wheat couldn't use the neutralized nitrogen, even though it was there. That's what we couldn't figure out. Spectroscopic analysis showed there was plenty of nitrogen in the soil, and yet plant tests showed that nitrogen deficiency was the cause of the brown-out."

Nick shook his head. "It's diabolical all right. But there's more, isn't there?"

"Yes. The first day I was in Mawabi I discovered a twenty-hectare crop of healthy wheat. It came from the genetically altered seed that had the reverse sequester spliced into its DNA. It freed up the nitrogen the doctored fertilizer had neutralized."

Doherty scrolled forward through the next few pages, then nodded and continued with his narrative.

"Baine took his proposal to Claude Rydell who runs the African desk at the CIA. They'd been watching Baku and had concluded that his regime posed a threat to U.S. interests. He had been democratically elected and had massive popular support, but had alienated the country's power elite, and the U.S. corporations that operated in Mawabi. He was supportive of the Palestinians, and friendly with leftist governments in Cuba and South America. When uranium was discovered it put U.S. Intelligence on red alert. They worried that he might sell yellowcake to Iran, and they wanted things back the way they were under Pierre Loyuba who had ruled the country with an iron fist for nearly twenty years before his brutal policies provoked a revolution. Operatives were put in place. They planted, then 'discovered' forged documents and other evidence that would prove the brown-out was the direct result of government corruption and collusion with Curtiss James. Once the wheat crop failed there would be famine, riots, widespread chaos and desperation. That's when Loyuba was supposed to return from Chad and save the country by restoring order. He would then hire Lang & Baine to replant the cash crop with patented seed that could reactivate the neutralized nitrates in the soil."

Doherty looked up. "Any questions so far?"

Nick asked, "It's ingenious all right, but isn't it a little like overkill, all that work, that investment, all those disrupted lives, maybe a civil war, just so Baine could take back a contract he'd lost to Curtiss-James?"

"If that's all it was, it wouldn't have been worth the trouble, but Mawabi was just the test Proto-Triticum. L&B's fertilizer doctored with NS2-7 has been shipped to every major wheat-growing area on earth. In a matter of months Baine will control the world's wheat market, or ninety percent of it. Almost all the wheat growing on earth will die and be replanted with L&B's patented Proto-Triticum. No one else will be able to grow wheat, and no one will have figured out why. With help from Rydell at the CIA, the Defense Intelligence Agency and Homeland Security, skewed statistics and fake reports will be disseminated for each wheat-growing area of the world. This will persuade almost everyone that the gene pool the world's wheat draws on for new strains, local adaptations and other necessary developments has been seriously and irreversibly degenerated. L&B will offer their genetically engineered seed as a benign solution, when in fact, the dominance of a single strain would destroy, forever, an ancient seed resource from which new strains could be developed."

There was a stunned silence. Vanessa said, "That's insane, Sean. It's madness."

Doherty nodded. "Yes, it is."

Vanessa asked, "Is there anything in those files about the nerve gas shipment to Chad?"

Doherty scrolled through to another folder that contained Sarbitt's contractual arrangements with the Pentagon, the CIA and the Department of Defense.

He scanned them quickly and nodded. "Looks like Sarbitt developed the gas with federal money. The shipment that was sent to Chad was bought from Sarbitt and paid for by the CIA." He paused, read a little further and a distraught look crossed his intent features. It was almost a minute before he spoke. "I'm sorry to have to say this, but the invoices and bills of lading for the Complianex-3 nerve gas shipment were signed by Kenneth Lang."

Instead of being shocked, Vanessa looked thoughtful. "That couldn't be right. You say the CIA was using forged documents to build a case against Baku?"

"Yes, and Baine was going to use them too, to set up a disinformation campaign that would spin his takeover of the wheat market as a move to save the world from starvation."

"Kenneth would never have signed those documents. There's got to be some way to prove that."

"Well, the documents in this file are just computer scans. You can probably track down the originals and have them checked out. I'll help all I can, but right now we need to save that wheat crop or there will be total disaster for the people of Mawabi and we'll have another dictator sending out death squads and sucking up foreign aid tax dollars."

Tamas had been standing by the window, smoking his Sobranies. He'd been unobtrusive but was listening intently as Doherty unraveled the complex details of Operation Stealth Seed.

At this last somewhat impassioned speech, Berenyi clapped his hands in approval and came forward. "Well done. Well said. I couldn't agree more. You're going to need copies of these materials, yes?"

Vanessa and Doherty both nodded. She was smiling. "Thanks, Tamas, you've been brilliant. You've averted a major international catastrophe. I'll do all I can to see that you receive an appropriate reward."

Tamas smiled back. "I've not been much for rewards, Vanessa, but I come from a country that knows a lot about tyranny, and understands the value, also the fragility, of human freedom. The Stealth Seed Agenda is too large a file for DVD, it will have to be on a flash drive. I can make many as you need. I will also save to my external HD for safekeeping. And if you and your companions have time, may I propose a brief celebration?"

They looked at each other, then Doherty said, "That would be super, but may I use your modem to access the Curtiss-James mainframe at our research division in London? If I send them the research materials, they should be able to synthesize enough of the reverse sequester to spray the entire area by the end of the week. That will release the nitrogen in the soil and get the wheat growing again."

"Of course. But that's a too big file for the email. Let me set up so you can send it by the cloud."

Tamas tapped the keys and explained the procedure to Doherty, then he got up and disappeared into the small kitchen.

Nick turned to Vanessa who had withdrawn into her private thoughts. He touched her lightly on the arm.

"I know this is hard. But I need to ask you something. We're going to need help with this. Baine's got heavy, high-level support. Do you know anyone with political clout you can tell our story to, maybe get the justice department to investigate?"

"Let me talk to someone I know in Washington, an old friend of Ken's. It may seem hard to believe sometimes, but they're not all corrupt or self-deluded. Some of them can actually think straight and act like human beings."

Tamas came in from the kitchen carrying four glasses and an open bottle of wine. He was smiling.

"In Kentucky, you have the front porch, and the sipping whisky after dinner, no? In Hungary we have this, Pauleczki-Vin Tokaji Aszúeszencia 2000, very rare, from the Muscat Lunel grape."

Tamas handed around the glasses, filled each one carefully, then raised his own. "Let fortune smile on Kamoro Baku and the peoples of Mawabi."

68

It was already dark and had begun to rain—a full-blown summer thunderstorm—and they were drenched by the time they got down six flights of stairs and across the open courtyard. There was no door at the entrance to the street, just a tall, wrought iron gate, and as he reached to open it, Nick thought he saw a speck of red light swimming through the white spatter of rain strafing the sidewalk. He yelled, "Incoming! Get down!" and dove to his right, pulling Vanessa back from the lamplight and onto the ground.

But it wasn't a flashback. Gunfire tore across the concrete and climbed up the gate, spitting off hot sparks and ricocheting from the tiled walls and vaulted ceiling. The staccato thwack and whine of automatic rifle rounds echoed in the passageway and Doherty was hit. The impact turned him around and he fell, face forward, already losing consciousness before he landed and sprawled out, one arm pinned under his body.

Nick dragged him out of the light, had some trouble unholstering his Beretta from under the sling that held his left arm, but pulled it free and returned fire, though he could only guess at where the assailants were positioned.

Doherty was still breathing, but his eyes had rolled back into his head and he seemed unaware of his surroundings. Nick turned to Vanessa who had gotten back on her feet and was leaning against the bank of brass mailboxes.

"Are you all right?"

"I wasn't hit, but I've been better."

"Okay, I need you to call 911. Tell them it's a 10-13, there's an officer present, and if they ask for it, give them my name and badge number."

She nodded, looked eager to help, then annoyed, angry. "Damn it! I can't. Left my cell in the car."

"It's all right, you can use mine."

He reached into his jacket pocket, but it ripped, and when he looked down he saw that a ricochet had torn through it and his cell-phone was a blasted mess.

"Looks like we're not going to get any help unless one of the good citizens hereabouts calls it in."

He bent down, raised his pant leg to unsnap the ankle holster and came up with a Glock 26 9mm, which he handed to Vanessa.

"You know how to use one of these?"

She grinned. "I grew up in West Texas. I could shoot before I could ride a bike."

"Great. This one's locked and loaded. It's got ten in the clip and one in the chamber. I returned their fire so they know there's a weapon in here and I don't think they'll come storming across the street, but if they do..."

She nodded. "I won't shoot till I see the whites of their eyes!"

Tamas had poured himself the last of the Tokaji when he heard the unmistakable staccato of an M-16 on full auto. Given the gravity of what he'd just hacked into, he was not surprised.

He got on the phone and called 911. He told them he'd heard assault rifle fire down on the street and gave them an address. They asked him if he was in danger, if he was on the street, if there were others in danger, and who was he, and could you spell that for me please, and was he sure it was gunfire he heard, and did he see who was shooting, on and on until he just hung up, went to the bedroom closet and took out his SKS carbine with ten rounds already in the stripper clip. He climbed up to the roof, walked around to where he'd heard the shots and peered down into the blinding rain.

There was another short burst of rifle fire off to his left, then a third and he could see that the muzzle flashes were daggering from the street-side windows of a Lincoln Town Car parked near the corner of 77th Street and Cherokee Place. A man wearing camo fatigues climbed out of the back door, stood on the sidewalk and fired toward the entrance of the building over the roof of the vehicle. His head and shoulders were visible and unprotected. Brerenyi worked the bolt of his SKS, slid a round into the chamber, released the safety and rested the barrel on the tiled overhang of the roof. He let his breath all the way out, lined up the shot and slowly squeezed it off. The shooter's head twisted and he fell out of sight behind the Lincoln. Berenyi pulled away from the edge of the roof as another shooter got out of the passenger door and fired back.

Nick came out of the 78th Street entrance of building two and flattened himself against the tan brick facade. If the attackers knew the area, one or more of them would be coming from 77th up Cherokee Place and around on 78th to get in behind them the way Nick had just come out. As he stood there wondering what to do next, there was more gunfire from 77th Street. Two short bursts, then a single shot. He thought that might be Vanessa, but it didn't sound like his Glock, more like a rifle round, and it puzzled him. It was followed by a third burst from an M-16. He waited for a full minute but nothing else happened. He saw no one and heard nothing but thunder and the driving rain.

He broke into a run, sprinted east to the end of 78th Street and across Cherokee Place into John Jay Park, which ran south all the way to 76th. Using the trees and iron benches for cover, he worked his way down to where the park extended west, about twenty yards, along 77th. There were four handball courts in that corner and as he came around one of their concrete walls, he immediately recognized the silver Lincoln Town Car. It was parked on the corner where 77th dead-ended into Cherokee Place, across and to the right of the entrance that had been strafed with rifle fire. Nick checked his clip. He had nine rounds left. If he could get a clear line on the Lincoln that should be enough. He crouched and duckwalked around the concrete wall till he had a better view through the park entrance flanked by the wrought iron fence and a border of waist-high shrubbery.

Someone in combat fatigues was standing on the sidewalk, leaning against the passenger door and aiming an assault rifle with a laser scope up at the roof of the apartment building. Nick put two rounds in his upper back, but he didn't go down. *Fuck! I should have known. Body armour!* Nick thought as the Blackwater contractor turned and sprayed the park. Bullets tore through leaves and twigs, dinged and sparked off the fence and skimmed off the concrete wall above his head. Nick rolled onto his back and shot the man in the neck. The M-16 kept firing erratically till the clip was empty and the shooter slumped against the car, then slid down onto the sidewalk. But not before another shooter bolted out of the back door, firing a handgun as he came. He vaulted over the wrought iron fence and sprinted into the park. Nick recognized the big, heavily muscled mercenary who'd survived the firefight in the supply yard.

It was hard to see through the rain, but Nick thought he saw him disappear behind the concrete wall of the other handball court. Nick ran across the open space and flattened himself against the edge of the wall, then, very slowly, inched around till he could see the other side. There was no one there. He started to pull back, but before he had moved more than a few inches he felt the muzzle of a gun behind his left ear. A large hand gripped his right wrist and a voice rasped, "Release the weapon, slowly."

Nick let him have the Beretta and Clay Noireau stepped back but kept the FNP-45 aimed at Nick's head. He was smiling.

"They let you cops run around with fancy Eye-talian popguns? Thought you had to carry Glocks or SIG Sauers." He shook his head. "Don't know what the NYPD is coming to. No discipline." He released the clip and it fell to the ground. He kicked it off the court into the grass and threw the pistol over some trees into the swimming pool. He stepped out into the open court and lowered the -45 to his side.

"You been a real pain in the ass, Cortese. I oughta just off you, but that would be too quick. So, what I'm gonna do, I'm gonna take you apart. One piece at a time."

He laid the FNP down on the ground and kicked it behind him. Then he set up in a combat stance. Noireau was six-five or -six and built like an ox. He was still smiling.

"Let's see what the pussy psycho's got."

As he spit out the words, Nick spun and kicked. He was aiming to crush his nose, which would make his eyes tear up and blur his vision for a moment or two, but the sling kept him off balance and it went high, hit Noireau forehead and bounced away. But it stopped him long enough for Nick to turn and land a straight right on his jaw. It had no effect. Noireau grinned and shot out a doubled jab to set up his right but Nick came in under it and stabbed the stiffened fingers of his right hand into the big man's Adam's apple. He felt some cartilage give way and backed off just in time to avoid a leg kick, which he countered with a chop to the nose.

Blood streamed from Noireau's left nostril and he cursed. He was no longer smiling. He snarled, "Fuck this!" bent at the knees and pulled a Ka-Bar with a seven-inch blade from an ankle sheath. He lifted the knife in a high feint, then brought it quickly down and up in an underhand strike. Nick caught Noireau's wrist and held it. But the man was incredibly strong and Nick had only one good arm. He knew he wouldn't be able to keep the knife from piercing his ribs for much longer. He let himself fall backwards pulling Noireau with him. As his back hit the ground, he lifted his knees and threw the heavier man over his head, releasing his grip on Noireau's knife hand. But as he did, the blade sliced across the heel of his palm.

Noireau rolled and got to his feet. Nick was already up, in combat stance, with one arm in a sling and a hand that was dripping blood. He moved only when Noireau moved. They circled each other. Noireau feinted, swiped at Cortese, dodged and lunged but missed. Nick knew he had to keep focused on the other man's eyes, not on the K-blade. His only chance was to anticipate one of Noireau's moves and kick the knife away. Even then it was not an even match and he knew it.

Through the downpour he heard something move to his left, in the grass near the kiddie swings. At first, he thought it might be one of the mercenaries. He kept circling, away from Noireau's weapon hand, then a voice cut through the sound of the rain.

"Put down that goddamn knife. Put it down! Now!"

It was Vanessa and she was behind Noireau. He turned halfway so he could still see Cortese. He smiled when he saw her emerge from the shadows of the trees that lined the sidewalk on that side of the handball court.

"Oh," he said, "it's you. The Texas belle. Hey, I got no beef with you. Get back in your Mercedes and fuck off."

She shook her head.

"I know who you work for. You killed my husband, you prick."

"Look, lady, I'm kinda busy right now. Why don't you just go sit on one of those benches over there. I'll get to you when I'm finished with this sorry excuse for a soldier."

"I'll get to *you* a lot sooner than that if you don't drop your weapon and get down on your stomach with your hands behind your back."

Noireau laughed, a loud, contemptuous burst that sounded like real surprise.

"Whoa, heavy talk, very heavy. Tell you what. You put down that peashooter and wait your turn, or I'll have to come over there and take it away from you. After that we'll do a little dance and it won't end up with wedding bells, darlin'."

He took a step toward her, with the knife held out menacingly in front of him. He was smiling an arrogant, male, combat soldier's smile. It cracked into another laugh when she fired once, over his head.

"Good. Very good. You remembered to take the safety off." His voice turned ugly. "Now put that fucking thing away, or it winds up in your cunt."

"One more step. There are a lot of places I can shoot you. But I don't want to shoot you, asshole, I want you to go to jail."

He stood there, sizing her up. Her eyes were very clear, very deep and very blue. He shrugged. "You'd better shoot to kill, girl, if you know how, and if you have the stuff, which I doubt. Even if you hit me once, or twice, I'll be on you faster than you can blink and then you're dead meat, so just give it up, right now."

Vanessa backed up one step, then two, she almost tripped on the edge of the sidewalk, but regained her balance just as Noireau began his rush. Then he stopped, flipped the knife so he was holding it by the blade as he raised it behind his ear and started the throw. She fired one shot. It took him over the right eye and shattered his skull.

That's when they heard the sirens. There were two of them coming from different directions. Nick wondered what Baxter Chase would have to say about this one. And as the sirens came closer, he felt an overwhelming urge to track down Jeremy Baine, let him know what it felt like to have his life torn apart, do serious damage to his living quarters and all the high-end accessories he almost certainly surrounded himself with, then break a few ribs, mess up that smug, well-groomed face he remembered from the TV interview, and get blood all over his expensive clothes. He turned to Vanessa, touched her on the arm that held the gun.

"Are you all right?"

She nodded. "Yes, I'm fine, but I really didn't want to kill him."

"I know, but he was armed, he attacked you, and he was trying to kill a police officer, so there won't be a question about that."

"And how are *you*, Nicola, you're bleeding."

"It's just a flesh cut, no serious damage, but…uh, can I ask a favour?"

"Of course."

"I need to talk to Jeremy Baine. Do you know where he lives?"

Vanessa hesitated. She started to ask a question but decided not to. Then she said, "He has a place out on the Island, in the Hamptons."

Nick waited for her to give him the address, but she looked thoughtful for what seemed a long time before she said, "Believe me when I say I know how you feel, truly, I do, but do you think this is a good idea?"

He knew it wasn't, but he was past caring, until he started to think about what would happen after he beat Baine to a pulp. It wasn't a pretty picture. It would cost him his job. He'd have to do jail time, and everything Vanessa Lang had done to help him would be wasted.

Besides, he was an NYPD detective, not a gangland thug. He gave her a weak smile.

"Good question, Vanessa. Thank you. That's the second time tonight you saved my butt."

69

The next morning Nick called Claire as soon as he got to the office. He wasn't sure what to tell her, whether it was safe to come back or if she should stay a bit longer. The big black man Vanessa had killed was clearly the leader of Baine's Blackwater mercenaries, and Doherty had thwarted the CIA's plan to depose Baku by saving the wheat crop. An invasion now would not only be an act of naked aggression without the humanitarian excuse provided by famine and riots and rumours of corruption, it would also face fierce resistance from Baku's presidential guard who would not be distracted helping the police restore order to a disintegrating regime. But even though his master plan was in ruins, Baine could still be dangerous. He might decide someone had to pay for his failure.

She answered her cell on the third ring.

"Nico! Are you okay? I was beginning to worry."

"Yeah, I'm fine, except for a flesh wound in the shoulder. We've made serious progress on the case. I think it's safe to come home now, today if you want."

Silence. Then she said, "We're on speaker. Terry wants to talk to you."

"Hi, Pops. Glad you're okay. Did you get shot or what?"

"Yes, I did. I got shot in the left arm, the fleshy part, above the elbow."

"Wow! Did it hurt?"

"Sure did, hon, but it's better now. All stitched up and sterilized and bandaged. I've even got a sling, a blue one."

"Cool. So, I hear the coast is clear and we can come back to New York."

"Right."

"Okay. Well, I guess...the thing is, Claire and I have decided we'd like to stay here and hang out, till next weekend."

It was not at all what Nick expected and he waited a beat before he answered. He wanted to see them, but he was also elated that they were getting along so well. And the case was far from over.

"No problem, hon. Glad you're enjoying your new status as Manhattan exiles."

Terry laughed. A bright, musical sound. "We're not exiles, Dad, we're runaways, and we love it!"

They chatted for a few minutes longer and when they rang off Nick felt the weight of the job return. The first thing he had to do was finish the report he'd started before he left to meet Vanessa Lang at The Cherokee. And he'd have to write up another one about what happened there, though that was clearly a continuation of the firefight at the supply yard in the Bronx. It took an hour-and-a-half. He wondered if there would be more violence, and if anyone else would be killed before it was over.

After he filed the reports, he called the hospital to check on Eddie Mifflin and Sean Doherty. Mifflin was in intensive care but Sean's condition was listed as stable, though he wasn't well enough to have visitors or to talk on the phone. It wasn't good news, but it wasn't as bad as it might have been.

Nick put it out of his mind and began working on a summary of the evidence they had against Baine. Vanessa would courier a copy to Senator Alvin Tillis. He already had the Operation Stealth Seed files but wanted to carry as much weight as possible when he met with the intelligence oversight committees and the attorney general.

The clearest and most damaging evidence of what Baine had done in Mawabi was contained in the files they'd recovered the previous evening. But the authorization for funding was signed by Kenneth Lang. Baine could claim he was just following orders. He'd still be chargeable as an accessory, but not for the murders of Lang, Tomlinson, Ramirez, Duplessis and Rhea Carson, or for attempts on the lives of several police officers, Sean Doherty and Vanessa Lang. There had to be some way to prove he was responsible for those crimes. The strongest link was Malcom Duplessis. The wire tape implicated Baine as the one who hired him, but it was damaged and didn't reveal who he was hired to impersonate or what else he was hired to do.

Nick thought for a moment, then picked up the phone and called Lazlo Kaprisky at the Bellevue morgue. He answered on the second ring.

"Hey, Nicola, how ya doin'? Heard you got shot."

"Yeah, left arm, not too serious. And we took down the whole goddamn Blackwater goon squad, so I'm feeling okay, but a little good news about Duplessis would make me feel a lot better."

"Don't know if that's gonna happen. There is news but it's not break-out-the-beer-and-pretzels kind. The program did work, but the results weren't really conclusive. There wasn't enough left of his new face to get a definitive reconstruction of the reconstruction, if you know what I mean. What we do have is half a dozen probables, with positives on the eyes, ears and hair. You wanna see them?"

"Can't hurt, sure, send them over."

"Okay, I'll email you the jpeg files."

"Good. But Lazlo, could you also pull printouts on photo paper and send them by courier?"

"Don't see why not, you gonna frame them or somethin'?"

"Nah, we're getting some help from Washington, believe it or not, and I'm putting together an evidence file."

"Ah, well, in that case I'll make them eight-by-tens. Anything else you need?"

"Can't think of anything at the moment, but I'll drop by if something comes up."

"Drop by anyway, whenever you can. I've got a new coffee machine and a nice cognac, VSOP."

Nick laughed. "Will do, my friend. *Hasta luego*."

After he hung up Nick went back to his notes on Duplessis and found the number for Dr. Murray Gimmelman. The receptionist answered.

"This is Detective Cortese of the NYPD. I'd like to speak with Dr. Gimmelman if he's back from the Ba*hay*mahs."

"Doctor Gimmelman returned two days ago. I'll see if he's free."

She put him on hold and several minutes went by before she came back on the line. Nick started to ask if she had a nice lunch while she was gone but restrained himself.

"He's just finishing up with a patient. I'll connect you as soon as he's able to take your call."

When Gimmelman finally picked up he sounded rushed and not overjoyed to be receiving a call from the boys in blue.

"Gimmelman here. What's this about?"

"You performed reconstructive surgery on a patient named Malcolm Duplessis. We'd like to see his file and any before-and-after photos you may have taken."

"Never took any. We don't do that sort of thing. It's an ad hype and we don't need it."

"How did you decide what alterations to make in his appearance?"

"Usually we discuss this with the patient, explain the procedures, but this was an unusual case."

"How so?"

"He came in with detailed instructions and an artist's sketch of what he wanted to look like."

Nick felt a spurt of adrenalin. "Great, that's great. Exactly what we need."

"I'm sorry, but I can't let you see the file. That material is protected by doctor-patient privilege."

"I understand, but Malcolm Duplessis is dead, had his face shot off, so there's no patient left to protect."

He wondered if Gimmelman was going to buy it. There was a lengthy silence and when the doctor spoke again he sounded pretty sure of himself.

"I'll have to check with my lawyer, but I don't think his being dead changes anything."

Nick let it hang for a moment, figured he still had some work to do.

"You certainly have the right to do that, Dr. Gimmelman, and I wouldn't advise against it, but if you're not comfortable letting us see the file, we'll have to subpoena you as a witness and you'll have to come in and testify before the grand jury. You'd be there when court opens in the morning, you'd have to wait till it's your turn on the stand, then hang around in case you need to be recalled. It could end up wasting two or three days of your valuable time. Wouldn't it be more efficient if you sent us the file?"

Gimmelman gave a long, exasperated sigh that sounded more like a growl. Then he said, "Yeah, I guess it would. I'll courier it to your office this afternoon."

Nick had almost finished writing up the evidence, but there were a number of factual details he had to check. He unlocked the bottom drawer of his desk and rummaged among the miscellaneous papers he'd stashed there. As he did, he uncovered something he had forgotten. It was the autograph album he'd taken from the compartment in the wainscoting at the Charles Street apartment. He lifted the heavy nine-by-twelve scrapbook out and laid it on top of his desk.

The first thing he noticed was that there was nothing on the cover, no title, no information of any kind. He opened it to the first vellum page and began to study its contents.

Most of the autographs were undecipherable, but several of those that could be read were names he knew he'd heard before, though he couldn't place them. Except for the last one in the book. It was both legible and familiar.

70

It took Vanessa a little over an hour to drive from Greenwich to the New York Port Authority in Manhattan. She was shuttled from office to office until she found herself in a large, dingy room crammed with filing cabinets, two desks and a metal packing table separated from the entrance area by a counter. She reached over and hit the plunger of the chrome handbell.

After a while, a gaunt old man with a bony face and a shock of steel-grey hair came shambling out from behind a row of library stacks stuffed with dusty file folders and old boxes. He was not happy to see her. He was even less happy when she began to ask questions about his files.

"Who the fuck are you, anyway?"

Vanessa smiled. "I represent a group who would like to donate a substantial amount of money to the Longshoreman's Association."

The man's thin, creased face was still suspicious, teetering on the brink of a smile when he asked, "Just what do you mean by substantial?"

She pulled an envelope containing five one-hundred-dollar bills from her purse and handed it to him. He counted it quickly, his eyes a little wild, and slipped the envelope into his work-shirt pocket.

"'preciate it. Now what do you want? I'm a busy man, ya know."

Vanessa explained what she was looking for and the old seaman disappeared around a corner among the stacks and filing cabinets. A short time later he returned with a sheaf of papers, which he laid out on the counter.

Vanessa studied them carefully and shook her head.

"This doesn't make sense," she said in a thoughtful whisper. Ken couldn't have signed this three weeks ago on a Friday. He took me out to the Russian Tea Room for blinis and caviar. We spent three hours eating from the zakouski and drinking vodka.

She asked the old-timer if the dates and times on the bills were accurate. "Bet your life. They're all fucking-A-correct. We're not stupid, ya know."

It was obvious the cranky old salt enjoyed pissing people off. But it had the opposite effect on Vanessa, who laughed out loud. Her burst of merriment caught the old man off guard and he started to laugh too. She saw the opening and took it.

"Let me ask you one more question."

The old man shrugged his shoulders, his thin crack of a mouth still curved in a smile. "Who was on duty when these bills were signed?"

"Anything that big would have been checked by Bill Higgins on days and Andy Sciorra on the graveyard shift."

Vanessa asked for their phone numbers, but the old man stiffened up again. He was adamant. It was against policy to give out the phone numbers of Port Authority personnel.

Vanessa offered him a hundred-dollar bill, then another when he didn't respond. His left eye crinkled up while he considered the moral complexities. After about five seconds, he nodded.

"Okay," he said, reaching for the money, "I can't give you Bill's number but I can tell you he lives in White Oaks."

Vanessa used the cellphone in the Jaguar XKE to call Inspector William Higgins. When she told him who she was, he said, "I was very sorry to hear about your husband, Mrs. Lang. He was a very important individual but he never put on airs and I liked him. But why are you calling now? What I mean is, I contacted the police three times. No one responded and when I phoned again, I was referred to somebody by the name of O'Hare. He said the case had been taken over by the Feds and it was closed."

"I see. Well, I'm trying to get it reopened. Would it be all right if I came by for a chat?"

"Sure. You come over anytime. It's my day off."

Bill Higgins came to the door carrying a can of Budweiser. He was a large man, with a square, open face and an easy manner. He was wearing a plaid shirt and an old pair of jeans.

"Come in, come in. Can I get you something?"

Vanessa asked for a soft drink and when they were settled around the coffee table in the sunken living room, she said, "Mr. Higgins…"

He waved his hand back and forth, shook his head. "Please, just call me Bill."

"Okay. Bill. What was it you wanted to tell the police?"

"I was pretty sure the man who came in to sign for that shipment to Africa wasn't really your husband. He looked like him all right, and at first I didn't pay much attention, but he seemed different, I mean, the way he acted."

Higgins paused, took a pull from his Bud.

"You see, over the years I sort of got to know Mr. Lang. I don't mean socially or anything, I just got to recognize his walk, how he spoke, his humour and generally how he handled himself. He'd always say a few words, ya know, pass the time of day, very relaxed, but this guy hardly says a thing, just a grunt for a hello and instead of talking he uses hand gestures and a lot of head moves. He's with someone else from L&B, his partner, I think, but they don't communicate much and when we go outside to check on the shipment, he's walking in front of me up the stairs to the loading platform, and I see something that convinces me I'm right. This joker is not Kenneth Lang."

"What did you see?"

Higgins was getting excited as he recalled the details. His voice rose and he nearly shouted, "Elevator shoes!" He paused, a slightly stunned expression on his flushed features. "Pardon my French, but there's no fuckin' way that guy was Mr. Lang."

Detective Cortese had told her that he suspected Duplessis was hired to impersonate her husband. He was right and it looked like Higgins could prove it.

"I wonder if you'd be willing to testify to that in court?"

"You're damn tootin', Mrs. Lang."

She smiled and held out her hand.

"Please, just call me Vanessa."

71

Nick filled out the application for Line of Duty Injury leave and signed it. It didn't look like his signature because the knife wound on the heel of his right hand was swollen, throbbing and heavily bandaged, but it would have to do. Now he'd have to get Baxter Chase to approve it.

Chase looked up when Nick knocked on his open office door.

"Oh, Cortese. Good. I wanted to talk to you about these reports you just filed."

Nick didn't like what he heard in the captain's voice. It sounded like reprimand and interrogation. It annoyed him. "What about them? You find a spelling error?"

"Sit down, Cortese."

Nick came into the office and stood in front of the desk. He did not sit down.

Baxter stood up and barked at him. He was almost half a foot shorter than Nick and he looked like an agitated terrier yapping at a Great Dane.

"I said sit the fuck down, that's an order."

This wasn't going well at all and Nick really wanted that LoDI leave. There were things he had to do and he needed some free time. He raised both hands as well as he could, given the splint, in a gesture of surrender. Then he took a seat and waited.

Baxter sat down too and pointed at the report on his desk.

"Says here one of the people who was killed at the supply yard was DHS."

"That's what she said."

Chase bristled. "She was Agent Angela Sommers. She identified herself as DHS, and you shot her."

Nick shook his head.

"Read it again. She lied, said we were designated enemy combatants and she never showed any ID. Said she had the authority to execute me if I didn't order the other members of my crew to disarm and show themselves, but we'd been ambushed and fired on. Several of my men were wounded, one of them severely. My best read was that they had attempted to kill us and she was going to finish the job."

"So, you shot her without asking for confirmation of her status."

"Malone shot her. Her status was armed assailant threatening a police officer and the men in his command. She had come in with the rest of that Blackwater mob. DHS or not, she was one of them, and none of them said who they were or what the hell they wanted. They just started shooting. Even if she *was* DHS, which I doubt, she waited way too long to say so. She might just as well have claimed to be the president or the chief of police. Nothing she said at that point was credible."

Chase nodded, closed the file and put it aside.

"This is not over. We've sent copies to all the appropriate agencies. If they confirm that she was DHS, you and the others will be interviewed and your actions investigated. Now, what did you come in to see me about?"

"I'm putting in for an LoDI leave." He handed Chase the application. Chase read it and shook his head.

"I can't sign this, Cortese."

"Why the hell not? I've got a bullet hole in my left arm and a knife wound in this hand." He held up the bandage that had begun to seep blood and needed to be changed.

"I can see that, for chrissake. It's not the injury part I have problems with. You had the afternoon off, you were on your own time. What the hell were you doing up there, anyway?"

"We were casing out that warehouse where Altieri was killed."

"What for? It was declared a righteous shoot."

"Donovan lied, pulled strings. I think I have enough to file an appeal."

"You think, but you don't know for sure?"

"Not yet. That's one reason I need some time."

"What's the other reason?"

"You don't want to know."

"Yeah, I do, so just spit it out."

"You told me there was no case, but there is."

Nick told him about the files they'd recovered from the Lang & Baine mainframe, the CIA, Department of Defense and Homeland Security involvement in the plot to depose the President of Mawabi and Baine's scheme to take control of the world's wheat. Baxter Chase looked like he'd just been poleaxed.

"Jesus!" he said. "And that's why you were ambushed by private security contractors?"

"Mercenaries, yes. Blackwater, then Xe, then Academi. But these goons were freelancing, probably recommended by the Feds but paid by Baine."

"I told you to stay the fuck off it. You could've been killed. They the same crew who kidnapped your daughter?"

"Yeah, they wanted a tape Rhea Carson found in a safe deposit box and gave to me. When the kidnapping failed, they killed Rhea and set me up for her murder."

Chase nodded. "You have to understand, I had my orders, from the chief of police, the mayor, the governor of New York. And that's the way things work here. I deferred to the Feds, I told you what came down from upstairs, I ordered you off the case because everything had already been turned over to federal jurisdiction. There was nothing I could do. I just got on with my job. But this is un-fucking-believable. A mercenary force shooting up detectives under my command? How does shit like that happen?"

"I dunno. But it did. And they're not gonna walk."

Chase laughed, a snort of dark humour. "Guess a lot of 'em won't do much walking now, you put their lights out."

"Yeah, but the big kahuna's in the wind and I'm gonna nail him. We've got some help from Washington, Senator Alvin Tillis, so maybe it will get done."

"We. Who's we?"

"Vanessa Lang. She's the one who shot that Blackwater thug, Noireau. He's probably the one who killed her husband. And there's one more thing—Officer Finch, he's a mole for Homeland Security. Don't know how they recruited him, but I'd suggest keeping an eye on the little weasel."

"Will do."

Chase looked like he was about to say something else, then he picked up the leave application and looked at it hard.

"I still can't sign this. What I will do, though, is send it upstairs. The borough chief will have to make the decision, and that's Jen Hendricks. She's got a lot more flex with technicalities than I do. In the meantime, take a few days off. It bothers me to have to say this, Cortese, but it's true. You've earned them."

When Nick got back to the squad room, Malone was downloading the digital photos from the Pentax onto his computer and he called Nick over to look at them.

"These are great, Chaz, exactly what we need. All five of the SWAT team positions you shot from had a clear view of the warehouse roof and the vent where Buzz and I entered the building. Now let's hope that loading zone security camera caught us going in, and that the tape hasn't been erased. It's been a long time since the shooting."

"Most of 'em get up to ninety days and that should do it. Want me to track that down?"

"No, I'll do it. Chase kicked me loose for a few days but you're still on the job, and he won't sign LoDI leave apps for any of us, says we weren't on duty when we got shot. I was on my own time and the rest of you weren't pursuing the cases you'd been assigned."

"What a prick!"

"Yeah, that's what I thought, but if you and the others submit the forms, he says he'll send them up to Hendricks and let her decide. I guess Corbie was right, as usual."

Malone looked confused.

"About what?"

"About Chase, said he was a rule-book desk jockey, but an all right guy under the bullshit."

72

Tri-State Transfer and Cartage handled, warehoused and transported a wide range of products, from individual packages to autos and heavy machinery. Their clientele was centred in New York, New Jersey and Pennsylvania, but also included Connecticut and other states both west and south. Though the five-storey building across from the warehouse looked like an abandoned factory, a short internet surf revealed that Tri-State was a complex, busy operation, and Nick decided the best approach was to visit the place in person rather than play phone tag with a voicemail network.

He parked on Kingsbridge Road, as he had done the day before, and walked around the block looking for the entrance. There didn't seem to be one, so he went around back and climbed up onto the loading dock that ran across the entire width of the building. There were crews loading and unloading half a dozen semis and they all pretended he wasn't there till he flashed his badge. One of the men pointed to a door near the end of the platform.

The first floor was an open warehouse with flimsy plywood partitions along one wall that only reached halfway up to the ceiling. They'd been painted white a long time ago and never cleaned since. He walked over and knocked on one of the open doors. A young woman in blue jeans and a white blouse looked up from a pile of manila folders and raised her eyebrows in a way that said, *who are you and what are you doing here?* Nick smiled.

"Hi. Wonder if you can help me. I'm Detective Cortese, NYPD. Who do I talk to about your surveillance installation?"

"Oh, that would be Todd, Todd Jaworski, I'll see if I can find him." She smiled back and picked up the phone. Buttons were punched, lights flashed and blinked, and the frown over her eyes deepened as she tried to track him down. Then the frown disappeared; she spoke briefly before she hung up and turned back to Nick.

"Todd's kind of our utility infielder, you never know where he's at, but he's always fixing something. He'll be by in a minute or two."

She went back to her manila folders and Nick stepped outside to wait. The place was huge, took up almost an entire New York city block, and the rate at which materials were entering or leaving it was impressive. Todd came out from a narrow corridor between stacked crates, and held out his hand. His body language communicated a cheerful exuberance. He was probably in his mid-thirties, but he looked like a kid, blond and skinny, his blue eyes on full alert.

"I'm Jaworski. Let's grab a coffee."

Nick followed him to a small room with a coffee machine, Styrofoam cups, a large container of nondairy creamer, packets of sugar and white plastic spoons. There was no place to sit, so they stood, leaning against the outside wall. Nick spoke first.

"I have some questions about your security camera, the one that overlooks the loading zone. First of all, is it working? It looks a little the worse for wear."

Jaworski laughed. "Yeah, like most everything else around here. Not slick and trim, but it gets the job done."

"And how long do you keep the tapes?"

"We don't use VCRs any more so we don't have tapes, but our data logs usually run for about six months before we reset them. Christy said you're a detective?"

"That's right. NYPD."

"So, is this still about the break-in?

"Break-in?"

"Yeah, eight, ten days ago. They chloroformed the night watchman and boosted a whole shipment of cigarettes. But we already sent the pictures to the B&E squad at the 49th."

Nick felt his pulse do a flip. The 49th was Donovan's precinct. If they started scanning the surveillance and discovered shots of him and Altieri entering the warehouse...

"Will they send that stuff back when they're through with it?" Jaworski asked.

"No way, they keep it, in case arrests are made and the DA needs it when she goes to trial."

Nick tried to think of a way he could get into the evidence room at the 49th. There was an officer he had worked with during his stint in Operations, but he didn't know the man that well and hadn't done any big favours he could call in. He might try asking for the pics in connection with the firefight at the supply yard, but that was pretty thin. He'd already included the licence plate of the semi in his report, and he didn't need to ID the assailants—they were all dead. He thought hard but couldn't come up with anything the camera might have caught that would be relevant. There was one more possibility. It was a long shot, but it was all he had left.

"Guess I could go over and check it out with Donovan, but, uh, you wouldn't have kept a copy here, you know, for the company archives?"

"Well, actually, you know it's digital, right?"

Nick nodded.

"So, it doesn't get erased when we send it over to their computer."

"You mean you still have a copy here?"

Jaworski smiled. "That's what I said, yes."

"Good, and you also said there's a six-month data log."

"Correct."

"If I give you a date and approximate time, do you think you could find the stills I need and copy them for me?"

"No problem. Everything that comes off the camera is date stamped. Just give me a few minutes to set up the scan."

They walked across to a small office on the other side of the large room and Jaworski sat down at a desk with a computer keyboard and a large monitor. Nick gave him the information and he typed it in. The machine clicked and whirred for several seconds, then a screen came up with the first grainy black-and-white photo. The camera shot a still every six seconds so the sequence was quick and jerky, but the warehouse roof was clearly visible near the top of the screen. The photos whizzed by and nothing came up but the empty roof.

Nick wondered if he'd been wrong about the time. Could have it been later? Earlier? Maybe the date was wrong, but he had checked it carefully before he left the precinct. He felt a mounting tension in his chest and shoulders and when he saw Altieri's head and shoulders appear above the edge of the low wall that surrounded the roof he almost yelled, "Stop there, that's it!"

Jaworski backed up and set the scan to run one frame at a time, Buzz coming onto the roof, then Nick, then Buzz opening his Swiss army knife, removing the air vent, climbing into it, and Nick climbing in after him.

73

The Honourable Brian Cullen Williams was hard at work on a stack of trial motions when Nick entered his chambers. He was a small man, with fuzzy hair and a short, cropped beard. His eyes were dark, but lively with a keen intelligence. He closed the manila folder and the yellow notepad he'd been writing on. His smile suggested that he was not all that unhappy to be interrupted.

"Afternoon, Nicola, come in, have a seat. Can I get you something?"

"No, Your Honour, I'm fine, thank you."

"Very good, then let's get started. From what you told me on the phone, there's a good chance you've got enough to support a warrant. I'd like to see your documentation."

Nick opened the package he'd brought and took out the evidence he'd collected, one piece at a time. He tried to keep his descriptions short but realized they also had to be clear and relevant.

"This may take a while, but please interrupt with any questions you may have."

"Okay," the judge said. "For starters, have you discussed the case with the D.A.?"

"With her assistant, yes, and she suggested I come to you."

"Fast tracking. All right, continue."

"This is a transcript of a tape that was recorded by a homicide victim, Malcom Duplessis. He wore a wire while he was being hired to impersonate someone. Unfortunately the tape is damaged and we don't know who that someone is. It also refers to another skill he was being hired to utilize, but that's not made explicit either."

"That's not even proof of a misdemeanour, and you say people were threatened and even kidnapped to recover it? Kind of ironic, isn't it?"

"Sure is, and the attempts to recover it were seriously counter-productive. They called attention to things that should have been left in the shadows."

"I expect you've got more. Has the other voice on the tap been identified?"

"It was Jeremy Baine, junior partner of the agro-giant Lang & Baine."

"And has this been confirmed?"

"We compared it to an interview he did for CNN. It was a perfect match." Nick removed another document and an eight-by-ten sketch of a face.

"We have an affidavit from Inspector William Higgins at Port Authority. He will testify that the man who accompanied Jeremy Baine, represented himself as Kenneth Lang and signed papers that authorized the shipment of nerve gas to Chad, was in fact not Kenneth Lang."

"What does he offer in proof of that assertion?"

"The man was four inches shorter than Lang but was wearing elevator shoes."

The judge picked up on it right away. "Duplessis, and the other skill was forgery."

"Exactly. And this sketch is what Duplessis brought to the plastic surgeon as a model of how he wanted to look. It's a sketch of Kenneth Lang."

"Do you have expert evaluations of the signatures on those shipping papers?"

"No, not yet, but there's corroborating evidence." Nick brought out another sheaf of papers. "This is a photocopy of what I thought was an autograph album. I recovered it from a compartment hidden in the wainscoting of the apartment on Charles Street." He turned to the last page. "When I saw this I realized that the book wasn't a collection of autographs, but an archive documenting Duplessis's expertise. The final entry is the signature of Kenneth Lang, and though it hasn't been analyzed yet, I'm certain it's a forgery."

"Do you have a money trail, any transfer of funds or securities, to substantiate the relationship between Duplessis and Baine?"

"It's not a slam dunk, but Duplessis had $645,000 in L&B bearer bonds in a safe deposit box. Of course, they could just be something he bought as an investment, and there's no record of a transfer from anyone else, but the circumstance is damaging."

Judge Williams nodded. "Anything else?"

"Well, we believe Baine hired the men who killed Kenneth Lang and the security guard at L&B's office building on Fifth Avenue."

Nick went on to explain Operation Stealth Seed and Baine's connection to federal agencies that were interested in deposing Mawabi's president, Kamoro Baku.

"We also believe DHS and the CIA put Baine in touch with the team of ex-Blackwater contractors who kidnapped my daughter, attacked my squad and mounted the assault at the Cherokee."

"But there's no hard evidence to support these allegations?"

"No, Your Honour, but we'd like to make an arrest anyway, if you think we have sufficient cause."

"I do. Conspiracy to commit identity theft under article 190.80 and forgery under 170.10. They're both Class D felonies."

Judge Williams took a form out of his desk, filled it out and signed it. He folded it, slipped it into an envelope with the court's logo on the front and held it out. "This will authorize the arrest. Good luck with the rest of your case and I'd appreciate it if you'll keep me informed of your progress."

"I will, Your Honour, and thanks for expediting the warrant."

As he came out through the tall columns of the Supreme Court Building into the sun and walked down the marble steps, the brief sense of accomplishment he'd felt in Judge Williams' chambers began to fade. He would arrest Jeremy Baine, but though the charges against him were serious, they were trivial compared to the crimes the man had committed, the harm he had done, the lives he had destroyed.

74

Lang & Baine was housed in a building of sheer white stone with windows like smoky X-ray film. It swept gracefully back from the street and up twenty-eight storeys. Nick stood before the thick, tinted glass of the automatic door, waited while it opened with a smooth hiss, and started walking across the spacious foyer with its trees and shrubs and fountains. It was impressive, but the air of tasteful affluence was marred by a large sign that instructed all who entered to report to the security desk to confirm appointments or show company IDs.

The uniformed guard was engrossed by what he saw on the computer screen and as Nick approached he held up one hand as though stopping traffic but did not look up. He was young, beefy and wore no hat over his blond buzz cut. Nick watched him for nearly a minute, then he yelled, "Yo, dude, hands in the air!" The look on the guard's face changed from annoyance to alarm as he turned from his laptop and saw Nick's NYPD badge held up to his face.

"Oh, excuse me, officer. Sorry to keep you waiting."

"It's detective and I'm here to see Jeremy Baine."

"Very good, sir. I assume you have an appointment."

Nick wanted to say, *don't need one, I have a warrant to arrest the sonofabitch,* but he'd already caused enough ill will with this guardian of corporate well-being and shook his head instead. "No, I'm sorry to say, I don't, but it is an urgent matter that may seriously affect Mr. Baine's future."

Dude looked skeptical and he scanned Nick's face for some clue as to what he was really doing there and how he should represent this upstairs. "Please be seated in the waiting area. I'll find out if Mr. Baine can see you."

He indicated an area beyond the fountain where black leather chairs were casually arranged around ebony coffee tables on which magazines and what looked like picture books of New York were placed. Nick stayed where he was while the guard dialed, punched a button, and spoke into the phone while keeping his eyes on Nick. After several exchanges, he nodded and hung up.

"I'm sorry, sir, but Mr. Baine is not available."

"And why is that, has he broken out in a rash or, no, don't tell me, he's in an important meeting, with, uh, the governor, or maybe a Saudi sheik?"

Dude was quickly losing his cool. His eyes hardened and his mouth looked like he'd just tasted something unpleasant.

"Mr. Baine is not in his office."

"Where is he then?"

"I'm sure I don't know."

"Fair enough. Just tell me how he can be reached."

"I'm afraid Mr. Baine did not leave a number."

"But you do know where he lives. Please give me his home address."

"I don't know where he lives and I certainly don't have his home phone number."

Nick felt his pulse speed up a bit. He decided to push it. He took the envelope with the Supreme Court of New York logo on the front out of his jacket pocket.

"This is a warrant for his arrest. If you continue to withhold information, I can arrest you for obstructing an officer in the pursuit of a felon. You will go to jail, dude, so tell me where the fuck he lives."

Dude finally began to look uncomfortable. His eyes darted around as if checking for someplace to hide or hoping for the sudden appearance of the cavalry. He spoke quickly and his voice had gone up a notch. "It's probably on the computer somewhere, but I'm not authorized to give out that information."

"Who is authorized?"

"I don't know, but I can call admin and put you in touch with our legal department."

Nick shook his head in disgust. He'd talked to lawyers before, more times than he cared to count, and he knew it was useless. Then he remembered something. He left the guard with his mouth half open and sauntered over to the waiting area. He sat in one of the very plush leather chairs and opened his cell.

She picked up on the second ring.

"Nicola, I'm so glad you called. I've been trying to reach you."

Nick felt a twinge of guilt.

"Sorry, Vanessa, I turned my phone off so as not to be interrupted hours ago and forgot to turn it back on. What's up?"

"Senator Tillis called. He's flying up to see me later this afternoon. If you're free, I'd like you to be here."

"Wow, that was fast."

"I know. It surprised me too, but I'm not sure what to make of it."

"Guess we'll just have to wait and see. What time will he get here?"

"Pretty soon now, around four."

"Okay, I'll leave right away. If I can beat the rush it should take a bit more than an hour."

He wondered if he ought to tell her about the warrant but decided not to. If Tillis had managed to get the attorney general on board, it would be irrelevant anyway.

75

Senator Alvin Tillis was almost as tall as Nick, a classically handsome man in his early sixties who looked a lot younger. Without waiting for an introduction, he moved across the veranda with the easy grace of a tennis player and held out his hand. His blue-grey eyes were intense and alert.

"You must be Detective Cortese. I'm glad you're here."

He wore a grey suit, white shirt, blue tie and looked every bit the senior senator, except for his hands. They were huge, rawboned, and his grip was the grip of a man who had spent much of his life working oil rigs throughout the southwest.

He looked away almost immediately and rubbed the back of his neck. He gestured toward the bar and smiled at Vanessa. "Mind if I help myself?"

She smiled back. "*Mi casa es tu casa.*"

He went over and poured himself a good shot of Jack Daniel's. "Anyone else?"

Nick was beginning to feel restless, impatient. He needed to know what was happening in Washington. Tillis wasn't being evasive, exactly, but he was clearly uncomfortable and this was not a good sign. On the other hand, he was not a man who could be rushed. Nick raised his hand as though he were a boy in school and immediately felt foolish.

"Glenfiddich."

That seemed to relax Tillis, who poured the drink and handed it across. Then they moved to the other side of the shaded porch and sat around a wicker coffee table. For a while no one said anything, then

Tillis cleared his throat and began to speak in a halting voice, choosing his words carefully.

"I should begin by emphasizing that no final decisions have yet been made, so what I'm about to tell you should be taken as a report on a work in progress." He paused, took a sip of whisky.

Nick said, "Doesn't sound like good news, Senator."

"Well, it's not so bad to not too good, then it goes to infuriating."

Vanessa filled the short silence, her voice a mix of encouragement and perplexity. "When we spoke on the phone you said you had briefed your contacts at the CIA, DHS, the NSA, DOD and the attorney general. I was surprised it didn't take much longer."

Tillis laughed. It was not a happy sound. "As you know, I'm chairman of the Intelligence Oversight Committee, also Foreign Relations. I consult with those agencies almost daily, so it wasn't difficult to arrange meetings. What was difficult, and what may prove to be impossible, was to weave through Washington politspeak and get a straight answer."

Nick wanted to cut to the chase, but he knew it was necessary to hear every bit of information Tillis could give him. He nodded and waited for the senator to continue.

"I brought the files you sent to my liaison at the CIA. My sense was, is, that he didn't have prior knowledge of Operation Stealth Seed, but also that it didn't surprise or worry him very much. The CIA has been interfering with foreign regimes for half a century. In spite of their name, their hidden but inadmissible mandate goes way beyond gathering information.

"There are layers and layers of special designations, black ops, paramilitary interventions, targeted assassinations, black flag attacks on friendly forces, and everything they do that violates international law or the platitudes of the USA as the champion of freedom is protected by fiercely maintained strategies of deniability. Rydell, head of the African desk, will receive what amounts to a slap on the wrist, but only because Baine sabotaged a British firm and MI6 was extremely displeased that they were kept out of the loop. If he'd gotten Baku out and Loyuba back in, Rydell would have been kicked up to deputy."

Nick expected something like that but there must have been a connection between the CIA and the security contractors Baine hired to do his dirty work.

"Will Rydell testify that he put Baine in touch with Blackwater?"

Tillis shrugged. "He might be persuaded to say he recommended them, but it wouldn't do much good. He claims he has no knowledge of what he calls 'Baine's domestic operations.'"

"What about Homeland Security? They kidnapped my daughter and one of their agents was with the group that ambushed and tried to kill me and my squad of detectives."

"Ah, DHS. They pretty much do what they want, and they're even more cloaked in secrecy than the CIA."

"But we know who the agents were—O'Hare and Sommers. I saw their IDs."

Tillis shook his head and sighed. "No such people exist, or have ever existed, were never born, never died and have no paper."

"They scrubbed their computer files."

"Right. Also city halls, hospitals, schools, universities, the U.S. armed forces and any other public or private record on which those names might have appeared. Hard to believe they could do that, but it looks like they can, and they did. But, of course, we'll never be able to prove it."

Nick was beginning to feel his pulse race. He got up from the wicker chair and paced back and forth as he spoke.

"The Defense Intelligence Agency came into the Sixth Precinct and collected all the evidence on the Lang/Tomlinson and Duplessis/Ramirez homicides. Surely there is some record of that and some way to get those materials back."

"DIA says they were just clarifying jurisdictional boundaries. I did manage to have a quick peek at what they've got and it looks to me like some strategic pieces have been either lost or misplaced. One thing I did notice was that Tomlinson, the L&B security guard, was killed with an M-NP16 and Kenneth took two slugs from an FNP-45, the newly issued army handgun.

There's no way the shooters were Mawabian terrorists."

"It was probably the Blackwater crew. We've identified their leader as one Clay Noireau, ex-Marine, special forces, who went freelance after his tour as a contractor in Iraq.

"Unfortunately, he's dead, and so are the others he worked with, so we won't be able to turn them. That brings us to the attorney general and the DOJ. Have you been able to establish any financial connection between Jeremy Baine and the Blackwater contractors? Anything? Fingerprints on dollar bills, stock transfers, deposits in overseas accounts, anything at all?"

Nick shook his head, slumped back into the wicker armchair. "We found Lang & Baine bearer bonds valued at $645,000 in a Duplessis safe deposit box, but no proof they were given to him by Baine. The connection is obvious, but even though it's irrefutably logical, it's not proof in a court of law."

Tillis nodded, looked thoughtful. "The attorney general is the only one I talked to who doesn't want this to just go away. He's keen to mount a case, but doesn't think he's got enough for an indictment, at least not yet."

"What about the Stealth Seed files?"

"He thought they were obtained illegally and would never be admitted into evidence."

Vanessa shook her head. "No, they weren't. As the major shareholder in L&B, which is Sarbitt's parent company, I had every right to those files."

Tillis brightened. "Of course, I should have known that. But I'm not sure it will make a difference."

"Why not, Alvin? Sabotaging a foreign company's wheat crop, then offering to take over their World Bank contract which Baine bid on but lost? Isn't that international fraud?"

"Sure, but that's the problem. It's not a crime that was committed on American soil or against an American victim, so it's moot. The

Brits are looking into it, but I doubt they will follow through. And Mawabi's already arrested Tumulu but they have no jurisdictional authority to go after Baine."

Vanessa's face had gone very pale and her voice shook with controlled anger. "I don't believe this. Are you telling us the trash who killed Kenneth will be allowed to go free?"

Tillis rose from his chair, came over to where she was sitting, leaned over and touched her on the shoulder. He looked directly into her eyes, then stood up, stiff with both frustration and an iron resolve.

"No, Vanessa, it's not over by any means. We've got forensic accountants digging into Jeremy's finances, we're checking phone records, we're searching his house, his office, Noireau's apartment and the rooms they rented all over town. We'll find something, and we'll nail the bastard. But it will take time, maybe a lot, and there's nothing more we can do right now." As he spoke Tillis looked less and less sure of himself and his voice trailed off.

"Maybe not." Nick was on his feet again. "I've got an arrest warrant for Jeremy Baine. Conspiracy to commit identity theft and forgery. That should hold the slippery little prick until we can charge him with kidnapping and murder in the first degree."

Nick thought the news about the warrant would restore some of the senator's enthusiasm, but Tillis seemed to shrink as he slumped back into his chair with a sigh of exasperation.

"That won't do it, Nicola. He's left the country and a New York warrant on those charges won't be strong enough to bring him back with an extradition request."

"Where is he?"

"He's at his fly-in hunting lodge in Canada. Shooting defenceless animals. I guess. But we can't go get him, and the only way your warrant can be served is if he comes back to New York voluntarily."

"Why doesn't he just disappear somewhere in Asia or South America or the Middle East?"

"I dunno. He probably thinks he's still protected by the Feds and is just waiting for this minor inconvenience to blow over."

There was a long silence, then Nick said, "I think I see a way out of this. What's your status with Sarbitt, Vanessa?"

"I'm the major shareholder."

"Good. I need you to get me something."

"My Sarbitt is your Sarbitt, Nicola."

He opened his cell and dialed a number. A woman's voice answered.

"This is Nicola Cortese. I'd like to speak with Mo Zimmerman."

76

The immigration official looked up from the passport. His voice was polite but had an authoritative edge to it. "Please remove your sunglasses, Mr. Peibach." He glanced down at the photo, then up again, and the small frown disappeared from his forehead. "And what is the purpose of your visit?"

"Pleasure, a fishing trip."

He stamped the passport and handed it back.

"Welcome to Canada, Mr. Peibach. Enjoy your stay."

At customs they looked through his backpack, but he had no checked luggage, so he walked past the carousels and into the arrivals area. A man dressed in jeans, a plaid shirt and a baseball cap held up a sign with his name on it, printed, not handwritten. For some reason he took this as a good omen, an indication, perhaps, of professional efficiency. When he made a gesture of acknowledgment, the man held out his hand.

"Russell Connor, I'm your driver."

They shook hands and walked out of the airport through a door with a sign above it that said Ground Transportation. The van was parked in the loading zone to the right of a line of taxicabs and limos. It was white, with Sunset Lodge, Red Lake painted on the side. The bottom half was covered with dust.

Russell lifted the tailgate, stashed the backpack, then came around and opened the front passenger door.

"The seat goes all the way back, so you can take a nap if you like. We'll be on the road for several hours."

"Thank you, but I wonder if we could make a stop first, at Winnipeg Outfitters?"

"Sure, no problem, but you know we supply all the gear you'll need—rods, reels, lures, boat and motor?"

"Understood. But I want to fish downriver and do some whitewater rafting. I don't think a sixteen-foot aluminum Lund would handle it."

"Well, you're right about that. And we don't have inflatables at the lodge, but we can offer you the use of an air hose at the marina. You'll need a motor, too, unless you want to return with the boat on your back."

At Winnipeg Outfitters he purchased a ten-foot Zodiac, a 9.9-horsepower Honda 4-stroke short shaft outboard, a motor tank with hose, a twenty-litre jerry can, a nine-inch hunting knife with sheath, a boreal forest survival kit, a mini-flashlight and a PD Model 190B breech-loading pistol.

The Trans-Canada Highway east was a very straight road that shimmered with reflected light and seemed to melt into heat waves at the horizon. The van hummed along at 140 klicks, and an hour-and-a-half later, just as they were approaching a bridge that crossed the Birch River, they slowed and pulled into a gas bar that was also a general store and a diner.

They ate fresh pickerel fillets fried in butter, baked potatoes, green beans and a tossed salad, with apple pie and coffee for dessert.

After that the landscape changed, from ancient lake bottom prairie, fields of grain, soybeans, flax and canola, to the aspen evergreen forest and granite outcrops of the Canadian Shield. It was cooler among the trees on the hilly, curving blacktop as they entered Ontario and the flittering mix of sun and shade through the trees was nearly hypnotic. They drove on Highway 17 fifty miles past Kenora, then turned north on 105. There was more and more a sense of wilderness as they passed through Perrault Falls, Goldpines and Balmertown. After that a gravel road brought them to a parking lot and small marina where they loaded Nick's luggage into an aluminum boat and set out across the lake in a breeze scented with pines and the occasional spray of fresh water that blew back from the wake.

Cabin three had a single bed, a small kitchen–living room area with a wood-burning stove and was finished, both walls and ceilings, in knotty pine. It wasn't the Sheraton, but it would do, it would do very nicely.

He unpacked the laptop and used the password Russell had given him to get on the internet. His Galaxy Maps toolbar responded slowly but brought up Northwestern Ontario in detail, one square at a time. He had no intention of fishing downstream, or anywhere else for that matter, but he needed to verify the route he would take on his expedition into Rathouse Lake and record the exact distances on his smartphone.

The next thing he had to decide was timing. He wanted to get to his destination early in the a.m. Or just before the evening meal. But he had no previous experience of the terrain and it was impossible to make more than a wild guess about how long the trip would take. An early morning arrival would require him to leave after sunset and travel almost all the way with a flashlight in the dark or get where he was going before dark and sleep in the woods overnight.

Not the most appealing option. He walked to the screen door and looked out over the grounds. Light on the water told him it was already mid-afternoon. He felt a strong urge to leave right away, but after thinking about it, he decided to wait until morning.

The sun had just edged up over the horizon as he inflated the Zodiac with the air hose at the marina, then filled the motor tank and jerry can with gas. He hooked the tank to the motor and attached the motor to the motor mount on the boat. As a precaution, he unwrapped the oarlocks, installed them securely and laid the telescope oars within easy reach. He had breakfast in the dining room and asked them to make up a box lunch.

Back at the cabin he spent half an hour studying his route, rehearsing it over and over till he had it memorized. He had no idea what it actually looked like, but he had detailed topographical maps of the area and if he could get a signal, he could always locate himself using his smartphone's GPS.

He loaded his gear, started the outboard and pulled out into Red Lake. The lodge was situated in a small cove with a curved point of land to the northeast. The first thing he had to do was get around that point and navigate between McKenzie Island and the east shore. The weather was clear and it took him less than an hour to reach the opening where the north end of the island came within fifty feet of the shoreline. He throttled back and steered slowly through the deepest part of the channel, then changed his heading to northwest, passed Gentles Island on the left and came to a stretch of open water. This was where he had to turn hard right, hug the shore and make his way through a long narrow passage that opened into a large bay.

There were rocks and dead heads in the water and he picked his way carefully around them until the Zodiac was clear. He was now in a part of the lake populated by dozens of islands and he tried to negotiate a path that would take him through them while continuing to travel north. The stream that led into the Little Vermillion chain of lakes was at the northwest corner of the bay, but when he came through to a wide stretch of water, crossed it and approached the shoreline, the stream wasn't there. He'd become disoriented navigating the maze of islands. He was lost.

He cut the motor, drifted close to shore and took out his topographical map of Red Lake. After studying it for several minutes he realized that a map is useless unless you know where you are, and he did not. He checked his smartphone. The GPS would show him where he was located on the map, and it would be a simple matter to find the stream because he knew he was close. But when he tried to access the internet, he was unable to get a signal.

77

For a moment he felt the onset of an anxiety attack. It began to blow his mind around, but he did a taekwondo breathing exercise until he was centred again and could assess the problem. He couldn't locate himself on the map, so that was his first priority. It was a bit like looking for a lost key. Where was the last time…? He restarted the Honda. He would follow the shore all the way around east and south, back to where the channel had opened into the bay. That was the last place he would recognize, and once he got located on the map he could chart a better course to the stream that led to Vermillion Lake.

It took him half an hour to get back to the island where the channel came into the bay. He turned off the motor, pulled the boat up onto a thin beach and looked at the map again. What he needed was a landmark that could help him locate the stream he had missed on the last run. If he hugged the western shore it would take him north and then east again, and as he traced this route with his fingernail, he found it—a small cove less than a kilometre from the passage to Little Vermillion.

Before he launched the Zodiac, he looked up at the sky. It was beginning to cloud over, but the sun was still visible. He figured the time to be early afternoon and decided to open the box lunch and get some nourishment while he looked at the map again to make sure he had it committed to memory.

This time he found the entrance to the stream without any trouble, but after a few hundred metres the way grew more and more narrow, and after several kilometres dwindled to a tight brook clogged with silt and reeds. It wasn't difficult to turn off the motor, raise it and drag the Zodiac around to a point where the stream was navigable again, but it took time, and the day was wearing on.

After a couple of kilometres, the channel opened into the first lake of the Little Vermillion chain. It was a large, almost square lake and a short, narrow strait in the northwest corner connected it to the main body of Little Vermillion. The way was clear, without any islands or sandbars, and the water was deep. He felt a little thrill of exhilaration as he began to cross open water again. He cranked the outboard to full and felt the wind in his face.

But before he had gone 100 metres, the wind started to gust and whistle, blowing up two- and three- and finally four-foot waves with white crests. Clouds covered the sun and the day turned cold. He kept the prow of the Zodiac pointed into the gusts to steady it through the high chop, but he was heading east-northeast, away from the transit into Little Vermillion. He tried to turn west, but the wind was so strong it blew him into a shallow inlet.

He cranked the outboard to full throttle and tried to get back to deep water, but it was too late. He was among sharp rocks and though the Zodiac had a very light draught, the motor slammed once, twice, and guttered out. Before he could get the oars into the oarlocks, the craft was blown up against a gravelly beach and he was pinned there. He reached back and raised the outboard so he could inspect the damage. The shaft was bent and the propeller looked like it had been crumpled in a giant fist. He pulled the start cord hard, once, twice, five times but the Honda didn't even cough. It's flooded, he thought, I'll wait five minutes, but he didn't believe it. When he tried again he got the same result.

He looked at the map, then he looked at the sky. Darker clouds and a shimmer of lightning near the horizon. And under that, grey veils of rain. The motor was badly damaged and there was no way he could repair it without tools and spare parts. He reached back and loosened the clamp screws on the stern bracket, lifted it from the transom and carried it ten feet back from the water line where he laid it down in plain sight. Maybe someone would find it and get it running again, but it weighed near 100 pounds and all it would do for him now was slow him down.

He returned to the Zodiac, walked it into the lake and used leg kicks to propel it to deeper water. Then he climbed aboard, fitted the telescope oars into the locks and began to row. He made some progress, but after twenty minutes the bullet wound in his shoulder began to throb and he had to stop. All he could do was watch as the wind blew him back to shore.

The strait that would take him into the main body of Little Vermillion was only half a mile away. He gritted his teeth and set out again, but after several hundred metres, his shoulder was so sore he could barely move it. He tried rowing with his right hand, first one oar then the other. He didn't get very far but he did manage to keep from getting blown ashore. When he'd rested his shoulder for ten minutes or so, he was able to use it again and after half a dozen short runs he made it to the channel.

As soon as he turned into it, the going got easier. Both shores rose to higher ground and he was protected from the wind, but when he pulled out into the main body of Little Vermillion, he was hit with a fierce blast and the boat veered out of control. He'd have to row directly across a mile of whitecaps before he reached the chain of streams and ponds that connected Little Vermillion to Rathouse Lake. As he looked out over that stretch of turbulent water he realized two things. The gale force wind had shifted from west-southwest and was now blowing directly south. It carried rolls of heavy cloud that strafed the lake with torrential rain and occasional stabs of lightning. Even with two good arms, he'd never make it.

78

The wind blew him south and he used the oars to steer the Zodiac to a small cove on the lee side of an island. He landed, pulled the boat up from the water and carried the boreal forest survival kit up the small rise till he came to a nearly level clearing. It was sheltered by shrubbery on the ground and a canopy of spruce, fir and aspen overhead. He strung a nylon line between two trees and used the tarp to fashion a crude tent open at both ends. He anchored it with stones, used the hunting knife to cut fragrant evergreen boughs and laid them across each other till he had several layers of a reasonably comfortable bed. Something he had learned while in Iraq and Afghanistan—get sleep whenever you can. It was the only useful thing he could do while the storm raged. He hoped it would blow itself out soon, but he'd just have to wait and see.

In his dream he was dragged underwater again, but this time there was no fear, only a kind of brittle urgency as he reached and reached blindly down until his fingers found and gripped the shirt of the child, and they rose toward the bright surface, broke into the light, and he was on his back, swimming, splashing ashore, and the child's terror sputtered out as he stopped struggling and began to smile.

When he woke, it was nearly sunset. There was still some wind, in mild gusts, but the sky had cleared and the water was only disturbed by occasional cross-hatch patterns that picked up tints of the dying light. He came out of the improvised tent and scanned his surroundings. A hundred yards away, a small black bear was prowling along the headland, making quick forays into the lake, trying to scoop fish up on the rocks.

Suddenly, he realized he'd eaten nothing since just after noon.

The survival kit had a fishing line, hooks and a small folding spade he could use to dig for grubs or worms as bait. There were waterproof matches and a mess kit which contained metal plates and flatware, and could be unfolded for use as a frying pan. But he hadn't brought any oil or butter, salt or pepper, and as he thought this he realized what a city boy he was. If he were really hungry he'd just boil the fish, or fillet it and eat it raw, but the whole thing seemed like too much work and he'd been delayed long enough.

He took down the tent, packed up the survival kit and found his way down to the Zodiac. The sun had set and the afterglow was quickly deepening into night. He launched the boat and as he began to row, he was surprised by the beauty of the fading light, how it caught in the curls of water that churned from the edge of the oars.

He pulled out of the cove into deep water and heard the loons begin their long tapering cries that echoed mournfully in the stillness. It was a long way across the main body of Little Vermillion, but the wind was light and he made it without mishap. But there was a problem. He knew he had been blown south to the island cove, but had no idea how far, and he was sure that as he rowed across open water he'd drifted even further away from the chain of streams and ponds that eventually connected with Rathouse Lake. He needed to find the entry point. After that, he'd be fine because there was no place else he could end up. He turned north and rowed along the western shore.

After almost an hour, he stopped to rest. The moon had come up. It was almost full and very bright. It lit up a scatter of algae particles in the water and he realized that they were moving slowly north. He started rowing again, and a few minutes later, he noticed that the algae had picked up momentum and continued to accelerate until they began to converge and flow toward shore. He angled the Zodiac to port and soon felt it pulled by the current as he entered the effluent stream.

He was now zeroed in on the final leg of his journey. There were no serious difficulties, though he had to take the boat out of the water and portage twice, around a beaver dam, then a fallen tree that blocked the stream. After that he had to negotiate a stretch of whitewater rapids but managed to stay afloat and arrived at his destination just as the sky began to shade toward grey.

The private hunting lodge was the only one on the lake and it was impressive. Three main levels of skinned varnished pine logs were built into the slow rise of the shore and connected through a covered passageway to a large boathouse and a long dock with a Grumman G-111 Albatross amphibious flying boat tied up at the deep end. The buildings were located a few hundred yards north of where he had entered Rathouse Lake, and his first plan was to go ashore, stash the Zodiac out of sight, and go overland to the clearing at the back of the lodge.

But that would mean crashing through underbrush in the half dark. It would be better to pull right into the boathouse and enter from there. If he rowed slowly, his approach would be almost soundless, and would be indistinguishable from small waves lapping the shore.

It was dark inside but after a few minutes his eyes adjusted. There were five berths where a twenty-foot Lund 208 Pro fibreglass, a thirty-seven-foot Sea Ray Sundancer and a two-passenger Sea-Doo rocked gently in the wake he made when he entered. To the right a storage area held wooden crates, cardboard boxes, folded deck chairs, rakes, axes, spades and other tools. On the rear wall, hunting bows hung from two horizontal rows of hooks and below them there were shelves stacked with arrows in boxes with plastic covers. To the left, a set of stairs led up to a landing and what looked like a steel door.

He got out of the Zodiac, walked up the stairs and knelt down in front of the door. He unfolded his tool pouch and laid it out on the landing. It was still fairly dark. He turned on the miniature flashlight and inspected the lock. It was a standard pin tumbler deadbolt. Holding the flashlight in his mouth, he selected a curved tension hook and a sawtooth comb. He was able to turn it and was inside in less than two minutes.

At the end of a longish corridor there was another door with a keyed lock in the doorknob. He worked a straight pick and tiny pressure wrench into the keyhole and had the door open in seconds. He closed it behind him and found himself in a large living room.

There were leather chairs and sofas scattered around several coffee tables made from sections of huge tree trunks cut at an angle and varnished with many coats of Varathane. They glowed in the early light. On the far wall, an enormous fieldstone fireplace rose up to the ceiling. To the right, a table held liquor bottles below a shelf of cut crystal glasses. He went over and poured himself three fingers of Macallan twenty-one-year-old single malt. He sipped it as he leaned against the mantelpiece and waited.

He was working on his second drink when Jeremy Baine came down the stairs in a gold bathrobe. When he saw Nick, his face showed the barest flicker of surprise and apprehension, but he masked it instantly and his smile was just one click short of a sneer.

"Ah, Detective Cortese. How nice of you to have come all this way for a visit. How did you get here, anyway? There's no road access, and I'm a light sleeper. I heard no plane or outboard. Did you swim?"

"Zodiac inflatable. Two oars. You should try it some time. Actually, officially, I'm in the Bahamas, but never mind."

Baine shook his head and his voice turned nasty. "You are one drunk, whacked-out puppy. What do you want?"

"Want? Well, I was hoping for a fireside chat."

"Oh, really, and what would you like to chat about?

"How about Operation Stealth Seed for starters, and the murder of your partner Kenneth Lang?"

Baine barked out a short laugh.

"That's classified, Cortese. National security. Too complex for your one-groove, low-level intelligence to comprehend. Ken was obsolete, a dinosaur. He had a narrow little mind, like yours, didn't understand that we could have ended starvation on this planet and insured the unchallenged, full-spectrum dominance of American democracy. Too bad you and your friends fucked it up."

"Fucked up your big bucks, too, didn't we?"

"This is entirely pointless. You have no authority here, and since you say you never arrived, I'm going to ignore you, have some breakfast, take out my bow and go hunting. I suggest you get in your paddleboat and go back where you came from. If you stick around you might be mistaken for a moose."

As Baine turned and walked toward the door that led into the kitchen-dining area, Nick reached behind him and removed the breech-loading pistol from his belt. He had grown up believing it was wrong to shoot a man in the back, but in this case, he decided to make an exception.

79

The room was flooded with early morning sun. They had just made love. Claire had her head tucked in between his right shoulder and his chest. He stroked her arm absently as they lay together in the sweetly comfortable silence. She was the first to speak.

"I was really disappointed when you called and said you'd be away for a week or ten days. Then I got really curious. I still am. You told me you went up to Canada and confronted Jeremy Baine. Now I want to know the rest of it. What happened after you shot him?"

Nick laughed. "I guess it must have felt like a bee sting. He turned around and looked really mad. When he saw me standing there with the pistol, he screamed at me. 'What the…? You shot me in the back? *With an air gun?!* You're out of your fucking mind, Cortese.'

"Then his eyes changed as the liquid form of the Complianex-3 Vanessa had gotten from Sarbitt began to work. There was a cubic centimetre and a half in the hypodermic dart and it would last for thirty-six hours. I just flashed my badge and gave him instructions. He was to fly directly back to his private dock on Long Island Sound and go immediately to his house in the Hamptons. Astonishingly, he did exactly as he was told. When he got there, Price and Malone made the arrest."

"That's astonishing all right, and I may ask you to guest lecture one of my criminology classes about it. But the evidence you have only supports two conspiracy charges, forgery and identity theft. He'll probably get by with three to five in a minimum-security lock-up and with his money he could live in relative luxury if he greases a few palms."

Nick smiled. "Ah, but the story doesn't end there."

After a long minute of silence, she poked him. "Dammit, Nicola, tell me or I'll pluck out your eyebrows!"

He laughed, pulled away. "Okay, okay! Well, it was another crime, still in the planning stages, that closed the door on Jeremy Baine. Would you like to hazard a guess, Professor?"

"No, it would take too long. Just tell me."

"That big black Blackwater dude was apparently planning to blackmail Baine when Operation Stealth Seed succeeded and he cornered the wheat market. It might have cost billions to keep him quiet."

"What did he have? If he agreed to testify against Baine he'd incriminate himself as well, and there's no way the prosecution would give him full immunity."

"Right. But he had recorded every one of their telephone conversations. It was a slam dunk. Conspiracy to commit murder, kidnapping, attempted murder of NYPD detectives, the whole ball of wax. There's no death penalty in New York, but Baine will get several consecutive life sentences without possibility of parole."

"Well done, Lieutenant!"

"Thanks, but it wasn't just me. There was Price and Malone, Mifflin and Trojas, Sean Doherty, Vanessa, Tamas Berenyi, the FBI team that found the tapes in one of Noireau's safe houses—lots of people made this happen."

Claire nodded, looked thoughtful.

"There's something I still don't understand. Why did you have to stay away as long as you did?"

"I knew Baine would claim that I had coerced him to return to the States and his arrest was therefore invalid. I had to have that covered. My passport would prove that I'd had a week of R&R in the Bahamas. If I were seen in New York, or anywhere but the Caribbean, my cover would have been blown."

She picked it up immediately.

"Mo Zimmerman!"

"Yes. The man is an artist. He changed the photo in my passport. Hector spent a week in the sun, healing his bullet wound, and calling himself Nicola Cortese. When he returned to New York, Mo changed the photo back."

"What about blood tests? Did Baine claim he'd been drugged?"

"Sure, but we stalled him, and by the time the tests were done they showed nothing."

"And what about your fishing trip? Did you have to row all the way back to Red Lake?"

"I got lucky. Baine's Lund fibreglass had a 135-horsepower motor, but it also had a smaller one that I guess he used for trolling. It was a 15-horsepower, but no one back at Red Lake noticed the difference. When I left I told them they could keep it along with the Zodiac."

"That must have made them happy."

"They said they couldn't offer me what the equipment was worth, but they'd accept it as payment for my stay."

"So. Another happy ending."

"True, but there's more. Remember I told you I'd filed an appeal of the commissioner's review committee ruling that the SWAT shooting at the warehouse was an 'appropriate application of deadly force'?"

"Yes. That was where your friend was killed."

Nick felt his eyes tear up. It still hurt. It hurt like hell. He nodded.

"The new evidence I sent with my appeal convinced them to reverse their decision. When the SWAT team heard about it, two of them reneged, said that Donovan had coerced them into signing the false report. As it turns out, it was Donovan himself who fired the first shot. That's why he stonewalled when I went to see him."

"Has he been charged?"

"Yes. Manslaughter, but it will be plea-bargained down to reckless endangerment. He'll still get his pension, but he'll have to do some jail time."

"Too easy. Was that because he's a captain in the NYPD?"

"Probably, and it bothered me too until I thought about his wife and kids. They didn't deserve to be homeless or destitute because of what he did. He won't endanger anyone else, and the point was made. Police can't do whatever they want. Even a captain's not immune.

Hopefully the gung-ho trigger-happy cowboys on the force will think twice before they use their weapons."

Claire was quiet for a while, then she said, "I'm glad things worked out so well, but I still don't know how to feel about the way this case invaded my life."

"I know, and I'm truly sorry. I know how I'd feel if it happened the other way around. I'd be very pissed."

Claire smiled at his bluntness. "That's one way to describe it."

When he answered, Nick's voice was filled with concern. "I've been thinking about that. A lot."

He paused, as though what he was about to say was difficult, momentous, and had to be carefully weighed. "If we're going to have some kind of life together, and I hope we can, I won't let work interfere with us again. I'm willing to resign from the force."

Claire was quiet for a long time before she answered.

"I'm not sure that's a good idea, Nico. What would you do? Besides, if you quit for me it wouldn't work and neither of us would be happy. I'm not even sure I want to live with you, or with anyone. I like being on my own too much. And I'm happy where I am. Aren't you?"

"Well, yes, but I thought..."

"You know, Nico, we can have a great time together but we don't have to set up house. We're not going to raise a family and neither of us cares much for formal dinners where couples sit around trading rumours and news. Can't we just keep going as we are and see what happens?"

Nick felt a lightness move through his body and he smiled. He loved this woman. She had just said what he never knew he wanted her to say until she said it. She grinned up at him.

"That wasn't so hard, was it? Let's do lunch sometime soon."

He grinned back. "How about today, are you free?"

She nodded. "Sure am, and I know this high-end hot dog stand on the west side of Central Park."

ACKNOWLEDGMENTS

I would like to thank Donald Hermiston for his contribution to the first tentative plot outline when the book was about Vietnam and did not include the PTSD theme; Robert Astle for suggesting PTSD and that the book be updated from Vietnam to Iraq/Afghanistan; my agent Rebecca Platt for help with a substantial restructuring and revision; Alison Preston for her detailed and immensely helpful feedback; and my editor, Douglas Whiteway, whose keenly intelligent questions, comments and suggestions targeted the lingering kinks and creases.

ABOUT THE AUTHOR

George Amabile has published his poetry, fiction and non-fiction in the USA, Canada, Europe, England, Wales, South America, Australia, and New Zealand in over a hundred anthologies, magazines, journals and periodicals including *The New Yorker, The New Yorker Book of Poems, Harper's, Poetry* (Chicago), *American Poetry Review, Botteghe Oscure, The Globe and Mail, The Malahat Review, The Penguin Book of Canadian Verse, Saturday Night, Poetry Australia, Sur* (Buenos Aires), *Poetry Canada Review*, and *Canadian Literature*.

Amabile has published twelve previous books, including the chapbooks *Flower and Song* (Borealis Press, 1977) and *Four of a Kind* (Pachyderm Press, 1994); the anthology *Five-o'clock Shadows* (Letters Bookshop, 1996); the poetry collections *Blood Ties* (Sono Nis Press, 1972), *Open Country* (Turnstone Press, 1976), *Ideas of Shelter* (Turnstone Press, 1981), *The Presence of Fire*, winner of the CAA Award (McClelland and Stewart, 1982), *Rumours of Paradise/Rumours of War* (McClelland and Stewart, 1995), *Tasting the Dark* (The Muses' Company, 2001), *Dancing, with Mirrors* (The Porcupine's Quill, 2011), and *Martial Music* (Signature Editions, 2016); as well as the short-fiction collection *Small Change* (Libros Libertad, 2011). *Dancing, with Mirrors, Small Change*, and *Martial Music* were all awarded the Bressani Literary Prize. *Operation Stealth Seed* is Amabile's first novel.

Eco-Audit

Printing this book using Rolland Enviro 100 Book instead of virgin fibres paper saved the following resources:

Trees	Energy	Water	Air Emissions
6	10 GJ	2,000 L	368 kg